CASSIDY

CASSIDY

LEE NELSON

Council Press

Council Press
P.O. Box 531
Springville, Utah 84663

ISBN 0-936860-30-8

Printed in the United States of America
First Printing, September 1992

Readers respond
to Lee Nelson books

One night at the dinner table I was telling my mother about Lee Nelson's books. I picked up one of the books to show her some of the pictures. I thumbed through the pages a full five minutes before I realized there were no "real pictures," only the word pictures created in my mind.

David Noyes
Preston, Idaho

I have never read any books that I have enjoyed more than the ones of Lee Nelson.

Ann Hone
Rawlins, Wyoming

Walkara, by Lee Nelson, is truly one of the most interesting, educational, and fascinating books I have read. Once I got into it, I simply didn't want to put it down until I had reached the final page at 3:30 a.m. this morning.

Judge Donald Nicholson
Corsicana, Texas

I am a teacher of 8th grade reading. Mr. Nelson's Storm Testament books are the most widely circulated books in our school library.

Janet Carroll
Hyde Park, Utah

Lee Nelson's books captivate me to the point where I do not want to put them down. It gives me much pleasure to sit down and get lost in one of these stories. My favorite authors are Shakespeare, Dumas, L'Amour, Twain, and now Lee Nelson.

Janet Howard
Hampstead, Maryland

My favorite Lee Nelson book is Storm Testament V. I have read this book at least a dozen times, and love it every time.

Ryan Stout
Colorado Springs, Colorado

Lee Nelson is the best western writer of them all. When I read one of his books, it puts me in the saddle right next to the main character all the way through the book. One of the marks of a good writer is the pain and suffering the reader goes through when the book is finished and there is nothing more to read. Lee Nelson does this.

Scott Morrison
Provo, Utah

Oh how much I enjoyed a borrowed copy of Walkara. I hate to give it back. I keep thumbing through it. I bought the rest of the Storm Testament series, thinking they would provide an entire winter of reading, but I found I could not leave them alone, and was finished long before the snow melted.

Elaine Freestone
Bountiful, Utah

To Marvin,

who is blessed with the same traits of
kindness, generosity and immagination
which set Butch Cassity apart from
the other cowboy outlaws of his day.

Chapter 1

It was evening when Robert LeRoy Parker arrived in the sleepy Mormon community of Milford, Utah Territory. It was mid summer, 1879. Parker was 13 years old, but he looked older. Though he had not yet reached his full height, his shoulders were broad, and the muscles in his arms were hard. He was a boy accustomed to hard work.

He had hired out for the summer on the nearby Pat Ryan Ranch at Hay Springs. In his trousers jingled the most money he had ever had at one time, ten silver dollars--pay he had received for his first 20 days work at the Ryan Ranch. A top hand with cattle would normally get a dollar a day, so it wasn't unusual for a boy to get half that.

As young Parker trotted along, bareback on Babe, his bay mare, he knew exactly what he was going to buy with the first real money he had ever earned. Upon arriving at the Ryan Ranch a month earlier, he had brought only one pair of coveralls with him. His mother had just patched the holes in the knees and seat, but now, a month later, there were new holes which were both embarrassing and troublesome. His entire life he had always worn hand-me-down and patch-up jeans and coveralls. Today he would buy his first pair of brand-new store-bought coveralls.

His blue-gray eyes squinted against the evening sun. He had a frank, open face with a square jaw. His sun-bleached hair, barely covering his ears, looked like it hadn't been combed in days, perhaps weeks. He was riding alone, the corners of his mouth turned up in an unmistakable smile. Being from a poor family, and having to do a man's work at an early age didn't make him unhappy. His face radiated youthful optimism.

Upon entering the town, he slowed the mare to a walk. He was looking for the dry goods store, hoping it would be open in the evening. It was still hot in the street. Not very many people were outside. Mr. Ryan had told the boy he would find the dry goods store across from the post office which had an American flag over the doorway. Young Parker spotted the flag, then the dry goods store.

He slipped to the ground, then tied his mare to the hitching rail in front of the store. After checking his pocket to make sure the ten silver dollars were still there, he hurried up the wooden steps. The door was locked. Through the window he could see a sign that said the store was closed.

The ride to town had been too far, and his expectations for new coveralls too high, to just get back on his horse and return to the ranch. He wondered if someone might be inside, perhaps stocking shelves or cleaning floors. Maybe the back door to the store was not locked.

He walked to the corner of the building, jumped down from the wooden porch, and started up the alley between the store and another building. Upon finding an open window, he had momentary hope that someone was still inside, that the back door might indeed be open, but when he reached the back of the store, the door was as tightly locked as the one in front.

Chapter 1

He stood there for a moment, thoughtfully rubbing his chin, wondering what to do. He still didn't like the idea of returning to the ranch empty-handed. He needed new coveralls, and he needed them now. Not tomorrow or the day after. He had worked hard for his money and was determined to spend it.

Slowly, he started walking back through the alley towards the street. He stopped at the open window, knowing that somewhere beyond that window, not very far away, he would find piles of new coveralls.

He wiggled through the window. He had no plan to steal anything, not with ten dollars in his pocket.

There was enough light coming through the windows that it was not necessary to light a lantern. In fact, he found a huge pile of coveralls on a table beside the window he had crawled through.

One by one, he began unfolding the coveralls and holding them up against his chest. The first dozen or so pairs he held up were too large, but finally he found a pair that seemed just the right size. Quickly he slipped out of his old, worn trousers and stepped into the new coveralls. The stiff new material felt solid and substantial against his skin. He enjoyed the smell of new denim as he marched back and forth to see how the new coveralls felt when he moved. The coveralls were a little large, but that would allow room for shrinkage.

He began looking around for a sign of some kind that would tell the price of the coveralls. There was no price marked on the pair he was wearing, nor on any of the others. For a minute he thought he might leave two or three of his silver dollars. That would probably be too much. He remembered someone saying the price of new coveralls was only about a dollar and a half. He didn't have any quarters or fifty-cent pieces, only silver dollars.

It occurred to him that if he left money behind, perhaps it might not get into the hands of the owner of the business.

3

Maybe someone coming in early the next morning to clean, or buy something, might pick up the money.

Though he wasn't sure what to do about the payment for the coveralls, he fully intended to wear them back to the ranch.

He walked over to the cash register. He looked around until he found a piece of paper and a pencil. At the top of the paper he printed, "I.O.U. for one pair coveralls." Then he signed his name. Below that he wrote that he was working at the Ryan Ranch, and would pay for the coveralls the next time he came to town. Carefully, young Parker placed the note on top of the cash register where the owner of the store would be sure to see it. It didn't occur to him that he might be doing something wrong. He crawled out the window and returned to his horse.

The next day as young Parker was leading a team of horses out of the barn to hitch to one of the hay wagons, he noticed two riders approaching along the road from Milford. It was common for strangers to come out to the ranch looking for work, so he didn't pay much attention to the men as he began hitching the team to the wagon.

The two riders tied their horses in front of the ranch house, then walked inside. A minute later they came back outside, Mr. Ryan accompanying them. They were headed straight for the boy, who was not aware of their approach until Ryan said, "Roy, the sheriff wants to talk to you."

The boy turned to face them. He was glad he had left the I.O.U. note in the store so they could not accuse him of stealing the coveralls. The sheriff was a tall man with a long handlebar mustache, and piercing black eyes. The other man was short and heavy, with a red face. Both of them were frowning, like they were involved in some very serious business. Mr. Ryan hung back, letting the two men have their way with the boy.

"Are you Robert LeRoy Parker?" the sheriff asked.

"That's me," Roy answered, responding to their scowls

with a nervous grin.

"Looks like you've got some new coveralls," the sheriff said. Roy nodded.

"Mr. Miller here says you got them from his store and didn't pay for them. That's stealing."

"I left a note saying I'd pay for them later."

"That's not the way we do business around here," Mr. Miller said, his voice loud and angry. "Especially not with strangers and children."

"Can you pay for the coveralls?" the sheriff asked, trying to ignore Miller's outburst.

"How much?" Roy asked. There was a note of uncertainty in his voice. He still believed he had done nothing wrong. Still, he sensed he was in some kind of danger.

"Two dollars," Miller said. Roy reached in his pocket and pulled out two silver dollars. He gave them to the sheriff who in turn handed them to Miller.

"Can I go now?" Roy asked. The sheriff looked at Miller to see if the merchant was satisfied.

"The boy has to be taught a lesson," Miller said, a sternness in his voice that made Roy feel cold, even though it was the middle of summer.

"I'm not going to arrest him," the sheriff said.

"The boy should spend a night in jail," Miller said.

"How old are you?" the sheriff asked Roy.

"Thirteen."

"The boy's paid for the coveralls," the sheriff said. "As far as I am concerned the matter is finished."

"That's not good enough," Miller whined.

"I'm not locking up a kid. Not when he's paid for what he took."

"How about giving him a licking?" Miller suggested.

"Not me," the sheriff said.

"Then I'll do it," Miller said, stepping over to the wagon Roy had just hitched the team to. Miller reached out and took hold of a buggy whip that was resting against the

5

side of the wagon.

For a moment Roy thought it might be best to run. He knew the chubby merchant could never catch him. He looked at Ryan, who was staring at his feet, kicking dust into a pool of fresh tobacco juice.

"Turn around and grab that wagon wheel," the sheriff urged. "Let him have a couple of licks, then this whole thing will be over."

Roy started to turn towards the wagon wheel, then stopped. He looked back at the sheriff.

"I didn't steal the coveralls," Roy said, his voice high, but his words clear. His fists were clenched, and his eyes had narrowed to where they looked like little more than knife slits. "I will not be whipped for something I didn't do."

"We'll see about that," Miller said, raising the whip above his head. Roy held his ground as Miller stepped forward to strike the first blow.

A shot rang out. The whip shattered about six inches above Miller's hand. Everyone looked towards the barn to see who had fired the shot.

Standing beside the barn door was Mike Cassidy, a cowboy who had recently hired on to work with the stock. Nonchalantly, he returned the smoking Colt .44 to the holster on his belt. Cassidy sauntered forward, grinning.

"Who are you?" the sheriff asked. There was a tone of uncertainty in his voice.

"Cassidy, Mike Cassidy," the cowboy said, continuing to walk forward. Miller was glaring at the Cassidy, but seemed too surprised or frightened to do anything. Ryan was kicking dust into another puddle of tobacco juice.

Roy wondered why Cassidy had come to his rescue. The two hardly knew each other, even though they shared the same bunkhouse with a half dozen other men.

Cassidy was the first to speak. "Sheriff, I'd like to report a crime, a theft." When the sheriff did not respond, Cassidy continued.

Chapter 1

"Mr. Miller here stole four bits from my friend, Roy."

"I did not," Miller protested.

"What are you talking about?" the sheriff demanded.

"I was in Miller's store a few days ago," Cassidy explained. "He said I could have any pair of coveralls in the place for a dollar and a half. He just took two dollars from Roy, and didn't give the boy any change. Four bits is a lot of money to a kid. I demand you arrest Miller for stealing. It'd do him good to spend a night in jail."

"I won't do that," the sheriff said.

"Then maybe we ought to give the fat man a thrashing," Cassidy grinned, suddenly whipping the .44 back out of its holster, and pointing it straight at Miller. Cassidy ordered the merchant to turn around and place both hands on the top of the wagon wheel. He told Roy to run to the barn and get another whip.

"Stay right where you are," the sheriff roared at Miller, sounding like a man who had just figured out what he had to do.

"Give me four bits," the sheriff said, stepping towards the merchant, ignoring Cassidy's gun. When Miller started to protest, the sheriff told him to shut up. The merchant reached in his pocket and handed a fifty-cent piece to the sheriff who tossed it to Roy, who by now was grinning.

"As far as I am concerned, this matter is finished," the sheriff said. Then turning to Miller he said, "I'm getting on my horse and riding back to town. You can come along, or you can stay here and take your chances with Cassidy." The sheriff turned and walked towards his horse. Miller followed. Ryan returned to the house.

When the sheriff was mounted, he turned to Cassidy.

"Cowboy, it's just a matter of time until you get into trouble with that gun of yours. I'd just as soon it didn't happen around here."

"I'll behave myself, sheriff," Cassidy said.

"Why don't you behave yourself somewhere else?" The

sheriff turned and rode away, a disgruntled Miller following close behind.

"Always wanted to see the country east of Beaver," Cassidy said, mostly to himself. "Maybe I'll take the man's counsel and move on."

"Can I go with you?" Roy asked. "My family has a homestead in Circle Valley. I want to go home."

"Then we'll ride together," Cassidy grinned. "I'll take you home. We'll leave in the morning." The two started towards the house to collect what Ryan owed them.

Chapter 2

It didn't take Roy long to decide that riding with Mike Cassidy was preferable to working in the Ryan hay fields. Cassidy was unlike any adult Roy had ever met. With a good horse under him, a Colt revolver in his belt, and money in his pocket, Cassidy didn't have a worry in the world. He and the boy didn't get up in the morning until they felt like it. They didn't hit the trail until after they had cooked up a big breakfast. Cassidy was under no pressure to go anywhere, or get anything done.

Upon entering Beaver, Cassidy treated Roy to a steak dinner and a hot bath in a copper tub. That night they slept in a hotel room between clean sheets. Roy enjoyed every minute. He had never slept in a hotel before. His father would never spend money on unnecessary luxuries. Mike was different. He had plenty of money, and didn't mind spending it. He even bought Roy his first glass of whiskey. The boy didn't like the burning in his throat, but he drank the glass empty anyway. If his new friend Mike was generous enough to buy him a drink, he would darn well gulp it down.

The next morning, after stuffing themselves on eggs,

fried potatoes and salt pork, Mike and Roy headed east into the mountains. Roy was riding bareback. His meager personal belongings were in a gunny sack tied to a rope looped over one shoulder. A gray wool blanket tied up with string hung over the other shoulder. Cassidy led a packhorse carrying his bedroll and camp gear.

"Why are we heading into the mountains?" Roy asked, knowing the shortest way to Circle Valley was south around the mountains.

"We need to get you a saddle," Mike answered.

"There are no saddles in the mountains," Roy responded.

"No, but there is the means to get saddles."

"I don't know what you mean."

"Mavericking."

Mike didn't need to say any more. Roy knew exactly what the cowboy meant. Mavericking was something every cattleman did, from the largest land baron to the smallest homesteader. Without fences, herds of cattle spread far and wide, getting mixed up with other herds. It was impossible to prove ownership of a free-roaming cow or horse that didn't carry a brand. Whoever could catch and brand a previously unbranded animal became its proud new owner.

The large ranchers were always trying to pass laws allowing only themselves to brand unbranded stock. But the homesteaders ran cattle on the range too, and argued they had just as much right to catch and brand strays. The argument always ended in a stalemate, meaning unbranded cattle and horses were fair game for anyone who could catch them, and slap on a brand. Going after these animals was called mavericking.

Mike Cassidy had everything he needed to go mavericking--a fast horse, a stout saddle, a lariat, and a branding iron.

"Can you throw a rope?" Mike asked.

"A little," Roy said, remembering how he had caught a few calves and colts in the corral at home.

Chapter 2

Cassidy uncoiled his rope and started giving Roy a roping lesson. First he showed the boy how to make a loop, extending the hondo (the eye through which the rope passes) about two feet from the hand holding the loop. He showed Roy how to take the kinks out by swinging the loop forward or backward in a complete circle.

He demonstrated how to swing the loop overhead in a natural swinging motion, the hand turning upside down as the loop passed over the left shoulder. Mike said most beginners used too much wrist in a short jerking motion, but that good ropers used the entire arm, plus the wrist. He told Roy that when letting go of the loop, he should follow through with the arm, like he was trying to reach out and touch the critter he was trying to rope.

Later that same day Mike spotted the sun-bleached skeleton of a dead cow. Some of the bones had been carried off by coyotes, but most were still in place. Mike and Roy stopped their horses and dismounted. Mike picked up the white skull and tied it in an upright position to the end of a fallen juniper log. Then he walked over to his horse and got his rope. No sooner had Mike made a coil, than it began hissing around his head. Then it shot forward, the loop round and flat, falling easily over the horns on the bleached skull. Mike jerked the loop tight. He threw a few more times to show Roy how to do it. Sometimes the loop would settle over the entire skull, other times just over the horns. Mike always said before he threw whether he was going for a head catch or a horn catch, and the loop always caught just what he said it would catch. He said when he was going for a head catch he dipped the front of the loop lower as he was swinging it over his head. When going for the horns only, the loop was flatter, and slanted slightly over his right shoulder. Then he handed the rope to Roy.

"I want you to throw a hundred loops every morning, and another hundred every night," Mike explained. "In a week you'll be a pretty good hand with a rope. In a month, with me teaching you, you'll be as good as anyone in these

11

parts.''

Roy didn't throw very many successful loops during the first practice session. He wasn't surprised. But he believed with time he would become good with a rope like Mike said he would. Roy promised to throw the hundred loops every morning and every evening just like Mike asked him to do. Before getting back on their horses Mike removed the skull from the log and slipped it in his pack where it would be available for future practice sessions.

As Mike and Roy rode higher into the mountains they began to see more and more cattle. They rode among the grazing stock, checking brands.

On the second day as they entered the high, rugged country, they found two bulls and a cow that had not been branded. They rounded them up and began pushing the unbranded animals ahead of them as they continued the search for more. By the end of the next day they had six unbranded animals, including two large calves not yet weaned from their branded mothers.

"Ever seen a bull busted?" Mike asked.

"No," Roy responded.

"Watch."

Mike removed the lariat from his saddle, formed a loop, and galloped into the little herd of cattle. The biggest of the bulls began to run away from Mike, but the fat beef was no match for Mike's horse.

The horse, without any coaxing from Mike, lunged to a position behind and to the left of the fleeing bull. Mike's loop shot forward, dropping around the bull's horns. Mike jerked the loop tight as the horse and bull continued running. What happened next was a surprise to Roy.

Mike urged his horse closer to the bull until he was running almost parallel to the animal, on the left side. Reaching out with his right hand, Mike flipped the slack rope over the right side of the running bull. The rope now extended from the bull's horns down its right side, around its hind quarters, and up the left side to Mike's hand.

12

Chapter 2

With everything just the way he wanted it, Mike wrapped or dallied the end of the rope around his saddle horn, then turned his horse sharply to the left. As the rope jerked tight the bull's head was pulled to the right while its hind quarters were jerked to the left. If the animal had been standing still it could have given in to the rope by just turning in a circle, but such movement could not be accomplished on the run. The bull lost its footing and began to roll.

By the time the startled animal ground to a halt, Mike had galloped around a nearby aspen stump and back past the bull, at the same time making a loop with his spare rope. By the time the bull figured out what had happened and decided to get back on its feet, Mike had a second loop over one of the bull's hind legs. Quickly the horse backed up, pulling both ropes tight, making it impossible for the helpless animal to get on its feet.

Mike dismounted and retrieved his branding iron from one of his saddle bags. The horse knew exactly what to do without Mike giving commands. When the bull began to struggle against the ropes in an effort to get up, the horse leaned backwards, tightening the ropes even more. When the bull relaxed, the horse leaned forward just enough to relieve some of the tension.

Roy dismounted and helped Mike build a hot fire in which they placed the branding iron.

"This will go a lot faster," Mike said, "when you have a saddle and can help catch them. You'll rope the heads, I'll catch the heels, and we'll stretch'm out between us." He said that when he busted an animal he usually just jumped off his horse and tied its feet before it had a chance to get up, but with bulls he preferred staying on his horse until the animal was securely tied.

Mike's brand was a simple one, a C for Cassidy. When the heat of the fire had turned it reddish-orange, Mike picked up the handle with a gloved hand and hurried over to the now-quiet bull. Without any hesitation Mike slapped the hot end of the iron down on the bull's left hip.

Cassidy

The animal bellowed and struggled as the savvy horse backed harder against the ropes. Mike held the iron firmly in place as the air filled with smoke and the smell of burning hair and flesh. The bull continued to struggle but was no match for the horse.

"Sometimes an old bull like this will go on the fight when you let him up," Mike said when he was finished, tossing the branding iron towards the fire. "Guess if I'd just been branded on the ass I'd be mad too."

Mike walked around to the front of the bull and looked at its face. At the sight of Mike the animal began grinding a hole in the ground with one of its horns. Its eyes were wide. It let out another angry bawl.

Roy walked over and got on his horse. He did not want to be on foot when this beast was set free. Mike rubbed his chin, thoughtfully.

"Guess we have no choice but to take the fight right out of him," Mike said, pulling his skinning knife from the sheath on his belt. "Steers sometimes bring a better price anyway."

Quickly bending over the bull's hip, Mike reached between the hind legs and grabbed the scrotum. Almost before Roy realized what was happening, Mike had sliced the sack open, cutting one testicle free, then the other. The old bull twisted and bellowed.

Mike clucked for his horse to step forward, then removed both ropes from the now quiet beast. It remained on the ground as if it didn't know it was now free.

After coiling up both ropes and hanging them over his saddle horn, Mike picked up one of the discarded testicles. After dusting off some grass and a few pine needles, he bit off a large chunk and began to chew, grinning at Roy as he did so.

"Kind of slippery tasting," Mike said, his mouth still full. "But I strongly recommend it."

"No thanks," Roy said. As he watched Mike continue to chew and swallow, he asked, "Do you really like those things?"

14

Chapter 2

"Not particularly," Mike answered. "I suppose I just hate to see them go to waste."

"Why's that?"

"Think about it," Mike said, thoughtfully, holding the partly eaten testicle out in front of him so he could get a good look at it. "This slimy piece of flesh is the only difference between a powerful, aggressive, majestic bull and a dull, cowardly, fat-ass steer. This small piece of bloody flesh was the source of his manhood and virility." Mike paused, seemingly surprised at his eloquence.

"It just seems a shame," he continued, "to just throw away something so significant. By eating it, I am saving it from being wasted. By eating it, I am showing respect for what it stands for. By eating it, I hope the courage, strength and virility of that bull will somehow become mine. Some of the Indians and mountain men believed that. They ate raw testicles too."

"Do you think that really happens?" Roy asked.

"I don't know. If I had a wife I would tell you to ask her." They both laughed.

"Throw me the other one," Roy said. Mike picked up the second testicle, brushed off some dried grass, then tossed it to Roy. Without hesitation the boy ripped off one end with his teeth and started chewing.

Mike and Roy chewed in silence, watching the emasculated and branded bull struggle to his feet and wander back to the other cattle. Finally, Mike walked over to the fire and threw on some more wood and placed the branding iron in the hottest part of the fire. Then he got back on his horse.

"Let's bust the rest of them," Mike said. "If we can brand all of them tonight, tomorrow we'll trail them back to Beaver and see what we can do about getting you a new saddle and a rope or two."

"Sounds fine to me," Roy answered. They galloped towards the grazing cattle.

Chapter 3

A few days later as Mike and Roy were driving their little bunch of freshly branded cattle towards the mining town of Marysvale, Mike excused himself to take care of some personal business in a thick bunch of junipers. Roy stayed with the slow-walking cattle, knowing Mike would soon catch up.

As Roy pushed the cattle around a rocky ledge into an open meadow he saw three riders coming towards him. All three carried guns and they were riding straight for Roy. He understood all too well how the large ranchers frowned on mavericking. The men were middle-aged. They rode like they owned the country.

For a second Roy wondered if he might be better off turning and running away, but he and Mike had worked hard for this little herd. He decided to stay. He pulled his horse to a halt and waited for the riders to reach him.

"Do you have a bill of sale for these cattle?" one of the strangers asked. He was a tall, square-chinned, over fed man with a drooping mustache and blood-shot eyes. He wore a ten-gallon hat and a blue coat. His voice was gruff and to the point. Roy wasn't used to people not offering a greeting before they got down to business.

"No," Roy said, "but they've all been branded."

"Brand don't mean nothin' without a bill of sale," the man said.

Roy didn't know what to do. He wished Mike would hurry along. Mike would know what to do.

"They're all legally branded," Roy said. "If you want to buy some, I'll stay and talk. Otherwise I've got to be moving."

"We're not interested in buying stolen cattle," the man in the blue coat said. Roy guessed he was in big trouble. They thought he was a cattle thief. He'd heard plenty of stories of suspected cattle rustlers being hung on the spot, right where they were caught. It was too late to run. The three armed men would have no trouble shooting him down at close range.

"Is that your brand?" the man in the blue coat asked.

"No," Roy said. He didn't know how much to say. He didn't want to get Mike in trouble by saying the brand belonged to Mike Cassidy. Roy was beginning to feel sick. He wished the men would leave, or let him continue with the cattle.

"Who does the brand belong to?" one of the other strangers asked. Roy stared at the cattle, not answering.

"Mike Cassidy's brand is on them cattle," shouted a rider emerging from the junipers. It was Mike. He had a happy smile on his face as he rode up to Roy and pulled his horse to a halt.

"They said the cattle are stolen," Roy whispered.

Mike's smile vanished. He glared at the three strangers. "Nobody calls Mike Cassidy a cattle thief," he growled, at the same time pushing back the side of his coat to uncover his Colt .44 resting in a leather holster at his side. The three strangers exchanged uneasy glances.

"Mike Cassidy is ready. Go for your irons, boys," Mike challenged. Roy couldn't believe what was happening.

Mike was challenging the three strangers to a gun fight. Roy felt sicker than he had felt earlier. He thought he was going to throw up. He looked at Mike's face. The easy-going cowboy stared intently at the three strangers.

"Fill your hands boys," he said. "I guess it's time to turn the wolf loose." Mike seemed eager to fight. Roy wondered why.

"Look, Cassidy, we didn't know they was your cattle," one of the strangers offered, an unmistakable note of hesitation in his voice. The man in the blue coat remained silent.

"Just bring'n in some strays," Mike said, "but if you men want to call me a cow thief, I'm ready to go for it."

"Nobody called you a cattle thief," one of the men offered. "We just asked the boy where these cattle came from."

"You're saying that maybe there's been a misunderstanding," Mike suggested.

"A big one," one of the strangers said.

"Good," Mike said, letting his coat move forward to cover the handle of his revolver. "Like to invite you men for a bite to eat, but we're in a hurry to catch up with our main herd. If you find any rustlers, shoot one for me." Mike tipped his hat to the strangers and started riding towards the small herd. Roy followed, glancing uncomfortably at the strangers as he trotted by.

"Damn range hogs," Mike growled, when the strangers were out of sight. "Just because they own a few cattle, they think they own the whole country. Unmarked strays belongs to whoever can get a brand on them first. That's the law."

"How did you know they wouldn't fight?" Roy asked.

"The one in the blue coat had me a little worried," Mike responded.

"Because he talked so mean?"

"No. Had blood on his spurs. Got a mean streak. Don't want to ever let a man like that get an upper hand."

"But how did you know they wouldn't fight?" Roy

asked again. "There were three of them and only one of you. I don't have a gun."

"I reckoned they'd recognize my name. I said it twice."

"I don't understand."

"Most everybody in these parts knows Mike Cassidy is good with a gun."

"You're a gunfighter?"

"No. Never shot a man. Just do a lot of shooting. Turkey shoots, demonstrations in rodeos, that kind of thing. Never met a man who could out shoot me, on moving targets with a pistol. People respect that, and don't want to mess with a man who's good with a gun."

Roy was impressed. He had seen Mike shoot the whip in the merchant's hand back at the Ryan Ranch, and hadn't thought much about the incident. Now, three armed men had backed down because they were afraid of Mike's gun.

"Will you teach me to shoot?" Roy asked.

"Not today," Mike said, thoughtfully. "Learn to rope first. When you can catch everything you throw a loop at, then we'll talk about shooting a gun."

Roy uncoiled his rope and began throwing loops at passing bushes and rocks. He was determined to throw a hundred loops a day until he was as good as Mike. Then he would learn to shoot. He was glad he had met Mike Cassidy.

The next day they drove their tiny herd into Marysvale, the mining boom town of southern Utah Territory. Mike had no trouble selling the cattle to the head cook at the big mine. They rode back into town where Mike bought Roy a brand new saddle, a Navajo blanket to go under it, and a new rope. Before paying for the saddle, Mike made sure the rawhide tree was sound so the saddle wouldn't get ripped apart when Butch started roping bulls.

"Got to make sure the tree is good," he said to the clerk. "This boy'll be roping bulls someday."

Roy could never remember feeling happier in his entire life, as they rode south out of Marysvale that afternoon. He found it hard to believe the new saddle was his.

The new hemp rope was stiffer than the one Butch had been using, making it easier to catch targets. He was finding it easier to swing a flat loop over his head, enabling him to rope objects on either side of his horse.

With the new saddle he could now practice dallying, securing the tail end of the rope to his saddle horn after roping something. This was accomplished by making a quick loop or two around the horn, thereby enabling the roper to hold onto whatever it was he had caught.

"Don't forget to keep the thumb up," Mike said, reminding Roy of the first rule of dallying. He said ropers who didn't keep their thumbs up tended, over time, to get one or more fingers caught between the rope and the saddle horn, and if a lunging bull happened to be at the other end of the rope, those fingers were inclined to disappear.

"Thumbs up," was Mike's repeated caution as they continued their journey towards Roy's home in Circle Valley.

Chapter 4

Roy had been away from home a little more than a month, but to him it had seemed like years. So much had happened. He was eager to share with his family the adventures he and Mike had had, and show them his new saddle and how well he had learned to rope. He was still a long way from doing what Mike could do with a rope, but he had caught a couple of yearlings while his horse was galloping and he was very proud of that. Someday he would be as good as Mike.

Roy entered the cabin, Mike following close behind. Everything looked the same as Roy remembered it. The ceiling was covered with inexpensive white cloth, called factory, covering the hand-hewn beams and planks that made up the ceiling. Except for the cooking area, the plank floor was covered with hand-tied rag rugs tacked down over straw padding which had to be replaced every summer. Heavily starched lace curtains covered the window openings. The little organ with the foot pedals was standing in its usual place beside one of the windows.

"Came for some fresh bread," Roy said, his nose

telling him his mother had been baking. "With butter and bullberry jam."

"LeRoy, is that you?" called a female voice from the back bedroom. It was Roy's mother, Annie Parker.

"Sure is," he said, hurrying to meet her. He was strong for his age, so not only did he give his mother a hug, but he lifted her off her feet and swung her around in a complete circle, taking her breath away.

"Meet my new friend, Mike Cassidy," he said, when he finally let her have her footing again.

She looked at Mike, and back at her son. She knew about Mike Cassidy. He was a good cowboy, but he was not a Mormon, and he carried a gun. He was a cowhand who never stayed at a job very long. Some people thought he was a rustler. It concerned her that her oldest son was traveling with such an unsteady character.

"Mike and I found some strays," Roy boasted. "We sold them in Marysvale and bought me a new saddle. Come and see it."

Annie followed her son outside and quietly admired the new saddle.

"I understand they are looking for some help at the Marshall Ranch," she said to Mike, hoping to get the cowboy to move on. She didn't want him to stay. Though she couldn't put her finger on anything specific, she felt uneasy with Mike around. It was not that she feared for her or her children's safety, it was just that he and her oldest son seemed too close. She sensed Cassidy was somehow competing with her for the love and loyalty of her child. She didn't like that, and the sooner she could get rid of Cassidy, the better.

"Maybe I'll just head up that way," Cassidy said, sensing the woman's desire to have him gone. "How about a piece of that fresh bread to eat on the way? Haven't had any fresh bread in a long time."

As Annie hurried into the cabin to fix the bread, Cassidy put his arm around Roy's shoulders and offered some friendly advice.

Chapter 4

"Sometimes a Ma and Pa will work a strong boy like you until he don't know there's anything else in life but sweating and grunting like an ox."

"I don't mind work," Roy said, "as long as I can have some fun once in a while."

"I just want you to remember one thing," Mike said, "something your folks will never tell a boy like you."

"What's that?"

"If you got a fast horse and a good saddle, and know how to use a rope and gun, you'll never have to work for anybody as long as you live."

"I'm not sure I understand."

"There's hundreds of ranches between here and Canada, and strays everywhere. With a fast horse, a good hand with a rope can catch and sell enough strays to keep money in his pockets, like we did on this trip."

Roy knew what Mike was talking about.

"Remember, a fast horse, a good saddle, and a sure hand with a rope and a gun."

"I've got the horse and saddle, and I'm learning to use a rope. But I don't have a gun."

"That will come later," Mike said, looking towards the house. He didn't want the woman overhearing what he was telling her son. "I'll get work at the Marshall Ranch and check in on you once in a while. Keep throwing a hundred loops a day. Catch a critter or two every day too. Remember, thumbs down when you throw, and thumbs up when you dally. Take your rope everywhere you go. Catch bushes, trees, rocks, anything that comes along. Rope until putting that loop on a thing is no different that reaching out and touching it with your finger. When you are that good I'll see you get a gun and learn how to use it."

"You mean it?" Roy exclaimed. He didn't know any boys his age who owned their own gun.

"That's a promise," Mike said.

"A promise for what?" Annie asked. She was walking towards them, two big slices of bread, covered with bullberry

23

jam, in her hands.

"I told him if he practiced roping every day, someday he would be as good as me," Mike said, carefully avoiding the subject of the gun. Roy also knew better than to mention getting a gun around his mother.

"Remember what I said," Mike reminded Roy as he got onto his horse. "Thumbs down when you throw, thumbs up when you dally."

"I won't forget what you told me," Roy said. Annie handed Mike the bread and jam.

"Thanks Ma'am," Mike said, pulling his horse around and easing it into a smooth gallop, taking a big bite of the bread and jam as he did so.

"I'm glad you're home," Annie said, as she began walking back to the cabin with Roy.

"Me too," he said. "Where are the kids?" He was the oldest of seven, and it was unusual not to have children playing near the cabin.

"Down by the pond," she said. "Old Jack died yesterday. The children said they were going to bury the old horse. Maybe you should go down and help them."

"I will, as soon as you fix me another piece of the bread and jam," he said, pushing what was left of the first piece in his mouth.

A few minutes later Roy was riding towards the pond, looking for his little brothers and sisters. He was a few hundred yards away when he saw them. They didn't see him because they were intent on dragging the partially bloated remains of Old Jack into a freshly-dug shallow grave. Blanche and Dan were doing most of the work, while the smaller children tugged and pushed as best they could.

Had the horse been on level ground the children would not have been able to drag it, but since there was a downhill slope to the grave, they were able to jerk it along an inch or two at a time. Roy urged his horse into a gallop, eager to help his brothers and sisters.

As the children turned towards the approaching

hoofbeats, the first thing Roy noticed was how dirty their faces were. All had been crying. All had been wiping away tears with dirty hands.

"Bob," Blanche called, recognizing her older brother. While the parents called their oldest son by his given middle name, LeRoy, the brothers and sisters called him by his first name, Robert, or Bob.

"Old Jack died," sobbed five-year-old Eb.

Roy leaped from his horse as the children gathered around. Reaching out with his strong, young arms he drew them to him. All of them were talking at the same time, for the most part saying things about Old Jack and how bad they felt that he died.

"Come on," Roy urged, a brief minute later, "I'll help you put Old Jack to rest." The children hurried back to their work. With Roy helping, the horse was soon in its final resting place.

Roy was amazed at the size of the hole his little brothers and sisters had dug for their horse. Though it was shallow compared to a human grave, it was plenty big. The children had worked long and hard, taking turns with the two family shovels and a pick.

"Somebody should say something before we cover him up," Blanche said, looking at Roy. Several of the children nodded their approval. Roy was the oldest. He should say the words. Besides, he had spent more hours riding Old Jack than anyone else in the family.

Roy removed his hat and looked down at the horse he had known so well. The old gelding had been with the family for many years. It was on Old Jack's back that Roy and the older children had learned to ride. Roy guessed the animal died of old age, though no one knew how old the horse was.

Roy hesitated. He wasn't nervous or frightened at being called on to give a funeral sermon for a horse, not in front of his brothers and sisters. It was a matter of not being sure what to say. Looking down at the dead animal, he hoped he could think of something that would make his brothers and sisters feel better.

Roy, like his father, was not a regular church attender, but he had been to several funerals and guessed the words spoken over the human dead, might work at a horse funeral too.

"Lord," he began, slowly, "some of us Parkers are gathered around Old Jack today to pay our last respects, and to dedicate this hole as his final resting place."

Roy realized the children were still and silent, except for a few sniffles. They were listening to every word. They waited for him to continue. He didn't disappoint them.

"Lord, we don't know if there is a heaven for horses," Roy continued, "but if there is, Old Jack ought to go there. He pulled our wagon over rocky roads, jerked our stumps out of the ground, pulled our plow over a hundred miles, and helped raise us Parker children. He never complained, not even when four or five of us crawled on his back at the same time, not even in the winter when we ran out of hay and he had to nibble sage brush." All the children were sniffling now. Roy had a choking feeling in his throat as he forced out more words.

"Lord, if there's a heaven for horses with green valleys and knee-high grass and cool, clear water running in sparkling streams, then Old Jack deserves to go there." Roy hesitated, but as he continued his voice became stronger.

"But don't let him go there as an old, worn out gelding. Give him his nuts back and let him be young again, galloping through those green valleys as a powerful stallion, leading his own band of mares who bear him new foals in the eternal springtime of that beautiful place." Roy was surprised at his eloquence.

"Let it be so. Amen," he concluded. He picked up one of the shovels, scooped it full of sandy, rocky soil, and reverently sprinkled it over the remains of the horse. The rest of the children, the older ones using implements, the younger ones using only their hands, began pushing the soil over Old Jack. None of them spoke until their work was finished--Old

Chapter 4

Jack neatly covered with a mound of orange dirt, circled neatly with white river rocks.

"That was a nice prayer," Blanche said as Roy boosted the three smallest children onto his mare and started walking back to the cabin.

Roy didn't answer. His thoughts were elsewhere. Burying the old horse had stirred up some strong feelings. He didn't want to spend his life toiling over a poor piece of land at Circleville, Utah. He wanted adventure, excitement and money. He wanted to see new places and meet new friends. He didn't want to be like his parents, and Old Jack, grunting and toiling for meager survival. Robert LeRoy Parker would have something better. Mike Cassidy had given him a taste of what he thought was the good life. He wanted more. He would learn to rope. Then he would learn to use a gun, and before very many years would pass, he would mount a strong, fast horse and leave this hard country and go to better places.

Chapter 5

With nearly a month left before the beginning of school, Roy's life fell into a predictable routine. Upon getting out of bed each morning he threw 50 or 60 loops at a cow skull lashed to the end of a log. Some days he practiced roping only the horns, other days the whole head.

After breakfast, while his mother and one or two of the older children milked the two family cows, Roy rode up to the land his father wanted cleared. There he chopped and sawed at the stubborn trunks of juniper trees until his arms became weak and rubbery. Then he got on Babe and dragged the freshly fallen trees to the edge of the clearing. On the way back he would toss loops over clumps of purple sage or rabbit brush. After dallying his rope around the saddle horn he would cluck the mare forward, jerking the unwanted plants out of the ground. Such work became play, Roy imagining the clumps of brush to be wild cattle, buffalo or even the burly store owner who had tried to have him whipped.

About mid-day when Roy returned to the cabin for dinner, he didn't mind if the food wasn't ready. That gave him time to throw more loops at the cow skull. His brothers

Chapter 5

and sisters soon learned if they ventured near Roy while he was practicing with his rope, there was a good chance their feet or heads would become targets for his friendly loop. But even the slap of the most gently thrown loop tended to sting and burn, so the children generally stayed out of range. In the afternoons Roy did chores around the yard and moved irrigation dams. Between tasks he practiced roping.

It wasn't long until the two family cows, Sal and Hutch, began finding themselves on the receiving end of Roy's loops. At first they ran from him, but the boy's attempts to catch them were so persistent that the cows soon realized that getting roped wasn't as hard on them as running away. In time they just stood still and let the boy throw loops at them as often as he pleased.

It wasn't long until Roy's search for roping targets began leading him to the open range where he had no trouble finding plenty of two-horned targets. Of course, the range cattle didn't belong to the Parker family, and were branded, but that didn't stop Roy. He wasn't stealing them, just catching them and turning them loose. At first his targets were calves and yearlings. Because the younger cattle didn't have fully developed horns, it was necessary for him to catch the entire head. By the time school started, he was roping cows, and an occasional bull.

One afternoon as Roy was about to turn loose a yearling bull he noticed the animal had no brand. He hesitated. He remembered the first winter his family had moved to Circle Valley. They had brought nearly fifty head of cattle with them, but winter storms had been so severe, and with no hay put away, all but the two cows, Sal and Hutch, had died. In the yearling bull, Roy saw an opportunity to accelerate the growth of a new family herd.

Roy left his rope on the little bull and began driving it ahead of him back to the ranch. Whenever it tried to run back around him to join its former companions, Roy would dally the rope around the saddle horn and jerk the calf to a halt. It

29

would fight the rope for a minute then stand still as Roy worked his horse in position to begin driving it again. After a while the young bull realized there was no advantage in fighting the rope, and trudged sulkily ahead of the boy rider.

Roy knew his mother wouldn't be very happy with him for bringing in an unbranded stray off the range. She would argue that even without a brand, the stray belonged to the owner of its mother. Roy knew that morally she was probably right, but according to the law, the calf belonged to the person or outfit putting the first brand on its hide. Not wanting to discuss the matter with his mother, Roy herded the bull directly into the corral, stretched it out on the ground, built a fire, and applied the family brand. Then he turned it in with Sal and Hutch who welcomed a male companion. Now it would no longer be necessary to take Sal and Hutch to Mr. Kittleman's every spring to be bred. Roy walked into the house and told Annie what he had done.

As he anticipated, she was strongly opposed. She insisted he return the bull immediately. He told her he had already branded the animal, that it was too late. He argued that his father would no longer have to work at the mines and carry mail when the family herd was large enough to have beef to sell every year. Mavericking was the only way he knew to get his father and her husband living at home again. Besides it was perfectly legal.

Annie still insisted he was wrong. But the idea of having her husband living at home again was the most persuasive argument of all. Perhaps in this instance, the ends justified the means. She agreed to let Roy keep the bull.

If school hadn't started, the family herd would have grown more quickly. Roy was already more skilled with a rope than most of the men in Circle Valley. He didn't miss very often. His horse, Babe, was fast enough to catch any cow around, even in rough country. But between school and chores, about the only time he could get out to look for unbranded cattle was Saturdays and Sundays.

Of course, Annie objected to her son going mavericking

30

Chapter 5

on Sundays--the Lord's day when every good Mormon was supposed to be in church worshiping with the Saints. Roy had been ordained to the priesthood and it was time for him to receive more responsibility in the local church organization.

Roy didn't agree. Whenever the discussion came up as to whether or not he would go to church, he would remind his mother how a church court had ruled against the family in a dispute over some land when they first moved to Circle Valley. Roy agreed with his father that the decision had been unjust, favoring a local member of the high council. Such talk made Annie defensive.

Roy never mentioned the real reason he avoided church meetings because he didn't think she would understand. He simply could not stand sitting all day in boring, stuffy meetings while unbranded cattle were wandering the open range, just waiting for someone to catch them. Besides, Sunday was the best day for mavericking. The large ranchers, and most of their hands, usually spent the day in church.

When it came time to go to meetings each Sunday, Roy always managed to have an irrigation dam that needed changing, or something in need of urgent repair--like a broken fence that would allow the cattle to get out if not repaired immediately. But as soon as Annie and the children were out of sight, Roy stopped whatever he was doing, saddled Babe, and gallopped off in search of unbranded cattle.

By Christmas Roy had increased the family cattle herd to nineteen animals, all carrying the Parker brand. When Roy's father came home for Christmas and saw how his cattle herd was growing, he expressed concern. He told Roy to stop mavericking because sooner or later one of the neighboring cattle ranchers would accuse the boy of cattle rustling. Max, however, did not tell Roy to get rid of the nineteen head already gathered. Obviously, he was pleased with the initiative his boy had demonstrated.

For Christmas that year Roy received exactly what he wanted, two new hemp ropes. He had worn out all the others, not so much from roping cattle, but from the incessant throwing at cow skulls lashed to logs.

Every time a rider approached the Parker homestead, Roy's first hope was that Mike was coming to visit. Roy was always disappointed when the approaching rider was someone else.

With the coming of spring Roy grew increasingly restless. He had roped every cow a hundred times, and nearly every critter on every neighboring farm at least once. He had roped every kid in school, and most of their dogs. Robert LeRoy Parker, though still in his mid teens, was possibly the best hand with a rope in Circle Valley.

One spring afternoon, as Roy hurried home from school, he noticed a strange horse tied in front of the cabin. He knew in an instant the animal belonged to a serious cowboy. Not only were three coiled ropes tied to the saddle, but extra leather was wrapped around the saddle horn to protect it from excessive wear from frequent dallying.

Roy hurried inside, and was not disappointed. Mike Cassidy was seated on a wooden chair by the stove, sipping a tin cup of hot coffee. Annie was temporarily out of the room. Mike was the first to speak.

"Your Ma tells me you're a pretty fair hand with a rope." Grinning, he stood up to shake Roy's hand.

"Step outside and I'll show you," Roy responded.

Continuing to sip at the cup, Mike sauntered towards the door, Roy leading the way. By the time Mike stepped outside into the bright sunshine, Roy had already swung into the saddle and was galloping towards some grazing cattle.

Mike watched with interest as the boy uncoiled his rope and formed a small loop in his right hand. Seeing the approaching rider the cattle began to scatter. Roy headed for the nearest cow, his horse gaining rapidly.

When they were nearly upon the fleeing cow, Roy began swinging the rope over his head, the loop quickly increasing in size as he allowed more rope to feed into the loop. As the boy's hand shot forward the loop settled gracefully, but quickly over the cow's horns, the rope whipping around to the left as the horns stopped its forward momentum. Before the returning end of the loop could settle over the cow's neck, Roy's right hand shot back in a low, sweeping motion, jerking the slack from the loop which was now tight around the cow's horns. Still holding onto the rope, Roy's right hand shot forward to dally the rope around the saddle horn as his horse began to stop.

Upon releasing the cow, Roy galloped proudly back to Mike, who had set the tin cup on the window sill, and was scratching his chin, thoughtfully. He was both surprised and impressed with the boy's roping skill. He knew some hands who were unquestionably better than Roy with a rope, but he knew no one who had learned so much in such a short period of time.

After bringing each other up-to-date on what each had been doing since the previous summer, Mike invited Roy to accompany him on a cattle drive to the Henry Mountains, one of the most remote areas in the Western United States. Cassidy didn't say who the cattle belonged to or why he was taking them to the Henry Mountains.

"Not on your life," Annie shouted, suddenly appearing in the doorway. Apparently she had been listening to their conversation from inside the cabin.

"He's just a boy, and he's still in school," she added.

"Hold on," Mike said, trying to calm an excited mother. "I'll take good care of the boy. We'll be home in five or six weeks, and I'll pay him well, five cows, in advance. Besides, I don't know where else I could get a good hand like Roy. I need him."

"Don't sweet talk me, Mr. Cassidy," she responded. "The boy belongs in school, and that's all there is to it. He cannot go with you." To end the conversation, she turned and marched back into the cabin. Roy knew it would do no good to try to persuade her to change her mind now, so he didn't try. He just shrugged his shoulders and looked at Mike.

"I'll be leaving from the Kingston Ranch at daylight," Mike said. "If you can get your Ma to change her mind, I'd still like you to come along."

"I don't think she'll change her mind," Roy answered.

Mike walked over to his horse, motioning for Roy to follow. After tightening the cinch he unbuckled one of the saddle bags and invited Roy to look inside. Resting in the bottom of the saddle bag was a brand new Colt .44 revolver, resting in a leather holster wrapped in a gun belt with a large silver buckle. Roy knew better than to reach in and take it out. His mother might see, and the sight of a revolver would only make her more determined to keep her son away from Mike Cassidy.

"I picked it up last winter," Mike whispered. "I was going to teach you how to use it on this trip to the Henries. Bought a whole case of bullets too. Figured we'd have shinin' times, shooting and roping. If you got good enough at the shooting, I was going to give you the gun."

"I can get Ma to change her mind," Roy said, a determined, but desperate look on his face. "Look for me at first light. Don't leave without me."

"I won't," Mike said, swinging into the saddle and galloping south towards the Marshall Ranch.

Chapter 6

Mike Cassidy didn't know whether to be surprised, or not, when Roy arrived at the Kingston Ranch the next morning. Babe was freshly shod, and Roy's bedroll was tied tightly behind the saddle. Two ropes and a canteen were hanging from the front of the saddle.

"How did you get your Ma to change her mind?" Mike asked.

"I didn't," the boy answered. "I just snuck away in the middle of the night."

"Don't know if that was a good idea," Mike said, concern in his voice. "Maybe she'll send somebody after you, maybe the law."

"She won't. Parkers handle their own business, and Pa won't be home for a couple of weeks. By then it will be too late to come after me."

"I don't know."

"I left a note. Said I was almost a man, that I'd be careful. Told her I loved her, but she had to let me do this. She'll be fine."

"I hope you're right," Mike said, "but no use worrying about it now. Let's get this herd moving."

After cutting out five cows for Roy, and talking one of the Kingston cowboys into driving them up to the Parker place, Mike and Roy rounded up the 60 or so head of cattle they were taking to the Henry Mountains, and started driving them up the east fork of the Sevier River towards Otter Creek, which they intended to follow upstream for several days before cutting east to the Fremont River, which would lead them to the northern slopes of the Henry Mountains.

Their camp outfit was loaded on a black mule named Andy, who was in love with the sorrel mare Mike was riding. Wherever the mare went, Andy followed. It was not necessary to lead him. He just tagged along, his lead rope tied to the side of his pack, nibbling at brush and grass whenever he felt like it. Mike turned a couple of geldings in with the cattle so he and Roy would have fresh mounts.

It felt good to Roy to be on the trail again with Mike. Even with the responsibility of driving 60 head of cattle, Roy felt light and free, like burdens and worries had been lifted from his shoulders. No school. No irrigating. No little brothers and sisters to care for. No junipers to chop, and no roots to tear out of the ground. No cows to milk or dishes to wash. It was great to be on the trail with Mike.

Riding on opposite sides of the herd most of the time, there was not a lot of opportunity for talk the first day. Several times Roy thought about asking Mike when they would start shooting the guns. Instead he just waited. Mike would know the right time.

That night as they were unsaddling their horses, Mike reached in his saddle bag and removed the new .44 revolver, still wrapped in the gun belt, and tossed it to Roy.

"Might as well start getting used to this," Mike said. Roy didn't need any coaxing. Quickly, he unwrapped the belt and strapped it on. He drew the pistol out of the holster and checked the cylinder to make sure it was empty. His father

Chapter 6

had taught him that.

"We're heading into some of the wildest country in the world," Mike said. "Never know when you're going to need a gun."

"Indians?" Roy asked.

"Injuns usually mind their own business," Mike explained. "It's mostly rustlers and outlaws that worry me."

After a supper of canned peaches, boiled salt pork and coffee, Mike gave Roy his first shooting lesson. He threw the empty peach can on the ground in front of them and told Roy to shoot it as many times as he could.

After two misses, Roy finally hit the can. It hopped five or six feet further away. After another miss, he hit it again, and once again the can bounced further away. After Roy hit it five or six times, Mike walked out to bring it back.

Even though Roy guessed Mike was still a young man, in his late 20's or early 30's, he walked like an old cowboy. There didn't seem to be much movement in his hips or ankles, and his knees seemed more inclined to bend sideways than back and forth like knees should. Mike had spent a lot of time in the saddle.

"Before this trip is over," Mike said, when they had finished shooting, "I'll be throwing peach cans in the air and you'll be shooting holes in them before they hit the ground."

While Roy was cleaning the gun, Mike walked over to his gear, rustled around for a minute, then tossed a coiled up rope back towards Roy. It landed at his feet, remaining coiled because it was tied together in three places with new white string.

"What is it?" Roy asked.

"A rope, of course," Mike responded, smartly.

"I know that. But what kind?" The coils were too smooth and white to be hemp or horsehair. Roy had seen Maguey ropes before, the kind the Mexicans made by hand from cactus fibre. He was familiar with the look and feel of rawhide rope too. The new rope was not made of anything he

37

had ever seen before.

"Silk Manilla," Mike said, proudly. "The best there is. You'll think you've gone to ropers' heaven."

Roy untied the strings, loosened the coils and tried to form a loop. The rope was too stiff.

"It's stiff because it's new," Mike explained. "Tie it tight between two trees tonight, then drag it behind your horse tomorrow. In a couple of days it'll be the best rope you ever threw, and it will stay that way. Won't get soft like hemp. Won't break like rawhide. Won't wear out your hands and horn leather like horsehair and Maguey."

Even though it was April, Roy felt like it was Christmas. A new gun and holster and a new rope, all in one day. There was a smile on his face as he went to sleep that night.

The next morning Roy was awakened by the hoarse braying of Andy the mule. After rubbing the sleep out of his eyes, the boy propped himself up on one elbow and looked towards the animals. Mike had tied the horses and mule close for saddling and packing and was letting each horse nibble oats out of his hat. With all the noise, Andy was just making sure he got his share of oats.

The second day didn't go as smoothly as the first. One of the big steers got a little tender in his front feet and decided he didn't want any more to do with the cattle drive. He merely turned and headed off at a ninety degree angle away from the herd. When Roy galloped out to head him back, the old steer refused to be driven, and when Roy persisted, the old fellow just lowered his head, closed his eyes and charged. Roy got out of the way, but not before one of the long horns raked Babe across the hind quarter. Repeated efforts to drive the steer were answered with charges. The animal was firm in his decision to leave the herd.

When Mike rode over to lend a hand, he wasted no time throwing a loop over the steer's horns. It charged him a few times, but Mike's alert horse managed to stay out of range,

Chapter 6

gradually pulling, jerking and pushing the animal back to the herd, where they turned it loose with the other animals and resumed the drive.

A half hour later the old steer headed off into the brush again. And again Mike roped him and began working the stubborn animal back to the herd.

"Won't he just wander off again when we turn him loose?" Roy asked.

"Nope," Mike answered, suddenly turning his mare to the right and making a complete circle around a juniper tree. He then pointed his mare towards the tree and told her to back. The steer on the other end of the rope didn't want to be pulled into the tree, but every time he shook his head in protest, the mare took another step back, drawing him closer to the tree. In ten minutes the steer's head was snubbed up flush against the tree.

Mike handed the end of the rope to Roy and told him to keep it tight. Mike got off his horse, removed an old Maguey rope from the back of his saddle, and approached the wide-eyed steer.

After removing his knife from his belt, Mike dropped to his knees, the trunk of the tree between him and the stubborn steer. Leaning to his right, reaching around the tree, Mike grabbed the steer by the nose, maintaining a firm hold until the animal stopped jerking and thrashing. Then quickly, Mike thrust the point of his knife three or four inches up the right nostril and sliced through the cartilage separating the two air passages. When he pulled the knife free, blood began to flow from the steer's nose.

After returning the knife to his belt, Mike uncoiled the Maguey rope and formed a loop over the steer's horns. He took the other end of the rope, the pointed end which was not tied in a knot, and pushed it carefully into the steer's right nostril. He had no trouble pushing the rope through the incision he had just made. Reaching into the bloody left nostril he pulled the end of the rope back out, completing the loop

39

through the steer's nose. Being as careful as possible, because he knew what he was doing was painful for the steer, Mike fed the entire rope through the hole in the steer's nose, until all the slack between the horns and the nose was gone.

Mike got on his horse, dallied the bloody end of the Maguey rope around his saddle horn, and told Roy to let the steer go. As soon as the beast realized the first rope wasn't holding him to the tree, he backed away five or six steps, spun around and headed for the hills, not realizing the Maguey rope, which passed through his tender nose, was dallied to the horn on Mike's saddle.

By the time the steer reached the end of the 60-foot rope, he was at a full gallop. Mike's mare had dug in with all four feet anticipating the jerk, which spun the steer around and caused him to roll completely over. He came up bellowing in anger and pain, and charged Mike's horse, which jumped out of the way, just as the steer closed his eyes for the anticipated impact. The horse braced itself for the second jerk, which spun the steer around again.

The fight was suddenly gone from the steer. He had no desire to charge, or flee. His only interest now was to avoid more pain in his already throbbing nose. Mike turned his horse and headed back to the herd.

It took a minute or two for the slow-witted steer to figure out what leading was all about, but in a little while he was following the horse like a sulky pup.

"You don't plan on leading him all the way to the Henry Mountains?" Roy asked when they reached the herd.

"No, we'll let Andy do that," Mike responded as he approached the grazing pack mule. He tied the free end of the Maguey rope to the back of the mule's sawbuck. When the herd started moving again, Andy was close on the heels of Mike's mare, and the steer reluctantly followed the mule.

About an hour later, right after Andy had jerked hard on the steer's lead rope while jumping a little gully, the steer offered his protest, and tried to vent his frustration by

Chapter 6

suddenly charging at the mule. Andy saw the steer coming, laid back his ears, and let fly with both hind feet, striking the steer square in the shoulder. Defeated and bewildered, the steer offered no more trouble the rest of the day.

That evening, before unpacking the mule, they tied the steer to a tree, leaving plenty of slack so he could get something to eat. The next morning they tied him to the sawbuck again. During the morning hours the old boy was so cooperative and agreeable that by noon Roy suggested they remove the rope from his nose and allow him to rejoin the herd.

"Think he'll behave himself?" Mike asked. Roy thought he would, so they removed the rope from the steer's horns and nose and let him rejoin the herd. He behaved himself the rest of the afternoon, but late the next morning, as they were pushing the cattle through a narrow canyon, the steer darted into a thickly wooded side canyon. Junipers, pinion and oak made the canyon an impenetrable barrier for a man on horseback. The steer wiggled and pushed his way into the thickest part of the forest where it would be impossible for a horse to follow.

Roy looked at Mike and said he was sorry for suggesting they take the rope out of the steer's nose. Mike responded, suggesting they give the critter a name, something they could remember him by after they had to shoot him. Rather than leave the animal behind, it was Mike's intention to shoot it and throw a slab of fresh meat on Andy.

"How about Gadianton?" Roy suggested, sensing it would be appropriate to name the rebellious bovine after the arch villain in the Book of Mormon.

"Good," Mike said. "Gadianton it is, but before we kill him, let's try one last time to get him out of the brush. Mike got off his horse, and with rope in hand, began pushing his way into the thicket. It was easy to see the animal, the spring leaves still not fully developed. But it was also easy for the steer to see and hear Mike. It didn't have any trouble

41

staying out of reach of a cowboy on foot. After a while Mike returned to Roy.

He told the boy to build a fire while he went to get some bullets for his gun. They were going to eat Gadianton for lunch. After their shooting practice the previous evening, Mike had neglected to reload the gun on the gun belt. When he returned with a new box of bullets, Roy had a nice fire going behind a large boulder which sheltered the fire from a brisk spring breeze blowing down the side canyon. Mike dropped to one knee beside the fire and began loading his gun.

"Think I can get him out of the brush without shooting him," Roy suggested. Mike continued loading his gun. He knew if he couldn't get the steer out, certainly Roy couldn't.

"Give me ten minutes," Roy said as he disappeared up the side canyon. Mike stretched out on the ground by the fire, wondering what Roy was about to do.

A few minutes later the air over the boulder was filled with smoke, but not from the little fire by the rock. It was coming down the canyon. The spring sun and wind had dried the old grass and leaves from the previous year. Roy had gone upwind to the head of the canyon and set some dry grass on fire.

Mike grinned, holstered his pistol, and leaped on his horse. He rode a short distance from the edge of the thick brush and got his rope ready. He didn't have long to wait. The big steer had had enough of the smoke and was headed down the canyon to join the rest of the herd. Mike got a loop over the horns and trailed the steer back to the herd. Roy wasn't far behind.

"Do you think he'll behave himself now?" Roy asked.

"I think he'll head off into the next thick patch of brush we come across. Don't think we'll be so lucky with the wind next time."

"Should we tie him to Andy again?" Roy asked.

"First, let's try something a Mexican told me would

42

keep a critter out of the brush," Mike said. He still had a hold of the rope that was looped around the steer's horns. Mike rode a circle around the nearest tree, and began cinching the steer up tight against the tree as he had done the first time he roped it. While he was doing this he asked Roy to cut two green oak sticks about as big around as pencils, sharp at both ends, and about three inches long. He didn't explain why, and Roy didn't ask as he rode up to the nearest oak, took out his pocket knife and began cutting the two sticks. By the time he finished, Mike had old Gadianton's face cinched up tight against the tree. This time the steer didn't fight like he had done the first time.

"When a critter goes in the brush, he closes his eyes," Mike explained. "When he comes after you or your horse, he'll close his eyes just before he hits you."

"What do the sticks have to do with that?" Roy asked.

"The Mexican said if you propped his eye lids open with sharp sticks, a critter wouldn't go in the brush, or wouldn't try to hook you."

"Don't know if I believe that," Roy said.

"I don't know either, so I thought we could give it a try and find out if it works." He took the sticks from Roy and crawled under the tree up next to the steer's face. After carefully cutting a little hole with his knife in each upper and lower eye lid on both eyes, Mike inserted the sticks with the sharp ends sticking into the little holes. The edge of the sticks did not touch the eye ball, so Mike guessed there wouldn't be much pain for poor old Gadianton. Mike loosened the rope and let the steer go.

Gadianton walked in circles, shaking his head for a minute or two. When he realized he could not get rid of the sticks, he returned to the herd, carefully keeping his face away from the brush. As the drive continued, Mike and Roy noticed that old Gadianton avoided getting close to anything that might touch his face, including other cattle. Gadianton was finally subdued, and offered no further trouble.

Cassidy

That evening as Mike and Roy were crawling into their blankets, Roy asked Mike if he thought Gadianton would be able to sleep with his eyes open.

"Know some people who can do that," Mike said. "Suppose old Gadianton will have to learn to do it too." He rolled over and went to sleep.

After a week on the trail, they began getting glimpses of the snow-capped Henry Mountains, far to the east and south. A few days later Roy asked why they were continuing straight east, when it appeared they could get to the Henries a lot faster by going in a straight line.

"Because that's not where we're going," Mike said. Roy didn't know what to think.

"But you said we were going to the Henries," Roy said.

"I lied. Didn't want folks to know where we were taking these cows."

Roy had heard all the rumors about Mike being a cow thief. He hadn't known whether to believe them or not. Mavericking was one thing, outright cattle rustling something else.

"We're going to the Roost country," Mike said, pointing to the northeast.

"What's there?" Roy asked.

"Some friends of mine," Mike explained. "They'll take the cattle on to Telluride."

"Why Telluride?" Roy asked, figuring he might as well find out all he could.

"A thousand gold miners eat lots of beef. Mine pays almost double the market. I'm getting rich taking beef to Telluride."

"Why did you tell me we were going to the Henries?" Roy asked.

"Didn't want the Mormons to find out about the high beef market in Telluride. If they knew how much money could be made, every Mormon in the southern part of the

44

Chapter 6

territory would be trailing a herd this way. Besides, the Roost isn't far from the Henries, just a little to the north.''

Mike went on to tell Roy what he was going to do when he became rich. Said he was going to Argentina and get himself a big ranch. He said the land was practically free, the *señoritas* friendly, and the law didn't ask very many questions.

"Take me with you?" Roy said.

"Nope," Mike answered. "But when you are old enough, if you want to come down, that would be fine with me.''

"How could I afford a trip that far?" Roy asked.

"Not by staying home. Get a job in Telluride. A strong boy like you can earn $5 a day.'' From that moment on, Roy started making plans to someday go to Telluride.

Less than a week later, Roy and Mike pushed their herd of cattle into the head of the gentle canyon leading to Roost Spring. Mike's friends hadn't arrived yet, so Mike and Roy set up camp, and waited. There was plenty of feed and good water. The cattle needed little attention, freeing Mike and Roy for serious shooting and roping lessons.

By now Roy's new silk Manilla rope was broken in. Mike had lashed two large bull skulls to a log, and they practiced roping for hours at a time, first the horns, then the whole heads, then the horns again. Mike showed Roy how to swing a larger loop, letting it dip over his left shoulder, and how to throw such a loop in front of the hind legs of a critter to catch both hind feet. After practicing on the ground they saddled their horses and practiced on live cattle.

When they tired of roping, they got the pistols out and started shooting. When it came time to practice at moving targets thrown into the air, they lowered themselves by rope into the lower part of the canyon where they could shoot against a backdrop of steep sandstone walls.

Mike insisted there was a good reason people couldn't hit moving targets. When practicing shooting at something in the air, if they missed, they couldn't tell if they were shooting high, low or to the side, or by how much they were missing. If a target was thrown into the air next to a sandstone wall, the missed bullets striking the sandstone would let the shooter know immediately where the bullet hit in relation to the target, allowing the shooter to make adjustments before taking the next shot.

When it was time for Roy to shoot, Mike would walk up next to a wall, usually carrying an empty cans, and begin throwing it straight up in the air for Roy to shoot at. As Roy was shooting, Mike would keep his back to the wall so the splattering sand and rock chips wouldn't get in his eyes. Roy was far enough back so as not to have to worry about flying debris. After two or three sessions, Roy was hitting the cans a good percentage of the time.

Next, Mike started teaching Roy to shoot from the back of a running horse. Mike said, that in addition to lots of practice, there were a few tricks one needed to know. First, he said it was absolutely necessary for the rider to stand in the stirrups while shooting, letting the knees absorb the up and down movements of the horse. He said this was the reason Indians, hunting buffalo on horseback with bows and arrows, used stirrups, even though they were skilled bareback riders.

Secondly, he said a skilled shooter on a galloping horse doesn't try to hold a steady aim at his target before pulling the trigger. Instead, the rider, in an almost throwing motion, thrusts his barrel down towards his target, pulling the trigger at the moment the barrel passes over his target. A good horseback shooter never tries to hold his aim perfectly still because he simply cannot do it. After three or four days of practice Roy could gallop through camp, hitting one of the bull head roping skulls almost every time.

Roy and Mike had been practicing their shooting and roping for nearly a week when Mike's friends finally showed up to get the cattle. They were two young cowboys named Bill and Morris. As soon as they gave Mike his share of the

Chapter 6

money from the last drive to Telluride, they began rounding up the cattle.

"Why were they in such a hurry?" Roy asked, when the cattle were gone.

"Can't wait to get their money and spend it on women and whiskey," Mike responded. "I'm save'n mine for Argentina. They'll still be poor cowboys when I'm a wealthy land owner in the beautiful foothills of the Andes Mountains. Let that be a lesson to you, boy."

For a minute, Roy thought Mike sounded like his father. The boy didn't ask any more questions as they began packing up their belongings and saddling their horses for the trip back to Circle Valley.

Chapter 7

The cattle drive with Mike Cassidy to Roost Canyon and the Henry Mountains changed Roy forever. He knew it was just a matter of time until he would leave Circle Valley. He figured his first stop would be the mines at Telluride where he would earn enough money to do something with his life. He didn't know if he wanted to join Mike in South America, but he was determined to have the means to at least visit his mentor and friend.

Roy knew the day would come when Mike would leave. Whatever Roy was going to make of himself, he would have to do it on his own. In the meantime, he continued practicing his roping and shooting at every opportunity. He still toiled at clearing land for his father, and helped his mother with the chores and the smaller children, but in time he found his skills with a horse and rope in increasing demand. Local ranchers were discovering that when it came time to round up cattle, rope and brand, and drive herds, young LeRoy Parker was a good hand to have around.

Roy appreciated the confidence, the money he earned

Chapter 7

from the work, and the associations with the other cowboys. Whenever there was a roping or shooting competition, Roy won most of the time. The pay he received from his cowboy jobs was usually spent on new ropes and bullets.

He worked for a while in the mines at Marysvale where the pay was better than what he could earn as a cowboy, but the work wasn't nearly as much fun.

During the summer of his seventeenth year, anticipating he would need good horses when he finally left home, he made a deal with his neighbor, Jim Kittleman, to breed Babe to a fine thoroughbred stallion. Kittleman had the finest horse herd in that area of the territory. Roy had hopes the new colt would be bigger and faster than Babe.

During the following winter Roy learned to play the harmonica. He caught a magpie, built a cage for it out of willow sticks, and taught it to say a few words. He began to attend dances in Marysvale and Panguitch. Though his interest in members of the opposite sex was sincere, he didn't want to think about settling down, or as Mike put it, being tied down with a woman.

Roy's energy seemed boundless. Except for an occasional fight, he managed to keep out of trouble, at least until the summer when he turned 18.

The year had started out good, with Babe dropping a fine horse colt in late spring. The size and conformation of the foal indicated it would be both big and fast, and hopefully have some of its mother's intelligence and sense. Roy named the foal Cornish.

Soon after the colt was born, Mike dropped by to offer his final farewell. There were rumors from Panguitch that the sheriff was getting ready to file charges against Mike for cattle rustling. The local ranching community believed many of the cattle Cassidy was driving to Telluride were not his own, and not mavericks either, but stolen from the ranchers in southern Utah. It appeared enough evidence had finally been gathered to make the charges official, and Mike wasn't about to wait around to see what would happen. He had enough money saved up to buy his ranch in Argentina, and figured it was time to make his move. He told a number of people he was going to Mexico, and confided in Roy that this was merely a ploy to keep the law off his trail in the event people got serious about bringing him back to stand trial. Roy agreed to keep the confidence.

It was an emotional parting. In the absence of Roy's real father, who was away working most of the time, Mike had become a substitute father, a good friend too. Roy knew his most prized possessions--ropes, gun and saddle--and his ability to use them, came to him as a result of his association with Mike. By this time, Roy knew Mike had been rustling cattle. Roy had mixed feelings about Mike's refusal to include him in any of the rustling activities, except for the one trip to the Henry Mountains and Roost Canyon. On the one hand Roy appreciated Mike not wanting to help get a boy on the wrong side of the law. On the other hand, Roy would have liked to share in some of the money Mike was making. After all, Mike wasn't stealing from poor people, but from the big ranchers who could easily afford the loss of a few cows now and then.

"There's four things I want you to remember," Mike said as he untied his horse and prepared to mount. "I don't care if you forget everything else I ever told you. Just remember these four things."

As far as Roy was concerned, Mike Cassidy was the greatest man he knew. Mike was better at doing important things--riding, roping and shooting--than anybody Roy knew. The boy listened carefully.

"Don't be afraid to die," Mike began. "This is a wild, dangerous world. People who are too afraid of death never amount to anything." Roy was surprised. He hadn't expected Mike to talk about death.

"Second," Mike continued. "Friends are more important than money. A lot of people agree with this in principle, but few people live this way."

Mike placed his toe in the stirrup and stepped into the

saddle. "You said there were four things you wanted me to remember," Roy said, afraid Mike would ride off without finishing.

"Three," Mike continued. "There's nothing more exciting than a good horse race. And four, there's nothing more desirable than the love of a good woman." Roy thought Mike would continue, but the cowboy just smiled as he began to rein his horse away.

"What will you do?" Roy asked, not wanting the conversation to end. Mike pulled his horse in, momentarily.

"The first thing I'm going to do is find me a good woman," he grinned. "Then I'm going to get real serious about the horse racing business." Mike eased his horse into a gallop. Roy never saw him again.

After Mike's departure, Roy felt increasingly restless. He had just turned 18, and he knew it was time for him to go. What made leaving so hard was the fact that his family was so dependent on him. His father was still off working, and his mother leaned on Roy to do the man's work around the place. He thought he had been doing the family a favor by bringing in and branding wild cattle so the Parkers could get their own herd started again, but with Pa off working, Roy was the only one who could handle the cattle. It was tough to just pack up and leave. Besides, he got along well with his mother, brothers and sisters. He knew when he left he would miss them.

One afternoon in late spring, two small-time ranchers, Fred and Charlie, stopped by to ask Roy if he would help them rope and brand some spring calves they had rounded up and were keeping in a corral up at the Marshall Ranch. Roy knew Fred and Charlie were not very good hands with ropes, and he could do in a few hours what these two would need all day to do. He agreed to meet them at the Marshall Ranch.

The next morning as Roy began roping the calves so Fred and Charlie could brand them, he didn't have to be very smart to see what was happening. Many of the cows in the corral carried brands that did not belong to Fred and Charlie, yet the two men were branding all the calves with their own brands.

Roy asked them about it. Fred said they had bought the calves, range delivery, meaning the buyer was responsible to round up the livestock he had purchased. It was their intention, after the calves were branded, to turn the cows back on the open range and take the calves home to be fed by Fred and Charlie's milk cows. Roy guessed that if his two friends were challenged, they could not produce a bill of sale for the calves, but he was just working for them and had no intention of asking to see a bill of sale.

When the branding was finished, and Roy was turning the cows out onto the range, he noticed a rider approaching. Fred and Charlie were busy tieing the calves' feet so they could load them like sacks of grain in the back of a wagon. Neither had noticed the approaching rider.

Roy stopped what he was doing to see what would happen. By this time the cows Roy had turned out had surrounded the corral and were mooing for their calves, which in turn were bawling for the mothers.

The rider had just about reached the mooing cows when Roy recognized him as Pete Ream, a hand on one of the big ranches. Roy had worked with Pete. He was a good man with a rope, and he rode good horses.

Without a word, Pete rode among the cows, checking the brands. Fred and Charlie still hadn't noticed his arrival. Roy watched as Pete rode over to the wagon where Fred and Charlie were loading the calves. When they finally saw him, they stopped what they were doing. Both looked surprised. Neither said anything.

After checking the calves, Pete pulled some paper and a pouch of tobacco out of his shirt pocket and rolled a cigarette. Still, no one had said a word. Roy was wearing his Colt .44, but had no intention of using it to defend Fred and Charlie in the event trouble broke out.

Pete was the first to speak, after taking a long draw from his cigarette.

Chapter 7

"Looks like you boys have a mite of explaining to do," Pete drawled, looking at Fred and Charlie. "I'm head'n into town to tell the sheriff what I saw here today. Hope you got your affairs in order."

Pete took another draw from his cigarette then tossed it in the dust. Without another word he turned his horse toward town, and eased it into an easy gallop. He never looked back. Neither Fred nor Charlie had said a word.

When Pete was out of sight, Fred and Charlie jumped out of the wagon and ran over to Roy. Now they had plenty to say.

"We'll go to prison for sure," Fred cried. There were tears in his eyes. His voice was breaking.

"If they don't hang us," Charlie added, his voice high and squeaky. He appeared more frightened than Fred.

Roy was disgusted. Both knew the risks when they stole the calves. They should have been better prepared to handle the eventuality of getting caught. Roy knew Mike would not have acted this way had he been caught with stolen cattle. He would have taken it like a man. Fred and Charlie were acting like frightened children.

"We'd better go straight to Mexico," Fred said, trying to get a hold of himself. "They'll never find us there."

"What about our wives and babies," Charlie sobbed. "We can't take them with us. Without us they'll starve."

"No they won't," Fred said. "The bishop will excommunicate us and give our wives to someone else, in polygamy." Both men started to cry. Roy felt sorry for them. At the same time he found their weakness laughable.

"We shouldn't have done it," Fred said. "I shouldn't have let you talk me into it."

"It was your idea, not mine," Charlie protested.

"I know how both of you can get out of this mess," Roy said. It was the first time he had spoken since turning the cows out. The men stopped crying and looked at him.

"When the sheriff shows up tomorrow," Roy explained, "just show him a bill of sale for the calves."

53

"We don't have a bill of sale," Fred said. "If we did we wouldn't be in this mess." There was a note of sarcasm in his voice.

"I could write out a bill of sale for you," Roy said. "When Sheriff Wiley gets here, just show it to him and there won't be a thing he can do to you."

"But where will you get the bill of sale to give us?" Fred asked. It still hadn't occurred to him what Roy was offering to do.

"I said I would write it out for you," Roy said.

"Then the sheriff would come after you," Charlie said. "And all you did was help brand the calves."

"Why would you do this for us?" Fred asked, suspicion in his voice.

"I don't suppose I'd be doing it for you as much as for me," Roy responded. They didn't understand. He continued. "I've been wanting to leave this place for some time, and just can't seem to bring myself to do it. If the sheriff was after me for cattle rustling, I suppose I'd have to leave."

Fred wasn't about to let this moment get away. He reached in his shirt pocket and pulled out a piece of paper and a pencil which he handed to Roy. The boy got off his horse. He flattened the paper against the side of his saddle and scribbled, "Sold to Fred and Charlie, nine whiteface calves, June 1884." Then he signed his full name, Robert LeRoy Parker. Without hesitating he handed the note to Fred.

Not wiating to give Fred and Charlie a chance to thank him for what he had done, Roy stepped into the saddle and headed for home. He didn't think to collect his pay for the day's work. He had other things on his mind. There was much to do, and little time to do it. He felt good. He was finally going to do what he had wanted to do for a long time. Robert LeRoy Parker was going to Telluride.

Since it was almost dark, he spent the night at home. He enjoyed the home-made bread and a home cooked meal more than usual, knowing it might be his last. He played with the children longer than usual that night, not telling them he would be gone the next morning.

It wasn't until after the children were asleep, and Roy was beginning to put his things together that he told Annie he was leaving. She tried to talk him out of it, but he wouldn't listen. When she persisted, he told her about the phoney bill of sale, and how he had to leave. She said his father would be home in a few days and could straighten things out. Roy said he couldn't take a chance on that. He didn't sleep much during the night, and neither did his mother.

The next morning both of them were up before the children awakened. Roy knew he had to be on the trail before his brothers and sisters found out what was happening, and began crying for him to stay.

Annie wrapped some fresh bread and a jar of bullberry preserves in a blue woolen blanket Grandfather Parker had made for her, and handed it to Roy. He tied the blanket behind his saddle.

He tied Dash, the family dog, to the fence so it wouldn't follow him, and he let Babe's new colt out of the corral so it could follow. He told Annie he would not be traveling alone, that his friend Eli Elder was going with him. Roy embraced his mother one last time, stepped into the saddle, and urged Babe into a gallop. He wanted to be through Circleville before anyone saw him.

Roy planned to pick up Eli at Marysvale. The two had talked often about going to Telluride, and Eli made Roy promise that if he ever went that way he would take Eli with him. Roy intended to keep his promise to his friend.

After passing quietly through Circleville in the early morning light, Roy headed straight for Marysvale, trying wherever possible to avoid travelers on the main road. He knew the law would be looking for him sooner or later, so he wanted to avoid contact with people as much as possible.

With the colt tagging along, Roy couldn't travel as fast as he could have otherwise, so it was almost dark when he finally reached Marysvale. He hid the horses in a patch of oak brush at the edge of town and hurried to the shack where Eli was staying with some other miners.

Eli wasn't there, but in jail. He had bitten off a man's ear in a fight. Roy's first thought was to continue to Telluride alone. But he figured as long as he was in Marysvale he might as well speak with Eli. He headed for the jail.

Finding the barred window to the cell, Roy called Eli's name. His friend answered immediately. Yes, he still wanted to go to Telluride, now more than ever, but he wouldn't get out of jail for probably another week. Roy couldn't wait that long.

"Then bust me out," Eli said. Roy laughed until Eli explained how it could be accomplished. Roy hurried back to his horses, saddled Babe, and rode back to the jail, the colt following close at his heels. The jailer was gone for the evening, leaving the prisoners alone.

The street was dark outside the cell window. Roy didn't waste any time. He rode up to the window and passed one end of his silk Manilla rope through the bars.

Eli didn't think the bars could be pulled from the outside window without attracting a lot of attention, so he pulled the rope across the cell and tied it to the inside door leading to the jail office. This door seemed much less substantial than the iron bars covering the outside window.

After tieing the rope to a bar next to the lock, Eli whistled for Roy to start pulling. Now Babe knew what it meant to lean into a rope and pull. She had been on the business end of a rope attached to many an unwilling steer or cow, and knew what it meant to dig in with all four feet and test the strength of a rope. She didn't know what the rope was attached to inside the jail, but when Roy gave her the signal to start pulling she popped the slack out of the rope and lunged forward with all her might. When she felt something give at the other end, she stopped. She had pulled the inside door from its hinges.

Roy coiled up his rope and returned to the oak grove where he had hidden the horses earlier. An hour later two riders showed up. One was Eli, and he had brought a friend,

Chapter 7

Heber Wiley, who wanted to ride with them to Telluride. Heber was the nephew to Sheriff Wiley.

Roy had no objection to more company. He swung into the saddle and headed for the same trail he and Mike had taken to the Roost Country. He hoped he was ready for what he guessed would be the greatest adventure of his life so far.

Chapter 8

Roy and his two friends, in their hurry to get on the trail to Colorado, failed to make adequate preparation for a journey which would take them hundreds of miles across what was probably the most desolate wilderness in North America. While each boy had brought along a gun, a knife and a blanket, they soon found themselves out of food and matches, and rapidly running out of ammunition, as they were forced to use up their bullets shooting rabbits to eat. Because they hadn't brought along rain gear, their sleeping blankets were soaked in afternoon thundershowers for two consecutive days, making sleeping very uncomfortable.

When Eli's horse threw a shoe and the foot became tender, they had no spare shoes or nails, or any horse shoeing tools. While the animal wasn't lame enough to abandon, it became necessary to lead the horse. The three boys began taking turns riding and walking.

Roy remembered the trip along the same trail with Mike Cassidy a few years earlier. The journey had been fun and easy because Mike had been prepared. Now, the same

Chapter 8

journey, the same time of year, was tough. Roy decided that as soon as he earned some money he would begin assembling his own pack outfit, and he would get a mule like Mike's Andy to carry it.

On the morning of the third day, after being unable to build a fire without matches in the early morning coolness, the boys forced down a breakfast of half-dried, uncooked rabbit flesh before hitting the trail.

Later that morning they spotted a herd of about 30 horses grazing next to a bluff about a mile to the west of the trail. They could see smoke from a lone campfire near the horses.

Because of their troubles with the law in Circle Valley and Marysvale, the boys had been careful to avoid other travelers, but sleeping in damp blankets and eating raw meat was rapidly wearing down their otherwise normal caution. They realized whoever had built that campfire might be cooking breakfast. Maybe bacon, eggs, coffee, and biscuits with gravy or honey. The boys had to investigate.

When the morning breeze carried the smell of boiling coffee to their eager noses, they quickened their pace. They could see a lone man hunched over a small cook fire. He seemed neither concerned nor alarmed at the approach of the three young cowboys.

"If you fellers don't mind sharing my only cup, you're welcome to some coffee," the stranger said when the boys were close enough to hear his voice. The man remained crouched by the fire. Using a leather glove to protect his fingers, he removed the steaming coffee pot from the glowing coals.

"Used up our last match yesterday," Roy said, cheerfully. "Had to eat raw rabbit for breakfast. That coffee looks mighty good."

Carefully, the man poured the steaming contents from the pot into a tin cup. After returning the pot to the coals, he stood to face his three young visitors. His clothing was soiled and worn, like that of a man who had been on the trail for

59

many weeks. He was a middle-aged man with healthy, sun-tanned skin and jet black hair, except for a streak of silver on both sides. Even though the stranger was smiling, there was an unmistakable fierceness in his eyes that made Roy a little more cautious than he otherwise might have been.

"The name's Cap Brown," the stranger said as he handed the cup to Roy.

"My name's Cassidy, George Cassidy," Roy lied. He knew the law would be looking for him sooner or later, and he didn't intend on making his trail any easier to follow than it already was. He raised the steaming cup of coffee to his lips.

"My name is William Shakespeare," Eli said, figuring if Roy used an alias, he might as well do it too, and William Shakespeare was the first name that came to mind. He spoke the new name just as Roy was beginning to swallow. Caught by surprise, Roy coughed, spraying coffee all over the stranger.

"Something wrong?" the stranger asked, seemingly undaunted by the mention of the famous English poet.

"Sorry," Roy said. "Didn't expect the coffee to be so hot. Caught me by surprise." Again he raised the cup to his lips.

"My name's Porter Rockwell," Heber said. This time Roy didn't choke on his coffee. He couldn't believe the stupidity of his companions. Maybe the stranger didn't know about William Shakespeare, but he would certainly know about Porter Rockwell, Brigham Young's enforcer, the west's greatest gunfighter and toughest lawman, by anybody's standards.

"Thought you died in seventy-eight," Brown said, looking directly at Heber.

"That wasn't me," Heber replied, after a moment's hesitation. "That was the real, or I guess I should say the first Porter Rockwell. I was named after him."

"You boys want some biscuits?" Brown asked, apparently unconcerned over the strange offering of names.

60

Chapter 8

All three young men nodded at the same time. After a breakfast of partially dried raw rabbit flesh, merely the mention of hot biscuits made their mouths water.

Brown picked up two tin plates. One was covering the other. He removed the top plate, allowing the boys to see nine golden brown biscuits. Eagerly, the boys waited for Brown to pass them out. Instead, the plate still in his hand, Brown turned around and began reaching into a canvas pannier.

"Don't have any butter," Brown said. "Too hot during the day to keep butter. But there's a jar of honey in here somewhere."

Finally finding a fruit jar half full of yellow honey, Brown removed the lid and poured a good portion of the contents over the biscuits while they were still in the pan. Finally, he handed the pan to the three hungry boys.

"Eat'm all," he said. "I've had my breakfast." Without another word, and without bothering to wipe their hands clean, the three boys reached for the honey covered biscuits and began wolfing them down. When they finished, it took them two or three minutes to lick all the excess honey off their fingers and hands.

"Will you sell us some supplies?" Roy asked, when they had finished licking up the honey. "We're headed over to Telluride to work in the mines."

Brown rubbed his stubbled chin, carefully looking over the three boys, then their horses. They were well mounted, he concluded.

"You can buy all the supplies you need in Hanksville," Brown said, carefully. "Charlie Gibbons has a store there."

"I know," Roy said, "but we need something to hold us over until we get there."

"Have you been to Hanksville?" Brown asked.

"Yes, with Mike Cassidy, a couple of years ago."

"Then your real name must be Roy Parker. Mike told me about you. Said you were a good hand with a rope."

Roy nodded. He guessed Brown knew all about Mike Cassidy, and how he rustled cattle to sell to the mines in

61

Colorado.

"I might be willing to let you take the mule and my whole camp outfit as far as Hanksville," Brown offered. The boys were listening. With Brown's outfit they could have hot biscuits and honey, with coffee, every morning.

"Why don't we ride together," Roy offered. "We could help you drive your horses."

"What I had in mind," Brown explained, "is letting you boys push the ponies to Hanksville for me, in exchange for eating my food and using my camp outfit. I've got some business in Salina. If you would do that for me, I could head over there today."

Roy looked at his two partners. They didn't see anything wrong with Brown's proposition. All of them shook hands. Brown gathered up some supplies and a blanket to tie behind his saddle.

"Just put the horses and mule in Charlie Gibbons' corral," Brown said as he stepped into the saddle. "Tell him I'll be along to get them in a few days."

When Brown was gone, the boys fried up some potatoes and onions, and boiled up another pot of coffee. When they were so full they couldn't eat any more, they loaded the camp outfit on the big brown mule Brown had left behind, and began to round up the 30 or so horses they had agreed to deliver to Hanksville.

As soon as they got close to the grazing animals, Roy noticed something very wrong. He recognized many of the horses. At least a dozen carried a small K brand on the left shoulder. That brand belonged to Jim Kittleman, Roy's neighbor and friend in Circleville. While Kittleman sold a horse now and then to raise cash, it was unlikely he would sell a dozen at one time, including his two favorite brood mares. Kittleman was a bachelor, and loved his horses like children. Roy knew the two old mares were not for sale at any price, yet here they were on their way to Hanksville.

"These are stolen horses," Roy said to his companions. "We can't drive them to Hanksville."

Chapter 8

"We promised Brown we would," Eli said. "It's none of our business where he got them. Maybe he bought them from a rustler, not knowing they were stolen."

"Twelve of these horses belong to Jim Kittleman and ought to be returned," Roy insisted.

"You're not proposing we go back to Circle Valley, not with all the trouble we're in."

"I've seen old man Kittleman feed these mares off his supper plate," Roy explained. "I've seen him lead them right into his cabin during a bad storm, or when they were about to foal. It would break the old man's heart to lose these animals."

"I'm going to Telluride, not back to Circle Valley," Eli said, his voice firm.

"Me too," Heber said.

Roy figured it was probably more risky for him to return than for either of the other boys. He didn't want to go back, but he couldn't help steal Kittleman's prize horses either.

"Here's what we'll do," Roy said, after mulling the matter over for a few troublesome minutes.

"I'm heading back with the twelve horses belonging to Kittleman. You two drive the rest to Hanksville as we agreed to do."

"You'll get arrested and thrown in jail," Eli warned.

"I won't drive them all the way home," Roy explained. "I'll push them in that direction until I find a cowboy who will take them the rest of the way. I'll give him a ten dollar gold piece. Then I'll turn around and head back this way, hopefully catching up with you two before you reach Hanksville. If I don't catch up before you get there, just wait a few days."

"I don't like it," Heber said. "We shouldn't split up. Besides, Eli and I don't know the way to Hanksville."

"You can't get lost," Roy said, pointing northeast to a big snow-capped mountain off in the distance. "The Fremont River flows east from there. Just follow it to Hanksville."

Cassidy

Roy shoved a few things to eat into the rolled-up blanket behind his saddle, and put some wooden matches in his shirt pocket. After cutting out the horses with the K brand on the left shoulder, he began driving them back towards Circleville.

Roy was still riding Babe. Her colt, Cornish, stayed close to her as Roy moved around Kittleman's horses and began the drive towards home.

That evening Roy found a good camping spot in a little side canyon leading to Otter Creek. There was plenty of grass and a good spring. The horses were tired and hungry after the day's journey, so Roy figured there would be no reason for them to leave the canyon before morning.

Roy set up his camp in a flat, sandy spot between two sandstone boulders, built a little fire and began to dress out a cottontail rabbit he had shot a few hours earlier. He planned to roast it over the fire on a green pinion pole.

He was seated on the ground, his feet towards the fire, his back against one of the boulders, beginning to run the green pole through the inside of the rabbit, when he heard the unmistakable click made by the hammer of a revolver being cocked back.

Carefully, he placed the rabbit and pole on the ground. He didn't want to make any sudden movements that might cause the person holding the gun to pull the trigger. Slowly, Roy turned his head in the direction of the sound.

Two men had emerged from behind a juniper tree, not 30 feet away. Both were pointing Colt revolvers at Roy. He didn't recognize the men.

"You're under arrest," one of them said. Roy noticed the man who spoke was wearing a silver badge. The other was not.

"What for?" Roy asked, not moving.

"Horse stealing," the man said.

"I didn't steal any horses," Roy said.

"Twelve animals with a K brand were rustled in Circleville night before last. We followed the trail to this very

64

spot, finding you and the horses. Looks like you're the feller we've been hunting."

Roy couldn't believe his bad luck with the law. He had been arrested for taking coveralls which he fully intended to pay for. He had been forced to leave home because the law thought he had stolen cattle which in fact his neighbors Fred and Charlie had stolen. Now he was being arrested for stealing Jim Kittleman's horses while he was trying to return them to the rightful owner.

"You may not believe this," Roy explained, deciding he should tell the truth. "I got these horses off a man named Cap Brown, and I'm returning them to Kittleman. Jim's a friend of mine."

"I suppose Brown started feeling guilty for taking so many fine horses, and asked you to return them for him," the man with the badge said.

"Not exactly" Roy said, sensing the officer was only playing with him. "Brown doesn't know I'm bringing them back."

"Save it for the judge," the officer said, stepping forward. The second officer kept his pistol pointed at Roy while the first one placed a pair of iron bracelets on Roy's wrists, and another pair on his ankles. The officer with the badge began cooking the rabbit, while the other disappeared into the brush to take care of their horses. Later when they offered Roy a piece of his own rabbit, the boy declined. He said he wasn't hungry. The officers said their names were Nephi Hackaberry and Moroni Lee.

It was a long night. Roy didn't sleep much. He wasn't cold because the officers had let him roll up in his blanket. After a while the shackles didn't bother him, but he still couldn't sleep. He figured he was probably going to go to jail.

The next morning, following a brief breakfast of jerky and water, and after the horses were saddled, the officers removed Roy's ankle bracelets, allowing him to mount his horse. There had been few words spoken since waking up. The officers were tired, and eager to get back home with their prisoner. Roy was discouraged at the possibility of going to jail.

It was early afternoon when they decided to stop for lunch. One of the men had shot a porcupine and they decided to stop and cook it.

Officer Hackaberry, the one with the badge, removed a bucket from one of the panniers on their pack horse and headed down to the creek for some water. The other officer gathered an armload of twigs and sticks and began to make a fire. Roy was sitting on the ground, his back against a flat rock, near the spot where the fire was being built.

Concentrating on getting the fire started, Officer Lee placed his rifle on the ground as he leaned forward to hold a wooden match under some small twigs. As the tinder began to smoke, he puffed gently to help the tiny flame spread.

As Roy watched, he realized he had an opportunity to escape, if he could push the unsuspecting Lee away from the rifle, pick it up, and get the drop on Lee. But Roy hesitated. Lee had a pistol in a holster on his belt. He might draw the pistol and begin shooting. If that happened, the other deputy down by the stream would enter the fight. Roy remembered the words of advice he had received from Mike Cassidy--don't be afraid to die.

It seemed like the most natural thing in the world to lift up his feet and thrust them into the deputy's side. So he did it, sending the startled officer rolling away from the fire. At the same time, Roy lunged forward, picking up the man's rifle, quickly cocking back the hammer and taking aim at the deputy who by now had stopped rolling. Roy was surprised the man hadn't yelled to his partner for help.

"One peep and you're dead," Roy hissed, doubting he would really be able to pull the trigger should the man yell. The officer remained silent. Roy told Lee to remove his Colt from the holster and toss it over. The man obeyed. Roy leaned back to his original position against the rock, placing the rifle and pistol at his side so Hackaberry, returning from the stream with the water, could not see them. Then he told

Chapter 8

Lee to resume building the fire.

A minute later, Roy had disarmed Hackaberry too, who reluctantly handed over the key to the shackles. It felt good to be free again. Taking the officers' guns with him, Roy got on his horse.

"You won't get away boy, we'll catch you," Hackaberry said.

"That won't be easy without saddle horses," Roy said, carefully untying their horses while keeping an eye on Lee and Hackaberry.

"You wouldn't dare leave us out here without horses," Lee said.

"You can ride Kittleman's horses," Roy said. "If you can catch them. I intend to scatter them down the trail ahead of you. Have no idea what you will use for saddles and bridles. Just make sure Kittleman's animals are returned."

Roy untied their pack horse too, and since it wanted to follow the saddle horses, he didn't attempt to lead it, as he headed back up Otter Creek to rejoin Eli and Heber. He guessed without saddles and guns, the officers would not attempt to follow him. By the time they got back home and assembled a posse, Roy and his companions would be so far away it would not be practical to follow.

When Roy caught up with Eli and Heber on the Fremont River, they were surprised he had returned so quickly. Heber had been worried they would never see Roy again.

"Where'd you get the extra animals?" Eli asked. Roy told them about his run-in with Hackaberry and Lee, how they had arrested him for stealing Kittleman's horses, and how he had gotten the drop on them and taken their horses.

It took Eli and Heber a minute to realize the full significance of what Roy was saying.

"Then we've been driving a herd of stolen horses?" Eli asked. Roy nodded.

"Cap Brown's a rustler?" Heber asked. Roy nodded.

"If we get caught with these horses we could go to

jail," Heber concluded. Roy nodded a third time.

"I'm getting out of here," Eli said. "Without the horses. I don't want the law after me for rustling."

"Me neither," Heber said. "Let's git."

"Just a minute," Roy said. "I been thinking. I have a plan. The law's not after either one of you, so just ride on to Hanksville without me, and wait for me there."

"What'll you do?" Heber asked.

"Since the law's already after me for cattle rustling, and now for getting loose of the two officers and taking their horses, I figure I don't have anything to lose in trying to dispose of these horses. Maybe I can get enough money out of them to get us a good start in Colorado."

"You can't sell them without a bill of sale," Eli protested.

"I'll write up my own like I did with the calves," Roy explained.

"Where will you sell them?" Heber asked.

"We're not far from Loa, I'll just drive'm up there."

"Will Brown come after us if he finds out we sold his horses and kept the money?" Eli asked.

"He might," Roy explained. "But I doubt it. They're not his horses to begin with, and he almost got me arrested and thrown in jail. We're the ones who ought to be looking for him."

"We'll wait for you in Hanksville," Eli said. He and Heber turned their horses east. Roy rounded up Brown's stolen horses and headed for Loa.

Loa was a Mormon farming community near the headwaters of the Fremont River. It had a saloon, general store, blacksmith shop, and a church which doubled as a school.

After stopping at a few ranch houses where no one was interested in buying horses, Roy drove his little herd right into the middle of town and ran them into a large corral next to the saloon. He went inside to make sure it was alright to leave his horses there, and to let the bartender know the animals were for sale for only $20 each, about half the market value. Roy figured the bartender might be able to get the word out to a lot of people fast. Next, Roy walked over to the general store to tell the men over there about the $20 horses, and that he didn't think they would last long.

When he was finished, he walked back to the saloon, which was also a restaurant, and ordered the only meal on the menu--steak, potatoes, onions and fresh bread with butter and desert holly preserves. As he was finishing up the steak, a middle-sized, middle-aged man, wearing clean but well used cowboy clothes, entered the saloon. Also, he was wearing a badge.

Sitting across the table from Roy, the man announced he was the sheriff of Wayne County, and that he would like to see a bill of sale on the horses in the corral.

Roy couldn't believe his bad luck. It seemed no matter which way he turned, he was getting into trouble with the law. The last time, with Hackaberry and Lee, Hackaberry and Lee, Roy had told the truth, and they had put him in shackles. He decided to lie this time.

"Raised most of them myself, so they don't have bills of sale," Roy explained, confidently. "Rest belonged to my neighbors. I'll be sending them the money when theirs are sold."

Rubbing his chin, between a thumb and forefinger, the sheriff looked Roy over very carefully. "What's your name? Where're you from? Why did you bring the horses here to sell?"

"My name's George Cassidy. I'm from Beaver, and I'm headed to Colorado to work in the mines. Seems everybody's selling horses where I'm from. Thought the market would be stronger along the way. It hasn't been. This is my last chance to get them sold before heading into the desert, so I lowered the price."

"Why is it I don't believe you?" the sheriff said.

Roy didn't say any more, wondering if it would have been better to just tell the truth. After all, it was Cap Brown who was the horse thief.

"Mind if I put you in jail while I run a check on these ponies?" the Sheriff asked.

"That'd be fine with me," Roy said, not backing down.

The sheriff looked at Roy for a few seconds, then began to smile. "Loa don't have a jail," he said. "Either have to tie you up, or trust you to behave yourself. What'll it be?"

Now Roy was smiling. "You can trust me to behave myself," he said. The sheriff nodded, turned and walked out the door. Roy finished his dinner and returned to his horses.

Now the law was pestering him, Roy wondered if he should still try to sell the horses, or if he should just try to get away to join Eli and Heber while he was free to do so. He guessed the Sheriff liked him. He decided to stick with his original plan and see how much he could sell the horses for.

Roy was sitting on the pole fence looking at the horses when a bunch of boys, seven or eight, came over to see what was happening. Most of them appeared to be two or three years younger than Roy. Two of them were tossing a baseball back and forth.

When they climbed on the fence to get a better look at the horses, Roy told them they could have any horse in the corral for only $20. Some said they would bring their parents back.

"You want to play baseball with us?" one of the smaller boys asked.

"You got a bat?" Roy asked.

"We got lots of bats, a backstop, bases, mitts and balls," one of the older boys said. "We've got everything but enough players."

"Let's play ball," Roy said, jumping down from the fence.

Excited at having a new player, the boys gathered around Roy, asking him lots of questions about his baseball experience, Then they hurried over to the diamond which was less than a hundred yards from the corral.

Roy spent the rest of the day playing baseball. He was

no stranger to the game. Circleville had a diamond too, and Roy had learned to hit a ball further and with more consistency than any one else in Circle Valley. The Loa boys had never seen anyone who could hit the ball as well as Roy. When evening came the game did not end. Eventually some of the fathers joined their boys. Mothers brought picnic suppers. They played until it was too dark to hit the ball.

When Roy returned to the horses, there were some men there, with money to buy seven head. Roy spent the night near his horses, rolled up in his blue blanket.

To his surprise, the boys returned early the next morning, ready to play more baseball. Roy was happy to join them. The game resumed.

A few times during the course of the day Roy noticed the sheriff watching over the fence. Occasionally, a man would come to the corral. Roy would leave the game to show horses. He sold seven more, all at the $20 price.

When evening arrived, Roy called the boys in for a huddle at the pitcher's mound. He didn't know if he should be worried about the sheriff, or not, but he was. He had sold all but four of the horses and was eager to be on his way.

"I've got to be leaving," Roy said. The boys moaned, not wanting the game to end.

"See those last four horses?" Roy asked, pointing over to the corral. "I don't want to take them with me, so I'll give a horse to each of the first four boys who can get a hit off my fast ball." Most of the boys stood their ground, looking at Roy, thinking he was teasing.

"I mean it," Roy said. "A free horse to the first four boy who can hit my fast pitch before striking out. Line up at the plate." This time the boys raced to home plate and lined up to get a chance at winning a horse.

Roy threw for a good half an hour before the fourth boy finally got a hit. After that all the players walked over to the corral together to participate in the awarding of the prizes.

Roy saddled Babe, swung into the saddle, said goodby to his baseball friends, then headed east towards Hanksville.

Cassidy

As he left Loa it felt good to feel the jingle of money in his pocket. The Wayne County Sheriff was not around. That felt good too.

Chapter 9

When Roy arrived in Hanksville, Eli and Heber were hard at work branding calves for Charlie Gibbons. The friendly storekeeper insisted Roy join his two companions until the work was finished. Gibbons said it wouldn't last more than a day, or two, at most.

Roy was reluctant. He said he was in a hurry to get to Telluride. Actually, he was worried about who might following him from the west, either officers of the law with a warrant for his arrest, or possibly Cap Brown, wondering what had happened to his horses. Eli and Heber didn't seem to share Roy's concern.

Reluctantly, Roy went to work branding calves with his two companions. While working he kept an eye out for approaching riders from the west, but none came.

Roy liked the friendly Gibbons, giving him one of the horses he had taken from the deputies, including the saddle. In exchange for that, and for the boys' help with the branding, Charlie Gibbons gave them enough supplies for their journey to Colorado. Roy gave Gibbons five $20-dollar gold pieces with instructions to give them to Cap Brown, along with an explanation of how Roy had been arrested, but still had been able to sell some of the horses in Loa. He said to tell Cap he was sorry for what had happened and that the $100 was probably all Cap would ever get from that herd of stolen horses.

"I wouldn't leave any money for a horse thief," Eli protested when he saw how much money Roy was handing over to Gibbons.

"We're in Cap's country now," Roy explained. "He knows these trails better than anyone else. Hate to have him trying to catch me. Besides, he makes his living trailing horses and cattle to Telluride. We'll be living there. Cap may want to look us up one day, and I'd rather have him wanting to fill us with whiskey instead of lead."

They packed the supplies on the deputies' mule and headed out. Gibbons, who had traveled to Telluride on several occasions with Brown, gave them careful instructions on where to cross the Green and Colorado Rivers. While they would see a few ranch houses along the way, they would not see another town of any size until they reached Montrose, which was a good day's ride from Telluride. They would be traveling south of Green River, Thompson Springs and Moab.

Gibbons warned that the Green and Colorado Rivers would still be swollen with spring run-off waters from the mountains and could be dangerous. He told the boys to attempt crossings only at the heads of rapids where the water was shallowest, and only where they could see trails leading into the water, the places cattlemen, Indians and travelers used to cross. He warned against crossing at places where no trails entered the water, no matter how calm and shallow the water might look. Such places might have submerged boulders, swift undercurrents, or large deposits of quick sand. The boys listened carefully. None of them had ever crossed anything larger than the Sevier River.

Gibbons told them if they were careful and didn't travel at night, they shouldn't have any trouble following Cap

Chapter 9

Brown's trail. He said Brown had been on the rustle for a lot of years and had been supplying the mines at Telluride with cattle and horses since the mid seventies.

As they rode east out of Gray's Valley, which later became known as Hanksville, Roy was finally beginning to enjoy the journey to Colorado. They had plenty of food, matches, bullets and rain gear. They were in the wildest country Roy had ever seen, no ranches or cabins, no lawmen. In the first three days they didn't see anybody but themselves, not even an outlaw or Indian.

After leaving Gray's Valley, they crossed the Dirty Devil River and rode to the head of what Gibbons called Happy Canyon. As they pushed onto the plateau at the top of the canyon, Roy saw some of the most spectacular country he had ever seen--endless desert canyons of red and purple. Now he knew why outlaws came to this forbidden place. It seemed he could see a thousand places where a man could hide and never be found.

Behind him the Henry Mountains rose from the desert floor to majestic, snow-capped heights. Ahead of him he could see the snow-covered LaSalle Mountains. He knew the trail he was following would lead him around the south end of those mountains, but before he got that far he would have to cross two mighty rivers, the Green and the Colorado.

Roy felt a choking sensation in his throat. There was something about this wild, rugged desert land that filled him with emotions he had not felt before. He knew this land could kill him, if he wasn't careful. But it could also offer protection and solace. Somehow the rugged beauty of the place left him with a feeling of peace, a feeling that his daily troubles were insignificant, when compared to all this spectacular desert wonder.

Picking their way down a rock slide the boys entered a long canyon that led them due east to the Green River. Upon reaching the river, they were in no hurry to cross. The rushing brown water had flooded the thick tamarisk patches and cottonwood groves along the side of the river, clear evidence the river had overflowed its normal boundaries. The river looked a hundred yards wide at the mouth of the canyon they had come down. It looked doubtful that either man or horse could swim that far through such a raging current.

Quietly, the boys made camp, no one wanting to share with the others the fear he felt concerning the upcoming river crossing. The uncertainty was the hardest thing to deal with. None of them had any experience at this kind of thing. Nobody had any idea how difficult or dangerous the crossing might be. Though all of them could swim a little, the result of playing in irrigation ponds, none of them were experienced, strong swimmers. Roy looked at his mare and wondered how strong a swimmer she would be. He was sure she had no experience crossing this big of a river. The irrigation pond at home had not been deep enough for her to swim. Crossing the Sevier River had never required swimming.

After supper Roy scouted up and down the bank, finding what he thought were old cattle trails leading down to the water. This was probably the spot where Cap Brown drove his herds across the river, but Roy couldn't be sure.

No one slept very well that night. It wasn't so much the incessant swarming of mosquitos around their heads as it was the worry of the crossing that kept them awake. After breakfast the next morning, no one seemed to want to be first to begin saddling the horses.

"I think we should wait," Roy said, hoping his friends wouldn't think he was a coward. "The water looks awful high. Maybe it'll go down in a couple of days. Maybe someone will come along, who has crossed here before, then we will know what we are up against."

Heber and Eli were quick to accept Roy's suggestion. Both seemed relieved that Roy felt as uneasy about the river as they did. The boys decided to go hunting. They had seen fresh deer tracks the night before.

That evening they feasted on fresh venison roasted over an open fire. Before rolling up in his blanket, Roy walked down to the river and pushed a stick into the sand at the water's edge. By checking the stick every morning and evening he would know if the water level of the river was rising, lowering, or staying the same.

The next morning when Roy checked the stick, he measured a six-inch drop in the water level. That was good news, he thought. In a week the river might drop three or four feet. He guessed that would be worth waiting for. He shared his discovery with Eli and Heber. Both were in agreement that as long as the water level was falling, they would wait.

The second day the boys moved their camp a few hundred yards away from the river to get away from the most mosquitos any of them had ever seen. In the afternoon, after rubbing the juice from wild onions over their faces, necks and hands to repel the insects, they returned to the river and caught a few catfish for supper. Then they explored some ledges where they found ancient Indian writings and some broken pottery. They discussed at length how the early Indians might have crossed the river, reaching no conclusions that increased their own confidence in crossing.

Late in the afternoon of the third day, as Roy was tieing a hind quarter of venison to a green pole in preparation for roasting, he heard the mule bray. Then two or three of the horses whinnied. Roy guessed someone was coming, and the animals were offering their greetings. He put down the meat, stood up, and looked up the canyon. He could hear the rustle of brush and the snapping of dry branches. It sounded like a large number of horses or cattle were coming.

A minute later he saw a dozen horses break from cover and gallop towards his camp. They were followed by a lone rider. Roy recognized the man. It was Cap Brown. Roy checked the .44 in his holster to make sure it was ready. He didn't know how angry Cap was going to be.

"Sure glad I caught you boys before you crossed the river," Cap yelled as he pulled his lathered horse to a stop. "Could use some help pushing these ponies across. How come you camped so far from the river?"

"Mosquitos are too thick by the water," Roy

responded, relieved that Cap didn't seem angry with him.

"Hate skeeters. Got any coffee?" Cap asked as he dismounted.

"Did you get the $100 I left for you at Gibbons' store?" Roy asked as he poured the coffee for Cap.

"Not much to show for 30 animals."

"You didn't tell us they were stolen. I almost went to jail," Roy said.

"Guess I should have told you," Cap said, taking his hat off. "But I didn't think three good Mormon boys would want to drive a herd of stolen horses. I didn't think the law would give you any trouble that far from Panguitch." Roy didn't tell Cap he had been arrested while trying to return Kittleman's animals.

Roy went back to work, preparing to roast the hind quarter of venison while Brown unsaddled his horse and unpacked his mule. While he was doing this, Heber and Eli returned from exploring upstream. Heber asked Cap when he thought it would be safe to cross the river.

"In the mornin'," Brown said. "Can't wait to leave all the skeeters behind."

"Isn't the water too high?" Eli asked.

"Not if you're a good swimmer," Brown said. The three boys exchanged looks of concern with each other.

"If any of you can't swim real good," Brown continued, "cut some punk wood out of the dead cottonwoods. I'll show you how to make a life jacket."

All three boys went to work gathering punk. When they had gathered a sizeable pile of the porous, half-rotten wood, Cap showed them how to tie pieces together in a belt that could be secured around their waists. He said in the event one of them got dumped in the river, the punk belt would keep them afloat while they paddled ashore.

The next morning after the horses were saddled, and the gear packed tightly on the mules, they drove the little herd of horses down to the river. All three boys had strings of punk wood tied tightly around their waists. The horses stopped at

Chapter 9

the edge of the water. Cap began instructing the boys in the art of crossing big rivers on horseback.

"Head straight for the opposite shore," he said, "We won't come out on the spot you are looking at, but down there somewhere." He pointed to a sandy beach about a quarter of a mile downstream.

"Stay on your pony when he starts to swim," he continued. "If you don't he'll probably try to turn around and come back. Get off only if he starts drowning, or if you're more than halfway and know he'll keep going to the opposite shore. If you get off, stretch out flat and hang onto his tail. If you get in front of him he'll paw you to death. You boys lead the way. I'll push the ponies in behind you. I'll come last to make sure nothing turns back. Let's go."

"Isn't that a long way for a horse to swim?" Roy asked. None of the boys had moved.

"Sure is," Cap laughed. "Good thing we'll only be swimming for 20 or 30 yards, unless somebody gets carried into the rapids. Most of the river is shallow enough to wade."

This news made the boys feel a little better. Because the water was so murky, it was impossible to gauge depth by just looking. They had assumed the river to be a lot deeper than it really was.

Roy spurred his mare into the water. The colt, Cornish, galloped up and down the bank, whinnying excitedly to his mother. Roy called to the colt as he pushed the mare further into the river. Finally the colt plunged into the water and splashed to its mother's side. Eli and Heber followed.

As soon as the three boys were in the water Cap began pushing the 12 horses in behind them. With the boys' horses in the water ahead of them, Cap's horses followed without a lot of coaxing. Cap came in after them, yelling and shouting at his horses to hurry them along. Last came the two mules carrying the camp gear.

Roy was nearly to the middle of the river when his mare's head suddenly disappeared under the murky water. He could feel her trying to swim. When her nose finally surfaced, it was stretched straight out in front of her. Roy could feel her legs churning vigorously in the brown water. She tried to turn downstream. Roy kept her head pointed straight for the far shore which was now moving from right to left at five or six miles per hour.

As soon as the mare's feet hit bottom again, she braced herself against the current and began walking towards shore. Her colt was about 30 yards downstream and hurrying towards the shore too, instead of to its mother. Cap managed to keep the swimming horses ahead of him, and in another minute all were safely on the bank.

The boys began removing their home made life jackets.

"Might want to keep them," Cap said. "We'll be crossing the Colorado tomorrow. It's bigger and swifter." The boys draped their strings of punk wood over their saddle horns.

Roy was glad Cap had come along to help them cross the river. He figured with what he had learned, he could do it on his own the next time. As he looked back, the river didn't look near as frightening as it had an hour earlier.

Crossing the Colorado River was about the same as crossing the Green, except the horses had to swim a little further, and one of the mules got too far down stream and had to flounder through some quicksand.

"Tell us about Telluride," Roy said as they were cooking supper that evening. Cap was seated on the ground leaning back against his saddle, letting the boys do the cooking while he nursed a bottle of Valley Tan. He hadn't offered any to the boys, after telling them they were too young to drink hard whiskey.

"Stay away from Pacific Avenue," Cap warned in a serious tone of voice.

"That's where the sheriff has his office?" Roy asked.

"Nope."

"What's on Pacific Avenue?" Heber asked.

"Twenty-six whore houses, and I've been in every one of'm," Cap bragged. "But if I catch any of you boys going down there I'll make sure your parents find out about it. That's a promise," he added.

"Pacific Avenue," Roy said, teasingly. "We'll have to remember that."

"And I'll tell your bishops too," Cap threatened. "If Diamond-Tooth Leona or Jew Fanny got a hold of one of you Mormon boys, I'd just hate to think what would happen." He took another drink from his bottle. There was a happy, far-away, look on his face.

"Who are they?" Eli demanded.

"Diamond-Tooth Leona owns the Pick and Gad, and Jew Fanny, the Senate," Cap explained. "Two places young boys should never go."

"Why not?" Roy asked. Cap looked at the boys for a minute, wondering whether or not he should attempt to answer what he thought was a dumb question.

"Telluride is the most beautiful city on the face of the earth," Cap responded, deciding it was time to change the subject. "If the good Lord asked me for a suggestion on how to make Heaven, I'd say make it like Telluride--surrounded by pine tree forests and jagged snow-capped granite peaks. There's lush, green meadows, even in the middle of summer, crystal clear running streams, full of trout, and three of the most beautiful waterfalls you'll ever see. The folks calls them Cornet, Bridal Veil and Ingrams.

"Because the nights are cool, even in summer, folks got their stoves going. They burn pine because there's so much of it. Other towns smell like outhouses in summer. Telluride smells wonderful, like pine smoke and horse shit--over a thousand horses and mules stabled right in town. If I died and could pick my own heaven, I'd pick Telluride."

The boys urged Cap to continue. They loved hearing him describe their new home.

"Lots of good people in Telluride," Cap continued. "People who don't go down to Pacific Avenue. They have a band with fifty trumpets, French horns and Spanish horns too. There's Germans, Irishmen, Swedes, Italians and Scotsmen--

and everyone of'm talks so funny you can't understand a word they say. There's a couple of dozen saloons with any kind of drink you can think of. They have ice, if you want it, even in the summer. There's dog fights, cock fights and fist fights Friday and Saturday nights, and horse racing every Sunday."
Cap took a deep swallow from his bottle. He was happy to be returning to Telluride.

"In the stores you can buy about anything you want, even oranges from California, onions from Salt Lake, beans from Mexico, sardines from Norway, and cashew nuts from Georgia. You can get your picture took for a dollar. The stage office has a telephone that works, the only one in town. I know, I talked to the sheriff in Montrose, and he talked back. Had some questions about brands on some of my cattle.

"When I'm in Telluride I go to church on Sundays at Hurley's Saloon. Of course, they hold church before the whore houses open up, and before the horse races start. Parson Hogg rides over from Silverton to preach hell fire damnation. His boy hits you on the knuckles with a willow stick if you don't put enough money on the collection plate. When the sermon's over you don't leave because Hurley opens the gambling tables. Parson Hogg always buys a stack of chips with the collection money and gives his flock a chance to win their donations back. If you ask me, that's a good way to run a church.

"In Telluride there's politicians, blacksmiths, gamblers, doctors, singers, fortune tellers, niggers, chinamen and Injuns. When the fancy ladies takes their dogs for walks they lead them on short, fancy ropes.

"And everyone is rich. Thousands of men earn five dollars a day at the mines. Everybody has plenty of money to buy drinks for his friends. Telluride's a wonderful place..."

Cap was through talking. He was snoring, undoubtedly dreaming of his next visit to Pacific Avenue.

Chapter 10

The next morning after breakfast, when the boys figured it was time to hit the trail, Cap announced there was some work to be done. He removed an 18-inch running iron from one of his panniers. The business end of the iron was curved like a spade, making it possible to burn either curved or straight lines. With a running iron, and a little skill, a cowboy could burn any brand he wished on the side of a cow or horse. Cap pushed the spade end of the iron into the coals left over from the breakfast cook fire.

"What's that?" Roy asked.

"You boys sure is green," Cap responded, shaking his head. "Never seen a brand before?"

"Not like that," Roy said.

"The best brand a man on the rustle could ever have," Cap said. "I calls it the full moon brand. Now you boys run out and catch them horses and we'll brand'm."

"Most of them are already branded," Roy said.

"Catch them anyway," Cap said as he threw an armload of wood on the fire.

The boys didn't ask anymore questions. One by one

they caught the horses and brought them in. Heber or Eli, mounted on their saddle horses, would lead the horse past the fire, the lead rope dallied firmly to the saddle horn. Roy would circle in from behind and rope the hind feet. The two riders would then stretch the horse out until it fell over on its side. They kept the head and heel ropes tight until Cap was finished burning his full moon brand over the top of any and all existing brands. After the initial circle was burned in the horse's hide, Cap used the edge of the brand to burn over the space inside the circle. When he was finished all signs of the earlier brands were gone. It took Cap and the boys about an hour to brand all Cap's horses.

"Now I can write out a legal bill of sale for every horse," Cap said when they were finished.

"Doesn't anybody ever challenge your fresh full-moon brand?" Roy asked.

"Not in Telluride," Cap grinned. "I'd never take a band of freshly branded full-moon horses to Salt Lake or Denver. The lawmen in those places tend to be more uppity and particular. In Telluride, as long as the brand is technically legal, no questions are asked."

Five days later as they headed south out of Montrose, they encountered a non-stop caravan of wagons traveling in both directions. The wagons coming from Telluride were full of high-grade ore to be loaded on rail cars at Montrose. The wagons returning to Telluride were loaded with lumber, hay, grain, whiskey, coal oil, horseshoes, hardware, food-- everything people needed in a booming mining town.

"You're looking at the most valuable dirt in the world," Cap explained as they passed a large ore wagon pulled by six mules. "Eight hundred ounces of silver and eighteen ounces of gold in every ton, plus zinc, lead, copper and iron."

It took the big wagons two days to make the trip from Telluride to Montrose, a day to change cargo, and another two days to return. A man on horseback or in a buggy or surrey could make the trip in one long day. Pushing his horses

Chapter 10

at a trot much of the time, Cap was determined to make the journey from Montrose to Telluride in a single day. Roy was surprised when Cap turned in at a ranch house about the middle of the day.

"You boys ought to keep your horses here," Cap explained, "unless you want to sell them." He said the going rate for stabling a horse in Telluride was a dollar a day, which was very expensive. They could leave a horse at one of the ranches along the Montrose road for about a dollar a month. That's why he had turned into the ranch.

Cap introduced the boys to Jake Butler, owner of the ranch, who agreed to keep Eli's and Heber's horses for a dollar a month each, and Roy's mare and colt for a dollar and a half. Cap gave Butler $3.50 to cover the first month's rent. Butler warned the boys if they didn't keep their pasture bill current, he would sell their horses to pay the bill.

Roy didn't like Butler, even though the rancher made some favorable remarks about Babe and Cornish. Butler could recognize well-bred horses when he saw them. Roy couldn't put his finger on it, but he guessed Butler was a selfish and mean man. He was tall, fairly good looking with black, curly hair, but Roy could feel no warmth in the man.

The boys threw their saddles on three of Caps full moon horses and soon were back on the road to Telluride. When they asked Cap about the different kinds of jobs available in the mining town, he said most men worked in the mines digging long tunnels through solid rock. He said the jobs in town--clerks, bartenders, and stable hands--didn't pay as much.

Cap said if he ever worked in Telluride, he would want to be a mule skinner, those who worked with horse and mule pack trains hauling the ore down the mountain from the mines in Marshall Basin. The mule skinners, in addition to earning as much as the diggers, got to work outside with the livestock, breathing fresh air and enjoying the beautiful scenery.

"That's the kind of job I want," Roy said.

"The problem with being a mule skinner," Cap said,

85

"is that everybody else wants to do it too. As I see it, not very many men can handle a mule. First, a man has to be smarter than the mule, and I've met darn few men who qualify, and the man is rare indeed who is smarter than a string of ten mules all together."

"Yup, I'm going to be a mule skinner," Roy said.

"A mule is like an ugly woman," Cap continued. "Spend some time winning her trust and respect and she'll do what you ask of her."

"What about pretty women?" Heber asked.

"They'll do as they damn well please, no matter how you treat them," Cap said.

Roy didn't know if Cap knew what he was talking about or not, as far as women were concerned, but the boy did know he would rather work with mules than dig tunnels through solid rock.

The sun had set when they reached Telluride, but there was still enough light to see the booming mining town was as beautiful as Cap said it would be, surrounded by jagged snow-capped peaks, lush green forests, crystal clear streams and roaring waterfalls.

As the three wide-eyed boys followed Cap up Colorado Avenue, laughter and music poured out the front doors and open windows of what seemed countless saloons, gambling houses and dance halls. Even though it was evening, all the businesses were open and busy, and the street was clogged with wagons, carriages, riding horses and pack animals. Roy was sure it was the busiest, happiest place he had ever seen.

Cap rented the boys an upstairs room at Hurley's Saloon, ordered them each a steak dinner with green onions, fried eggs, potatoes and orange slices, then headed off to Pacific Avenue, leaving strict orders for the boys not to follow.

The boys slept with their window open that night, not wanting to miss out on any of the exciting noises going on in the street below. As Roy drifted off to sleep he was glad he had left Circleville. He was glad he was in Telluride, and wondered what great adventures he was going to have.

Cap wasn't around when the boys got up the next morning, so they had breakfast without him, then started up Colorado Street together to check out the various mine offices to see what work was available. Because he was determined to get work as a mule skinner, Roy wore his spurs and carried his silk manilla rope. He wanted to look as much like a mule skinner as possible. He even rubbed a little coal soot on his cheeks and chin to make himself look like an older man who hadn't shaved in several days.

Getting jobs wasn't as easy as the boys thought it would be. There were no openings at the Liberty Bell, the Alta, Hidden Treasure, or the Smuggler mines. When Roy asked if there were openings for mule skinners, the usual response was there were none, but when there were such openings, they hired experienced mule skinners only. Because the trails were steep and rough, they couldn't let boys and greenhorns handle the stock. Roy concluded the soot he had rubbed on his cheeks hadn't fooled anyone.

Finally, at the Sheridan office, they were told there were some openings to replace several miners who were on a drinking spree and didn't show up for work. The mine needed gad hammerers, men who broke loose rocks into little pieces. The pay was $5.50 a day, if the boys agreed to be responsible for their own room and board, or $4.50 a day if they wanted to live in the company barracks at the mine. Heber and Eli accepted the later arrangement. They were instructed to follow the trail up the steep hill on the north side of town, leading to Marshall Basin where the Sheridan mine was located.

Roy passed, insisting he was going to get work as a teamster or mule skinner. Saying goodby to his friends he continued up Colorado Avenue alone, checking for work at the Pandora, Cleveland, and Union mines, finding no openings for mule skinners.

Finally he entered the office of the Tomboy, one of the mines located in Savage Basin, high on the mountain beyond Marshall Basin. The manager was in the front office, but he was too busy arguing with a man dressed like a cowboy, to take time to talk to Roy.

"I don't care how you do it," the manager was yelling at the cowboy. The manager was a bald, paunchy man, wearing a white shirt and red bow tie. His face was flushed with anger. "When you accepted the job you said you could haul anything we wanted up the mountain. That cable has been sitting out in the street for weeks, getting rusty. We want it up the mountain, now!"

"But it's an inch thick," the cowboy protested. "And it's four thousand feet long. It weighs over a pound to the foot. The biggest elephant in the world couldn't carry that much weight, and you want me to put it on a mule--which I could do if you would let me cut it in smaller pieces, but you won't."

"Why don't you roll the cable out on the ground, hitch five or six mules to one end, and try dragging it up the mountain," the manager suggested. Roy sensed the man was frustrated enough to scream.

"Too many switchbacks," the cowboy said. "It'd get hung up on the corners. "Besides, there's too much traffic coming down the mountain." Roy recognized a familiar tone in the cowboy's voice. He had heard it many times before, in other cowboys. Because the man had some experience in handling horses and other livestock, he thought he was somehow smarter and better than people who did not handle livestock. He felt contempt for those less fortunate human beings who did not have manure on their boots. It was obvious in the cowboy's tone of voice, he thought the office manager was no better than an old steer who had been kicked between the eyes too many times.

"If you can't drag it," the manager continued, trying hard to be calm. "Perhaps you could roll it out on the ground, lead a long line of mules alongside, lift up the cable and tie it to the sawbucks."

The cowboy started laughing. The stupidity of the manager had reached new heights. The wrangler couldn't wait to tell his cowboy friends about this dumb suggestion.

"Actually, it might work," the cowboy finally said, fighting to control his laughter. "If we put a mule every ten feet we would need only four hundred mules to carry your cable up the mountain." He burst into laughter again.

In frustration, the office manager surrendered. He turned away from the cowboy to see what other business needed his attention. He would worry about the cable later.

For the first time, the manager saw Roy who was dressed in his cowboy best, and was in no mood to talk to another cowboy. Still, he asked the young man what he wanted.

Every time Roy had asked for a job that morning, he had been not only rejected, but abused and insulted. Nobody wanted to hire a young teamster. Instead of just asking for a job, Roy decided to take a different approach at the Tomboy.

"I'd like to haul that cable up the mountain for you, in the morning," Roy said, surprising even himself with his boldness. He had an idea on how he might get the cable up the mountain. That was all.

The cowboy heard what Roy said, mumbled something about babes in diapers wanting to do a man's work, turned and stomped out the door. The manager looked Roy over, carefully, then began to smile. It was not a smile of ridicule, but one of genuine warmth.

"You have no idea how I wish I could believe you," the manager said. "Every mule skinner in Telluride is like that horse apple that just walked out of here. They all say it can't be done. How can I believe the words of a boy, and a stranger?"

"Give me four pieces of string, and I'll show you," Roy said, sensing the futility of words in trying to persuade the manager to trust him. He would just demonstrate how he thought the cable could be hauled up the mountain, then let the manager decide whether or not to give Roy a chance.

Upon receiving the four pieces of string, Roy unraveled his silk manilla rope, stretching it across the office floor.

Starting at one end of the rope, he fashioned three tight coils, tieing them with a string so they would not come undone. A foot or so up the rope he fashioned three more tight coils, tying them together with the second string. He did the same thing with the third and fourth strings. When he was finished there were four bunches of coils, all connected to each other in a straight line on the office floor.

"If you did the same thing with the cable, tieing up bunches of coils, about ten feet apart in a line down Colorado Avenue," Roy explained. "All you would have to do is lead the mules alongside, maybe ten at a time, tied to each other, head to tail, and lift the bunches of coils on top of their backs."

"How would you secure the coils?" the manager asked. It seemed to Roy, by the man's tone of voice, he was taking Roy's proposal seriously.

"The rope used to tie the coils together would be long enough to have a loop in one end which would fit over the sawbuck as the coil was lifted into place," Roy explained, slowly, thinking as he talked.

"Wouldn't the load be out of balance, too much weight on one side?" the man asked. He was familiar with all the objections the mule skinners had come up with on why cable couldn't be hauled on mules.

"Yes. Since the mules would be carrying empty ore panniers, I would throw some other kind of cargo in the pannier opposite the cable to help balance the load."

"I have a hundred 40-pound boxes of dynamite that need to go up to the mine."

"Good. When we saddle the mules we could throw a box in each of the right panniers as we put them on the mules."

"Have you packed cable before, at another mine perhaps?" the man asked, looking directly at Roy.

"No sir, I haven't," Roy said, truthfully, "but I've worked with horses and mules all my life. I'm confident we can do this."

Chapter 10

"Then you've got a job," the man said, extending his hand. "Seven dollars a day, if you succeed in getting the cable up to the mine tomorrow."

"I'll need four or five men to help tie the cable and load the mules. We'll need to get the cable coiled up and tied today so we can load the mules first thing in the morning."

"I'll have the men and lots of rope at the office here right after lunch. I'll have the dynamite delivered to the stables."

"That cowboy who was in here earlier..." Roy said, hesitating, "I don't want him around."

"You mean Slim. He's a good hand with mules."

"I'm sure he is," Roy explained. "But he said it couldn't be done, and he's going to be mad when he sees me doing it. Don't want him around, looking for a way to prove he was right. That's all."

"He won't be in the way," the manager promised. He extended his hand, introducing himself as Horace Nelson.

Roy hurried back to Hurley's Saloon, finding Cap out back trying to negotiate a sale for his horses. When the customer finally left, leading away three full-moon ponies, Roy explained his new job to Cap, and how he had promised to haul 4,000 feet of cable up the mountain the next morning. The old horse thief began to laugh.

"You don't think I can do it?" Roy asked.

"I'm laughing at Slim. Tried to get him to go with me once to rustle a bunch of cattle. He races horses quite a lot, so I figured he had grit. All he could do was come up with reasons it wouldn't work and how we would end up in prison. Did it all by myself. He was as sorry as hell when I came in here and sold the cattle for over $5,000. I thought he had learned a lesson. I guess he didn't. Now a boy has his job."

"Would you mix mules and horses, if they can't find enough mules?"

"Absolutely not," Cap said, without having to think about it. "If one or two horses spooked at the cable and got to bucking, they'd head down off the trail and pull the whole

91

string with them. They'd get all tangled up in the cable as they rolled down the mountain, the dynamite might start going off. I'd love to see it.''

"And if I don't have any horses in the string?" Roy asked.

"If a mule or two gets frightened by the cable or anything else, they'll just charge forward. If the panic spreads through the whole train, the worst that can happen is they will stampede all the way to the mine. I've never seen a mule stupid enough to jump off a steep trail and hurt himself, no matter how scared he gets. All mules, no horses.''

Roy borrowed Cap's good saddle horse to use in leading the mule train up the mountain, then headed back to the Tomboy office.

Roy's crew was waiting for him at the office, six men with gloves and knives, ready to start cutting up a pile of rope and start coiling the cable as Roy directed. It took them only two hours to unravel the entire spool of cable and tie it in bunches of coils about ten feet apart extending about 600 feet down Colorado Avenue.

When they were finished, Roy hurried back to the office to tell Horace he had 52 bunches of coils and would need 52 mules to carry them up the mountain. Horace said 52 of the best mules the company owned would be saddled and ready to go at 8 a.m., and there would be a box of dynamite in each mule's right pannier. There would be half a dozen men on hand to help Roy string out the mules and load the cable.

As Roy rode back to Hurley's Saloon he couldn't help but wonder what could go wrong the next day. Had he been too bold, tackling a job experienced mule skinners had shied away from? What did they know that he didn't know?

Suddenly he realized they were familiar with the trail leading to the mine, and he was not. Was there something about the trail that would make hauling cable difficult or impossible? He decided to find out. He turned his horse north toward the mountain, and the trail leading to the Tomboy Mine.

Chapter 10

It was after dark when Roy returned to Hurley's Saloon. While he hadn't ridden the entire distance to the mine, he had gone as far as Marshall Basin and hadn't found any obstacles that concerned him. While the trail traversed some of the steepest sidehills he had ever ridden across, it was well used and well maintained.

Heber, Eli and Cap were seated at a table eating supper when Roy arrived. Cap had already told them about Roy's new assignment. They were envious, having spent the afternoon hammering steel gads into solid rock. Both were nursing broken blisters on their palms and fingers.

After ordering a rare steak, Roy told his companions how he had landed the job, using his silk Manilla rope to demonstrate how he thought clumps of coils could be hauled on mules. He told them that the first day on the job he had been the boss of six men. Eli and Heber were impressed.

"Do you have anymore advice for me?" Roy asked Cap.

"Once you get started, go like hell and don't stop until you reach the Tomboy," Cap responded.

"Are you going to be around in the morning to keep an eye on things?" Roy asked.

"Wouldn't miss this for anything," Cap said. "I'll follow your string up the mountain."

When Roy was finished with his steak, Cap ordered a large bottle of whiskey. When the waiter brought it to the table, Cap stood up and began pounding the bottom of the bottle on the table until he had the attention of everyone in the room.

"I propose a toast," the horse thief bellowed. Some of the men cheered, and some walked over to the table, drinking glasses in hand, wanting Cap to fill the glasses for the toast.

"To Roy Parker, the Mormon boy from Utah Territory," Cap began, holding his glass high in the air, shouting loud enough for everyone in the room to hear him clearly, as well as some of the people in the street. Feeling embarrassed, Roy looked down at his plate. His cheeks blushed.

"Who tomorrow is going to haul 52 cases of dynamite and four thousand feet of cable to the Tomboy Mine on one continuous string of mules," Cap continued. The men cheered. Roy felt his cheeks blush even more. "First I propose a toast to the success of this bold undertaking." Everyone cheered, and those with glasses drank, some sipping, some gulping.

"And second," Cap roared, when he had removed the bottle from his lips, "I propose we drink to Roy's good health in the event one of the mules bumps a case of dynamite too hard against a big rock." The men drank heartily to the second part of the toast, some shouting words of encouragement to Roy, who felt like he was among friends. He was happy, but not for long.

Someone else began pounding a bottle on a table to propose a toast. Roy looked over and recognized the man. It was Slim, the mule skinner who had tried to convince Horace the cable could not be hauled on mules up the mountain.

"I propose a toast to the lying Mormon boy who fast-talked the Tomboy into turning the work of a man over to a boy," Slim shouted. There was a slur in his voice, indicating he had been drinking.

Suddenly the room was silent. All eyes were on Roy.

"You don't have to do anything," Cap cautioned. But Roy knew he did. It wasn't anything he had been taught, it was instinct, like when a young stallion, who has been getting too close to the mares, is challenged by the old herd stallion. The young stallion can stand and fight, or he can leave. Leaving is the same as defeat, but with less sweat and blood. By leaving the young stallion gives up breeding rights to the mares, at least for the present.

Telluride was a mining town, where the primitive laws of the wilderness held rule more so than the laws of civilized society. Roy knew this, and so did Slim. In this particular instance, it wasn't breeding rights, but Roy's manhood and status as a mule skinner, that was being challenged.

Chapter 10

Roy grabbed Cap's whiskey bottle and pounded the bottom of it on the table. He stood up, glaring at Slim.

"I propose a toast to the limp-hearted teamster, Slim," Roy growled, "who didn't have the gristle to haul cable, forcing the Tomboy to turn the job over to a boy who did."

Some of the men cheered, then the room remained silent. The boy from Utah had not only refused to back down, but had returned the insult. Now there would be a fight. Quietly the men began to place their bets. They knew Slim to be a mean fighter, but they knew nothing about the boy from Utah. The kid had shown courage in landing the job hauling cable, but talking and fighting were not the same.

Knowing there was no backing down now, Slim got up from the table where he had been drinking and began walking towards Roy.

"Duck out the back," Cap hissed. "I'll take care of Slim." Slim quickened his pace, apparently overhearing Cap's warning to the boy. The mule skinner wasn't about to let this kid with the smart mouth get away.

Roy rolled out of his chair, half turning towards the door, as if he intended to follow Cap's advice. Slim leaped to cut him off.

Roy might have kept going towards the door, had he not been raised in wild country, and taught from an early age that if he ever found himself in close quarters with a mountain lion, the worst thing to do was turn and run. A big cat would rather chase than fight, any day, and trying to run away would only trigger the cat's chasing instinct. A running man or boy was no match for a cat that could leap 30 feet without touching the ground. The sensible thing, when in close quarters with a big cat, was to stand and fight. Usually the cat would back down. Roy didn't know what triggered the thought of the big cat, but the mere thought made it impossible for him to run from his enemy.

Without warning, Roy suddenly reversed his movement, spinning back directly into Slim's path. As he did so, Roy's hand instinctively shot to his hip, grabbed his Colt .44, cocked back the hammer, and shoved the barrel straight ahead into Slim's skinny belly.

Slim stopped in his tracks. His face turned white. A small stream of saliva oozed from one corner of his mouth. His eyes were not looking into Roy's face, but down at the gun.

Roy realized too late that he had made a mistake. Slim was not armed. Roy did not want to shoot the sulking mule skinner, but neither did he want to just let the man go, after humiliating him in front of his friends. And Roy couldn't risk getting shot in the back a day or two later. He realized he had to figure out a way to let Slim escape without loosing too much face and pride. Roy decided to stall, by talking.

"If I catch you fooling with my pack train tomorrow," Roy growled, "I'll kill..." Roy hesitated. Mike had warned him against making threats with a gun you weren't willing to follow through on. "I'll kill your best race horse."

Roy remembered Cap telling him Slim raced horses. Slim didn't respond. He was still looking at the gun.

"You think you're a pretty good hand with stock," Roy said, his voice calmer. He finally figured out what he wanted to do. All he needed now was to get the words right.

"I'm better, and I intend to prove it to you and the whole town," Roy challenged. For the first time, Slim looked away from the cocked pistol. Carefully, Roy released the hammer, and returned the pistol to the holster.

"When I came to Telluride," Roy explained, "I brought a little bay mare along. With me on her back, she can run the socks off any horse you got. I challenge you to a horse race, a week from Sunday."

"Why not this coming Sunday?" Slim asked. He had taken the bait. Roy was delighted. Now, they didn't have to fight. Roy didn't have to kill the man.

"The mare's got a colt on her, and she's out to pasture at Montrose. I don't think I can get her here and have her ready to run by this Sunday."

Slim began to laugh. "The Utah farm boy unhitches the

Chapter 10

horse from his father's plow, rides to Telluride and challenges Slim Olsen to a race. Don't waste my time, boy, unless you can put serious money on the race.''

"How about a hundred dollars?" Roy challenged. "A half-mile match race, just you and me. We'll ride our own horses. Winner take all." Roy extended his hand.

"You got a deal," Slim said, shaking Roy's hand. Then to the others he said, "This'll be the easiest hundred dollars old Slim ever made." Before he finished talking, others began making bets. Slim swaggered out the door while someone was asking Roy where they could get a look at the mare.

"I'll bring her to town as soon as all that cable and dynamite is safely unloaded at the Tomboy," he said, nodding to Eli and Heber that it was time to get off to bed before anything else exciting happened. Roy had had about all a boy could handle for one day, and he figured tomorrow would be even more exciting.

Cap raised the bottle to his lips, gulped down the last of its contents, and followed the boys to bed. He had planned to go down to Pacific Avenue for the evening, but was finding life more exciting, hanging around Roy Parker.

Chapter 11

The thing that surprised Roy most the next morning was the crowd that appeared to see what everyone believed was the longest pack train ever put together in Colorado. The same six men who had helped tie the cable in coils appeared to help secure the cable on the mules, which began arriving at eight o'clock sharp. Each one had a box of dynamite in the right pannier.

Horace Nelson stood on the front steps of the Tomboy office, nervously chewing on a cigar he never got around to lighting. He made no effort to interfere as Roy walked quietly up and down the row of coils, offering encouragement and discussing problems and potential problems with his men.

As they began to load the mules, it quickly became apparent they needed two ropes instead of one to secure the cable to the sawbucks. Volunteers from the crowd joined in, cutting more rope and passing it down the line of mules. More volunteers stepped forward to help hold the mules while the animals were being loaded.

Cap was on his horse, riding up and down the street, keeping an eye on things. Roy had asked him to be on the lookout for Slim, and if the mule skinner showed up, to keep him out of the way. There was no sign of Slim.

It took about an hour to secure all 52 coils of cable to the backs of 52 mules. The lead rope from each mule's halter was tied to the tail or sawbuck of the mule in front. As the last four or five coils were being secured to the animals at the back of the line, Roy got on his horse and rode to the front of the line, taking the lead rope of the first mule. Roy knew the easiest way to get mules turned around or tangled in the cable was to let them stand, so the second the last mule was loaded, Roy turned his horse towards the mountain trail leading to the Tomboy Mine and started riding.

At first the mules seemed a little confused, feeling the stiff cable pushing and pulling against their loads, but it didn't take them long to figure out where to walk to cause the least amount of pushing and pulling. By the time they reached the mountain trail, most of the mules were walking briskly, the rest trotting. Cap was following the last mule. A half a dozen mounted riders followed Cap.

While he was constantly looking back, Roy never slowed down until he reached a gang of cheering miners at the entrance to the Tomboy Mine.

"Where do you want this cable dropped?" Roy shouted.

"Don't drop it anywhere," one of the men answered. He stepped forward. "I'm the foreman here, just hand me that lead rope."

Roy handed over the rope and reined his horse out of the way. Without giving the mules a chance to stop, the man hurried towards the entrance to the mine where he handed the lead rope to a miner who disappeared into the dark shaft, the mules following single file. The mules had been in the mine before. None hesitated going into the dark tunnel. A minute later all the mules were out of sight.

"Where's Slim?" the foreman asked.

"Had some differences with the office on how to haul cable, so Horace asked me to do it," Roy said.

"Might as well head over to the cook shack and get some breakfast," the foreman said. "It'll be about an hour before the mules are loaded with ore and ready to head back down the mountain."

Roy and Cap rode over to the cook shack where they filled up on pancakes, eggs, bacon and fried potatoes. Shortly after noon they were back in Telluride, each leading a string of 26 mules into the depot where a crew of men emptied the ore panniers into large wagons which would haul the ore to Montrose.

"I like this job better than I thought I would," Roy said to Cap as they rode back to the mine office to report the events of the morning to Horace. "I didn't know other men would do all the loading and unloading. All I had to do was sit on my horse and lead the mules up the mountain. And I will get seven dollars for doing it. I don't know things could get any better."

They did. Horace hadn't expected them back so quickly, not with 52 loads of ore. He was smiling brightly as he congratulated Roy, and thanked Cap for his help.

"The mules will be too tired for another trip up the mountain today," Horace said, "And we don't have enough fresh animals to put together a second train, so you might as well take the rest of the day off, with pay, of course. See you at eight in the morning."

While Cap headed back to Hurley's Saloon, Roy figured he might as well use the free afternoon to ride back to the Butler Ranch and pick up Babe--the sooner he started graining and conditioning her for the race, the better.

Cornish had been born early in the spring, so Roy decided he might as well wean the colt by leaving him behind at the ranch. It was after midnight when Roy arrived back in Telluride.

The next day Roy rode Babe up to the mine, leading a string of mules. He figured climbing the steep trails at the higher altitudes would be good conditioning for her. He noticed along the way that men, going up and down the trail, stopped and watched the mare, carefully. By now everyone in Telluride knew about the upcoming race between the Utah farm boy and the Colorado mule skinner.

"Do you think she can beat Slim's big gray?" someone would ask.

"I've got a hundred dollars on her," Roy would respond. "I wouldn't bet that kind of money on a horse I didn't think could win."

Roy gave the mare a full gallon of oats every morning and another every evening. Sometimes after work he would gallop her a few miles. He put new shoes on her, and for the first week or so, milked her a little every day or two to remove some of the pressure she was feeling in her milk bag from having her colt taken away. After about a week her milk dried up. She was ready for the race.

There was a lot of talk about Slim's big gray, the horse that had been beaten only twice in about ten races. Most felt the gray was the one to put their money on. More than once, men challenged Roy to race Babe against this or that horse, so they could see how well the mare could run. More often than not, the horses they wanted her to run against were horses that had raced Slim's big gray. Roy refused all such offers, telling the challengers they would have to wait and see.

Roy didn't tell anyone he had obtained Babe from Jim Kittleman, who had the finest herd of fast horses in the southern part of the Utah Territory, and that whenever there was a race at Beaver, Cedar City or St. George, it was usually a Kittleman horse winning the prize money.

Roy was content to let those who wanted, believe Slim's claim that Roy had unhitched the mare from his father's plow. Those who were good judges of horseflesh, and who looked closely at the mare, however, knew this bay mare was no plow horse.

Since Eli and Heber moved into the barracks on the mountain, Roy seldom saw them. He spent a lot more time with Cap, who had decided to stick around until after the horse race.

Cassidy

"We're friends, aren't we?" Cap asked one night as they were eating supper. He had already had two or three drinks.

"Sure," Roy answered.

"Then tell me, is Babe really going to beat the gray?"

"I've got a hundred dollars on her."

"I know," Cap responded, "but you had to make that bet to get out of a fight. If you want, I'll bet a hundred on the gray to cover your bet. Then you won't lose if the gray wins. I won't tell anyone."

"Look," Roy responded. "I grew up with this mare. She can run, and I can ride her. I feel good about having a hundred dollars bet on her. Whether or not she can run with the gray, I guess we'll find out next Sunday."

When Sunday finally arrived, it seemed to Roy the entire town turned out to watch the horse race. While hundreds of bets had been placed, no one seemed very sure of his bet, except Slim. The mule skinner acted like all he had to do was gallop down to the end of the straight-away and collect his money. The race course was Colorado Avenue, leading right through the middle of town.

"Don't let him scare you," Cap said, just before the race. "Slim's a bluffer. I've played poker with him. I know."

Still, Roy wasn't about to take any chances. He was determined to do everything possible to help Babe outrun the gray gelding. When he put shoes on her, he nailed on used, half-worn shoes that weighed only half as much as new shoes.

As the horses approached the starting line, Roy surprised everyone by jumping down from his horse and jerking off the saddle. He had never seen an adult remove a saddle to run a race, but racing against the kids his own age in Circle Valley, the horses that were ridden bareback always seemed to do better. Roy wasn't sure removing the weight of the saddle made as much difference as moving the weight of the bareback rider further forward on the horse's front legs. He was, however, certain horses without saddles ran faster, and he was determined to give Babe every advantage possible.

102

Chapter 11

He was a good enough rider that the lack of stirrups didn't bother him. Some bareback riders, whom Roy had raced against, tied ropes around the base of their horses' necks to hold onto, especially during the start, but Roy had always found the mane sufficient for his holding-on needs. From the talk before the race it was apparent that no one raced bareback in Telluride. Roy was pleased he could show them something new.

A man with a pistol was the designated starter. He was standing at the end of the straight-away. When everything was ready for the race to begin, the starter motioned for Roy and Slim to ride towards him, then turn their horses and start walking towards the finish line. There was no starting line. When the horses were even, the starter would fire his pistol, the signal for the race to begin.

At the other end someone had taken a can of lime and poured a straight, white finish line across the street. Most of the men who had wagered money on the race were gathered on both sides of the finish line. Still, there were lots of people on both sides of the street the entire length of the straight-away. Roy was sure everyone in town had turned out to watch. Many of the people, both men and women, were dressed in their Sunday best, having gone to church services earlier in the day.

It was a warm summer afternoon. The horses' coats were sleek and smooth, revealing rippling muscles underneath. The sides of the necks on both horses were dark with sweat. Both horses knew a race was about to begin, and they were ready and eager, but Babe seemed the calmer of the two.

Using his right hand, Roy grabbed a handful of black mane. He held the long, black leather reins in his left hand. As he turned the mare away from the starter towards the finish line, his knees tightened instinctively against the mare's shoulders. He leaned forward. Babe began prancing towards the finish line.

When the horses were even, Roy was aware that Slim was looking over at him. Roy didn't return the stare, but continued looking straight ahead towards the open street leading to the finish line.

The pistol sounded, the horses lunged forward with all their strength. Other guns went off. Long rows of people on both sides of the street began cheering and shouting. The ears on both horses were laid back, and noses outstretched as they charged with reckless abandon.

As soon as the horses were at full stride, Roy released the mane in his right hand and grabbed the loose end of the heavy black reins, and slapped them firmly across the mare's rump. It wasn't a hard slap, just enough to make sure the mare knew they were involved in a serious race.

Because the mare was shorter and stockier than the tall gray, she got off to a faster start, as Roy hoped she would, but she was leading by only half a length as the horses reached full stride.

Slim was swearing at his gray, applying both whip and spur. The gray was running as hard as he could, and began gaining on the mare. Roy slapped her on the rump a second time. She seemed to reach deep inside to find a little more speed. Still, she couldn't pull away from the gray who was slowly gaining on her.

At they reached the halfway point the gray was within a foot of taking the lead. Roy was beginning to worry that perhaps the gray's long legs were going to be too much for the little mare.

Then suddenly the mare's ears, which were already back, laid back even further on her neck. She turned her head slightly towards the gray, lifted her tail a little higher, and tossed her nose up and down, probably not enough for anyone on the sidelines to notice. But Roy noticed.

The mare had done this before in races at home. At first Roy had tried to jerk her head straight, thinking she was being distracted from the race. In time, however, Roy realized that when the mare engaged in this strange behavior, she usually won the race. After watching the mare in the pasture with other horses, when she made the same kind of gestures, Roy realized she was playing a dominance game, trying to establish herself at the top of the pecking order.

That's what she was doing now, with the gray. In the silent sign language of horses she was telling the gray that if he dared pass her she would kick his sides in as soon as the race was over.

Roy glanced over at the gray's ears, wondering how the gelding would respond to the mare's challenge. Instead of laying his ears back flatter against his neck to answer the challenge, the gelding moved out of kicking range and slowed his pace just a little. Roy was delighted. He slapped the mare on the rump again to get her mind back on the running. Slim increased his whipping and spurring, but it didn't seem to matter. The gray had already decided there was no way he was going to get in front and risk the wrath of this sassy little mare. Roy won by three quarters of a length.

Slim continued to whip and spur the gray after the race was over. The mule skinner was embarrassed and humiliated. He kept saying he couldn't believe he had been beaten by a boy on a plow horse. He continued to whip the gray, blaming the poor animal for his humiliation. Slim couldn't take his whipping like a man. The more he talked the worse he looked in the eyes of those who knew him.

"Shut up and pay your bet," someone shouted at Slim.

"Give the kid his hundred dollars," someone else yelled.

Roy rode over to Slim, figuring he might as well finish the business of the day by collecting his money. He didn't expect any trouble from Slim, not in front of so many people.

"I don't have the hundred dollars," Slim said, just loud enough for Roy to hear. "I can't pay you."

Roy didn't know what to say. Refusing to pay a legitimate bet was a serious breech of mining camp ethics. Refusing or being unable to pay the bet would bring even more humiliation and loss of face to the poor mule skinner.

"Will you take the horse and saddle?" Slim asked. "Full payment for the debt?"

105

Roy nodded. Slim dismounted and handed the reins to Roy. Without another word the mule skinner turned and walked away. Roy never saw him again, though word of mouth reached Telluride at a later date that Slim was packing ore at Silverton.

Roy worked through the fall and winter, packing supplies up the mountain to the Tomboy, and bringing back panniers full of the rich ore. He saw little of Eli and Heber, who eventually tired of chipping tunnels through solid rock and returned to Circle Valley. Roy didn't miss them. In his work he made plenty of new friends.

One afternoon, about a year later, Horace asked Roy to come in his office. He said the company wanted to increase production at the mine by opening a new shaft. Hiring and housing more miners wouldn't be a problem. What concerned company management was getting more ore down the steep trail to the roads at Telluride.

Rather than buy more mules and supervise more mule skinners, the company wanted to simplify its operations by hiring independent contractors to bring the ore down the mountain.

"Are you going to let me go?" Roy asked, not sure where Horace was headed.

"We'd like to," Horace said in a friendly tone of voice. Roy was confused. "We'd like you to be one of the independent contractors."

"What does that mean?" Roy asked.

"The mine is willing to pay you ten dollars a ton to pack the ore from the mine down to the road. The mine will do all the loading and unloading."

Roy did some quick figuring. With forty or fifty mules he could bring five tons off the mountain every day, for which he would get paid $50. If he built his own corral and shed, he could feed that many mules for $10 a day. For another $5 he could have a full-time man to help. If he figured another $10 a day to cover shoes, vet bills, repairing pack saddles, replacing injured mules, etc., he would net $25 a day, or $150 a week. He would be rich in no time at all, if he could find a way to get 50 mules and pack saddles.

"I don't have any mules and pack saddles," Roy said.

"Do you have any savings?" Horace asked.

"I could scrape together about $300," Roy said, "if I could collect the money friends owe me."

"Good. I could give you a letter from the mine expressing our willingness to contract with you to bring the ore off the mountain for $10 a ton. Take the letter and your $300 to the bank and ask them to loan you the money for the mules and saddles. I think they will do it. If they won't, then I'll have to start running all over the country trying to buy more mules, and I don't want to do that."

The next morning Roy walked into the San Miguel Valley Bank on Colorado Avenue. He hadn't been able to collect all the money people owed him, but he had $260 in his pocket.

This was his first time in the bank, and he was surprised to find the bank more lavishly decorated than any of the saloons or dance halls in town. The crystal chandelier was the biggest he had ever seen. There was polished mahogany trim wherever he looked. There was beveled glass in all the windows, plus imported silk curtains. Even the bars protecting the tellers' cages were made of polished brass. Persian rugs covered the polished oak floors. Without question the lobby of the San Miguel Valley Bank was the most lavish place Roy had ever seen.

When he told the clerk he wanted to talk to someone about borrowing money, he was ushered to a chair outside the office of L. L. Nunn, president of the bank, and told to wait there until Mr. Nunn was free to talk to him. Roy sat on the chair and waited, watching over-weight mine owners, lily-handed gamblers, pimps with hair parted in the middle, pasty-faced bartenders and merchants smoking white-papered cigarettes, and prostitutes with paint on their faces. All these people had one thing in common. They were shoving the most money Roy had ever seen underneath the polished bars to the bank clerks. Roy watched with wonder as bag after bag of wrinkled greenbacks and piles of jingling gold coins were shoved towards the tellers for safekeeping.

Roy sat there a full hour. He wondered why a wooden chair seemed so much harder than the seat of a saddle. He wondered what the initials L. L. in the banker's name stood for. He wished he knew so he could call the man by his first name instead of Mr. Nunn.

"I lost $50 when your mare beat that gray gelding last year," were Nunn's first words when Roy was finally ushered into his office. Roy was glad the banker knew who he was.

"What can I do for you, Mr. Parker?" Nunn asked as Roy took a seat. They didn't shake hands. Roy felt very uncomfortable. Nobody had ever called him Mr. Parker before. He didn't like it. It was obvious the banker wanted to keep the conversation as formal as possible. Roy decided he might as well state his request and get out as fast as he could.

"I have a letter from the Tomboy Mine asking me to contract with them to haul ore from the mine down to the road," Roy said, handing Horace's letter to the banker. "I would like to borrow $4,000 so I can buy 50 mules and 50 pack saddles. I could pay the money back at a rate of $50 a week."

"What kind of collateral do you have?" Nunn asked, looking up from the letter.

Roy had been reading since he was five or six years old. His family spent winter evenings taking turns reading from the Bible and Book of Mormon. He had read a number of novels, including *Moby Dick* by Herman Melville. But he couldn't remember ever seeing or hearing the word collateral.

"I don't understand," Roy said.

"When the bank loans money, we like to attach the loan to some kind of valuable property," Mr. Nunn explained, in a slow deliberate voice, as if he were talking to a child. "If the borrower can't make his or her payments, then the bank takes the collateral in place of the money owed."

"I have $260 and three horses," Roy said.

Chapter 11

"Hardly enough collateral for a $4,000 loan," Mr. Nunn responded. "Ideally, we would like a piece of free and clear real estate, or $6,000 worth of gold we could keep in our vault until the loan is paid in full."

"If I had $6,000 worth of gold, why would I want to borrow $4,000 from the bank?" Roy asked, confused again. Before Nunn had a chance to answer, Roy asked another question. "What about the mules and pack saddles I buy with the borrowed money? Could they be considered collateral, along with my three horses and $260?"

"The problem with mules as collateral is they can trot away during the night," Nunn said. "A lot of livestock changes hands illegally in this uncivilized part of the country. If we loaned you the money, and you walked in here on a Monday morning announcing your mules had been stolen, where would that leave the bank?"

"It seems to me, Mr. Nunn," Roy said, feeling both frustration and anger, "that you are willing to loan me the money if I can prove I don't need it."

"The bank has to protect its capital," Nunn responded.

"Are you saying you will not loan me the money?" Roy asked.

"Not quite," Nunn hedged. "Come back next week after the loan committee has had a chance to discuss your request. I'll give you a firm answer then. Thank you for coming in, Mr. Parker."

The next day when Roy discussed the bank interview with Horace, the office manager agreed to stop by Mr. Nunn's office and put in a good word for Roy, which he did the next day.

The following week when Roy entered the banker's office, he was greeted with even more formality and reserve. Before he sat down in Nunn's office Roy felt that something was wrong, very wrong. He waited for the banker to speak.

"A loan committee is an interesting group of people," Nunn began. "You might think such an entity would consist only of bankers. Not so. We have the Telluride sheriff, Mr.

109

Wasson, on our committee. He sees a lot of things a banker would never know about. A rancher by the name of Mr. Butler sits on our committee too. He lives on the busy road between here and Montrose, and sees a lot of things a banker would never know about."

"He is probably the same Mr. Butler I keep horses with," Roy said. "Did he tell you my pasture bill has always been paid on time?"

"No, but he told me when you brought horses to his place you were riding with a known horse thief by the name of Cap Brown. Is this true?"

"Yes," Roy said. "Coming over from Utah I traveled with Mr. Brown." Roy was surprised to see the banker's formal style of talk rubbing off on him. "But I never rustled horses or cattle with him."

"Mr. Wasson tells me when you came to Telluride you shared a room with Mr. Brown, and were seen with him about town on numerous occasions."

"Did Sheriff Wasson tell you in over a year in this town I haven't been in any kind of trouble, unless you count the horse race with Mr. Olsen?"

"I would be absolutely insane loaning money to a traveling companion and side kick to Cap Brown. Might as well give the fox the key to the hen house. Now, don't waste anymore of my time, boy." Mr. Nunn turned away and started looking through some papers. Roy returned to the mine office to report his failure to Horace.

"Guess we'll just have to find the money somewhere else," Horace said in a determined voice. Roy liked Horace, a man not easily discouraged. Roy remembered how Horace insisted the cable go up the mountain, no matter how many times Slim told him it couldn't be done. The office manager was showing the same persistence now. Maybe that's why Horace had so much responsibility with the mine. He always seemed to find a way to get a job done, usually cheerfully and without a lot of fuss.

"There are private individuals in Telluride who might

be willing to become your silent partners," Horace explained.

"In what way?" Roy asked.

"The way it usually works is the silent partner puts up the money and you do all the work. You split the profits down the middle."

"Who would have $4,000 to buy mules and saddles?" Roy asked.

"Diamond Tooth Leona, for one," Horace said. Roy had heard the name before, from Cap. The lady owned one of the establishments on Pacific Avenue, the ones providing female pleasures.

"And next time my name comes up in Nunn's loan committee meeting, they'll say not only do I hang out with horse thieves, but I do business with whores."

"Hardly," Horace said. He knew something Roy did not.

"Why's that?" Roy asked.

"Diamond Tooth Leona is on the committee." Horace laughed.

Roy had to admit that as much as he disliked Nunn, the banker was shrewd, having not only Wasson and Butler on his loan committee, but a whore too. Nunn probably had a better feel about what was going on in town, and who was doing it, than anyone else. Still, Roy didn't like the man.

"No thanks," Roy said, turning to leave. "Give me a few weeks. Maybe I can come up with the money on my own."

That night Roy started graining Babe again. The next Sunday he led her over to Silverton, entered her in a horse race and won $200. The next Sunday he won another $150 in Ouray. A week later he picked up $300 in Sawpit. While no one in Telluride would bet against the bay mare after defeating Slim's gray, Roy didn't have any trouble finding strangers to bet against her in the neighboring mining towns, as long as he didn't bring her back a second time. He even took her to Montrose and Delta where there were races every Sunday. A new horse coming to town increased the excitement of the race by adding to the uncertainty. At such times betting activity increased.

In a little more than a month, Roy had accumulated nearly half the money he needed to buy a string of pack mules. But winning money with Babe was becoming increasingly difficult as news of her running ability spread.

Just when Roy was wondering where else he could take the mare to find people willing to bet against her, an opportunity to double his money came to Telluride.

A man named Mulcahy had come to town leading a young, black race horse, a stallion. No one had heard of Mulcahy or his colt before. The animal looked fast, but everyone knew looks could be deceiving.

Roy was in Delta when Mulcahy arrived in Telluride. The stranger didn't waste any time lining up a race with one of the local horses, a sorrel mare. Babe had raced the mare twice and beaten her easily both times. Mulcahy's black beat the mare by little more than a nose. After he collected $50 in winnings, Mulcahy said his stallion was still tired after a lot of traveling and should have beaten the mare by a much greater margin. He said after his horse had a chance to rest he would race it against the fastest horse Telluride could come up with, and if such a race could be arranged, he would bet some serious money on his horse.

Roy hadn't been back in town five minutes when he found out about the challenge. The next day he looked up Mulcahy. The race was set for the following Sunday. Roy bet all the money he had, $1,600. They put the wagered amount, all $3,200, in the safe at Hurley's Saloon, so there wouldn't be any question about the winner getting paid when the race was over.

Roy felt confident he would win. Babe had beat the sorrel mare easily, and the black had struggled. Roy wished he had more to bet, but with $3,200 in winnings, if he was prudent, he could get his string of mules together. Most of the horse race watchers reached the same conclusion Roy did and bet their money on Babe too.

No one was more surprised than Roy when the black won. The race wasn't close. The black took the lead in the beginning and continued to widen the gap, winning by four or five lengths.

"I have never been one to squawk about losing a bet," Roy said to Mulcahy after the race. "But did you hold the colt back when you raced the sorrel mare."

"You bet I did," Mulcahy said, surprising Roy with his frankness. "Would you have bet $1,600 if I had beat the sorrel by ten lengths?"

"Of course not."

"Look kid, the race with the sorrel was only a trick to set you up, and the whole town too. I made a lot of money. In a month or so I'll move on to Arizona or Montana and do the same thing again. See you around, kid."

Roy turned and walked away. He felt like a whipped pup. He felt cheated and deceived. But he should have known better. He would be more careful next time. In the meantime he would have to give up the idea of contracting with the Tomboy to haul ore.

A few weeks later Roy was surprised to learn two boys from Utah had brought a new horse to Telluride and had set up a match race against Mulcahy's black colt. The boys were betting everything they had on their mare. The bet with Mulcahy was $500. Roy decided to find the boys from Utah and have a little talk with them.

He found them in a saloon, where he learned their names. The one who owned the mare was Matt Warner, the other, his jockey, was Johnny Nicholson. Rumor had it Warner had killed a man in Utah, in a fight over a woman.

As Roy moved closer, he could hear Warner complaining that he didn't have anything else to bet on his mare. He wished he had brought another 20 horses with him so he could bet them on the race. He told a man he had even wagered his double-bottomed cowboy trousers for a pair of dude pants he knew he would never wear.

Warner was at the bar. Roy walked up to him. "I hear

you killed a man in a fight over a woman," Roy said to start the conversation.

"Not exactly," Warner said, looking closely at Roy, liking what he saw. "I'm from Levan, Utah Territory. Coming home from a church meeting one night, one of the boys tried to hold my girl's hand. I told him not to. He refused. We started fighting. I hit him with a board from a fence. He dropped like a wet rag. Figured I'd killed him, so I saddled my horse and headed for Vernal. Had an uncle running cattle there. I was fifteen. Found out later I had just knocked the kid out, but by then I had my own string of horses on Diamond Mountain. Didn't want to go back to school, church, adults always telling me what to do, so I didn't."

"I'm from Circleville, Utah Territory," Roy said. "Left when I got blamed for stealing calves."

Roy and Matt bought each other drinks. They had similar upbringings, similar ambitions. They had a lot to talk about.

"I know the Mulcahy colt," Roy said. "It has never been beat. You're going to lose."

"The hell you say," Matt responded, bristling. "How much you got to bet on it?"

"Not much," Roy said, "but I'll bet everything, which is three horses, my saddle, bridle, chaps, spurs and gun."

"Your riding outfit against mine," Matt said, offering his hand to shake on the wager. They bought each other another drink.

They got along so well that later that same evening Matt asked Roy to be one of the judges for the upcoming race.

"I'm a stranger, and I'm betting against you," Roy said, surprised at Matt's offer.

"I know a square-shooting cowboy when I see one," Matt said. "I'd rather have you for a judge, even if you owned the Mulcahy colt, than trust one of these city pimps or gamblers."

"If that's the way you feel then I'll be a judge," Roy

114

said. "I feel the same way about these lady-fingered city sneaks, especially the bankers."

Outfits from the surrounding towns and valleys began showing up for the race several days ahead of time. Those who came early claimed the best camping places. Some came from as far as 30 miles away.

The problem was that everyone wanted to bet on the Mulcahy colt, the black stallion that had never been beaten. Nobody knew anything about Matt Warner and his horse, Betty. Those who bet on Betty did so because no one else would bet against the Mulcahy black.

Just before the race, Roy was surprised to hear Matt tell Johnny, who was going to ride Betty, to beat the Mulcahy colt just enough so there wouldn't be any dispute among the judges. Matt said he didn't want to discourage future races by showing people what Betty could really do. Shaking his head in disbelief, Roy walked down to the finish line to join the rest of the judges.

As Roy waited for the race to begin, he thought back on the time not very long ago when he lost all his money to Mulcahy. He was sure the same thing would happen to Matt today. Like before, it seemed everyone in town turned out for the race. Matt and Johnny seemed to be the only ones who thought the black colt would lose.

Suddenly the gun sounded. The race had begun. Without any spurring or whipping Johnny eased Betty a half a length ahead of the black and won by that same margin. When the race was over, Roy noticed the mare was barely sweating. It had been an easy race for her.

Roy had never seen a more surprised crowd, but as soon as they got their breath, they began cheering for Betty.

Roy brought his entire outfit to Matt. His saddle was on Babe. The chaps, gun belt and spurs were hanging from the saddle horn. He had Babe's reins in one hand, the lead rope to the gray in the other.

"You look like a half-naked sheepherder," Matt said, "walking around without all your stuff."

"Here," Roy said, handing Matt the reins. "You won fair and square."

Matt took the reins and lead rope, then hesitated. "I'm giving it all back to you, pay for being my judge and handing me the race."

"I didn't hand you the race," Roy said. "Betty did that, and besides, they don't pay men for judging horse races. A bet's a bet, and I don't bellyache when I lose."

"How would you like to be my partner," Matt said, changing the subject. "Do match races with me all over Colorado. Betty can run a lot faster than she did today."

"I sure would like to trail along with you," Roy said, delighted at the offer, suddenly realizing he was getting tired of Telluride, and wanting to leave anyway.

"It's a bargain," Matt said, "and seeing as all this stuff is mine, and you're my partner, and I won't have a partner running around like a half-naked sheepherder, I insist you use this stuff as long as we are together." Matt handed the reins back to Roy.

"When do we leave?" Roy asked.

"In the morning, if that's alright with you."

"Can't think of a better time," Roy answered.

Chapter 12

It felt good to Roy to be on the trail again, seeing new country with new friends. He enjoyed his job at the Tomboy, leading mules up and down the mountain, but traveling the same trail every day had begun to get monotonous. He was sure racing horses with Matt Warner would not get monotonous.

They headed north to the Butler Ranch to pick up Roy's colt, Cornish, who was now big enough to start riding. After doing that their plan was to head south to Durango where a mare named Gypsy Queen was winning all the races. All the locals thought she was the fastest horse west of the Mississippi. Matt had over a thousand dollars in his money belt and planned to double it in one match race against this Gypsy horse.

When they reached the Butler Ranch, Matt and Johnny waited at the hitching rail with the horses and pack mule while Roy walked up to the front door to tell Butler he had come to get the colt.

Butler was home, and when he answered the door he

was his usual unfriendly self. Roy wondered what Butler might have said about him in the loan committee meeting.

When Roy said he had come for the colt, Butler excused himself, saying he would be right back. When he returned he was carrying a double-barreled shotgun, and he was pointing it at Roy.

"Don't have any use for horse thieves," Butler said as he backed Roy off the porch. "Get the hell out of here. Never want to see you in these parts again."

"Just came for my colt," Roy said, bewildered.

"I don't have any colt of yours," Butler responded. "Now git."

"I saw him in the corral by the barn," Roy insisted. "I've been sending you money to cover his feed bill every month."

"Sorry, Kid, I don't have any colt of yours, so you can be on your way."

Suddenly Roy realized what was happening. There was no misunderstanding. Everything was clear. Butler was stealing Cornish, and didn't figure there was a thing Roy could do to stop him. Butler was an established rancher, a friend of L.L. Nunn and Sheriff Wasson. In a dispute over the ownership of the colt, it was Butler who would be believed, not Roy Parker, the migrant mine worker with no roots in the area, and a known associate of the horse thief, Cap Brown.

"Git on your horse and git out of here before I send for the sheriff," Butler growled, pushing Roy further away with the barrel of the shotgun.

Roy didn't say any more. He turned and stepped into the saddle, then nodded to his surprised companions to lead the way out of the yard.

"When we're out of range of the scatter gun, I'll pull out my Winchester and drill him," Matt offered in a low voice so Butler couldn't hear.

"Better not," Roy said, "I'll just sneak back tonight and get the colt."

Three or four miles down the road, in a cottonwood

draw with a spring, they made camp for the night. Roy wanted to kill Butler, but he knew he wouldn't. Roy decided killing a man like Butler wasn't worth going to jail for.

Shortly after midnight Roy saddled his horse and headed back to the Butler Ranch. Before heading out he made sure Matt and Johnny had their horses saddled and ready to leave the minute he returned with Cornish. He was riding the tall gray, figuring the gelding would be less likely to whinny a greeting to other horses. Babe, who had female hormones running in her bloodstream, would be hard to keep quiet during a solo nighttime ride. Plus the gray would be harder to see at night, against a background of green meadows and blue sage.

He tied his horse to a fence about a quarter of a mile from the ranch house. As he approached on foot, Roy worried that Butler might have hidden the colt, anticipating Roy trying to steal it back. He was also worried dogs might discover his presence and start barking. He hadn't seen any dogs around the place earlier, but that didn't mean there weren't any.

Instead of walking through the front gate, Roy crawled through a fence and cut across a little pasture, then a fenced-in vegetable garden with well-tended rows of sweet corn, carrots, potatoes, and other plants he couldn't identify in the thin moonlight. The rows of plants were straight and neat, and there didn't seem to be any weeds.

Roy's boldness paid off. There were no dogs, and the colt was in the same corral where he had been earlier in the day. There were four more colts in the corral.

Roy crawled through the fence, walked up to Cornish and slipped the halter over his head. As Roy led the colt to the gate the others followed, not wanting to be left behind.

Roy let the gate open just enough for Cornish to get through, but as he was closing it on the other colts he realized they would start whinnying as soon as he started to lead Cornish away. He stopped, wondering how he might distract the other colts so they would not notice the departure of their companion.

Roy thought of sneaking into the barn and scattering a bucket of oats along the corral fence, then he had a better idea. He opened the gate to the vegetable garden, then the gate to the corral, then hazed the colts into the garden, closing the garden gate behind them. The colts were so occupied with all the new things to eat they didn't notice Roy leading their companion out the front gate.

Roy couldn't help but chuckle over Butler's reaction the next morning when he discovered the colts in his garden. The damage would be considerable.

Roy was certain Butler would make no attempt to get the colt back. The colt belonged to Roy, and Butler knew it. But Roy underestimated the rancher.

That evening after Roy, Matt and Johnny had finished their supper, Sheriff Wasson walked into their camp, pistol in hand, ordering the boys to put up their hands. He promptly arrested Roy for horse stealing, explaining that Jake Butler had sworn out a complaint.

"The horse I took was mine," Roy protested. "Butler pastured it for me while I worked in Telluride. He wouldn't give it back, so I took it. You can't arrest me for that."

"Explain all that to the judge," Wasson said. "But I doubt he will take your word over Mr. Butler's."

Since Montrose was closer than Telluride, Wasson escorted Roy to the Montrose jail, dropping the colt off at Butler's as they passed his place on the way to the jail.

The next morning Matt visited Roy at the jail. Matt had seen the judge who said without a bill of sale Roy would need some reliable witnesses, who knew both Roy and the colt, to get him out of this fix. The judge said if it came down to Butler's word against Roy's, Butler would win. Roy said the only witnesses who could testify the colt belonged to him were Eli and Heber, and they had returned to Utah. Cap Brown knew the colt belonged to Roy, but it probably wouldn't be a good idea to bring in a known horse thief to testify.

"Then I'm going to Utah to get us a witness," Matt said. "I'll ask the judge to hold off until I get back. Johnny will take care of the horses. You just take it easy. Maybe they'll give you some books to read. I'll be back in two or three weeks. Don't worry about a thing.'' A minute later Matt was on his horse and headed for Utah Territory.

Roy felt a lot better after talking to Matt. Maybe he wouldn't be hanged or sent to prison after all.

In the days to come, as Roy paced back and forth in his cell, pondering the events of recent weeks, he became more and more angry, not only at Butler, but Wasson and Nunn as well. Roy was sure when his name had come up in the loan committee meeting, Butler mentioned the fact that Roy had pastured horses at the Butler Ranch, and had paid his pasture bill on time. That would have been relevant information for a loan committee.

Roy was convinced Butler, Nunn and Wasson were good friends, willing to bend the law to take care of each other. All three were crooks and deserved to be shot.

When he had been in the jail about a week, Roy had a visitor. Horace came to Montrose to pick up some mules for the mine, and stopped to visit his former mule skinner. After Roy explained what had happened, Horace went to see the judge, who said he was waiting on a young man named Matt Warner to bring in some reliable witnesses from Utah. Horace passed this information back to Roy.

There were times when Roy wondered if Matt would ever come back. After two weeks it seemed to Roy he had been in the Montrose jail half his life.

But Matt did return, and he brought Roy's father, Max Parker, with him, also Roy's younger brother, Dan. Before going to the jail, Matt marched his witnesses before the judge, who promptly dispatched a deputy to the Butler Ranch to retrieve either the colt, or a bill of sale signed by Roy Parker. The deputy returned with the colt, and Roy was released from jail.

Max urged his son to return to Utah to clear up the problem with the stolen calves, but Roy didn't want anything to do with such a plan. He was going horse racing with Matt

Warner.

A few days later Max returned to Utah without either of his sons. When Roy rode south with Matt and Johnny, Dan went to Telluride to get a job. Roy told him to look up Horace Nelson at the Tomboy Mine.

A week later, Roy, Matt and Johnny were in Durango, wagering everything they had against the famed Gypsy Queen in an upcoming match race against Betty. Johnny was shy and didn't say much, but Matt and Roy had plenty to say about Betty--how they had found her on their uncle's ranch near Moab, how they had raced her against all the local cowboys and won. They figured their Betty could beat anything on four legs. They neglected, however, to mention the big race at Telluride. They didn't want anyone to think Betty had a real chance against Gypsy Queen. Within a few days, Matt and Roy had all the loose change in and around Durango tied up in wagers on the race.

Betty beat Gypsy Queen by the usual half length. The people of Durango weren't very happy about their horse losing. They felt cheated, and many were angry when they reluctantly paid off their debts.

"We'd better hurry and get out of here," Roy said, when they had collected their money.

"Hate to leave a town with everybody mad at me," Matt said. "Might have to come back through here again someday."

"Unless we set up another race and let Gypsy Queen win, I don't know how we could ever win any good will in this town," Roy said.

"I do," Matt said. "Follow me."

Matt led Roy to the nearest saloon and announced he and Roy were buying drinks for everyone in the house. While they were doing this, Johnny kept an eye on the horses. As soon as Matt had paid the bill, he and Roy moved on to the next saloon and bought drinks for everyone there too.

Before the day was out they had spent the better part of their winnings, and half the people in Durango were inviting

Chapter 12

Matt and Roy to go home with them to spend the night. After all the trouble in Telluride, it felt good to Roy to be so popular. It didn't matter that he had bought the popularity with whiskey.

A few days later they headed west over the pass to Mancos, where the local populace believed a home-grown horse known as the Cavanaugh Stud was the fastest thing in southern Colorado. They couldn't figure out how the two farm boys from Utah came by so much money to bet on a horse race, but without exception everyone in Mancos was more than obliged to bet on the Cavanaugh Stud. Besides, some thought the two boys from Utah needed to be taught a lesson, not to bet so much money on horse races.

Like before, Betty won by half a length, and as soon as Matt and Roy had collected their winnings from the stunned citizenry, they set about re-establishing goodwill in the local saloons.

The next afternoon, at the local dry goods store, Roy and Matt overheard a clerk refusing credit to a poor man and his wife who had walked fifteen miles to town, hoping to get a little food to get them through the winter. There were a lot of people in the store, so Roy and Matt saw an opportunity to elevate their status to the Robin Hood level. They bought the poor couple a team and wagon, and threw in enough supplies to get them through the winter. Roy was embarrassed when the woman kept trying to kiss his hands, and he was relieved when she and her husband were finally on their way back to the farm. The next day, as Roy and Matt rode out of town, they felt like the people of Mancos were actually happy Betty had won the race.

They continued west to Cortez, but no sooner had they begun asking about fast horses to match against their Betty, than they began hearing about their own racing adventures in Mancos and Durango. Word of their exploits had preceded them. While they could find people who wanted to run horses against Betty, they couldn't find anyone willing to bet against the mare.

123

"Maybe we need to go somewhere far away, like Denver or Colorado Springs," Roy suggested as they were discussing the problem in one of the Cortez saloons.

Suddenly, Roy realized Matt was no longer listening to him, but looking towards the door. A stranger was entering the saloon, a slim, smallish man with a lean face and quick movements.

"There's a natural born fighter if there ever was one," Matt howled. Then to Roy, "It's my brother-in-law, Tom McCarty."

Roy had heard a lot about Tom. Betty was a daughter to a race horse Tom and his brothers had shipped in from back east. Tom had married Matt's sister, Teenie, when Matt was 13 or 14 years old.

A few years ago, after Teenie died, Tom decided to embark on a great adventure to help forget his heartache over the death of his bride. Matt joined Tom in New Mexico. Together, with one of Tom's friends from Panguitch, Josh Sweat, they headed down into old Mexico to steal cattle. The Chisolm Ranch in southern Arizona was paying $3.50 a head, no questions asked, for Mexican cattle driven over the border.

In a matter of days the rustlers managed to round up 200 head, and drive them over the border. They collected $700 in cash. It was so easy they decided to go back for a few hundred more. This time, as they crossed the border, they were ambushed by U.S. border patrol officers, who chased them all the way back to Utah. Josh was wounded in the initial ambush, and traveled the entire distance with three bullet wounds. Matt insisted Josh was the toughest man he ever met. Tom agreed. Matt and Tom had a lot to talk about. Roy and Johnny listened.

As the day grew late Tom invited everybody to a cabin he was living in about eight miles out of town. He insisted they come out, not just for the night, but for a good stay, perhaps for the entire winter.

The next day Roy and Matt brought Tom up to date on their horse racing adventures, and told him how they were finding it difficult to find anyone to bet against Betty.

Tom said the Navajos down in McElmo Gulch would bet everything they owned against Betty. He said the Indians had a one-eyed pony named White Face that had beaten every Indian race horse within 500 miles. The Navajos believed White Face was unbeatable. Tom was absolutely sure the Indians would bet against Betty, even if they had heard about the races in Durango and Mancos. They decided to take Betty down McElmo Gulch to race White Face.

Tom brought his buckboard along. He said the Indians didn't have a lot of cash, but would bet their wool blankets, saddles, guns, and maybe even a squaw or two on the horse race.

They found the Navajos camped in a long grassy draw near the foothills of Ute Mountain. Wickiups providing shelter for about 200 men, women and children were scattered up and down the draw. There was tall timber on both sides.

"Injuns sure knows how to pick the best camping places," Matt said as they rode up the green valley. When they stopped, a dozen Indians gathered around to see what the white men wanted.

Tom pointed at Betty, telling them this mare could run faster than any Indian pony he had ever seen. He insulted them even more, asking why it was that Indian ponies couldn't run fast.

It wasn't long until a boy trotted towards the group, leading a sorrel gelding. There was a wide blaze on the horse's face. It had only one eye. Matt and Tom didn't let on they recognized the animal.

"White Face heap faster than white man horse," one of the braves boasted. He turned and departed, returning a minute later with an armload of hand-made wool Indian blankets. Tom dismounted and looked over the blankets. He placed some gold coins on the top blanket, his portion of the bet. The winner would take the coins and the blankets.

"One-eyed pony can't run," Roy said, extending his palm to show he had some gold to bet on the race. Within ten minutes there were enough blankets piled up to fill the buckboard. Other items bet on the race included snowshoes, a pile of beaver furs, an eagle feather headdress, a choke cherry bow with a dozen obsidian-tipped arrows and a rabbit fur blanket.

"Time for the race," Tom said. "We don't have anything else to bet."

"Yes we do," Matt said, walking over to White Face, looking closely at the animal. "Most muscled up horse I ever saw. We'll bet Betty against White Face. Winners keep losers' horse."

The Indians didn't hesitate. They were so sure White Face would win. Betty was a beautiful animal, and the Indians were glad for an opportunity to win her.

Johnny crawled on Betty's back, and one of the Indian boys scrambled onto White Face. They rode down the gulch about half a mile to the designated starting place. A minute later the horses started running back. The race had begun, the horses racing up the center of the valley, dodging wickiups and cook fires as they dashed madly for the finish line, a 30-foot gap between a large pile of blankets and the buckboard.

The braves sounded their war cries to encourage White Face to run faster. The cowboys hooted and hollered words of encouragement to Johnny and Betty.

Just before the finish line, Betty pulled ahead, winning by a length and a half. The cowboys cheered, the Indians stared in disbelief. It hadn't occurred to them White Face might lose. Instead of accepting the fact that Betty was faster, the feeling among the Indians was they had been tricked and cheated by the cowboys. Surprise turned to anger. But Tom didn't seem to notice any of this.

"Looks like a lot of bucks is going to be shivering tonight," Tom said, grabbing an armload of blankets and throwing them in the back of the buckboard. A big Indian grabbed the blankets and threw them back on the ground.

Now Tom was mad too. A riding quirt was hanging from his wrist. He had brought it along for Johnny to use in

126

Chapter 12

the race, but had forgotten to give it to the jockey. Using the leather quirt, Tom began whipping the brave, in front of the entire tribe.

Matt and Roy didn't exchange any words. Both knew Tom was making a big mistake. Both knew some cowboys were going to get scalped and massacred if they didn't get out of this place very quickly. Already mounted on their horses, Matt and Roy jerked their Winchesters out of the scabbards.

Instead of riding away, they cocked their rifles and rode towards the Indians, who by now were fighting mad. Johnny grabbed a rifle off the seat of the buckboard and joined them. Tom let go of the quirt, drew his revolver and pointed it at the nearest Indian, which happened to be the one he was whipping.

Each Winchester held 16 rounds, so the cowboys knew they could inflict terrible damage should the Indians decide to fight. The Indians knew they could win because there were so many of them against just four cowboys. The only question was whether or not the Indians were willing to pay the price of victory.

"Injuns move, white man shoot," Matt yelled.

Roy could see the fight fading from the eyes of the Indians. Tom put his pistol away and threw the blankets and other items the cowboys had won into the back of the wagon. Nobody moved, not even when Tom tied White Face to the back of the buckboard. Tom jumped onto the wagon seat and began turning the wagon around.

Keeping their rifles ready to fire, Matt, Roy and Johnny began backing their horses away from the Indians. Eventually they turned and joined Tom, who was trotting the team up the draw towards Cortez. As soon as the cowboys were out of sight of the Indian village Tom whipped the team into a dead run.

It was the middle of the night when they reached Tom's cabin. Tom was sure the Indians were on their trail, so after watering and feeding the horses and locking them in the barn, the cowboys barricaded themselves in the cabin and prepared for battle. Tom said Indians were superstitious about fighting at night, so he didn't expect any trouble before daylight.

As soon as it got light, 15 Indians rode out of the timber, heading straight for the cabin. The cowboys cocked back the hammers on their rifles, ready to begin the fight. But the chief held up his hand, waving towards the cabin. The Indians' rifles were resting harmlessly across the front of their saddles.

"Put your rifles down," Tom said to his companions. "They want to talk it over."

The Indians stopped in front of the cabin. The cowboys, carrying their weapons, walked outside.

"White man give White Face to Injuns," the chief said. "We be friends."

"Injun bet White Face," Roy said, stepping forward, his voice firm but calm. "White man win White Face. White Face belong white man."

The Indians didn't like what Roy said. Their faces were sullen and dark. They were determined to get their horse back.

"Injun come to take White Face," the chief said. None of the Indians or cowboys moved.

Tom was the first to decide there had been enough calm discussion. "Get out," he yelled into the faces of the Indians. "Race horse belong white man."

Without warning, the man Tom had whipped the previous afternoon, turned his rifle on Tom. Before the brave could cock the hammer back, Tom drew his .44 and fired. The red man didn't yell or jerk, or do anything except slide off his horse to the ground, like a wet rag.

While the Indians were watching their companion fall, the cowboys raised their guns, at the same time cocking back the hammers. The fight was gone from the Indians. They bowed their heads and slipped off their ponies. They lifted their dead companion, like a sack of flour, and tied him across his horse. Without another word, they turned and rode away.

"I reckon we better hit the trail and hide up awhile,"

Chapter 12

Matt said, when the Indians were out of sight. "The Indian agent will be right after us."

"The Indians won't even report it, fearing they will get in trouble," Tom laughed. He walked back into the cabin to look for a bottle. It was time to celebrate.

Roy, Matt and Johnny ended up spending the winter at Tom's cabin. It wasn't that they enjoyed each other's company so much as they just didn't have anything else to do. They weren't in the mood to take their race horses to anymore Indian reservations, and they were sure no white men within hundreds of miles would bet against either Betty or White Face. An extended trip to a far-away place like Denver or Salt Lake would have to wait until spring. As far as Roy and Matt were concerned, some of the former fun of horse racing was gone since the run-in with the Indians. They just didn't feel like doing it anymore, at least not right away.

As the boredom began to set in, the ideas for diversion and adventure became more and more varied. After Tom and Matt's run-in with the border patrol, no one wanted to go back to Mexico to steal cattle. They discussed at considerable length the prospects of picking up some horses and cattle, and running them to Telluride, like Cap Brown was doing. Roy didn't like the idea of trying to sell stolen cattle or horses under the nose of Sheriff Wasson.

It was Roy who finally came up with the idea, that not only caught everyone's undivided attention, but started an instant rush of adrenaline through their young bodies.

It started after supper one night. Tom was pacing the floor like a hungry cat, though he had already eaten. He wasn't hungry for food, but for something to do, a challenge, an adventure, anything to take the place of endless days sitting around the cabin doing nothing but talking, drinking and playing cards.

"I feel like I'm going to bust," Tom said, "if I don't find something to sink my teeth into."

"Let's rob the Telluride bank," Roy said, his voice calm and firm. He was not joking, and the others knew it.

129

"Telluride's a big town," Tom said, looking keenly at Roy. "Everybody carries a gun. Someone robs the bank and a thousand guns could be called into action in minutes."

"In minutes the robbers could be out of gun shot range," Roy said.

This was not a new idea for Roy. During those long weeks in the Montrose jail he had dreamed of getting revenge, not just on Butler, but also on Sheriff Wasson and the banker, Nunn. Roy considered everything from poisoning their horses to burning their homes, but the only idea that really set well with him was robbing their bank. After getting out of jail, he had pushed the idea to the back of his mind, as something beyond his reach--too hard, too dangerous, too many consequences.

"We're just a bunch of cowboys having a rip-roaring time," Matt said, thoughtfully. "Racing horses, drinking all night, killin' an Injun. We just been playing. Robbing a bank is serious business. Don't know if I want to make the jump from a happy cowboy to a serious bank robber. Right now the law throws us in jail if it's handy. After we robs a bank or two there'll be reward posters with our pictures on them. Marshals and bounty hunters will be looking for us all the time. Why should we want to live like that?"

"I've seen the San Miguel Valley Bank," Roy said, ignoring Matt's objections. "The inside is richer and fancier than all the saloons and whorehouses in Telluride. I sat in a chair for a whole hour watching barkeeps, mine owners, even pimps bringing in sacks of money, and shoving them under the gold bars to the tellers. I bet that bank brings in enough money in a day to fill a buckboard. If we got a little lucky we'd never have to work again."

"Count me out," Johnny said, speaking for the first time, getting up from the table and walking over to a window. "I'm a jockey. I don't want to get shot in the back or spend time in prison. I'm leaving in the morning." He stretched out on his bunk, facing the wall, pretending to go to sleep.

"L. L. Nunn, the president of the bank is a horse's

130

ass," Roy continued. "Sheriff Wasson, Jake Butler and a whore named Diamond Tooth Leona are on Nunn's loan committee. If there was ever a bank that deserved to be robbed, it's this one."

"It'd be something for three cowboys to waltz into town and take all that money right out from under the noses of all those city dandies," Matt said, starting to get used to the idea of actually robbing a bank.

"Are we really going to do it?" Tom asked. "I don't want to spend all winter talking about it, then not do it. Talk is cheap, but to really do it, to ride into town and hold up a bank is something else. What'll it be, talk or action?"

"I want to rob the Telluride bank," Roy said, his face as sober as a preacher at a funeral. "And I'm as ready to do it now as I'll ever be."

"Count me in," Matt said.

Tom walked over to the cupboard, opened a drawer, and pulled out a large black book. He carried it over to the table and put it down.

"You boys is from religious homes," he said. "So am I. Each of you put a hand on this Bible and repeat after me."

Tom placed his palm on the book. Roy and Matt reached out and placed their hands beside Tom's, looking into the older man's face as he began to speak.

"I swear I will not be yellow, chicken-hearted or cowardly," Tom said in a serious voice. The two boys repeated his words.

"I swear I'll walk into the Telluride bank next spring, take all the money I can get my hands on, then ride like hell bent for leather, in Jesus name, Amen," Tom said, finishing the oath. Roy and Matt repeated his words.

"We're going to rob the San Miguel Valley Bank," Tom shouted, removing his hand from the Bible. "We'll start making plans in the morning. In the meantime I've got to see a man about a horse." He stepped out the door, his destination the nearby outhouse.

Chapter 13

After Johnny left the next morning, Roy, Matt and Tom had a serious talk about robbing banks. Tom reminded Roy and Matt that once they took a sack full of money from a bank, the bloodhounds of the law would never quit looking for them. It would be like the entire state of Colorado and the whole United States had declared war on them.

"We could stick with rustling cattle and earn enough in a couple of years to retire," Tom said. With all night to sleep on it, Tom was hesitating, even though they had taken an oath.

"If we rob the bank we can earn enough to retire in one day," Roy said, feeling none of Tom's reluctance. "I've seen piles of money in that bank, and we'll have it all."

"Just thinking about it almost takes my breath away," Matt said. "I didn't sleep last night. I wasn't scared, just too excited to sleep. This'll be the greatest adventure of our lives. We'll be famous, and rich."

"We don't know nothing about them cities," Tom said.

Chapter 13

"They're nothing but man traps. Every smart-ass in Telluride packs a rod. Before we could get out of town a thousand men could be shooting at us. We can't fight a whole town."

"Maybe all those city dudes really are smarter than us greenhorn cowboys," Roy said, trying to get Tom mad. "I watched all those pimps, gamblers, and barkeeps hauling sacks of money into the bank. Never saw a cowboy with that kind of money. We're just not as smart as those city dandies in their white shirts and little round hats."

"That's a lot of bull and you knows it," Tom roared.

"Then let's show'm there are three cowboys smarter than all the city dudes in Telluride."

That settled the question. The three men pulled up chairs around the table and began making plans. There was a lot to discuss.

First they had to pick a time. Since the mines operated year around, they decided there would be plenty of money in the bank regardless of when the robbery took place. To facilitate their get-away, however, they wanted to pick a time when the mountain passes were free of deep snow. April or May would be about the earliest they could get through the passes. But in the spring the rivers were usually flooding over with spring run-off waters, making crossing difficult and sometimes impossible. Usually around mid June, stream flow was back to normal. They decided to hit the bank sometime in late June.

Next, they discussed the best time of day to hold up the bank. None of them knew what time the bank opened for business, so they decided to do it later in the day, after many of the customers had made their morning deposits. They decided to do it during the noon lunch break when the number of employees and customers in the bank would be at the lowest level.

They discussed how they would carry the money. Roy described the piles of money he had seen pass through the windows into the tellers' cage. If the robbers were fortunate enough to hit a good day, ten saddle bags wouldn't hold all

133

the money they would find. Tom said, at his family's ranch in LaSalle, there was a big pile of tanned buckskin. Since the robbery wouldn't take place until June, there would be plenty of time to ride over to LaSalle and sew up some big money sacks that would fit neatly across the front of their saddles. While they were doing that, they could check out possible escape routes.

They debated at some length whether or not to wear bandannas over their faces to keep from being recognized.

"If we ride into town wearing bandannas, we might as well carry a big sign that says we're bank robbers," Tom said.

"We won't pull up the bandannas until we've pulled our guns out to start the robbery," Matt explained.

They decided they would wear cowboy outfits, not the clothes of working cowboys, but dressed up cowboys coming to town to tangle with wild women. That would draw the least suspicion.

Of course, they decided to ride their fastest, toughest horses, which included Betty and White Face.

"What do you think White Face will do the first time he sees a town?" Roy asked. "Do you think a lady in a fancy silk dress, or a big dog on a leash, or a big red sign, or the smell of a butcher shop might spook him?"

"Except for Betty, our best horses is range horses," Matt said. "It'd be damn embarrassing, after stealing all that money, to have our horses buck us off before we can get away."

It was decided, since Roy was the most familiar with Telluride, he would take their get-away horses to town several weeks before the robbery to get them used to all the strange sights and smells of the city, and to give them plenty of practice galloping up and down Colorado Avenue, through traffic.

They decided, since the distance from Telluride to the Mancos Mountains was only about 35 miles, they would not station relays of horses along the way. They figured once they got to the mountains, they could lose any posse that might follow them. From there they would ride to Tom's cabin where pack horses would be waiting to carry their outfits on an extended journey to the Blue Mountains south of LaSalle, Utah Territory. If the posse by chance followed them that far, they could head north to Moab, cross the Colorado River, and disappear into the remote Robbers' Roost country where Cap Brown hung out.

When spring arrived, Matt convinced Johnny to come back and keep an eye on a herd of horses he had been running in the Mancos Mountains, while he and Tom headed over to the Blue Mountains to make the buckskin bags and check out the intended escape route. At the same time Roy worked his way back to Telluride, leading Tom's and Matt's get-away horses, and riding his own.

With money from the sale of the Indian blankets, Roy stabled the horses and got himself a room at Hurley's Saloon. The next morning he walked into the San Miguel Valley Bank, opened a savings account, and deposited $10.

All the time he was in the bank, he could feel his heart pounding. The excitement matched the feeling one had during the final minutes before a big horse race. Every few days, Roy returned to the bank, either to deposit a few more dollars, or to withdraw some money from his account. Every time he felt the same excitement as he memorized additional details about the bank--the names and faces of employees, locations of cash drawers and vaults, windows and doors, the number of customers coming in and out, etc.

Once Mr. L. L. Nunn walked by. He looked at Roy, but offered no greeting, or showed no sign of recognition.

Roy put each horse on a ration of two gallons of oats a day. Also, he rode them every day, up and down Colorado and Pacific Avenues, getting the animals used to all the city noises and sights. He galloped the horses long distances to condition them. He even tied each horse to hitching rails, backed off twenty or thirty yards, then ran towards the animal, yelling and shouting, leaping into the saddle. In time the horses learned to stand still while he did this. Townspeople who watched these antics figured this cowboy had had too much to drink.

One afternoon Roy stopped by the Tomboy office to see Horace. Earlier, the office manager had gotten Roy's brother, Dan, on at the mine. Horace had been busy buying more mules to pack ore down the mountain, having been unable to establish satisfactory contracts with mule skinners to do the work. Horace said the mine was still willing to contract with Roy to haul ore if he could find a string of mules. Roy said he thought the day would come when he would get money out of the San Miguel Valley Bank. He thanked Horace for keeping the contract offer open.

"Kindness, hell," Horace said. "When you were packing for us there was no trouble. You were cheerful, even when there were problems, and you didn't bellyache about anything. Anytime you want to come back to work I'll make a place for you. Do you want a job?"

"Not today," Roy said. When Horace asked him what he was doing, he said he was training horses. Horace didn't ask what he was training them for, and Roy didn't explain.

On June 22, Roy checked out of his room, picked up his horses and rode down the river. About five miles from Telluride he found Matt and Tom's camp. The next day was occupied shoeing horses, cleaning pistols and rifles, and discussing the upcoming bank job. They tried to think of all the things that could go wrong, and what they would do in each case. They spent considerable time fiddling with the buckskin money bags Tom and Matt had made, trying to guess how much money could be carried in each bag.

"What if we can get only two or three thousand in each bag?" Matt asked.

"I'd guess we could get almost thirty or forty thousand in each one if all we take is greenbacks," Roy said.

"But we don't want to leave all that gold behind," Tom added.

None of them ate very much that day, and nobody

seemed to be able to sleep that night.

"Just think," Roy said, sometime in the middle of the night. "By this time tomorrow we might be the richest men in Colorado."

"By this time tomorrow we might all be dead," Tom added.

The next morning, after filling their horses with oats, they saddled up and headed for town, after turning loose the two extra horses and the mule Tom and Matt had brought with them.

All three were wearing fancy cowboy shirts Roy had bought in town a few days earlier. They were wearing chaps, high heeled boots, and jingling Mexican spurs. All three wore red bandannas and five gallon hats pulled down over their faces to make them harder to recognize in the event someone they knew might see them riding into town. There were silver-studded bridles on the horses. They were cowboys in their Sunday best, a common sight in Telluride. Cowboys generally dressed up when they wanted to drink, gamble and tangle with the women on Pacific Avenue.

There was another reason for the exaggerated dress. They were about to engage in a match of wits and courage between three cowboys and all the city smart alecks of Telluride. It was the cowboys against the dudes, and they didn't want anyone to miss this point.

"I sure feel uneasy," Tom said as they began their journey down Colorado Avenue. There were carriages, freight wagons, and strings of pack mules. There were men everywhere--some in work clothes, some in black suits. Nearly all the men were carrying guns.

"We're riding into one big trap," Matt said. "When the yelling and shooting starts how will we get past all these men with guns, without getting our heads blown off?"

"Sure glad I brought these horses to town early to get them used to things," Roy said. The horses weren't bothered by any of the city sights and noises.

"Hi there, cowboys," a man yelled from one of the

wooden sidewalks. Tom nodded back. Matt waved to two women hanging out a second story window. "Look," he said, "they're giving me the glad eye and an invitation to be a sucker."

It was shortly after noon when they reached the bank. Matt and Roy dismounted and walked inside. Tom stayed with the horses, mounted and ready for action.

As soon as they walked through the door, Roy realized they had picked the right time. The bank was empty, except for the cashier, who was sitting behind one of the barred teller windows. A lot of money was stacked in piles in front of the cashier.

Trying to act like regular customers, Matt and Roy sauntered towards the window, laughing and making small talk like they weren't noticing anything in the bank.

The cashier smiled at the approaching cowboys, expecting to receive a deposit from them. Trying to be as nonchalant as possible, Roy and Matt kept looking to see if anyone else was in the bank. They couldn't see anyone except the cashier.

"What can I do for you?" the cashier asked when they reached the window. Matt responded by whipping out his .44 and tucking the barrel under the cashier's nose before the poor fellow realized what was happening. At the same time Roy leaped around the end of the counter and into the cashier's cage. Without being told to do so, the cashier raised his hands high over his head. He had a scared look on his face. His mouth was twisted, like he was about to throw up or cry.

While Matt continued to point his cocked pistol at the cashier's face, Roy, with a sweeping motion of his arm, pushed the piles of money off the counter into one of the buckskin bags. When the bag was nearly full he shoved it under the bars to Matt, then headed for the open door to the vault where he found a big pile of tightly wrapped bricks of greenbacks.

Matt kept looking over his shoulder, towards the door. It seemed Roy was spending all day in the safe. Matt could hardly believe their good luck when no one entered the bank. He pulled his bandanna over his nose and mouth, and called to Roy to do the same. Eventually Roy hurried out of the vault, carrying a huge sack of money.

"I could put some more in your bag," Roy offered. Matt shook his head. It seemed to him they had spent too much time in the bank already.

They decided ahead of time there was probably a hidden alarm button, and a gun, somewhere in the teller's cage. They weren't about to leave the cashier behind, and they hadn't brought rope to tie him up, so they shoved him ahead of them out the front door.

They didn't think to tell the frightened fellow to put his hands down as he left the bank. Then it was too late. Someone across the street saw the cashier with his hands up, and began yelling, "Bank robbers! Bank robbers!" All of a sudden it seemed like everyone in town was yelling and shouting, and Tom was the loudest.

"On your horses," he screamed. Matt and Roy, dragging their sacks of money, pushed the cashier to one side, grabbed their horses' reins and swung into the saddle. In spite of all the commotion, the horses behaved themselves until Roy and Matt were mounted. There was no time to tie the money sacks to the saddles.

Expecting everyone in town to start shooting at them, the three cowboys spurred their horses and headed up Colorado Avenue like they were in a horse race, dodging around wagons and surprised people.

The cowboys were amazed. While everyone seemed to be yelling "Bank robbers," no one was shooting at them. As they raced by, the faces on the sidewalks looked surprised and helpless. In a minute the cowboys reached the end of Colorado Avenue and headed for open country.

"It was too damned easy," Tom shouted, when they had covered about five miles, and there was still no sign of a posse. "The city crowd is a bunch of babies."

"Wait'll they get organized," Roy cautioned. "We took

a lot of loot. They'll be trying to get it back."

"How much did we get?" Tom asked.

"About a hundred thousand," Matt said.

"Did anybody recognize you?" Matt asked Roy.

"Don't think so," Roy said. "Didn't see anybody I knew riding in, and coming out, our bandannas were up."

About an hour later as they dropped over a steep bank onto a road, they realized when it was too late to turn back that there were two riders in the road, two men leading some mules.

"Roy Parker," one of the men shouted. "Where're you headed in such a hurry?" Roy pulled up his horse to see who the man was. It was Horace Nelson, bringing some mules back to the mine. In that instant, when Roy was trying to decide whether to acknowledge the greeting or ride on, Matt and Tom began spurring their horses into a full gallop away from the strangers. Still, Roy hesitated. It didn't serve any purpose to run, now that Horace had recognized him. Roy turned his horse towards Horace.

"The way you're all dressed up," Horace said, his voice friendly, "Looks like you should be headed into town instead of the other way."

"Dressed up for a meeting at the bank this morning," Roy said, grinning.

"With Mr. Nunn?" Horace asked.

"He didn't make it, but I got the money anyway."

"The loan for the mules?" Horace asked, still not getting Roy's message.

"Enough to buy a thousand mules," Roy shouted. Horace looked confused.

"And the nice thing about it," Roy laughed. "I don't have to pay any of it back." He spurred his horse into a gallop after his fleeing companions, leaving the bewildered Horace to figure out what Roy had been saying.

Chapter 14

As Roy, Tom and Matt rode higher and higher into the Mancos Mountains, they kept looking back over the country they had passed through, looking for a posse, or anybody who might be coming after them. They saw nothing.

"If I'd known it was going to be this easy, I'd a started robbing banks a long time ago," Tom said.

"It ain't over yet," Roy insisted.

It was after dark when they finally stopped for the night. Their supper consisted of parched corn, dried fruit, and water. They did not build a fire, and they did not unsaddle their horses, though they loosened the cinches. Without the light of a fire, they had to wait until morning to count their money. Not having slept the night before, and having been in the saddle most of the day and evening, they were about as tired as men could get. Still, they made sure one of them was always awake while the other two slept. Those who slept wrapped themselves in rain slickers that had been tied behind their saddles.

At first light, after carefully scrutinizing the country behind them and finding no sign of pursuit, they spread out one of the rain slickers on the ground and dumped the contents of the buckskin bags onto it. For a minute or two they just stared at the biggest pile of money any of them had ever seen, and it was all theirs if they could avoid getting caught.

"At least a hundred thousand," Matt said. Tom and Roy didn't disagree, neither having any idea if Matt's guess was high or low.

"It'd take a hundred years to spend that much money," Tom said.

Dropping to their knees, they divided the pile of money into three more or less equal portions and began to count. It didn't take long to realize Matt's estimate of their wealth had been greatly exaggerated. They had $31,000, plus a handful of gold coins. They counted again and came up with the same number. Matt was mad.

"I volunteered to become one of the most wanted criminals in Colorado for a lousy ten grand," he said.

"Still looks like a lot of money to me," Tom said, as they began to sort the bills and coins into three equal piles so each could take his third and put it in one of the buckskin bags.

Once the money business was taken care of, they walked out on a rocky point and studied the trail they had taken the previous afternoon. When they were as certain as they could be that no one was following, they got on their horses and headed for the horse camp in the top of the Mancos Mountains where Johnny Nicholson, Neils Olson, and George Brown were tending Matt's horses.

Upon finding the camp, they made no effort to hide what they had done from the wranglers. Another man was at the camp, Bill Maddern, who had a store in Mancos. While Matt was telling about the robbery, Tom kept saying he couldn't get over how easy it had been. While Matt and Tom talked, Roy stood near the edge of a hill, keeping an eye on the trail they had come in on.

At the end of the day there was still no sign of a posse.

Chapter 14

Nevertheless, the three outlaws agreed to stick to their original plan, to move on to the Blue Mountains. When they gave Bill a list of the supplies they needed from his Mancos store, he said he didn't have some of the items on their list. He offered to ride into Telluride the next day to get their supplies. At the same time he would find out why a posse hadn't been sent after them, or if there were any plans to put one together.

Everyone thought this was a good idea. Bill headed for Telluride at daylight. While he was gone, the men took turns watching Bill's trail. Tom, Matt and Roy caught up on their sleeping and eating.

Matt, figuring the law would probably confiscate his horses and turn them over to the bank, made out a bill of sale, giving the animals to Johnny. It didn't matter that Johnny couldn't pay him.

"A fool's trade," Matt said after he had turned the bill of sale over to Johnny. "I am giving up twenty thousand dollars worth of horses so I can run off with ten thousand in bank loot."

The next day, Johnny, who had been on the lookout, ran into camp yelling that Bill was coming on the dead run, and it looked like half the state of Colorado was a stone's throw behind him.

The bank robbers saddled their horses while Neils and George threw a camp outfit and some supplies on the mule. A minute later the outlaws were headed west towards the Blue Mountains.

When the posse arrived, the wranglers acted glad to see them. When Sheriff Wasson started to arrest Bill for helping rob the Telluride bank, the three wranglers insisted Bill had been with them at the time of the robbery, and had left the previous day to go into Telluride for supplies. When asked if they had seen Roy Parker, they lied, saying they hadn't seen him all summer.

While Wasson was talking with the wranglers, one of his deputies, who had been riding in a big circle around the wrangler's camp, discovered the fresh tracks of three shod horses and a mule headed west. The race was on.

For a while the outlaws hoped the posse would lose their trail at the horse camp, but their hopes of an easy get-away were short lived. About an hour after hitting the trail they spotted the posse coming over a sandy ridge.

"Must be 50 of them," Tom said. "Most have Winchesters."

"They're leading a few pack mules," Matt said. "With supplies they'll be able to stay on our trail for some time. We'll have to go a lot farther than the Blue Mountain to lose these boys."

Tom led the way, planning to head northwest until he hit the trail that led to the place where Roy had crossed the Colorado with Cap Brown a few years earlier. That trail would lead them across the river to the desolate Roost Country where they hoped the posse would not follow.

The outlaws pushed their horses hard, but didn't seem to increase the gap between themselves and the main part of the posse. During the middle part of the day the men leading the posse's pack mules had fallen behind the main body.

During the afternoon Roy began to wonder if they would be able to recognize the trail leading to the river. The sandstone bluffs and juniper forests looked familiar, but he could find no distinguishable landmarks. Tom was sure the trail was still ahead of them.

Later in the afternoon they ran onto a cowboy leading a string of five horses. Tom knew the man, called him Jess. When they asked Jess if he was familiar with the trail leading to the river, he said he was, but advised against trying to cross. He said the spring run-off was late, and both the Colorado and Green Rivers were too high and fast to cross. He said if they wanted to get over the Grand, a name many of the old timers still used in referring to the Colorado River, they'd better head for the ferry at Moab.

No sooner had the outlaws changed the direction of their flight, than Roy's horse started limping. He was riding the tall gray he had won from Slim in that first horse race. At first the limp wasn't hardly noticeable, but it continued to get worse, and as it did, the posse began to get closer.

Coming out of a juniper forest, at a spot where they were out of sight of the posse, they made a sharp right turn across a big patch of volcanic cinders. They knew their tracks would be almost impossible to follow through the broken rock. They finally stopped at the base of a little hill in the middle of the field of cinders. After hiding their horses in the thickest part of the junipers they climbed to the top of the hill to monitor the actions of the posse.

They watched for a long time and saw nothing. They knew their tracks led to the edge of the rocky cinder bed. If the posse tried to cross the cinders in daylight, the outlaw position could be easily defended. If the posse didn't reach the cinder bed by dark, the outlaws figured they could slip away under cover of darkness, unless the posse had enough men to totally surround the cinder bed.

The longer they waited, the more sure they were they had made a mistake. In time, they were certain the posse was watching them from the cover of the juniper forest. It was now obvious the posse had no intention of crossing the cinder bed in daylight.

Tom was the first to spot movement. Pointing to the east, he got the attention of his two companions. They could see a horse moving at the edge of the junipers.

"I'll bet I can plug him from here," Matt said, raising his needle gun to the shoulder. Matt had picked up the rifle at the horse camp. Made in France, it was longer than a Winchester. The bullets were longer too, holding more powder. The gun was designed for long-range shooting.

"Wait," Roy cautioned. "First let's see who's riding the horse."

As the horse neared the edge of the junipers they could see that it was a paint, and that it was not carrying a rider, no bridle or saddle either. Eventually the horse started across the cinders towards the outlaws.

"Maybe they hazed the paint onto the cinders to see if

145

we would shoot at it," Tom said. "Since we didn't, maybe they'll follow."

"Maybe it's just a stray Indian pony," Roy said. The paint, a mare, continued walking towards the portion of the juniper hill where the outlaws' horses were tied.

"What should we do?" Tom asked, when the mare reached the hill, working its way into the trees to join their horses.

"You two stay here and keep an eye on things," Roy said. "I'm going to catch the mare. If my gray gets any lamer I'll need a replacement."

By the time Roy walked down the hill the mare was rubbing noses with the outlaws' geldings. When she refused to let Roy get close enough to put a halter on her, he removed his silk Manilla rope from his saddle and threw a loop over her head. Then he tied her to a tree. The way she fought the rope told him she was about two-thirds wild, and very spirited. She was small, hardly 14 hands tall, and thin, not much of a riding horse for a man needing to cover a lot of country.

Roy walked over to the gray to see if he could discover the cause of the limp. It was the animal's left front foot that had been giving it trouble. Roy knew the foot was still tender because the left knee was bent to keep weight off the injured hoof.

Looking at the leg and hoof, Roy could see nothing that would cause a horse to limp. He picked up the foot and looked at the bottom of the hoof under the shoe. He couldn't believe his good luck. A flat piece of red shale was wedged between the frog and the inside of the horse shoe. Roy wanted to kick himself for not looking at the bottom of the hoof earlier. He opened his pocket knife and pried the rock free. When he let go of the hoof, the big gelding placed it gently on the ground. Roy untied the animal and led it in a circle. It did not limp.

After dark Matt and Tom crept down the hill to the horses. There had been no sign of the posse all evening, only

146

Chapter 14

the appearance of the paint mare. It had been too quiet. They were sure the posse knew where they were. Their trail to the edge of the cinder bed would have been easy to follow. Undoubtedly, some of the posse members would have circled the cinders to see if there were tracks leaving. When they didn't find any they would know the three outlaws were holed up on the little hill in the middle of the cinder bed.

"We're trapped, like fish in a barrel," Tom said. "Bet they have a man stationed every 20 feet around the cinders. Not a chance in hell we could sneak past them."

"Got to try," Matt said. "Can't sit here and let'm tighten the noose."

"If they'd only showed themselves, or opened fire on us, then we'd know where to make our break," Tom said, a worried tone in his voice. "They got us cornered, we're trapped."

"We might be cornered, but we're not trapped, not yet," Roy said, thoughtfully.

He had an idea. He opened his knife and started cutting at the base of a large limb on a pinion tree until he had cut the limb free. Then he removed a rope from the mule's pack saddle, tieing one end to the green limb. As he tried to tie the other end of the rope to the mare's tail she started kicking at him. Roy ended up holding her head while Matt tied the rope to her tail. When they were finished Roy told Matt and Tom to get on their horses.

"What are you doing?" Matt asked.

"Ever tied a can to a cat's tail and watched it run?" Roy asked. "This mare's our cat, and when I let her go she ought to run like crazy into whatever kind of trap the posse has prepared for us. In the dark, they won't know it's a mare with a tree on her tail. They'll think it's us."

Roy removed the rope from the mare's neck and slapped her over the rump with it. As she lunged forward the tree limb jumped after her. The frightened mare stampeded back the way she had come across the cinder field, the tree crashing and bumping behind her.

147

"Never thought one little mare could make such a racket," Matt laughed. Then he stopped and listened. In the distance, he could hear men shouting. "There they go!" "That's them!" "Shoot the sons o' bitches!" "Get your horses!" "Don't let'm get away!" Suddenly guns began firing.

Fortunately the paint was headed back towards Telluride, the posse scrambling after her in the dark. Roy, Matt and Tom had a good laugh as they left the little hill, headed north towards Moab. No one bothered them as they left the cinders and entered the cedars.

They rode all night. Though tired, the gray horse didn't limp. They reached Moab an hour or so before daylight. They were worried the posse might have sent a few men ahead to cut them off at the ferry crossing. While they were holed up on the little hill there would have been plenty of time and opportunity for the posse to send a few men ahead as a safety precaution in the event the outlaws got away.

When they got close to the river they got off their horses and began prowling about like cautious animals of the night, looking for the ferrymen, while worrying about deputies.

Just as the sky was beginning to turn gray, they found the ferrymen in two beds, spread out on the open ground near the bank of the river. Matt and Tom were worried they might be walking into some kind of trap, but could see no sign of anyone else being around. Matt walked up to the beds, cocked his revolver, and said "Stick'm up." His voice was soft, but intense.

All at once, three ferrymen sat forward on their rumps, their hair messed up, their eyes wide with surprise and fright, their hands high in the air--looking like three scared rabbits staring out of a bush.

Matt and Tom had crossed the river many times at Moab. They knew all three--Lester Taylor, Jimmy Wright, and Adam Steele. When the ferrymen recognized Matt and Tom, they didn't know why the guns were pointed at them.

148

Chapter 14

"Keep your hands up," Matt warned. "Where's the deputies?"

"Ain't no deputies around here," Taylor said.

"If that ain't true," Roy said, coming up from behind, his gun in his hand, "you fellers better correct it now while you still can."

Taylor still insisted there were no deputies. A minute later the outlaws were leading their horses onto the ferry. A short time later they were on the other side of the river. As they were leading their horses off the boat, Matt handed Taylor some gold coins.

"You fellers ain't seen no outfit cross this river tonight," he suggested to the ferrymen.

"We sure ain't seen no outfit cross during the whole night," Taylor said, winking to his pals.

Two days later as the outlaws approached Thompson Springs, a little railroad town east of Green River, Utah Territory, they climbed a little hill and scanned the country they had passed through. They hadn't seen any sign of the posse since crossing the river at Moab, and they could see no evidence of a posse now.

Not daring to ride into town where they might be recognized, they turned north into one of the rugged desert canyons leading to the McPherson Range and Hill Creek, finally making camp at a little spring feeding into a large, shallow pond.

The next morning, after climbing up in the cliffs and scanning the horizon in the direction of Moab, and seeing no sign of a posse, Roy picked up Matt's needle gun, thinking he would try it out. He had never seen a bullet as long as the one he slipped into the chamber.

"Take care," Matt warned. "Butch packs a wallop."

"Why do you call it Butch?" Roy asked as he walked towards the edge of the pond. He had never heard of anyone giving a name to a gun before.

"You'll find out," Matt laughed.

Finding himself in mud at the water's edge, Roy

stepped onto a flat, sloping rock. The surface of the rock was wet and slippery.

"Bet you can't hit that rock in the middle of the pond," Tom challenged.

Roy raised the rifle to his shoulder and fired. He never saw if the bullet struck its intended target. The kick of the rifle was so severe, and the surface of the rock so slippery, that he lost his footing and fell backwards into the mud.

Matt and Tom roared with laughter until their sides hurt. Roy pulled himself and the gun out of the mud and spent the rest of the morning cleaning himself, his clothes and the rifle. As Matt and Tom continued to laugh and tease Roy over his inability to handle the needle gun, they began calling him Butch, a name that stuck with him the rest of his life.

Chapter 15

There was still no sign of the posse when the outlaws packed up and continued west the next morning. While they were getting ready to break camp, Matt and Tom called Roy by his new name, Butch. Ordinarily, Roy might have objected, but ever since Horace had recognized him the day of the robbery, he knew he would have to change his name if he ever wanted any peace. Officers all over the west were going to be looking for Roy Parker. If his friends wanted to call him Butch that was as good as any other name, he thought.

They hadn't been on the trail more than an hour when they noticed a cloud of dust off to the south and west. Matt grabbed the field glasses from his saddle bags, dismounted, and crawled to the top of a large rock where he thought he could see the cause of the dust.

"What is it?" Tom demanded, after Matt had been looking through his glasses for what seemed a long time time.

"A rider?" Matt said, continuing to look through the binoculars.

"What's he doing?" Butch asked.

"Looking through his field glasses," Matt answered.

"What's he looking at?" Tom asked.

"A cowboy on a rock, looking through field glasses," Matt answered.

"He's looking at you?" Butch asked.

"Yup, and I'm looking at him."

"Is he alone?" Tom asked.

"Nope. There's five riders with him, and I'd guess they're asking him what he sees, the same as you two are asking me."

"Are they deputies?" Butch asked.

"Yup," Matt answered.

"What makes you think that?" Butch asked.

"The feller's put his glasses away, and they are headed this way on the dead run." Matt slid off the rock onto his horse. The three headed for the nearest canyon to the north, hoping it would lead them to the rugged Hill Creek country. As they entered the canyon, the posse wasn't far behind.

"Don't think they're the boys from Telluride," Butch yelled to his companions.

"Why not?" Matt responded.

"Only six. Horses don't look familiar," he answered.

"Think you're right," Tom said. "Whole country must be out looking for us by now."

The valley they entered was wide at the mouth and reasonably flat, except for frequent patches of blue sage, and an occasional sandy wash. The outlaws were making good time, but so was the posse.

As the canyon began to narrow, the posse started to make its way to the left side. There were several gentle side canyons leading off in that direction that looked like excellent escape routes, while on the right side, where the outlaws were riding, the canyon wall was a sheer cliff extending two or three hundred feet straight up into the blue desert sky.

Seeing the canyon was eventually going to narrow, possibly into a box canyon, the outlaws tried to get their horses to run faster so they could work their way over to the

Chapter 15

left, where they had the option of whether or not to turn off into one of the gentle side canyons. But the posse had gotten too close. As the outlaws began to veer to the left they realized they would soon be easy targets for the deputies with Winchesters.

"Let's turn around, and charge right at'm," Tom yelled. "If each of us gits two, we're done."

"Better'n getting shot in the back," Matt responded. All three grabbed for their Winchesters.

"Wait," Butch yelled. "Look right."

There was a break in the sheer cliffs they hadn't been able to see earlier. A canyon with a smooth bottom was leading off to the right, or east. Then it appeared to turn north. They knew it could be a box canyon, or it could lead all the way to Hill Creek. They had no way of knowing.

Turning their horses sharply to the right they headed into the canyon. Their pack mule stayed with them, not wanting to be left behind.

After they had gone about a mile, they suddenly found themselves facing a sheer wall, almost too high for a pheasant to fly over, extending from one canyon wall to the other. They were hopelessly trapped.

No one needed to discuss what to do. They dismounted, tied their horses to a juniper tree, then dove into some boulders to prepare for their final stand.

"I won't be taken alive," Tom said, grimly, as he pumped a bullet into the chamber of his Winchester.

"Me neither," Matt said.

"There's only six," Butch said. "Maybe we've got a chance."

"Only twice as many as us," Matt said.

"Must be setting up a defense at the mouth of the canyon," Tom said, when the posse didn't appear. "Maybe they're going to wait until we run out of food and water."

"How do they know we can't climb up a crack somewhere and get away?" Butch asked.

"Too many questions," Tom said. "Let's fight." He

got on his feet, in a crouching position, and began stalking down the canyon. Matt and Butch, their rifles ready, followed close behind, expecting the shooting to start at any moment.

As they rounded the bend they could see clear to the mouth of the canyon. There were no deputies in sight.

"If they could see us, they'd start shooting," Matt said.

"Maybe they're waiting to see the whites in our eyes," Tom said. He crept forward while Matt and Butch covered him. They were sure the shooting would start at any moment, but it didn't.

"They'd have to be blind not to see us ride in here," Matt said.

Tom walked all the way to the mouth of the canyon, not only looking for deputies, but studying the ground as well to see if any horses other than their own had come in or out of the canyon.

A few minutes later Tom hurried back to join Matt and Butch. "They never entered the canyon," he said, "unless their horses can fly. There's no tracks except ours."

"It don't make sense," Matt said.

"Maybe they didn't know it was a box canyon either," Butch said. "The way it bends around to the north, maybe they figured they could beat us to the top by staying in the main canyon. That way they could ambush us as we came out the top."

"That's what they done," Tom said.

"Why didn't they split up," Butch asked, "leaving some of their men here? They didn't know it wasn't a box canyon. That way they would have blocked both ends and we'd be trapped in the middle."

"You don't know much about posses," Tom said. "Everybody in posses thinks outlaws is bad men." Butch didn't understand.

"There's only six of them," Tom explained to his young companion. "If they split up they would have only three men at each end of the canyon. That would make an even fight. Three against three, whichever way we decided to

154

Chapter 15

fight our way out. If you were a storekeep or a farmer who got swore in as a deputy, would you want to go even numbers against Tom McCarty, Matt Warner and Butch Parker?''

"They are scared of us?" Butch asked.

"That's right. Trapping us like fish in a barrel, six against three is one thing. Take'n us on three-on-three is a different matter...and when we don't show up for the ambush at the other end, they'll start down the canyon looking for us. Better get to the horses before they do.''

"The money's on the horses," Matt screamed, starting to race back up the canyon. Tom and Butch weren't far behind. They didn't slow down, driven by the possibility the deputies might beat them to their money.

There was no sign of any deputies when they reached the horses. A few minutes later the outlaws raced out of the side canyon, then the main canyon, but instead of turning west towards Green River, they headed east towards the White River Indian country. Now they knew posses in Utah Territory were looking for them too, they guessed they might be safer in the remote Indian country of northwest Colorado.

That evening, after finding an isolated, well-concealed camping spot with plenty of feed and water for their tired horses, Matt and Butch went to work cutting up the buckskin money sacks. After much trimming and sewing they finished three buckskin money belts which could be secured around their waists. Now, they would never be tempted to leave their money on their horses. They stuffed ten thousand dollars into each of the belts and tried them on.

"Never thought ten thousand dollars could be so heavy," Matt said.

"Or so bumpy," Butch added.

"At least the buckskin is soft," Tom said.

The next morning as they broke camp each was wearing a bulging ten-thousand-dollar money belt under his shirt. Guessing the posse from the day before might not be far behind, they pushed their horses at a fast trot, the money belts bouncing up and down, wearing sores on the tender skin

155

around their waists. Under the burning July sun, with salty sweat running down their sides, the money belts became unbearable. There were times when Butch and Matt were sorely tempted to rip off the belts and throw them on the ground, but neither did.

"The skin'll toughen up in a few days," Tom said, trying to comfort his miserable companions. "In the meantime try to think about something else." He began to describe a beautiful woman he had once seen in Price. She was loading supplies into her buckboard on what Tom guessed was the hottest afternoon of the summer. He said the woman's sweat gave the fabric of her dress a transparent quality and caused it to stick to her firm body in a way that could drive a man out of his mind.

Matt and Butch listened, trying to picture in their minds the scene Tom was describing, but the bouncing of the money belts against tender skin kept reminding them they were not in Price watching a beautiful woman, but in the wild desert country near the Colorado border, being skinned alive by heavy buckskin money belts.

The next morning, Matt was sick. He had diarrhea during the night, and had thrown up twice. His face was pale gray like a lizzard's belly, and he could hardly stand up. Roy asked Tom if he thought they should hide up for the day and give Matt a chance to get over his sickness.

"We ride," Tom said, his voice sober. "When a posse's on your tail you ride. If you got a broken leg, you ride. If you got three bullets in your side, you ride. On the outlaw trail a man's no better'n a dog or a horse. When he can't go any more he's left behind. If he dies, he dies, and is supper for the coyotes."

Without complaining, Matt crawled into the saddle. Except for frequent stops during the morning to relieve himself, he hunched over the front of his saddle, leaning forward, supporting himself with his hands and arms. His horse followed the others. In silence Matt suffered. He did not complain about his sickness or the relentless bouncing of his money belt as it wore deeper and deeper wounds in his tender skin.

The irony of the situation, which Butch thought about often, was that each man was carrying ten thousand dollars, enough money to buy the best comforts civilization had to offer, yet they pushed relentlessly forward, doing without the comforts they could easily afford.

Even the simple pleasure of a hot meal was something they couldn't enjoy every day, only when they were camped where they knew their fire and its smoke could not be seen. On such occasions they cooked enough beans and bacon to last for days. The next noon, or night, when they felt a fire was too risky, they would shove the pasty leftover beans in their mouths without the benefit of warming them up.

The three outlaws were on constant lookout for formations of exposed bedrock and sandstone. They went miles out of their way to cross such formations where horses' shoes did not leave tracks. When they found a stream or river heading more or less in an easterly or northerly direction they rode in the streambed for miles, knowing there would be no tracks for a posse to follow. If streams were rocky, horses lost shoes, and valuable travel time was lost shaping replacement shoes on rocks and nailing them in place. And each time a shoe was lost, it was harder to nail the new one in place because the hoof was wearing down faster than it was growing. After four days of hard travel, all the horses had at least one tender foot.

The only exception was the mule. Not only were his feet harder in the first place, but he also seemed more careful than the horses as to where he placed his feet. Even without shoes, the mule's feet did not get tender. He didn't get tired like the horses either. The mule browsed as he traveled, grabbing mouthfuls of bunch grass along the way. When there was no grass he would nibble at brush and even twigs. While crossing particularly barren stretches of terrain it wasn't unusual for him to pick up, chew and swallow an occasional chunk of dry cow manure. Horses wouldn't do this. But while the horses wore down more and more each day, the mule seemed to maintain his flesh and strength.

When they stopped for the night the three outlaws would stake their horses out on long ropes. This way they always knew where the horses were so they could be caught and saddled in a hurry. If the outlaws suspected a posse might be near, they frequently left the saddles on the horses and the pack saddle on the mule. Of course, they removed the bridles from the horses. Sometimes they would tie the tether rope to a halter, but usually to one of the animal's front feet where there was less chance of getting tangled in the rope and suffering a laming rope burn behind one of the rear hocks.

In selecting campsites they looked for a spot with feed and water for the horses, good cover for men and horses, and no nearby trails that might lead other people to the camp. Cook fires were built in daylight only, with carefully selected wood that made the least amount of smoke. Willow and cottonwood was best. The men fed their infrequent fires with small sticks and twigs so the fire could be quickly and easily extinguished. They never threw big logs on their fires.

At night when it was time to sleep, the outlaws avoided sleeping together in the middle of the camp. Each man would wander off a short distance, finding a good hiding place under a tree or boulder, often an elevated spot with a good view of the surrounding area. Loaded rifles and pistols were always within easy reach.

Even after a long, tiring day on the trail, the outlaw did not sleep soundly. His ears analyzed every sound--the whinny of a horse, the tumbling of a rock, the scolding of a squirrel, the snapping of a twig, or the stomping of a horse's foot.

Their horses were on the verge of collapse when the outlaws reached the White River Indian country. On three occasions they spotted groups of men riding in the distance. While they couldn't be sure, they assumed the men were deputies looking for the Telluride bank robbers.

One afternoon, while following the White River, they rounded a bend and found a band of Indians camped in a

Chapter 15

cottonwood grove. A herd of horses was grazing on a grassy
bench above the river. Matt was gruff and irritable as he
traded his race horse, Betty, for a fresh horse. It made him
angry when he had to give some gold coins to boot. He
couldn't seem to convince the Indians how fast this mare
would be as soon as she had a chance to rest and heal. The
outlaws traded off all their horses. All they kept was the pack
mule. As soon as the trading was finished, they saddled up
and were on their way.

As they left the Indian camp they had to lead the mule
until it got attached to the new horses. At first, it kept trying
to return to its old friends at the Indian camp.

The outlaws continued north for a day, then turned back
to the west. Matt told Butch and Tom about his good friend,
Charlie Crouse, at Brown's Hole on the Green River. Charlie
had done a little rustling on his own, as had almost everyone
in that remote corner of the country, where no one seemed to
have very much love for the law.

Not only was Brown's Hole a remote and hard to get to
place, but the boundaries of three states or territories came
together at the Hole--Wyoming, Utah and Colorado. If
officers from Colorado went there to arrest someone, it was
a short ride into Wyoming or Utah where the officers had no
jurisdiction.

Any worries Tom or Butch may have had about Charlie
Crouse, quickly evaporated upon meeting the man. The old
cowboy greeted Matt as if the outlaw were his own son. He
offered food, supplies, fresh horses, anything the men needed,
and refused to accept any pay.

"What we need is a place to hide," Matt said. "Seems
there are posses everywhere. We need to lay low, give the
deputies a chance to get tired of looking for us and go home."
He pulled up his shirt and showed Charlie the red sores the
money belt had worn around his waist.

"We need to rest and heal our wounds," Butch added.
Charlie led them to a cabin about ten miles from the Hole.
There didn't seem to be any well-used trails leading to and

from the area. The cabin was surrounded by thick forests, yet there was plenty of grass for the horses, and a good spring. It was a perfect hideout. The trapper who had built the cabin had died several years earlier.

When Charlie left, he promised to return in about a week, to check on them and bring fresh supplies. Tom's last word to Charlie was to be sure to bring some whiskey.

For the first time since the robbery, Butch felt like he could relax. It felt good not to have to wear the money belt. It felt good not to have to spend all day in the saddle. It felt good to sit at a table and eat a hot meal, two or three times every day. It felt good not to have something urgent to do, to just sleep, talk, eat and take it easy.

The third day Tom found a deck of cards and the three began to play poker. Each took a bundle of dollar bills from his money belt and put it on the table. They played all afternoon and most of the evening, never more than a hundred dollars changing hands.

It must have been almost midnight when Butch drew what he thought was a pretty good hand, three queens. They were playing five card draw. The previous hour or two the game had become increasingly boring, and he had found himself distracted by the itching sores around his waist.

Without warning Butch grabbed his money belt and slammed it on the table. "I bet my whole wad," he said.

Matt's and Tom's eyes widened in amazement. Tom, who was sitting on Butch's left, looked carefully at his cards, then at the money belt in the middle of the table. "I fold," he said, placing his hand face-down on the table. He looked at Matt.

Carefully, Matt eyed his cards. Then he looked across the table into Butch's grinning face.

"If I fold, will you show us your hand?" Matt asked.

"Hell no," Butch laughed. "You got to call to see it."

"Then I call," Matt said, reaching for his own money belt and tossing it on top of Butch's.

Butch drew two cards. Matt did the same. Each guessed

the other was drawing to three of a kind.

"I called you. Show me your cards," Matt said.

"Let's see yours first," Butch responded.

"Lay'm down together," Tom said. "On the count of three." He counted to three, and Butch and Matt, at the same time, spread their hands on the table in front of them. Butch had three queens. Matt beat the queens with four jacks.

"Guess it's not my lucky day," Butch said, starting to get up from the table to turn his back on the ten thousand dollars he had just lost.

"Wait a minute," Matt said. "I've been tricked and I don't like it. I think you cheated."

Had Matt lost, his words would have been taken seriously. They would have been fighting words. But because he won, Butch and Tom didn't know how to react. They didn't have any idea what Matt was trying to say. It wasn't normal for the winner to accuse someone of cheating.

"If you think you can use a card game to trick me into carrying two money belts instead of one, you're plumb loco," Matt said. "We've got a lot of riding ahead of us and I refuse to carry your money too. You can't give me that heavy money belt, not even in a poker game. I won't take it." Butch began to laugh. Matt and Tom joined in.

When Charlie arrived the next week he did not bring any supplies, but rather news that a large posse was on its way to Brown's Hole in search of bank robbers.

Grateful for a week's rest, the three outlaws strapped on their money belts, saddled their horses, packed their mule and headed south towards what they believed to be the most desolate, uninhabited, and remote corner of the world, Robbers' Roost.

They rode over Diamond Mountain to Vernal, then on to Nine Mile Canyon. After riding to the top of the Tavaputs Plateau, they followed Rock Creek to the Green River in the heart of Desolation Canyon. They met no travelers in this remote country, only an occasional cowboy. Every few days they would kill a deer or antelope, keeping them in fresh meat.

A short distance below the mouth of Rock Creek they found a wide, shallow section of the Green River at the head of a raging rapid. Here, they crossed to the east side where traveling was easier.

It was a strange, quiet land, the mighty river winding silently through fields of boulders, cottonwood groves, and white sand beaches where a weary cowboy could take his clothes off and stretch out on the warm sand, letting the quiet gurgling of the river sing him to sleep.

They saw little game, but plenty of sun-bleached antlers, indicating the land they were riding through was a wintering ground for deer and elk. They crossed an occasional stud pile where a wild stallion had emptied his bowels in the same exact spot week after week to mark his territory, and warn other stallions to stay out. Yet the wild horses were not here now. It was probably a wintering ground for them too.

"The animals are up there in the summer," Tom explained, breaking the silence. He was pointing to a flat-topped mountain rising five or six thousand feet above the river. "Moonwater Point. Best summer range a man ever saw up there," he said. "Thousands of acres of lush grass that stays green all summer. Groves of quakies and oaks. Plenty of fresh water. Biggest elk and deer a man ever saw running all over the place, almost begging to be shot."

"Why don't we go up there and hide out?" Butch asked.

"Too close to Hill Creek," Tom explained. "Some sheep and cattle are up there too. We'll be hid out better in the Roost country.

That night they stayed at the Jim McPhearson Ranch near the mouth of Florence Creek. Jim seemed to be a little reserved when he saw the bulging money belts around his visitors' waists. He didn't say whether or not he had heard about the Telluride robbery, and they didn't volunteer to tell him what they had done. Still, McPhearson was friendly, cooked them supper and put them up for the night.

Chapter 15

The next morning Butch traded horses with McPhearson, giving a little gold to boot. McPhearson seemed pleased. Butch was glad. He knew if he spent much time running from the law in this remote country, McPhearson was a good friend to have.

Waking up the ferryman in the middle of the night, they crossed to the west side of the river at Green River, then hurried through town in the dark, hoping no one would recognize them. By morning they were headed south into the Robbers' Roost country. Two days later they set up camp at the head of a steep, winding trail, on a grassy table-top mesa. There was only one trail leading to the top of the mesa, making it easy to defend their camp.

After placing a juniper tree across the trail to keep the horses from leaving, they turned their weary animals out to graze. There was a good spring near their camp. Butch had hoped they might run into Cap, but there was no sign of anyone else on the mesa. Butch knew the old horse thief would enjoy hearing about the Telluride bank robbery.

Butch was amazed how quickly Tom seemed to forget the hardship and danger of their flight from Colorado. Once more, Tom began making comments on how easy the robbery had been. He could hardly wait to plan and execute a second bank robbery.

Butch did not share the old outlaw's enthusiasm. By now the whole state of Colorado and most of Utah Territory knew Roy Parker had robbed the Telluride bank. Horace had seen his face, and the mine office manager wasn't a good enough friend to keep quiet. Everyone probably knew by now that Roy Parker was a bank robber.

He wondered how his parents, and brothers and sisters would react. He was sure they would be very disappointed, even ashamed. Although he had sent home a portion of his wages while working at the mine, he decided not to send them any of the stolen bank money. He guessed his mother wouldn't want it.

With each passing day Butch felt worse about what he

had done. While he still felt Nunn and Wasson deserved to have their bank robbed, Butch was sorry he had taken the big step outside the law.

While Butch was feeling down and out, Tom was making plans for the next robbery, at Butte, Montana. Butch avoided Tom's planning sessions.

After about three weeks they started to run out of supplies, and had shot up nearly all their bullets in target practice. Since Tom and Matt were both well known in Green River, Butch offered to ride in for supplies. Charlie Gibbons' store in Gray's Valley was closer, but the selection was better in Green River. Leading the pack mule, he headed north.

Three days later when Butch returned he was excited and nervous. While buying supplies he had seen Sheriff Tom Fares walk past the front of the store. Someone said Fares had come to town looking for clues as to the whereabouts of the Telluride bank robbers. Fares was an old, English gentleman, turned cowboy. He was tall, thin, and wore a long, white handlebar mustache. Even though he had been in America for nearly ten years, he spoke with a strong British accent. His personality was a combination of bulldog and mule. He was a tough old brute who didn't easily change his mind.

While leaving the store Butch ran into an old acquaintance, Dan Gillies of Circle Valley. The two men recognized each other, and chatted for a minute or two.

Immediately following the conversation Butch was on his horse heading back to camp, knowing Gillies would talk about the encounter, especially when he heard Roy Parker was involved in the Telluride robbery. By the time Butch reached camp he was sure it was just a matter of time until Tom Fares rounded up a posse and followed his trail.

The outlaws discussed at some length whether or not they should flee. The spot where they were camped was easily defendable. Unless Fares got to tracking Butch right away, while his tracks were fresh, the camp would be very difficult to find. With the weather as hot as it was, one wrong turn and a posse could find its horses dying of thirst.

Chapter 15

The three knew if they hit the trail to go somewhere else, there was a good chance they might run into another posse looking for them. By now it seemed to them the mood of the whole country was to join posses and go looking for bank robbers. They decided they had a good hideout, and there being a good chance Fares would never find it, they would just wait and see. But they would keep a careful lookout.

Everyday one of them would saddle a horse, drop down the steep trail off the rim, and ride in a wide circle looking for any signs of posses. They hoped that by doing this, if a posse came, they would have the advantage of finding it before it found them.

The fourth day after Butch's arrival from Green River, Matt discovered three sets of fresh tracks about five miles from their camp, heading up a draw towards their camp. He knew at a glance the tracks were made by shod horses, and because they maintained a steady course, they were being ridden by men with a purpose. Matt raced back to camp and warned Tom and Butch.

They rode to the head of the draw where Matt had seen the tracks. They could see signs of riders coming out of the draw, so they dismounted and prepared to ambush what they guessed was a posse coming to find them.

They hadn't been waiting long when they spotted three riders coming up the draw. The three outlaws found comfortable places behind rocks and ledges where they had steady rests for accurate shooting with their Winchesters, and good cover to protect them from return fire. This would be like shooting fish in a barrel, and with only three men in the posse, the outlaws were sure they would be victorious.

To the surprise of the outlaws, just before reaching the best place for the ambush to begin, the posse turned south into a rocky side canyon. Butch had explored that canyon earlier. It led to a desolate, easy-to-get-lost country, where there was not water. It wasn't noon yet, and the temperature was already nearly a hundred, they guessed. It appeared this foolish posse was going to meet disaster without a single shot having to be fired.

Butch was surprised at his reaction to this apparent stroke of good luck. While a moment earlier he and his companions were preparing to ambush and gun down the three men in the posse, now Butch didn't like the thought of knowingly letting the men die of thirst.

"Maybe we ought to warn them," Butch said. "There's no water up there. If they go too far, or get lost, they'll die."

"We could show'm the way back to Green River," Tom said, sarcasm in his voice, "so they could throw us in jail."

"I suppose it'd be a Christian thing to give'm some water before we shoot'm," Matt added.

"They don't deserve to die," Butch said, his voice serious. "Not for trying to do a job."

"You've been riding around in the sun without a hat on," Tom said, looking closely at Butch.

"Maybe if we save their lives and lead them to water," Matt said, "they'll be our friends, and won't want to take us in."

"I sure wouldn't arrest anybody who had saved my life," Tom added.

"We must be crazy," Matt said. "But I feel like it's what we ought to do." Butch agreed. Tom was more hesitant. Matt got on his horse and hurried down the trail. When he was almost to the side canyon where the three lawmen had turned off, he tied his horse to a juniper tree and climbed up a rocky point overlooking the side canyon. His Winchester was in his hand.

In the distance, Matt could see the three riders working their way up the canyon. He pointed his rifle in the air and fired. When the three riders looked back at him, he waved his hat in the air, motioning for them to come to him. They hesitated a minute, then turned their horses around and started back.

Matt scrambled back down to his horse, where he

166

removed a paper and pencil from his saddle bag. He wrote, "Death if you go south. Follow me to water." He folded the paper, wedged it between the forks of a stick, then stuck the stick straight up in the middle of the trail leading out of the south canyon. Then he stepped into the saddle and hurried back up the trail to the top of the rim, telling his partners what he had done.

Butch and Tom got on their horses and hurried back to the spring, hiding in the boulders above the spring. Matt stayed at the edge of the rim to watch the three riders dismount and read his note.

When they finished reading, he waved at them again. They got back on their horses and started up the steep winding trail towards the rim. By now Matt was sure the leader of the posse was Sheriff Fares. No other lawman, that Matt had ever known, was bull-headed or stupid enough to ride into what appeared to be an obvious ambush. The three men worked their way up the trail to the rim. Matt galloped to a series of ledges about half a mile away, where he waited to wave to them again.

When the posse saw him there, Matt raced to the spring ahead of them, hid his horse behind some desert holly bushes, ran to the spring and hid behind a boulder. He wanted to be close to the spring so he could hear what they said as they drank the water. Butch and Tom were further up the hill, watching from their hiding place.

When the lawmen reached the spring, they leaped from their horses, falling on their bellies in the mud to drink. Their horses buried their noses almost to the top of the nostrils as they sucked in huge gulps of the cool water. It was apparent both riders and horses hadn't had water in a considerable length of time. It was also apparent the outlaws had saved the lives of these lawmen, led by the bull-headed Tom Fares. And the lawmen knew it.

Keeping a sharp lookout for outlaws, the sheriff and his deputies tied their horses to some brush to keep the animals from filling their gaunted bellies too fast. Every minute or two the deputies and the sheriff would return to the water to swallow some more. Only men, who thought they were going to perish for lack of water, drank the way these men did. When they had returned to the water four or five times, they let their horses come back for more. Then the men filled their canteens, found a shady spot under the edge of an east-facing boulder, and began to eat some lunch.

"I think we ought to head back home," one of the deputies said. "And say we didn't find any outlaws."

"Me too," the second deputy said.

"Hi'm the sheriff," Fares said in a strong English accent. "Tom Fares na'er goes back without 'is man."

"But they saved our lives," the first deputy said.

"You'll bloody well do as I says," Fares insisted.

By this time, from his nearby hiding place, Matt had heard about all he could stand. He had just saved a man's life, and now that man wanted to take him to jail.

Knowing he would bust if he didn't do something, Matt jumped out from behind his boulder, pointing his cocked pistol straight at the sheriff and deputies. "Stick'm up," Matt yelled.

While the lawmen guessed they were being watched by outlaws, they had no idea one might be so close. The two surprised deputies jumped to their feet, their hands high in the air. Sheriff Fares, on the other hand, seemed calm and in control as he carefully stood up, and slowly raised his hands. He looked as if he were calmly waiting for Matt to look away, thereby giving the sheriff an opportunity to turn the tables.

"Turn around," Matt yelled, anger in his voice. When the three men turned their backs towards him, Matt stepped up close and took their guns.

As he was pulling the revolver from Fares' holster, Matt was so mad he cocked back the hammer and pulled the trigger. The gun roared, the bullet sped harmlessly through the air, missing Fares ribs by an inch or two. The old Englishman didn't yell that he'd been shot, as Matt hoped he might. The sheriff didn't even flinch. He had nerves of steel like everyone said. Matt was impressed, but he was still mad at the man's lack of gratitude.

By this time Butch and Tom showed up to see what the shooting was all about. Matt repeated the earlier conversation between the sheriff and his two deputies, and mentioned trying to scare Fares by firing the sheriff's pistol behind his back.

Now Tom was mad too. "Let's kill the dirty snake," he said.

"Would you really take us to jail, after we saved your life?" Butch asked, looking directly at Fares.

"Tom Fares na'er goes back without 'is man," the sheriff said, defiantly. "Your turn's a come'n."

"You might be as tough as nails, and as stubborn as a mule," Butch yelled, "but you are dumber than a fence post."

Then to Tom, Butch said, "Go ahead and shoot him."

The outlaw raised his cocked pistol, pointing it directly at the sheriff's nose. Fares didn't even blink as he stared down the barrel at Tom.

"Wait," Matt said. "You think we got a lot of posses on our asses for robbing a bank. Just wait'll we kill a sheriff. Time passes and folks forgets a bank robbery. Nobody forgets kill'n a sheriff. I don't like it."

"Then take your damn English pants off," Tom yelled at the sheriff.

"If you are going to shoot, you can do it with me pants on," Fares responded.

"Why do you want his pants off?" Matt asked.

"Teach the skunk a lesson," Tom said. "Let's make him ride home without his pants."

Butch started to laugh. He liked the idea of the tough old Fares riding into town without his pants. Why, that would be the best trick anyone in these part had ever seen.

"Let's take his saddle too," Matt said. "He can ride bareback and bare butt, all the way home. Then the tough old buzzard won't be so tough, at least not on the bottom end."

The three outlaws began to laugh so hard they could

hardly keep from rolling on the ground. It appeared the deputies wanted to laugh too, but they didn't dare.

Reluctantly, the old sheriff removed his pants and climbed onto the bare back of his horse. Fares' shorts were too large. It looked like his white, spindly, legs were bell clappers hanging out of huge flour sacks. The three outlaws laughed until their sides hurt as they led the posse to the edge of the rim and herded them down the steep trail back the way they had come. Fares continued to cuss the outlaws the entire way.

"Tom Fares always gets his man," Butch teased.

"You're bloody right," Fares said. "And your bally turn will come next." Butch couldn't help admire the old man for his grit.

When the posse was out of sight, Butch hung Fares' pants in a juniper tree beside the trail. He attached a note to one of the buttons which read, "Tom Fares never goes back without his man, but sometimes without his pants."

Later, the outlaws learned Fares went to Hanksville instead of Green River. He became so sore he ended up walking most of the way. When one of the deputies offered to loan the sheriff the deputy's saddle, Fares responded by saying that any sheriff, dumb enough to let two-bit bank robbers get the best of him, deserved to lead his horse all the way to hell.

As the three approached Hanksville, one of the deputies offered to ride into town ahead of the sheriff and bring back a pair of pants.

"To 'ell with the pants," the sheriff responded. "Won't do them natives a bit of 'arm to see a man without pants."

Huntsville has never had a very large population, but on that summer afternoon everyone turned out to see Tom Fares parading into town. His shorts were covered with trail dust, and had lost their whiteness, but were still flapping in the afternoon breeze. Fares' tongue had lost its sharpness too. He stumbled into town, stumbling awkwardly along, too tired to walk like a man, too sore to sit on his horse. Some of the

Chapter 15

onlookers commented that it looked like a couple of cowboys were herding in a lunitic off the range.

Chapter 16

The outlaws knew when the news got around that three bank robbers sent Tom Fares home without his pants, it was just a matter of time until a larger posse would be sent out. It was time to pack up and leave, but there was no consensus on where would be the safest place to go. Butch convinced his companions they ought to run down to Hanksville to see if the storekeeper, Charlie Gibbons, knew where Cap Brown was hanging out. If they could find Cap, Butch was confident the old horse thief could show them places to hide where no posse could ever find them.

Upon arriving in Hanksville the next day, they discovered everyone was still laughing about the day Fares stomped into town without his pants. Until now the outlaws assumed Fares had gone back to Green River, not Hanksville. Fortunately, as soon as Fares had purchased a new pair of trousers, he had headed north, and was not around when the three outlaws arrived.

Gibbons said Cap Brown had left the area some months earlier after telling the storekeeper he had bought a cattle ranch just outside Lander, Wyoming. He had purchased the ranch with the money he had earned selling cattle and horses in Telluride. The old horse thief told Charlie he intended to find a squaw, settle down and become a more-or-less honest rancher.

"Let's go to Lander," Butch said to his companions. "Cap will hide us out."

"Maybe we ought to continue south," Tom said, reminding his partners of the big posse that had come looking for them at Brown's Hole.

"By now every lawman in the west knows we took Fares' pants at the Roost," Butch reasoned. "They probably knew we were at Brown's Hole a few weeks before that. If they tried to figure out a pattern, it would seem we were working our way south. I'd think Lander would be about the last place they'd expect us to go now."

Butch won out. That evening they began the ride north to Lander, traveling mostly at night, hiding during the days, traveling the most remote trails possible to avoid posses and other travelers who might recognize them.

The second day on the trail Matt began talking about the two times in his life he had gotten involved with women.

"Probably wouldn't have become an outlaw if I hadn't let myself get involved with that girl in Levan," he said. He described in detail how he had hit his friend over the head with a board from a picket fence when the friend tried to hold his girl's hand. Thinking he had killed his friend, Matt left town and became an outlaw. He was only 15 at the time.

"Second time, just a few years later," he explained, "while running horses on Diamond Mountain, took a shining to a young filly in Brown's Hole. Feller named Toliver wanted the same girl and that led to the most wicked and bloody rough-and-tumble fight I was ever in. We used our fists and feet like wild animals. Nearly murdered him, and that convinced me I better leave women alone."

"It was downright disgusting," Tom said, entering the conversation.

"Don't know if I'd call it disgusting," Matt countered, "but I would sure call it ugly."

"Not talking about the fight," Tom explained.

"That's what Butch and I are talking about," Matt said.

"No, you're talking about women," Tom explained, "and it's downright disgusting how you fell in love with that girl in Brown's Hole."

"Didn't fall in love," Matt protested. "Just wanted to have a little fun."

"We'll let Butch be the judge of that," Tom said, reining his horse between Butch and Matt, so Matt wouldn't interrupt what he was about to tell Butch.

"Soon as he starts seeing this little gal," Tom began, "the first thing he does is start rubbing grease on his hair. Then he starts washing his face every day, whether he needs it or not. And if that ain't enough, he has to wear a different shirt every week. Every time he goes to see this little gal he puts on his best spurs. If that ain't love, then I guess I don't know what love is. It drives a man loco."

Tom's argument was too persuasive. Matt conceded that he had indeed fallen in love with the girl. "The minute I laid eyes on her all my resolutions against women oozed out of me like I was bleeding to death," he explained. "But after I near killed Toliver, I told him he could have her. Something about that fight that brought me back to my senses."

"I figure as long as I am an outlaw I won't give women serious consideration," Matt continued. "They don't fit in my way of life, and it isn't fair to the girl. I want to stay free to range the whole earth without being hitched to anybody or anything." He advised Butch to adopt the same philosophy.

Tom put it a different way. "Have your fun," he said, "but don't let a gal put the lasso on you."

A week later, early in the evening, they reached the front gate to Brown's ranch. Their journey had been uneventful, having seen no signs of posses. They figured any lawmen still after them had probably gathered at Green River to converge on the Roost hideout.

Chapter 16

As they reined their horses in at Cap's gate, they felt safer than they had at any time since holding up the Telluride bank.

"Wait," Tom said, as Butch began to lead the way onto Cap's ranch. "Why don't we ride into Lander and spend some of this money that's been wearing sores on our sides?"

"No," Butch said. "Too risky. No tellin' how much they are still watching for us."

"Good gawd!" Tom yelled, suddenly exploding. "Is this thing got to last forever? I would rather be dead than have thousands of dollars on me I can't spend. I'm going to take a chance."

"Every dollar is screaming to be spent," Matt said, taking sides with Tom. "And I ain't going to pass up a chance like this, if we have to blast our way though a line of deputies."

"It's your funeral, and I ain't going with you," Butch said. "I'm going to Brown's."

As it turned out, Matt and Tom should have stayed with Butch. Sensing a need for caution as they entered town, Tom and Matt tied their horses and pack mule behind the first saloon they came to, instead of in front.

They had barely gotten inside and called for a couple of drinks, when an old, weather-beaten cowpuncher saunters through the front door and over to the bar where they were standing. He leaned over like he had a secret to tell, and started whispering.

"A posse just rode into town asking about some strangers they been trailing. Maybe it ain't you, but I ain't going to stand around and see no sneaking deputies grab good cowboys."

Tom grabbed the old man's hand and nearly shook it off while Matt ordered the cowboy a drink.

"Don't stop for that," the cowboy said. "They'll be in here any second."

As the deputies came in the front door, Tom and Matt raced out the back. The posse chased them through town then

175

into the nearby mountains. That night Tom and Matt made a fireless camp in thick timber.

The next morning as they were preparing to break camp, they nearly went to pieces when they heard bloodhounds on their trail. Neither one of them had ever been chased by dogs before. As they got hold of themselves, they both thought it strange how a new danger, though no worse than any other way of getting caught or killed, tended to scare a man into losing control.

An hour later, after crossing a clearing, Tom and Matt pulled their horses to a halt at the top of a little hill. Quickly, they grabbed their Winchesters, dismounted, and took dead rests on fallen trees. A moment later, when two bloodhounds entered the clearing, Matt and Tom opened fire, killing one dog instantly, wounding the second and sending it howling back the way it had come. Tom and Matt concluded that men with Winchesters didn't need to be afraid of dogs.

It was beginning to snow, and without the dogs on their trail, they soon lost the posse. They headed for the divide leading to the Mormon community of Star Valley.

The next day, as they crossed the divide, the snow was already a foot deep and still falling. They knew if the snow continued the valley would soon be closed for the winter, nobody coming in or out. The snowfall continued, and as Tom and Matt rode into Afton, they knew they would be safe from the law, at least until spring.

They bought a cabin at the edge of town and fixed up an old barn to stable their horses. They told people they had just sold a ranch in Montana, and were looking for another. They said their names were Tom Smith and Matt Willard.

As the snow continued to fall, deer and elk came down from the mountains. For a while all a man had to do to keep meat in the pot was step out his front door, take aim and pull the trigger. But in time the animals left, and food became scarce.

The owner of the only store, a fellow the Mormons called Brother Burton, refused to give credit to his customers

Chapter 16

when food became scarce. Since no one could get in or out of the valley, Burton's store was the only place to buy groceries. Those who ran out of money became desperate.

Tom and Matt entered Burton's store one day to find it crowded with people. The Mormon bishop and his two counselors were trying to persuade Burton to extend credit to the needy families in the valley. The stubborn storekeeper refused.

Tom and Matt listened for a while, eventually becoming disgusted with Burton. They decided to take matters into their own hands.

"Looky here," Matt said, stepping up to Burton. "Us two hombres come from civilized country and ain't used to indifference to human suffering. We are going to show you right now how white men handle situations like this."

"Yes," Tom roared. "We are going to distribute your goods to these folks, and we're going to pay you half price on everything that's handed out."

Tom and Matt pushed their faces up close to Burton's, their hands on their guns. The bishop and his counselors looked startled, but did not interfere. Someone in the crowd gasped. Burton turned white and tried to back away. His jaw dropped.

"This is a stick-up," he screamed. "Somebody call the constable." Nobody moved.

"This ain't no holdup," Tom yelled. "Us fellers is going to pay half in cash for everything that's handed out. Burton's charging twice as much as he should anyway."

"Are you going to take it standing up, or on the floor?" Matt asked Burton.

The crowd seemed paralyzed, until Matt asked, "Who needs flour?" Some people stepped forward. Tom handed them bags of flour while the bishop's counselors recorded the transaction in a book.

Word spread quickly. Soon there were too many people to fit into the store. Supplies were handed out until the shelves were almost bare. The bishop urged moderation as the people cheered for Matt and Tom. When the prices marked on everything were added up, the total came to $2,300.

Up until now Burton was looking like he was sick enough to die, but when he saw Tom and Matt open their wallets and pull out wads of greenbacks, he suddenly felt better. He actually seemed pleased when they handed over $1,150 in cash, enough to pay half of the marked price on everything handed out.

After that the Star Valley Mormons rolled out the red carpet for Matt and Tom. The outlaws stuffed their skins with so many woman-cooked meals, they hardly had to do any cooking on their own. They were invited to all the dances and social functions. The end result was that both lost their convictions to steer clear of women, and before winter was over, as described by Matt later, both of these unbranded, long-eared maverick outlaws got tied to Mormon wives, which greatly complicated their bank robbing adventures in Oregon beginning the following summer.

Back in Lander, Butch followed a more cautious track. After hearing about the posse chasing Matt and Tom out of town, Butch packed up his things and headed south to Brown's Hole. He figured that would be a safer place than most to spend the winter, and he thought there was a chance Tom and Matt might show up, if the posse hadn't caught them.

It was snowing when Butch arrived at Charlie Crouse's cabin. The old horse rancher assured Butch there would be no need to hide out now. There hadn't been any sign of a posse in over a month, and he was sure there wouldn't be before spring.

Butch had plenty of money and didn't need to work, but after a few weeks, needing something to keep him busy, he landed a job on the Herb Bassett Ranch. Immediately, Butch felt like he had found a home away from home. Mrs. Bassett was an educated, religious woman, like Butch's mother. Immediately he began borrowing some of the many books she kept on shelves in her cabin.

Chapter 16

Butch shared the bunkhouse with three other cowboys, including Buckskin Ed Whitworth, an old cowboy with a reputation for training fast race horses. The other two hands were Elzy Lay and Al Hainer, young cowboys about the same age as Butch who took an immediate liking to him. Everyone at the Bassett Ranch, thanks to Charlie Crouse, already knew about the Telluride robbery, and how the outlaws had hidden out in the mountain cabin. Since everyone in the Hole seemed to do a little rustling from time to time, deputies were not welcome. When there was a chase, local sympathy was on the side of the chased rather than those wearing the stars.

Elzy was from Ohio, and had a background similar to Butch's. He had been raised in a large family where all the children were taught to read and write by a religious mother. Elzy had come out west to be a real cowboy. He was friendly, articulate, and eager to learn how to do things. He and Butch became best friends in a matter of days.

Al Hainer was quieter than Elzy. He was a cowboy's cowboy. He didn't read or write very well, but when it came to horses and cattle, Al knew about everything there was to know, but he didn't know much else. His biggest accomplishments in life, which he would only talk about after a drink or two, both happened in his fifteenth year. First, he had saddled and rode his horse every single day, 365 consecutive days. Second, he roped a sow grizzly as she sent her two cubs scampering up a tree. He said if he had roped her feet instead of her head she wouldn't have been able to come after him, and he wouldn't have lost his rope.

When Butch hired on there was some fall branding and castrating to do. Al and Butch did most of the roping, both heads and feet, while Elzy and Buckskin Ed kept the fire blazing and did the branding and doctoring. If the weather was warm, the Bassett girls helped too.

When the branding was finished, there wasn't much else to do. There were no fences to mend because the stock roamed freely through the Brown's Hole bottoms. There was no hay to feed because the Hole was low enough in elevation, and protected from winter storms by the surrounding mountains, to allow grazing year around.

When the weather was bad, Butch spent a lot of time reading the books he borrowed from Mrs. Bassett. When the weather was good he helped Buckskin Ed train a sorrel colt they both thought might be faster than anything around, including Charlie Crouse's race horses. They didn't have a stop watch, but by using the second hand on Butch's pocket watch, to time the horse over various distances, they knew the animal had legitimate speed.

They knew the only way they could make any money on a winter race would be to match the colt against one of Charlie's race horses. Since there wasn't much going on in Brown's Hole this time of year, they guessed there would be a lot of local interest, and therefore a lot of betting against any horse that would dare race against one of Charlie's race horses.

One afternoon Butch rode over to Charlie's and threw out the challenge. Butch guessed all he had to do was tell the truth. He said he and Buckskin Ed had a colt they figured could outrun any of Charlie's race horses. Butch said he had enough confidence in the colt's speed to bet $3,000 on the race.

"Let's put the horses on the line too," Charlie said, rising to the occasion. Charlie took great pride in having the fastest horses. He knew Butch had raced horses with Matt Warner in southern Colorado. Matt's race horse, Betty, had been bred and raised on Charlie's ranch. Charlie knew the new colt must be good if Butch and Buckskin Ed were willing to bet that much money. Charlie wanted the colt, and by including the horses in the bet, he would get the colt, and $3,000.

Butch and Charlie shook hands. They set the date of the race about ten days away, on a Sunday, so those living several days away would have time to hear about it and get to the Hole on time. Charlie didn't feel bad about taking Butch's $3,000. After all, the boy hadn't earned it. He had just stolen

Chapter 16

it from a bank.

It was decided Butch would ride the colt. Buckskin Ed warned him about one of Crouse's tricks that often proved helpful in winning big races. His jockey would face the horse away from the finish line just as the race was to begin. This would distract the opposing jockey, who usually thought the Crouse horse was not ready to start the race. What the opposing jockey didn't know was that the Crouse horse was trained to start races this way, to whirl and run at the sound of the gun, catching the opposing jockey and horse off guard.

Butch and Buckskin Ed decided to teach their colt to whirl and run too. As far as they knew no one, other than Charlie, had ever done that. Maybe they could catch Charlie's jockey off guard, and get a little bit of an advantage.

When the day of the race arrived, Butch had nearly $5,000 bet on the sorrel colt. It seemed everyone wanted to bet on Charlie Crouse's proven race horse, and not on an unknown colt. It surprised Butch that he could find so much betting money in a place like Brown's Hole.

Butch was also surprised at how many people showed up for the race--probably every homesteader, cattleman and horse thief within a 40 mile radius. Everyone seemed to be having a good time, feasting on picnic lunches while they laughed and talked. There was a lot of drinking.

When it came time for the race, people lined up on both sides of the main wagon road leading through the Hole. About half were congregated at the finish line.

Butch caught Crouse's jockey off guard with the whirl and run trick. The sorrel colt got off to a faster start. Butch could hear the thundering hooves of the Crouse horse behind him, but he never looked back. The colt laid back his ears, stretched out his nose and ran faster than he had ever ran before, beating the Crouse horse by two lengths.

Unlike the races Butch had been involved in at Durango, Mancos and Cortez, nobody seemed mad or angry over the outcome of this race, not even Charlie Crouse who lost his best race horse and $3,000. Butch guessed people weren't mad because they knew him and Buckskin Ed. Strangers hadn't come to town and taken their money. They had lost to people they knew. That was somehow better than losing to strangers.

To show he wasn't sore over losing the race, Charlie invited everyone to a dance at his place that night. He had brought down a fiddler from Rock Springs. He had killed a beef that was already roasting on a green, lodge pole spit. There would be plenty to drink too.

Butch knew if he went to the dance, Charlie's daughter, Minnie, and Josie Bassett would want to dance with him. He liked both girls, but the way they looked at him sometimes made him nervous, and he didn't know why.

Sometimes he felt the most powerful aching and yearning to be with a woman, but whenever he went to a dance, his palms began to sweat until they felt as slippery as a fresh caught fish. About that time a young lady would walk up and offer to take his hand to lead him to the dance floor. That's when he felt like a cat in a kennel, or a colt crossing a frozen river for the first time, waiting for the ice to break through at any moment. Breathing became difficult and he couldn't wait to get outside.

Butch was sure something was wrong with him, especially when he was around other men who bragged about their swooning skills and their courageous exploits in places like Pacific Avenue in Telluride.

But sometimes Butch thought the way he felt wasn't necessarily bad. He remembered Matt's warning against getting involved with women. A man on the rustle shouldn't let that happen. Still, Butch sometimes felt an emptiness and lonliness as big as an ocean, and he knew it could only be satisfied by a woman. When he felt this way the only thing that seemed to offer relief was to go outside and throw three or four hundred loops at a cow skull, or saddle a green colt and head out at a full gallop.

Having won the race, Butch knew he would be the guest of honor at Crouse's dance. Against the persistent coaxing of

Chapter 16

Elzy and Al, Butch stayed home that night. Said he wanted to count his winnings and do a little reading.

After the race, winter settled in at Brown's Hole. Things became too quiet for Butch. One morning he packed his things on his mule, saddled his horse and headed for Rock Springs, a coal-mining and railroad town about 75 miles to the north. He thought maybe he would look for a job, though he didn't need the money, and if the opportunity presented itself, line up another horse race.

It was mid afternoon a few days later when Butch rode into Rock Springs. Having been in the saddle all day, he dismounted and led his horse and mule into the town. Instantly, he knew he was entering another mining town. Like in Telluride, there were lots of saloons.

But Rock Springs was different than Telluride. Whereas the Colorado mining town was nestled among majestic peaks and raging waterfalls, Rock Springs was surrounded by sagebrush flats and brown rocks. The main business in Telluride was digging fortunes in gold and silver, while the main business in Rock Springs was digging dirty, black coal for the railroad.

As Butch led his horse down the middle of the main street, he noticed other differences between Telluride and Rock Springs. There were no fancy carriages, no fancy women in fine dresses leading dogs on gold chains. Instead of white picket fences and tidy yards, there was trash along the side of the street. Telluride was a gold town, Rock Springs was a coal town.

Hearing a snarling sound, Butch looked quickly to his left. A huge brown and white dog, whose breeding appeared to be half St. Bernard and half wolf, had emerged from a lean-to dog house and was carefully scrutinizing the cowboy who was leading his horse and mule too close to the dog's territory. Butch dropped to one knee, smiled at the dog, and snapped his fingers, inviting the dog to come to him.

It did, but not the way Butch anticipated. With more of a roar than a growl erupting from its throat, the now raging beast lunged at Butch. With one hand, Butch tried to hang onto the lead ropes to his frightened horse and mule. With the other hand he reached for his gun.

Fortunately he didn't have to kill the dog before it tried to rip his throat out. It hit the end of its chain about ten feet short of the target. Butch began to laugh. The excitement he thought he might find in Rock Springs had found him.

"Before I leave this town," Butch said, shaking his finger at the still growling dog, "you and me will be pals. That's a promise."

Continuing down the street, Butch stopped to gaze through the open doors of a large building called the Helsinki Saloon. Even though it was afternoon, the place was packed with men shouting, laughing and singing in words Butch did not understand. He had heard hundreds of men from Finland worked the coal mines at Rock Springs. He guessed the Helsinki Saloon was where they hung out when not working.

Just beyond the saloon was a butcher shop with a poster in the window advertising fresh sausages. He wasn't sure what a fresh sausage was by Rock Springs standards, but he hadn't had a meal all day, so he thought he might try some. His mouth began to water. The sign above the door said, "Gottsche's Butcher Shop." Butch tied his horse and mule to the hitching post and walked inside.

To his surprise there were a lot of people in the shop, waiting to get meat. An older woman with black hair all tied in knots on the top of her head was scolding the butcher for making her wait so long. Her black dress was too tight, squeezing in mountains of fat. It looked to Butch that if the buttons on her dress were suddenly cut away the poor woman would spread to death. He smiled.

"Mr. Gottsche, you must hire some help," she scolded.

"All uv de men vorks in de mines," the butcher apologized in a voice with a heavy German accent. "I can't pay dat much." The man was red-faced, middle aged and over weight.

"I'll help you," Butch said in a happy voice, stepping

behind the counter and picking up a knife.

"Vait just ein minute," Gottsche said, not sure he wanted this friendly young man behind his meat counter. "Vat's your name?"

"George Cassidy. Some of my friends call me Butch. I don't like to dig coal, but I like to cut meat. Pay me whatever you think is fair."

"Ve gif you a try den," Bottsche said, smiling, but still cautious. "You can sleep up der." He pointed to a stairway beside the meat counter.

By the end of the next day Mr. Gottsche figured he had made a good choice in hiring Butch. The young man was friendly and helpful with the customers, a hard worker, and though he hadn't had any commercial meat cutting experience, he learned quickly and cheerfully.

Butch figured the job was a perfect disguise. Even if a posse came to town looking for cowboy-bank robber, Roy Parker, the butcher shop would probably be the last place they would expect to find their man.

Butch enjoyed making deliveries about town--to the saloons, restaurants, cook shacks at mines, and private residences. He talked to a lot of people, and saw a side of city life he hadn't seen before. He knew he would eventually get restless and want to get out in the open again with cattle and horses, but for the winter months he couldn't think of anything he would rather do, or a better way to hide from the law.

One afternoon, after Mr. Gottsche had made more fresh sausages, Butch was working at the counter filling customer orders. The fresh pinkish-tan sausages were large, a full inch or more in diameter and five or six inches long, and usually sold out the same day they were made.

A well-dressed man in a black overcoat entered the shop and ordered some sirloin steaks. While Butch was slicing the meat, the two began to talk. The man's name was Douglas Preston, a local attorney. He was a young man, perhaps thirty. He was losing some of his hair. There was an intense look in his eye, and Butch thought he moved with unusual confidence and strength for a man who worked in an office.

Preston was feeling bad because one of his clients, a Finnish miner, had just been sentenced to five years in prison for killing a man in a drunken brawl in the Helsinki Saloon. The man's Finnish friends were angry over the conviction, and wanted Preston to give back the money they had collected and given to the lawyer for their friend's defense. Preston refused. He told Butch he was going to leave town for a few days to let the Finns cool off. He said he would rather tangle with Pedro than with an angry Finn.

"Who's Pedro?" Butch asked.

"A brown and white dog at the edge of town. Very mean. Have to walk past him on my way to and from work every day."

"He's on a chain and lives in a lean-to dog house?" Butch asked.

"That's Pedro, belongs to an old man who doesn't want to be bothered by anybody, and because of Pedro, he isn't."

"When the dog lunged at me the other day, I promised him we would be friends before I left town."

"You must plan on staying a long time," Preston said. "Pedro doesn't have any friends. Men have tried to tame him and have scars to prove it didn't work."

"That only makes me more determined," Butch grinned. He wrapped one of the fresh sausages in a piece of paper and handed it to Preston.

"I didn't order sausage," the attorney said.

"It's for Pedro. Slip it to him on your way home. I'll give him another tomorrow. Any dog can be tamed with the right kind of food, and Gottsche sausages, or vurst as he calls them, are the best food in this town."

Preston grinned and slipped the sausage in a pocket under his overcoat. "I gif de vurst to der doc," he said, imitating Gottsche's German accent. After paying for his sirloin, Preston left, feeling better having chatted with the cheerful young man behind the meat counter.

186

Chapter 16

Fifteen minutes later, while Butch was slicing some back straps into steak for a restaurant, a lot of noise began coming from the saloon next door--breaking glass, crashing furniture, shouting and swearing. Another drunken brawl had begun in the Helsinki Saloon. Without thinking to put down his butcher knife, Butch ducked out a side door to get a better look at what was happening.

As he stepped through the front door of the Helsinki Saloon, he saw there was no brawl after all, just two men fighting. One of them was a huge Finnish coal miner. The other was Douglas Preston, the attorney Butch had just sold the steaks to. Somehow the Finns had lured the lawyer into their saloon and one of them had started a fight with him.

What surprised Butch most, was that the young attorney, in his white shirt and fancy black overcoat, was winning the fight. His fists were much quicker than those of his half-drunk opponent.

It wasn't long before the Finn was semi-conscious on the floor. Preston was the winner, but his victory was temporary, at best. About fifteen friends of the man on the floor had formed a circle around the fighting men. Half of them had bottles in their hands. Two held knives. Butch hadn't been in town very long, still he had no trouble reading these men's faces. They intended to kill Preston.

Butch regretted he was not wearing his gun. The circle began to close on Preston. The attorney knew the danger he was in, and as he looked into his enemies' faces he seemed determined not to go down without a fight. The problem was they were all going to converge on him at once.

The only friendly face the attorney could see was that belonging to the young man from the butcher shop who had a butcher knife in his hand.

Butch thought of running for the marshall, but guessed Preston would be dead by the time the marshall arrived.

"I'm not through with you," Preston shouted at the man on the floor, the one he had just whipped. The circle of men paused in their forward movement. They had thought the

187

fight between Preston and the man on the floor was finished. Maybe it wasn't.

"When I lick a man I like to make it final and decisive," Preston said. It occurred to Butch the lawyer might be up to some kind of trick, or at least be stalling for time.

"You're the vurst excuse for a man I have ever seen," Preston yelled at the man on the floor. As Preston said "vurst" instead of "worst" he glanced at Butch, then quickly looked away. Butch realized the cornered attorney was trying to tell him something. But what?

"There is one thing vurst than being whipped by Preston in a fight," the lawyer continued, using vurst a second time, again glancing over at Butch.

Butch didn't know what to do. The lawyer was trying to tell him something that had something to do with sausages or vurst. Did the lawyer want Butch to run back to the butcher shop and grab an armload of sausages to hand out to the angry Finns. Butch knew that wouldn't quench their thirst for Preston's blood, and Preston ought to know that too.

"When I whip a man I pee on him, the vurst insult of all," Preston yelled, reaching inside his overcoat. It looked like he was unbuttoning his trousers so he could do what he just said he was going to do.

The circle of men stared in silence. Some shook their heads in disbelief, thinking only an unprincipled lawyer like Preston could stoop so low as to urinate on a man he had whipped in a mostly fair fight. As far as they were concerned, Preston was signing his own death warrant with urine--but they were content to wait and see if he would really do such a thing.

Butch was amazed too. If the smooth-talking Preston had ever had a chance to talk his way out of this tight spot, it was gone now. Was Preston crazy? Why did he keep saying "vurst?"

It wasn't until Preston pushed the pink sausage through the front of his overcoat that Butch realized what the attorney had been trying to tell him. At least he thought he knew.

Chapter 16

Butch could hardly keep from laughing at the brilliant and devious mind of his newest friend.

"Nobody pisses on my Finnish friends and gets away with it!" Butch shouted, suddenly leaping forward, his fist gripping the razor-sharp butcher knife.

Preston held perfectly still as Butch raised the knife high in the air and slashed down at the exposed sausage, slicing it in two, the front end falling to the floor. Everything happened so fast in the dim light of the saloon that only Preston and Cassidy knew that a sausage had been cut in half, and not Preston's ability to procreate the human species.

The circle of men was stunned at the bold act of a stranger. They approved wholeheartedly, making no effort to stop Preston, who by now was bent over, holding himself, screaming in pain as he staggered from the saloon.

After Preston had made his exit, Butch was concerned the men would recognize the half-sausage on the floor for what it really was, and decide to kill the butcher's helper. To prevent this from happening Butch scooped up the sausage and popped it in his mouth.

"Who's going to buy me a drink to help wash this slippery thing down?" he asked, his cheeks bulging, his mouth full of squashed, cold uncooked sausage.

Suddenly all the men in the room were yelling, shouting and cheering for the young hero who had magnificently defended their national honor. Every one of them wanted to buy Butch a drink. The butcher's helper was pleased to have so many new friends.

Later that same evening Butch stopped by Preston's home at the edge of town. The lawyer sincerely thanked him for saving his life.

"The sausage idea was smart thinking," Butch said.

"Exceeded only by your brilliance in figuring out what to do with only one clue," Preston added. "By the way, how did you keep the Finns from recognizing the sausage on the floor for what it really was?"

"Ate it," Butch said, grinning. They both began to

laugh.

"You shouldn't be working in a butcher shop," Preston said. "You would make a great trial lawyer. You should be going to law school."

"Not me," Butch said. "Something always bad happens when I get too close to the law." He changed the subject by telling the lawyer how the Finns in the bar had bought him drinks. "Made a lot of good friends today," Butch said.

"They won't be your friends if they find out what really happened tonight," Preston said.

"I'm not telling, and I hope you don't," Butch said.

"Don't worry, I won't tell anyone, unless..." Preston paused.

"Unless what?" Butch asked.

"Unless the women start giving me a wide birth." They both laughed until their sides hurt. The next day Preston left town for a few days as planned. He told Butch he didn't think it would hurt for the Finns to think he needed a few days to lick his wounds--a comment that made them laugh again.

While Preston was out of town Butch visited Pedro every day, giving the dog meat scraps from the butcher shop. While the big dog gladly ate the food that was thrown to him, he refused to let Butch touch him, and whenever Butch got within reach of the chain, Pedro tried to bite him.

After about a week, with no signs of improvement, Butch had about decided to give up on Pedro. That's when Al Hainer and Elzy Lay came to town. They had ridden up from Brown's Hole to visit Butch and have some excitement. One of Charlie Crouse's black and white stock dogs, a bitch in heat, had followed them. Her name was Tina.

As Butch led his friends on a tour of the Rock Springs saloons, Tina followed. Because of her female condition, however, half the male dogs in Rock Springs were soon trailing her, happily sniffing and wagging their tails.

As Butch and his friends came out of the second saloon, and were watching the dogs compete for Tina's favor, Butch suddenly had an idea. He tied a rope around Tina's neck, and

190

Chapter 16

led her to the butcher shop where he locked her in a pen and rubbed some of her bloody issue, the result of her female condition, on his boots and hands.

"What in the world are you doing?" Elzy asked.

"Just a hunch," Butch said. "Come to the edge of town with me. I want you to meet Pedro."

That evening Butch, Elzy and Al visited every saloon in Rock Springs. But they weren't drinking. Once inside, Butch called to get everyone's attention. Slurring his voice like he had had too much to drink, he announced that in just a little while he was going to make friends with Pedro, the dog everyone feared. He said he intended to let the dog lick his hand while he patted its head. About this time the men would start jeering him. No one believed he could do it.

"I've got hard cash that says I can do it," Butch challenged. "Put up or shut up. My friends here are accepting all wagers. Minimum bet, five dollars."

After visiting every saloon, Elzy counted up the wagers. Rock Springs saloon patrons had bet $785 dollars that Butch Cassidy couldn't pet Pedro.

After a quick stop at the butcher shop, where Butch sneaked unobserved into Tina's pen to rub more of her female perfume on his boots and hands, they marched to the edge of town to visit Pedro. The men who had bet against Butch, and about a hundred more, tagged along. Some of the men carried torches so everyone would be able to see what happened.

The men formed a half circle just outside the reach of Pedro's chain. The dog was crouched by his lean-to, the hair on his neck standing straight up, a rumbling sound deep in his chest.

Butch had some doubts. So many men, at night, with lanterns. The dog might be too frightened to act like it should. He waved the men to silence, then held up a wet finger to test the wind. After moving to a spot where he was directly upwind from the growling dog, Butch stepped within the half circle defined by the end of the dog's chain.

Pedro was just as aware of the limitations of his chain

191

as were the men. He knew Butch was within striking distance, and started to lunge forward, his upper lip curled back.

But then he stopped. The smell coming from this man was different, awakening within the beast feelings of love and passion, while suppressing the dog's normal feelings of hate and anger. He recognized this man as the one who had been bringing good things to eat. And the smell coming from this man on the evening breeze was more delicious than anything the dog had ever eaten.

Pedro didn't like all the other men being so close, but at least none of them were within the circle of the chain. There were too many of them, but they were giving him the respect he deserved.

Pedro inched forward, his lip still curled back as a warning to the men, and the hair on his neck still up. But behind the fierceness he was feasting on a smell delicious enough to charm the heart of even the most ferocious of beasts.

Stiff-legged and proud, Pedro worked his way nearly to the end of his chain until he was standing directly in front of Butch, who by now had dropped to one knee, and was speaking kind, gentle words to the dog. The men in the crowd stood still, amazed and silent.

Their amazement increased when Pedro put his nose to the ground and began licking the toe of Butch's boot. Never had the dog tasted anything so wonderful. Butch held out his hand. Pedro licked that too, at the same time letting Butch touch the top of his head with the other hand.

A moment later, as the men began to cheer, Butch withdrew quietly outside the circle. Pedro backed away, the rumble returning to his chest, the hair on his neck becoming more rigid.

While the men returned to the various saloons, Butch, Elzy and Al went to the butcher shop and divided up their winnings. Even though the whole scheme had been Butch's idea, and it was Butch's money that had been bet, he still divided equally with his two friends. Neither one had ever had

192

Chapter 16

that much money at one time in his entire life. They didn't complain.

"Let's spend it," Al said. "I'm thirsty enough to drink an ocean."

"Me too," Elzy added.

"Go ahead without me, I'll catch up," Butch said.

After Al and Elzy had gone, Butch wrapped up a big steak and tucked it under his arm. As he started to leave, he hesitated, thinking of something else. He stepped out the back door, tied a rope around Tina's neck, and took her with him to the edge of town where he treated Pedro to the night of his life.

Chapter 17

Before Al and Elzy started back to Brown's Hole they made Butch promise that when he decided to quit working at the butcher shop to go cowboying, horse racing or whatever, he would invite them to come along. He promised he would.

One evening a few weeks later, while Butch was swapping stories with some of his new friends around a table in the Fremont Saloon, he saw something that made him angry. It was payday at the biggest mine, and the saloons were crowded with miners eager to part with their money.

Butch noticed a miner drinking all by himself at one end of the bar. He was an old man, and so drunk he could hardly stay on his stool. The thing that caught Butch's attention was the man kept spilling his money, which consisted of a handful of gold coins, either on the bar or on the floor. Each time he spilled them, he would take a minute or two to pick them up. Instead of putting the coins in his pocket, he would pile them on the edge of the bar, and in a minute or two, spill them again.

The third time the old man knocked his coins to the floor, one of the bartenders walked around the end of the bar to help pick up the money. Butch watched closely, just to make sure they found all of it. The bartender stepped on one of the coins, but when he moved his foot, the coin was gone. Later, Butch saw the bartender reach down, remove something from the bottom of his foot, and slip it in his pocket.

Butch got up from the table, walked over to the bar, sat down by the old man, and waved for the bartender to come over.

"Give the old man his money back," Butch said, when the man was standing in front of him.

"Don't know what you are talking about," the bartender said, acting surprised.

"Do it now, before I jump over this bar, turn you upside down and shake them coins from your pockets," Butch growled. "You'll be mighty embarrassed when everyone sees the gum or pitch on the bottom of your boot, and how you used it to steal the old man's money."

The two men stared into each other's eyes. The bartender was trying to decide whether or not the cowboy was bluffing. Butch was waiting for the money to come forth. If it didn't he fully intended to leap over the counter and shake the man down.

After a long minute, the bartender reached reluctantly into his pocket and handed five or six $20 gold pieces to the old man.

"What's this for?" the drunk asked, having missed the confrontation between Butch and the bartender.

"It's yours," the bartender said. "Fell behind the bar."

"Thanks," the drunk said, warmly, his words slurred. "Can I buy you a drink?"

"Hell no," the bartender said, moving to the other end of the room. Butch remained by the old drunk until he finished drinking, shoved his money deep in his pockets, and staggered out the door. Thinking no more about the matter, and seeing his friends were no longer at the table, Butch sauntered out the door and back to his room at the butcher shop.

The next afternoon, while Butch was grinding pork

scraps for sausage, the Rock Springs Sheriff walked through the door and arrested Butch.

When Butch asked for an explanation, the sheriff said a number of witnesses had seen Butch follow an old drunk out of the Fremont Saloon the night before. Later, the old man's money had been stolen. When Butch protested, the sheriff told him to save it for the judge. In a mining town full of saloons it wasn't uncommon for thieves and drifters to take money from men too drunk to defend themselves, especially at night. In recent weeks there had been an increase in this kind of criminal activity in Rock Springs. Finally, the sheriff figured he had caught his man.

Butch was furious, but nothing he could say seemed to make any difference as they marched to jail.

The next day Douglas Preston stopped in to see Butch.

"I hope you can get me out of here," Butch said.

"Won't be easy," Preston responded. "Bill Ashworth is their main witness against you. He saw you side up to the old man when he spilled his money on the floor, then follow him out the door."

"Who's Bill Ashworth?"

"The bartender who was selling drinks to the old man."

"He's the one that ought to be arrested," Butch stormed. "Using gum on his shoe, he was secretly picking up the old man's coins and slipping them in his pocket."

"They figure you've been rolling a lot of drunks."

"Do they have any evidence?"

"Only circumstantial stuff," Preston answered. "They wonder why a young, strong fellow like you works in the butcher shop when you could be making twice as much in the mines. They figure you work in town so you can be close to the saloons to work over the drunks."

"Do you think I'm doing that?" Butch asked, looking directly into Preston's eyes.

"I consider you a good friend," Preston said. "And I mean that, but I have a number of friends who are not above

196

breaking the law, and I wouldn't be surprised if you are one of them. I don't know if you did it or not. I do know Gottsche doesn't pay you very much, yet you always have plenty of money to spend, including the hundreds of dollars you bet on getting that dog to let you pet him. Where do you get all your money if you are not rolling drunks?''

Butch was hurt. He had saved Preston's life. He thought Preston was a good friend, but now it was obvious Preston didn't know him very well at all.

''I want you to go to my room, above the butcher shop,'' Butch said. ''And look in a wooden box under the bed.''

''What for?'' Preston asked.

''Never mind,'' Butch said. ''Just take a good look at what you find under the chaps, then come back here and we'll talk.''

Preston asked again what he was supposed to find in the box, but Butch would not talk about it. The lawyer left the jail and walked over to the butcher shop. Mr. Gottsche let him into Butch's room, but not before giving the lawyer a piece of his mind.

''Dat boy ist honest az die day ist long,'' he said. ''He handles mein money effry day for ein month. Nefer ein penny missing. Die only ting he takes ist ein sausage sometimes for dat big doc.''

Preston waited until Gottsche was gone before he pulled the wooden box from under the bed. What he saw when he removed the chaps almost took his breath away. The bottom of the box was covered with neatly stacked piles of greenbacks and $20 gold pieces. Sitting down on the bed, he did some quick counting, stopping when he reached the $10,000 mark. There was still quite a lot more he hadn't counted. Carefully, he covered the money with the chaps and slid the box back under the bed where he had found it. He returned to the jail.

''Did you figure out how many drunks I would have to roll to fill my box?'' Butch asked.

"You didn't get that much money rolling drunks," Preston said.

"You can bet your life on that."

"What are you, a bank robber?" Preston asked.

"Let's just say, I don't need to beat up defenseless old men to get my spending money," Butch said.

"I would agree with that, now that I've seen what's under your bed."

"Do you still think I'm guilty?"

"I never said you were in the first place," Preston said. "I just said I didn't know if you were guilty, or not. Why did you let me see all that money?"

"I trust you. If you are going to get me out of here, you need to know I don't need to beat up drunks for spending money. What do you think now?"

"I think you are innocent of the charges against you, but you may be guilty of something far more serious than stealing money from a drunk old man."

"That depends on where your values are," Butch said. "I've never done anything worse than beating up an old man for his money. Can you get me out of here?"

"Tell me as one friend to another. Did you take the old man's money?"

"No. I did not."

"Good. I believe you."

"What do we do now?"

"I'll talk to the judge and try to get you out of here before the trail."

"And if we go to trial?"

"All the evidence against you is circumstantial. You have a good character witness in Herr Gottsche. That fat old German is the biggest tight wad in this town, and if he trusts you with his money, that says a lot for you. We'll win. You'll be free again."

Preston wasn't able to get Butch off without a trail, but when Butch finally appeared before Judge Jesse Knight, as Preston had predicted, the prosecution had no hard evidence to prove Butch had stolen the money from the old man.

"You can't send a man to jail because he happened to leave a saloon behind a man who was later robbed," Preston said in his concluding remarks, after Gottsche had testified that he would trust Butch Cassidy with his money, his daughter, and his life. In light of the lack of evidence, the judge had no choice but to rule in favor of Preston's argument. Butch was free to go.

"How are we supposed to maintain law and order in this town?" asked the city attorney who had worked very hard to get Butch convicted. He was a short, thin man with a face like a weasel, a long pointing nose, and no chin. "We finally catch a crook and the courts just let him go."

The sheriff, jailer and bartender expressed similar comments, all at once. The judge just shrugged his shoulders, reminding them his decision was final, unless more evidence could be presented.

Butch listened to all this, feeling more and more angry as the minutes passed. He remembered his first run-in with the law in Milford, when he was accused of stealing the coveralls. He remembered being thrown in the Montrose jail when he wouldn't let the rancher, Butler, steal the horse Butch had raised from a colt. He guessed he would probably be going to jail right now if Preston hadn't presented such a strong defense. It bothered him that so many of these people still thought he was guilty of stealing from an old man, even after the judge had ruled otherwise. Butch felt like fighting someone. Instead, he asked the judge if he could say something, before the court was dismissed. The judge agreed.

"I ain't going to sit here and listen to no two-bit cowboy," the bartender said, getting up to leave.

"The thief everyone is looking for is headed for the door," Butch said, pointing to the bartender. "By sticking gum on the bottom of his shoe, he was picking up the old man's money as he walked by, then sticking it in his own pocket. I stopped him."

"That's a lie," the bartender snarled, continuing to

walk towards the door.

"I'm surprised the owner of the Fremont hasn't caught you at your dirty tricks and sent you packing," Butch said.

"I am the owner," the bartender said.

Butch was caught by surprise, learning the thieving bartender actually owned the Fremont Saloon where Butch and his friends had spent so much money. This piece of news made Butch even more angry.

"The days of prosperity for your business are over," Butch said, an intensity in his voice few recognized.

"I'll have no threats in my courtroom," the judge said. "What is it you wanted to say."

"Two things," Butch said. "First, if the old man I am accused of robbing was destitute and hungry, and I had one $20 gold piece to my name, I would give it to him. That's the kind of man I am, and I am proud of it."

The sheriff and city attorney both yawned at the same time, on purpose, to show their contempt for Butch's comment. Butch continued.

"Second, in response to the attorney's comment that men like me need to be thrown in jail to maintain peace and order in this town, I'd just like to say they have arrested one more innocent man than they should have. The day is coming when they will beg for the peace and order they enjoyed before they arrested Butch Cassidy."

"Pretty strong words for a butcher's helper," the judge said. Butch ignored the comment. He turned and marched out of the courtroom and back to the butcher shop where he began packing his things. Gottsche and Preston tried to talk him out of leaving, but Butch would not listen. He had been burned by the law once too often. He was going to raise more than a little hell, and Rock Springs was going to be the target.

He paid Preston well for getting him out of jail, and thanked Gottsche for letting him work in the butcher shop.

After getting on his horse, Butch headed south in the direction of Brown's Hole. He had promised Al and Elzy he would include them in his next great adventure, and he fully

Chapter 17

intended to keep that promise.

A warm breeze was blowing from the south. The snow was melting. The ground was thawing. Spring was just around the corner. It was time to get outside where a man belonged. Butch was glad to be leaving Rock Springs.

At the edge of town he stopped to throw a last sausage to Pedro. As the big dog gulped it down, Butch got off his horse and stepped inside the circle of the dog's chain. He dropped to one knee, snapped his fingers, and called to the dog. Butch thought he noticed a little bit of a wiggle in Pedro's tail as the dog walked cautiously towards the man. Pedro was not growling, his lips were not curled back over his teeth, and the hair on his neck was not standing up.

Butch didn't move. The dog stepped within petting range. When Butch's hand reached out, the dog lowered his head and let the hand touch him. Butch rubbed the ears.

"I'll never forget my three Rock Springs friends," Butch said. "Herr Gottsche, Douglas Preston, and Pedro. Wish you could come with me, boy."

Butch looked over at the house. A curtain fell back into place over the inside of a window. Butch thought about going up to the house and asking if the dog was for sale, but decided against it.

He got back on his horse and headed south, the pack mule carrying nearly $15,000, following close behind.

201

Chapter 18

On the way to Brown's Hole, Butch made a detour into a rocky canyon. About 50 feet up a south facing hill he hid his money in a dry spot under an overhanging ledge. He covered his cache with rocks. Not only was he tired of carrying the money everywhere he went, but too many people knew about it, and it was the evidence that he robbed the Telluride bank. He thought it would be safe under the ledge until he needed it.

Elzy and Al were excited when Butch showed up. Spending the winter in Brown's Hole had been like going to jail for them. They were ready and eager for the excitement and adventure Butch promised them.

Butch told them how he had been arrested for taking money from an old man. He told them how Bill Ashworth, the owner of the Fremont Saloon, had put gum on the bottom of his shoe to steal the drunk's coins.

Butch told Elzy and Al about his courtroom promise, that the Fremont Saloon would fall on hard times. Al and Elzy agreed to help Butch get his revenge. Using Butch's mule to carry their belongings, the three headed north.

Chapter 18

"We've got to call ourselves something," Elzy said, after they had been on the trail a few hours. "How about the Butch Cassidy Gang?"

"No," Butch said. "I don't want a gang named after me. Maybe a mountain or river or something like that, but not a gang."

"There's the Tom McCarty Gang, the Jesse James Gang, the Tom O'Day Gang," Elzy explained. "That's the way it's done. I can't see calling us the Elzy Lay Gang or the Al Hainer Gang. Butch Cassidy Gang sounds much better."

" Tom, Matt and I called ourselves the Invincible Three at one time," Butch said. "How does that sound?"

"Too stuffy," Elzy said. "Besides, if we let someone else in we would have to change the name to the Invincible Four. Then two of us decided to quit, we'd have to change it to the Invincible Two. I don't like it."

"Maybe the name should be tied in with what we do," Al said, finally entering the conversation.

"How about The Rascalian Rustlers?" Elzy said.

"We're heading to Rock Springs to bust up the Fremont Saloon," Butch said. "That has nothing to do with rustling. We can't have that in our name."

"What are we going to do besides bust up saloons?" Al asked.

"We'll do honest cowboy work when there's a lot of heading and heeling that needs doing," Butch said. "We'll bust up saloons, get in fist fights with city slickers, race horses, rustle a few horses when we need money, maybe even rob a bank or two. We'll do a bunch of wild stuff."

"How about The Wild Bunch?" Elzy asked.

"I like it," Butch said.

"Me too," Al agreed.

"Then we're The Wild Bunch," Butch said, "and Rock Springs is the first place where we'll be famous." The three cheered, throwing their hats into the air.

Two days later as they approached Rock Springs, they still weren't sure what kind of trouble they were going to take to the Fremont Saloon. They did know they wanted to sneak into town unobserved, so whatever they decided to do, it would be a surprise.

As they approached Rock Springs from the east, they came upon a large herd of cattle heading in the same direction, right through the middle of the town. Cowboys were taking the cattle from winter range on the Sweetwater to summer range near Fort Bridger. When Butch and his friends offered to help drive the cattle through town, the cowboys seemed grateful.

It was mid afternoon when the herd reached the Fremont Saloon. Butch had his silk Manilla rope over the horns of a two-year-old bull that had been trying to leave the herd by turning off into some of the side streets. The bull was learning to behave himself because Butch held the other end of the rope in his hand. Whenever the bull tried to leave the herd, Butch dallied his end of the rope around his horn and jerked the stubborn animal to an abrupt halt. After two or three such occurrences, the bull was gradually learning to respect the rope, but was still a long way from learning to lead.

Elzy and Al were busy with the cattle too, and there had been no recent discussion on what they were going to do at the Fremont Saloon. Al and Elzy assumed that subject wouldn't come up again until the cattle were safely through town.

It was the first spring day. There was plenty of bright sunshine and no wind. Many of the doors and windows were open, especially those facing the south and west. The high, double swinging front doors to the Fremont Saloon were open too.

As Butch rode by, he tried to look through the doors, wondering if Ashworth was in there. This was difficult in the bright sunshine. Feeling the tug of the bull on the rope, Butch suddenly had an idea.

He called to Al and Elzy. When he had their attention, he dallied the rope around his saddle horn, and turned his horse directly towards the high, double swinging front doors of the Fremont Saloon.

Butch spurred his horse up the steps, ducking low as he went inside. The young bull, weary of fighting the rope, followed stubbornly behind. With the bull leading the way, Al and Elzy had little trouble pushing another dozen to fifteen head through the doors behind the bull.

To Butch's surprise, the saloon was empty. He pulled the reluctant bull past the potbellied stove in the middle of the room into the narrow space behind the bar. Riding around to the other side of the bar, Butch leaned over and removed his rope. As he did so the bull decided he didn't like the close quarters behind the bar and tried to turn around and go back the way he had come. As he began to make his turn Bill Ashworth charged in through a back door, suddenly stopping, half paralyzed, not sure what to do about a saloon full of cattle.

As the clumsy bull persisted in turning around in a space too narrow, the shelves against the wall began to slpinter and fall, causing hundreds of bottles and glasses to tumble, some falling on the bull. The now frightened animal panicked as he finished turning around, and charged full speed out of the narrow space between the bar and the wall, his big feet slipping and sliding on spilled whiskey, olives, pickled eggs and broken glass.

Once out of the narrow space, he put his head down and charged. Had he looked where he was going, he might have gone right out the front door. As it was, he plowed head on into the potbellied stove, knocking it over, spilling ashes and soot on the floor, filling the air with coal dust. While the bull was doing this, the rest of the excited cattle were milling about destroying chairs, tables and anything else that got underfoot. The excitement of being in a strange place had caused a dramatic increase in body functions. The polished plank floor was quickly becoming too slippery to maintain stable footing.

While the cattle were doing their best to destroy the

saloon, Butch kept a close eye on Ashworth.

"Just delivering the meat you ordered," Butch said, calmly.

Ignoring the comment, Ashworth stepped forward, waving his arms in a feeble attempt to drive the cattle from his saloon.

"Better watch where you step," Butch cautioned, "or you'll have something besides gum on the bottom of your boots."

Ashworth, suddenly showing some purpose and determination, started towards the bar. Butch guessed he was going for a gun hidden somewhere behind the bar. Butch drew his .44 and pointed it at Ashworth, who stopped and raised his hands.

"You wouldn't shoot me," the bartender whined.

Butch cocked back the hammer and pulled the trigger. The gun exploded, sending the cattle stampeding back the way they had come, out the front door.

"I missed," Butch said, as the bullet struck a crystal chandelier hanging from the ceiling, directly above the spot where the potbellied stove had been standing. Butch cocked his pistol a second time and fired.

"Oops, missed again," he said as the bullet shattered the large front window just south of the double doors. Butch fired a third shot, missing Ashworth again, but striking a grandfather clock on the north wall.

The saloon was beginning to fill with smoke. While it was a warm afternoon, and the potbellied stove had no fresh fuel in it, there were still coals from the morning fire, which had been spilled on the floor when the bull had tipped over the stove.

"Fire!" Butch yelled, spurring his horse back through the double doors and out into the bright sunshine. Somewhere down the street a fire bell started ringing. As Butch galloped down the street he was joined by Al, Elzy and the black pack mule. Butch would have liked to stop and chat with Preston and Gottsche, perhaps pick up some fresh sausages, but there was no time for visiting now. He didn't want to spend any more time in the Rock Springs jail.

The Wild Bunch headed east, riding hard through the remainder of the afternoon and evening, making a dark camp that night in the event a posse was on their trail. The next morning they continued east. There was no sign of a posse. Butch guessed Ashworth wasn't a well liked citizen in Rock Springs, and that it would be difficult to find volunteers to chase the men who had busted up his saloon. Apparently, Butch's hunch was right. No posse ever came.

A few days later, as they were discussing what to do next, Al suggested they try to hire on at the Two-bar Ranch, one of the largest cattle outfits in Wyoming, with over a hundred thousand head of cattle and almost three and a half million deeded acres. The spring roundup would soon be underway and Al was confident they could land jobs.

"If we can't get on there," Elzy said, "I once met Bob Divine, foreman of the C Y outfit. Almost as big as the Two-bar. Bob will put us on. And there's always the K C outfit up by Buffalo."

A few days later as the three approached the Two-bar headquarters it appeared there was some kind of celebration going on. Everywhere they looked, saddle horses and teams hitched to wagons were tied to fences and posts. People were gathered around a large arena, cheering and shouting. A rodeo was in progress.

They found out that prior to the spring roundup, the Two-bar was sponsoring a rodeo for the hundred or so cowboys in the area to show off their cowboy skills. The main events were team roping, saddle bronc riding, calf roping and bulldogging.

Festivities were just beginning, so The Wild Bunch headed around behind the chutes to enter some of the events. By the time the afternoon was over Butch had teamed up with a young cowboy by the name of Walt Punteney to win the team roping. Walt caught the heads and Butch the heels. Al got second in the saddle bronc riding, and Elzy third in the bulldogging.

Just when they thought the rodeo should come to an end, a cowboy carrying an empty coffee can, walked to the middle of the arena and placed the can, upside down, over the top of a snubbing post that was planted there.

Walt told Butch to hurry and get his gun if he wanted to enter the shooting contest. Butch said he had never heard of shooting contests at rodeos before.

"The Two-bar don't hire a cowboy who can't use a gun," Walt explained.

"Do they shoot the cows they can't catch?" Butch asked.

"Rustlers, nesters, squatters, sodbusters, sheep men. Lots of enemies. Lots of fighting. Two-bar cowboys are expected to use their guns."

One at a time, cowboys armed with either rifles or pistols, galloped past the can, shooting at it as they went by. Some hit it, some didn't.

After checking his .44 to make sure there were six cartridges in the cylinder, Butch got in line with the cowboys waiting to demonstrate their shooting skills.

When it was Butch's turn, not feeling very challenged by a single shot at a big coffee can, he decided to add a new twist to the contest. Instead of riding in a straight line past the post as the other riders had done, he reined his horse into a circle around the post, firing his .44 six times, each bullet striking the can. As he galloped out of the arena the spectators cheered. No one had ever seen that kind of shooting before.

When all the cowboys had had a turn, Butch was asked to do it again. This time he put two bullets through the can as he galloped towards it, and hit it four more times as he galloped in a circle around the post. He then drew a second pistol and placed two more bullets in the can as he galloped away.

When the shooting was over, three Chinamen started bringing food from the cook shack--large tubs of roasted beef, buckets of barbecue sauce, baked potatoes, fresh bread with

208

tin plates piled high with butter, cans of chokecherry and serviceberry preserves and a huge tub of ice cream. The cowboys ate until everything was gone.

As Butch was polishing off his third bowl of strawberry ice cream, the first he had had since leaving Telluride, he noticed a handsome, middle-aged, well-dressed cowboy walking towards him. The man introduced himself as Bob Divine, foreman of the C Y outfit. The two men shook hands.

"Interested in hiring on with the Wyoming Cattlemen's Association?" Divine asked. His voice was deep, confident and strong.

"My friends and I rode in here thinking to hire on with the Two-bar or C Y outfits. We're cowboys," Butch responded, cautiously.

"You can make twice as much with the association," Divine said.

"Doing what?" Butch asked.

"Law enforcement. Driving rustlers and undesirables out of the country. Pays $5 a day, plus incentives."

"Seems like that ought to be the job of marshals, sheriffs and their deputies," Butch said.

"Should be," Divine agreed, "but things has gotten out of hand around here, forcing the cattlemen to do their own enforcing. We're looking for hands like you who can use a gun."

"I won the team roping. I like cowboy work."

Divine invited Butch to a meeting that same evening. He said some of the cowboys working for the association would be there for Butch to meet. Divine added that if Butch hired on with the association, Elzy and Al would be sure to get steady work at the C Y. Butch agreed to come to the meeting.

Butch felt nervous and cautious as he entered the big ranch house that evening. A dozen men were seated on fancy chairs in the front parlor. Butch took a seat next to a tall cowboy who introduced himself as Ben Killpatrick, from Texas. He said most of the cowboys in the room were Texans too. He complimented Butch on his shooting and roping performance earlier in the day.

When it was time for the meeting to begin, Bob Divine walked to the front of the room and turned to face the men. The first thing he did was introduce Butch Cassidy as the newest member of the group. Butch didn't think he had accepted the job, but didn't say anything.

All of a sudden, Divine got serious. He looked as if he were about to deliver what he considered to be a very important speech.

"Between here and Montana there's a dozen or so small plots of ground with little fences around them," he began, his voice soft, but growing stronger as he continued.

"Inside the fences are headstones, crosses or nothing at all to mark the graves of those buried there. Who are these people? Brave men, women and children who came to this magnificent land when it was wild and untamed. They fought the Cheyenne, the Sioux, the Arapaho. They survived bitter winter storms and winds that seemed to last forever. They crossed flooding rivers and vast expanses of mud. And when the heat and draught of long summers threatened to take away their sanity, they stayed, and fought, and refused to be driven back to the comforts and security of civilization.

"No sooner had these brave men and women gained a foothold in this wild land," he continued, the words coming faster now, "they went to work and raised a hundred million in capital to stock it with a million head of cattle. The cattle were bought in Texas, branded with a T L on the left side, then driven a thousand miles through some of the most desolate wasteland our God in heaven ever created. The risks were frightening, the hardships almost unbearable. Many of those original Texas seed cattle are still roaming these beautiful valleys and mountains.

"And when it looked like prosperity and good times were finally to be enjoyed by these brave men and women, Mother Nature double crossed them with the winter of 1886 and 1887, the worst winter in recorded history. First came the heavy snow, up to a horse's belly. Then came the warm south

Chapter 18

winds, turning the snow to wet slush, then the sub-zero temperatures, turning the slush to a blanket of solid ice, five hundred miles wide and five hundred miles long. Unable to paw through rock-hard ice the cattle died. The horses died. The elk died. Some of the brave men and women died too, but those who survived that bitter winter, started to rebuild.

"Today there are different enemies trying to destroy what these brave men and women have fought so valiantly to build. You men were hired to fight these enemies.

"There are those who steal our cattle in broad daylight, some hiding behind the skirts of the law, claiming the cattle they take are not branded. We are here tonight to stop the rustlers." Divine paused while most of the men cheered. Butch remained silent, thinking Mike Cassidy and Cap Brown wouldn't like this kind of talk.

"There are those who want to blanket this magnificent land with prairie maggots," Divine continued, his voice getting louder and more emotional as he approached the climax of his speech. "We are here tonight to stop the sheep men." The men cheered again.

"There are those who want to dig up our grass, steal our water and fence out our cattle. We are here tonight to stop the sodbusters, squatters and land grabbers." The men stood up, giving Divine a standing ovation. Butch stood with them, not because he wanted to pay homage to Divine, but because he didn't want to call attention to himself. He wished he hadn't come to the meeting. Still, he admired this foreman, Divine, for his eloquence and vision in wanting to preserve the vast empires of the cattle barons.

The land grabbers Divine talked about were homesteaders like Butch's parents and neighbors. The only thing Butch could agree on was getting rid of the sheep. Butch was a cattleman too. He hated the sight of a flock of hungry sheep covering a hillside like a wet, heavy, stinking blanket, destroying everything in its path.

When the meeting was over Divine walked up to Butch. "Ready to ride with us?" the foreman asked.

"My folks are homesteaders, over in Utah Territory," Butch said. "I was taught to ride, rope, shoot and swim big rivers by men who didn't mind doing a little mavericking. I have a hard time helping you go after people like these," Butch said.

"The Bible says if you are not for us you are against us," Divine said. "Are you saying you are against us?"

"I'd hate to see an ocean of stinking sheep ruin the land," Butch explained. "Could I work in that part of your operation?"

"You got yourself a job," Divine boomed. "Report for orders in the morning."

"What's the pay?" Butch asked.

"Five dollars a day," Divine explained, "plus a dollar bonus for every unbranded critter you bring in, and twobits for every pair of maggot ears. Of course the bonus money has to be split with the men you ride with."

"Of course, see you in the morning. Don't forget you promised jobs for my two partners."

"A promise is a promise," Divine said as he left the room. Butch hurried back to the camp he had set up with Elzy and Al, to tell them about their new jobs, and his own, thinking he could now call himself a prairie maggot exterminator.

At first Butch actually thought he was going to like clearing the land of sheep, until three days later when he and some of Divine's men found their first flock of sheep. As they watched the flock from a nearby ridge, they guessed there were somewhere between 1,500 and 2,000 sheep, and there was only one sheepherder and his dog tending the flock. The dog was watching the herder cook something over a fire. His horse and mule were tied to some nearby brush. The sheep were grazing peacefully on the hillside above them.

Butch followed the other four association deputies as they rode nonchalantly towards the sheepherder. The dog was the first to see the approaching riders. It began to bark at the riders who were already within 50 feet of the camp. One of the deputies drew his Winchester from his scabbard and shot the dog before any words had been exchanged between the deputies and the herder.

For all Butch knew, sheep dogs were the smartest, most loyal and hardest working animals on the face of the earth. Butch felt ashamed, being part of a group of men who would shoot a dog like that, with no good reason. He pulled away from the other men, watching the silent sheepherder run over to his dog, dropping to his knees and scooping the lifeless body into his arms. Butch thought the poor man ought to be dealing with the approaching deputies, not mourning a lost dog. Either the man wasn't very smart, or he had loved his dog too much. Butch felt sick, starting to turn his horse away. Two more shots were fired. He looked back in time to see the herder's horse and mule fall to the ground, mortally wounded. Still no words had been exchanged between the herder, who was still holding his dog, and the deputies.

While two of the deputies, guns drawn, herded the man away from his sheep, the other deputies galloped around the sheep until they had herded them into a tight, milling, mass of bleating wooly bodies. Some of the deputies began firing their guns into the sheep, while others dismounted and begun swinging clubs and axes as they waded into the sea of bleating, frightened animals. One of the men began to cut the ears from the dead animals and place them in a bag to be taken back to the ranch so the men could collect their bounty, two bits for each set of ears.

Butch had seen enough. For the second time he turned his horse away from the slaughter and began to ride. He didn't know where he was going, only that he wanted nothing more to do with this place.

He hadn't gone far when he heard hoofbeats approaching from behind. He wondered if one of the deputies might be coming to shoot him for desertion. Butch looked back. It was the tall Texan, Ben Killpatrick, the one who had sat next to him at the meeting. Butch pulled in his horse, and waited for Killpatrick to catch up.

"No stomach for this sort of thing?" the Texan asked, pulling his horse to a halt beside Butch, who continued to look straight ahead, not answering the question.

"I felt sick the first time too," the Texan said. "It gets easier."

"It won't for me," Butch said.

"Don't do anything foolish," Killpatrick said. "Don't want to get on the association's blacklist."

"Don't worry," Butch said. "I won't do anything more foolish than shoot a man's dog for no good reason and wade into his sheep with an axe." He urged his horse forward. Killpatrick remained where he was.

"Will we see you back at the ranch tonight?" Killpatrick asked. Butch did not answer.

A few hours later as Butch came to the top of a ridge he could hardly believe what he saw. Another flock of sheep, larger than the last. This time there were two herders instead of one. They had three dogs. Butch rode into their camp.

"You're not one of them deputies from the Wyoming Cattlemen's Association?" one of the herders asked when Butch pulled his horse to a halt. Both men had similar stocky features, though one was much older than the other. Butch guessed them to be father and son.

"That I am," Butch said, his voice friendly. "My job is to get rid of sheep."

"What if we don't want to go?" the older man asked. "This is public land. We have as much right to it as the cattlemen. We have rights too. We could take you to court."

"Don't think you'll have much luck suing the association after your sheep are gone," Butch said.

"They wouldn't dare steal our sheep."

"I didn't say they would steal your sheep. They don't want your sheep. They just want them gone."

"They can't make us leave," the man said.

Butch began to describe what he had seen earlier in the day. "First they shot the dog, then the horse and mule. When I left they were slaughtering the sheep, with bullets and axes.

They were cutting off the ears so they could collect the twobit bounty on each pair. They'll do the same thing here. You might get away with your lives, but don't count on it."

"Are you threatening us?" the man asked. He looked towards a rock where a Winchester was leaning.

"No," Butch said. "I'm just warning you, hoping I won't witness another bloody slaughter like the one I saw this morning."

"It ain't right," the boy said, his voice high, almost out of control like he was about to cry.

"I know," Butch said.

"I know a place in Nebraska where I could take my sheep," the older man said, beginning to bend.

"You're not very far from the railhead at Rawlins," Butch said. "If you could get there before the other deputies find you, you could get your flock out of here before you lose it."

"I don't have enough money to ship my sheep to Nebraska," the man said. "Rawlins is a cattle town. I couldn't sell enough sheep there to pay for the shipping."

"How many sheep do you have?" Butch asked.

"About 2,000 adult sheep, plus the lambs."

"How much to ship them to Nebraska?"

"Probably about $250."

"I think the Wyoming Cattlemen's Association might pay the shipping costs," Butch said, rubbing his chin.

"I find that hard to believe," the man said.

"If you'll cut the ears off a thousand sheep, and give them to me in a bag, I think they will give me $250." Butch said, explaining how deputies brought in ears from sheep they had killed to collect the twobits per pair sheep bounty.

"They wouldn't give the bounty to us," the man said.

"They'll give it to me, and I'll bring it to Rawlins," Butch said.

"Don't know if I can cut the ears off my beautiful ewes," the boy said.

"Don't cut off the whole ear, just the top half," Butch

215

said. "Either that or let the deputies slaughter them with axes."

"Why are you offering to help us?" the man asked.

"I hate sheep as much as the next cowboy," Butch said. "I also hate to see anything slaughtered with an axe. Most of all, I guess I hate to see the cattle barons walking over the little people. Makes me sad. Makes me mad."

The herders sent out their dogs to round up the sheep. Dragging a gunny sack behind them the man and boy waded into the sea of sheep, the boy grabbing and holding them one at a time while the man sliced off the ears and tossed them to Butch who kept a careful count as he dropped them into the gunny sack. It took them less than two hours to collect two thousand ears from a thousand sheep.

"I'll bring the bounty to the railhead at Rawlins," Butch said as he tied the sack of ears behind his saddle.

"We'll be there in three days," the herder said. "Thank you very much for helping us."

Butch leaped into the saddle and headed for the Two-bar Ranch at a full gallop.

"Didn't expect to see you again," Divine said when Butch entered his office.

"You didn't?" Butch responded, acting surprised. "Came to collect my sheep bounty."

"That might not be possible," Divine said. "The men told me you didn't help, that you deserted them when they started to step on the maggots."

"Damn right," Butch said. "Killing sheep is one thing, but shooting the herder's dog, horse and mule is down right mean. Leaves a nasty taste in a man's mouth. I left alright."

"Then what makes you think you've got some bounty coming your way."

"Oh, I don't want any of their bounty," Butch said. "After I left the men I went out and found my own flock of sheep. Collected two thousand ears all by myself." Butch picked up the blood stained gunny sack and dropped it in the middle of Divine's desk. The foreman was both surprised and

Chapter 18

impressed. He opened the sack and looked at two thousand sheep ears.

"Count them if you like," Butch said. "But I'm sure the 2,000 count is correct. I was very careful. I cut until I had 2,000, and just left the rest to rot."

"There were more?" Divine asked.

"A lot more," Butch said, enjoying the conversation. "Try cutting off two thousand ears sometime. You won't want to do any more, no matter what the bounty."

"How did you handle the herders, all by yourself?"

Butch pulled his .44 out of the holster, looking at it as he spun the cylinder. "Some things are better not talked about," he said, carefully. "If you know what I mean."

"Then I believe the association owes you $250," Divine said, cheerfully. "Want it now?"

"Yes. Got to meet a friend in Rawlins in a couple of days."

"Will you be coming back?" Divine asked as he walked over to a safe and pulled out a money box.

Butch knew he had to be careful. He didn't want Divine changing his mind about the bounty. But neither did he want to spend another day employed by the Wyoming Cattlemen's Association.

"You haven't seen the last of Butch Cassidy," Butch said.

"I guess I haven't. This is a lot of money for a cowboy," Divine said, handing Butch $250. "There's a lot more where this came from. Keep your eye out for sheep on the way to Rawlins."

"I will," Butch said, shoving the money in his pocket, turning and heading out the door.

"Hold up," a voice called as Butch stepped into the saddle. It was Ben Killpatrick, the tall Texan. He hurried over to Butch.

"Get on your horse and ride with me a while," Butch said.

"Heard you brought in two thousand maggot ears all by

217

yourself," the Texan said as they were riding away from the ranch.

"That's right."

"After this morning I didn't think you had the stomach for killing sheep," the Texan said.

"I don't."

"I don't understand."

"You don't have to kill sheep before you cut their ears off," Butch explained.

"You're telling me there's a thousand sheep running around somewhere without ears? I'll bet they look awful funny."

"They're on their way to Rawlins to catch a train to Nebraska where they'll be safe from you deputies."

"They're safe from us deputies already," Ben said. Now Butch was the one on the guessing end of the conversation.

"Why are they safe?" Butch asked.

"Because they don't have ears! The bounty's already been collected on them." They both laughed, then Butch explained how he was taking the bounty money to Rawlins to pay for shipping the sheep to a safer place. Ben thought it very funny that the Wyoming Cattlemen's Association was paying the freight bill on a bunch of sheep.

"Do you like working for the association?" Butch asked.

"It's a job. Pay is good."

"You could make a lot more mavericking," Butch said. "Instead of making a dollar a head for bringing them in, you could put your own brand on them and make $30 or $40 a head."

"The only problem with doing that," Ben said, "is men like you and me can't get a brand in this country. Only land owners with herds of cattle can register brands. The association controls that. That's why you see so many unbranded cattle around here."

"If I bought a ranch, stocked it with cattle, and

registered a brand, would boys like you bring in unbranded strays if I offered to split with you when the critters are sold? We'd put my brand on them.''

"I'd bring you cattle. So would Nate Champion, Tom Waggoner, Tom O'Day, Sang Thompson, Dab Burch, Ranger Jones, and a bunch more. If I were you I'd do it up by Buffalo, somewhere between the K C outfit and the Big Horn Mountains. Lot of good places to hide stock there.''

"When I get my sheep shipped, I'll ride over to Rock Springs, pick up some money, then see if I can buy me a place. Let the boys know, so they can start getting some cattle together,'' Butch said.

"Got to keep it small so the association doesn't get on your trail,'' Ben said.

"Maybe we can start to break their power,'' Butch said. "If we let'm get away with what they've started, this here won't be a free country any longer.''

Ben returned to the Two-bar while Butch rode on to Rawlins where he found his sheepherders and gave them the money to ship their sheep. Then he rode to the canyon south of Rock Springs and got a couple of thousand dollars of his Telluride bank money. From there he trailed to the rugged Hole-in-the-Wall country southwest of the K C outfit near the Big Horn Mountains. He bought a place with a cabin on Blue Creek, a tributary to Beaver Creek. Behind his cabin the majestic Big Horn Mountains reached to the sky.

After hiring a couple of hands to start on the holding and handling corrals near his cabin, Butch took a week to visit all the large ranches in the area, looking for hands he knew and trusted, inviting them to a meeting at his new ranch.

On the day of the meeting about a dozen men showed up, including Elzy Lay, Al Hainer, Ben Killpatrick, Nate Champion, George Curry, Tom O'Day, and Tom Waggoner.

"There are thousands of cattle in this country that aren't branded,'' Butch began, when he had everyone together. "They're wandering around on public land, eating public grass and drinking public water. The big cattlemen hired a bunch of Texans with guns to get everyone thinking public land, public grass, public water and the unbranded cattle belong to them. Well, they're wrong. Unbranded cattle on the open range belong to the first cowboy to lay on his brand. That's the law, and it's about time the big range hogs stopped pushing everyone around. If they're too lazy to brand their own cattle they deserve to lose them.''

"Men have been killed for saying a lot less than you just said," Ben Killpatrick added. "I know. I'm one of those hired guns from Texas."

"The cattlemen have a lot of guns on their side," George Curry said.

"We have guns too," Butch said. "And the law isn't on their side any more than ours. The association will pay men like you a dollar a head to bring in unbranded strays. I'll give you half of whatever the critter brings at the railhead, less expenses, and you can use my brand while you're bringing them in. There won't be any questions about ownership. Think about it. Instead of a dollar a head you'll be getting fifteen or twenty."

"The association doesn't seem to care what's legal and fair, as long as its objectives are met," Killpatrick said.

"We may beat them at their own game," Butch said. But before he could explain, Nate Champion asked if Butch had a brand.

"Yes. Registered it last week in Buffalo. The box double E." Butch took a stick and drew his new brand in the dirt for all to see.

"Why do you have two E's in your brand when your name is Butch Cassidy?" Curry asked.

"A lot of thought has gone into this brand," Butch said, proudly.

"When this country was opened up for cattle ranching, over a million head of cattle were driven up from Texas. Some of you helped on those cattle drives. Many of those cattle are still around. You've seen the brand that was burned on most of them before they left Texas, a big T L on the left side.'' Butch drew a T L in the dirt.

"While you're burning my box double E on strays, if you happen to have a few T L critters around, it's a simple process, if you've got a running iron, to change the T L to a box double E.'' Butch drew four horizontal lines on the T L changing it to a ᴛᴇ. Some of the men began to laugh. They were impressed with Cassidy's imagination.

"The possibilities are endless,'' Butch continued. The biggest outfit in Wyoming, the Two-bar, owned by the Swan Land and Cattle Company, has a hundred thousand head of branded cattle roaming the open range.'' He drew the Two-bar brand, ‾‾, then showed the men how easily this one could be converted to the ᴛᴇ.

"I'm aware of 19 brands on large ranches that a good hand with a running iron can change to the box double E,'' Butch concluded. He drew some of these in the dirt.

⊔ ☐ ⊓⊦ ⊓ ⊥ ⊤⊤

"If the association gets tough with us, we can get tough with them,'' Butch concluded.

Most of the men seemed excited about Butch's proposal. Tom O'Day joked that, thanks to Butch, they would all become rich enough to join the Wyoming Cattlemen's Association.

The only one that didn't seem pleased was the tall Texan, Ben Killpatrick.

"What's the matter?'' Butch asked, when they were alone.

"You are underestimating the resolve of the association to stop this kind of thing. You didn't work for them very long. I have, and I know how they work. As soon as you start selling hundreds of cattle with that cute little box double E brand, someone is going to figure out what you are doing.''

"They'll have a tough time proving it in court,'' Butch said.

221

"You don't seem to understand," Ben said. "They don't have to prove it in court. As soon as they think you are burning your double E over the top of their brands they'll put you on the blacklist. Next thing you know 20 riders will show up in the middle of the night, burn your cabin and shoot your horses. You'll be lucky to get out alive. That's the way the association works. I know. I work for them."

"The big problem, Butch," he continued, "you own a ranch now. You can't hide. They can come and get you, and they will. You don't have a stomach for killing sheep. Do you have a stomach for killing association deputies? That's the only way you'll stop them. Are you willing to die, or see your friends die, defending your little mavericking operation?"

"The association isn't making good use of its resources," Butch said.

"What's that supposed to mean?" Ben asked.

"They should send you around talking to all the squatters, sheepmen, and freelance cowboys they want gone from this country. If the association'd turn your golden tongue loose for a few weeks everyone would leave the country and the association would win its little war without firing a shot, and have everything all to themselves."

"If you won't let me talk you out of rustling association cattle, the least you can do is let me point out how stupid you are in launching your operation from this place."

"What's wrong with my little ranch?" Butch asked.

"The location. It's smack dab in the jaws of the dragon. You couldn't have picked a worse place."

"You're the one who told me to come here," Butch said.

"That's right, but I didn't know you were launching the best conceived, most organized cattle rustling operation in the history of the American West. If left alone, you're getting ready to run half the cattle in Wyoming through these corrals. The association is going to pounce on you like a cat on a lamb, and you couldn't be in a better place for them to do that. To the south is Bob Divine, the foreman who does the

222

dirty work. To the east you have the KC outfit where all this association stuff got started in the first place. To the west in the Big Horn Basin you have Otto Franc, who's paying more than his share of the association's bills, including the bounties. You're surrounded by your worst enemies. They're going to get you, Butch, sooner than you might think."

"Will you help them?"

"If they knew I was here today they would get me too. They won't get any help from me."

"Why do you care what happens to me?" Butch asked.

"Knowing I work for the association, why did you trust me to invite me here today?" Ben asked.

"Ever get a new horse or mule, and realized right away you could trust it, that it wouldn't try to hurt you?" Butch asked. "That's the way I feel about you. Don't know why. I just know Ben Killpatrick isn't going to burn my cabin or shoot me in the back, even if he is on the payroll of the association. What I don't understand is why you seem to feel the same way about me."

"It's the way you handled that sheep thing, collecting the bounty and giving it to the herder to get his maggots out of the country. Never met a man before you who would do a thing like that. That's part of it."

"What's the rest?"

"My old man was a sheepherder. Killed by cattlemen down in Oklahoma. Had there been men like you around he might still be alive. But don't make too much of it. I was a no-good son. Hated our sheep. Ran away to be a cowboy when I was 14."

Ben was through talking. He turned and walked towards his horse.

"Let me know if my name gets on the blacklist?" Butch said.

"If I can, I will," Ben said as he got on his horse and galloped away.

Two weeks later Butch and Al Hainer were awakened by a knock on the door in the middle of the night. Butch's

223

Winchester and .44 were cocked and ready to fire when he invited the unexpected guest to step inside.

"It's me, don't shoot," the visitor said. Butch recognized the unmistakable Texas accent. It was Ben. Butch released the hammers on his guns and put them down.

"Tom Waggoner is dead," Ben began. He was half out of breath and very excited. "And they shot the hell out of Nate Champion's place, but I think he got away. Ranger Jones, John Tisdale, Dab Burch, and Jack Bedford are dead too. Divine's gone crazy, like he's slaughtering sheep, but they're men. He knows you gave the bounty to the sheepmen. You're on the list. Don't be here tomorrow. I can't stay." He turned and disappeared into the night.

Butch and Al didn't try to go back to sleep. They dressed and began packing their things. By daybreak they had ten miles between themselves and their cabin. They were heading west towards Lander.

Chapter 19

Butch and Al, in their hurry to get away from their cabin on Blue Creek near Hole-in-the-Wall in the middle of the night, left a few things behind, including matches. Butch remembered doing the same thing a few years earlier when he left his hometown of Circleville in a hurry. He didn't figure they would build a fire the first day or so in the event the association had a posse on their trail. He and Al also intended to avoid other travelers, and ranch houses, to reduce the risk of word getting back to the association as to where they had gone.

In throwing their camp outfit together and loading it on the mule, except for a few leftover biscuits, the only thing Butch had thrown in for food was a big chunk of raw meat he had sliced off half a beef hanging in a tree behind the cabin.

When they finally stopped for lunch that first day on the trail, having skipped breakfast, they had nothing but raw beef and cold biscuits. They enjoyed the same fare that evening, and again the next morning. In an effort to improve the taste of the raw meat they sprinkled it with plenty of salt and pepper.

After crossing the Owl Creek Mountains they began following what the settlers called the Mail Camp Road. There had been no sign of anybody following them since leaving Blue Creek, so they decided it would be safe to start following the main roads. Their growing hunger for something good to eat helped them decide to stop at the first house they came to and get matches. They were determined not to eat any more raw meat.

As they approached the south flank of Owl Creek they spotted a ranch house on the side of the road. Smoke was coming from the chimney. They figured anyone living this close to a main road would be used to frequent travelers, and would hardly take note of two cowboys stopping to ask for matches.

As they got closer to the building, they noticed it was no ordinary ranch house. There was a sign out front advertising home-cooked meals, hot baths and sleeping rooms.

They approached with caution, dismounted, then tied their horses to a fence rail in front of the house, and knocked on the front door. They were greeted by a large fellow who introduced himself as Emery Burnaugh. He spoke with a German accent. Yes, he had food, and if they didn't mind waiting half an hour he would fill them up with steak, fried potatoes and onions, vegetable soup, apple pie and coffee.

After sustaining themselves on raw meat for two days, Butch and Al thought they had gone to heaven. With their mouths already beginning to water, they went inside and seated themselves on wooden chairs around a large plank table. The aroma of cooking food drifted in from the kitchen. Burnaugh gave them two glasses and a bottle of whiskey to keep them company until the meal was ready.

When the food finally arrived it looked every bit as good as it had smelled. After filling his mouth with potatoes and onions, Butch cut into his steak. He didn't like what he saw. While the meat was brown and juicy on the top, it was

Chapter 19

red and cold in the middle.

"I'm not about to eat another piece of raw meat," Butch said, putting down his fork.

"Me neither," Al said, calling to the big German to come out of the kitchen. When the cook didn't appear right away, Butch drew his .44.

"Ist der ein problem?" Burnaugh asked, suddenly entering the room.

"Our steaks aren't cooked," Al said. "Could you throw them back in the pan for a minute?"

The German didn't move, apparently objecting to the request. He started to mumble something about stupid Americans always wanting to ruin their meat by cooking it to death.

Butch wasn't in any mood to argue with a stubborn German over the merits of rare versus cooked meat. Butch cocked back the hammer on his .44, pointed the gun barrel at his steak and pulled the trigger. While the meat suffered only a hole in the middle, the plate beneath it shattered into a dozen pieces. The bullet stopped halfway through the plank table. Because the gun had been fired inside, the noise seemed double what it would have been outside, leaving everyone's ears ringing.

Al was staring at Butch in astonishment, so was Burnaugh. Neither had moved. Butch pointed his pistol towards the ceiling and gently blew at the smoke that was still coming from the barrel.

"I killed it," Butch said, calmly, looking at Burnaugh. "Now I'd like you to cook it." Butch returned the revolver to the holster. The German hurried to the table, scooped up the steaks and retreated to the kitchen.

When he returned with the well-done steaks, he brought his own glass and pulled up a chair to join Butch and Al. After pouring himself a drink, Emery let Butch know it was alright if he wanted to shoot a rare steak, but if he shot the *Schnapps* bottle there would be big trouble. Butch laughed. Al and Burnaugh joined in. Butch liked the big German, and the food too, now that the steak was cooked.

A week later Butch rode into Lander, went to the courthouse and registered his box double E brand. He had bought a small ranch on Horse Creek in the Wind River Basin north of town, and was getting back in the ranching business. He thought he had done the right thing putting some distance between himself and the Wyoming Cattlemen's Association, but he wasn't about to let the box double E concept sit idle. The problems with the association seemed to be centered in the Johnson County area north of Casper. He figured the risk of stirring up the ire of the association would be much less in the Lander area.

Al and Butch were going to run the ranch together. They hoped their friends would bring in plenty of cattle and horses to sell. They figured their operation would be very profitable with a lot of selling and very little buying to do.

In time their herds of cattle and horses, all carrying the box double E brand, began to grow and prosper. They picked up additional range on the Quien Sabe. Butch found himself in the saddle much of the time, checking on his livestock interests. He was a frequent traveler along the Mail Camp Road near the Owl Creek Mountains. Frequently he would enjoy a hot meal, and stay over with his new German friend, Emery Burnaugh on the south flank of Owl Creek.

One crisp morning as Butch sipped on a cup of hot coffee, while sitting on a stool by the wood stove in Emery's kitchen, he noticed that his new friend not only washed his face and put on a clean shirt, but was rubbing grease in his hair.

"Next thing you'll be putting on your best spurs," Butch said.

"Vy you zay dat?" Emery asked.

"Nobody rubs on grease, washes his face, and puts on a clean shirt, all in the same day, unless he is falling in love," Butch explained. "The next thing is putting on your best spurs."

"I don't haf spurs," Emery said.

Chapter 19

"Who's the girl?" Butch asked, thinking his German friend might be reluctant or embarrassed to talk about his romantic interests. Butch was wrong.

Emery said he was about to ride over towards Fort Washakie to visit Alice Stagner, the woman he hoped to marry. He invited Butch to come along. The request seemed inappropriate. Butch hesitated.

Emery explained that when he visited Alice, one of her friends was usually present, making romantic conversation difficult. If Butch were along, he could keep the friend busy, allowing Emery more time alone with Alice. With this explanation the invitation seemed reasonable. Butch agreed to go. His livestock business could wait. Emery laughed as Butch washed his face, shaved and put on a clean shirt.

As they were riding west towards Fort Washakie, Emery told Butch about Alice's friends, Dora Lamorreaux and Mary Boyd, both half-breeds. Dora had a French-Canadian father and a Cheyenne mother. Mary was the daughter of Bill Boyd, a local Indian trader. Her mother was Shoshone.

Emery explained that neither Dora nor Mary were as healthy and strong as Alice, but what they lacked in strength, they more than made up for in womanly beauty--full breasts, shapely hips and thighs, and eyes like deep pools in a mountain stream--that if a man dared look into them, he felt like he could fall in and get lost forever. For a man who had a hard time with the English language, Emery was very poetic.

By the time Butch and Emery reached the Stagner place Butch was feeling more excited than he had felt since robbing the Telluride bank. At the same time, he was so nervous about the possibility of being called on to entertain a young woman his own age that he almost wished he hadn't agreed to come along. But there was no turning back now.

When they knocked on the door it was Alice who answered. She was everything Emery had described her to be--tall, strong, pink cheeks, friendly, enthusiastic, and pretty too. She seemed happy.

Cassidy

When Butch entered the cabin he was reminded of the home where he grew up. Alice had little brothers and sisters who were seated around a big table enjoying their midday meal. There was a lot of noise. One of the boys was trying to tease Alice about having her lover coming to visit. Mrs. Stagner--a tall, thin, tired woman--was trying to keep the children under control. They were eating fried pork and sweet potatoes with butter, salt and pepper. Mr. Stagner was not present.

Butch was watching the children when he felt a tug on his arm. Alice was pulling him around. She wanted him to meet Dora Lamorreaux, who had just entered from another room.

Dora was as pretty as Emery said she would be, except Butch wasn't sure about Emery's comment that her eyes were the kind a man could look in and get lost forever. She had the eyes and facial features of her French father, and the smooth, dark complexion and black hair of her Cheyenne mother. She looked to be in her early twenties, the kind of woman men stare at. Butch was pleased.

The women insisted Emery and Butch sit at the table and eat some pork and sweet potatoes. Butch tossed a silver dollar to the biggest boy, asking him to unsaddle and grain the horses. The rest of the children followed, eager to help, and share the dollar.

Suddenly the cabin was quiet. Mrs. Stagner excused herself, retreating to the stove to heat up some water to do the dishes. Alice kept herself busy waiting on Emery, offering more butter for his potatoes, more salt and pepper for his chops, refilling his glass every time he took a drink, even bringing him a sharper knife so his meat would be easier to cut. Her smile was constant, and her eyes never looked away from Emery. Butch guessed before the year was through Emery Burnaugh would have himself a wife.

When Butch and Emery had eaten their fill, Alice suggested the four of them go for a walk. Butch didn't forget why Emery had invited him along. As soon as they stepped out the door, Butch asked Dora if she would like to go for a ride with him on the horses while Alice and Emery were walking. She said she would. Butch tossed another dollar to the children, asking them to throw the saddles back on the horses.

Butch could tell by the way Dora swung aboard Emery's horse she was an experienced rider. She sat her saddle comfortably and confidently, even in a full skirt, which by necessity had to creep above her knees as she straddled the horse, a detail Butch couldn't help but notice.

They rode out of the lane and down the road, but hadn't gone far when Butch noticed the Stagner children were following, some sneaking through the trees on the side of the road. He winked at Dora. They urged their horses into a gallop. Soon the children were far behind. They slowed their horses to a brisk walk.

When Butch asked her where she wanted to go, she suggested since they were already headed in the right direction, they pay a visit to her friend, Mary Boyd. This was fine with Butch. He was unfamiliar with the area and had no ideas of his own on where they might go. He remembered Emery had mentioned Mary Boyd's name, one of Alice's half-breed friends.

"Have you ever been with a woman in an intimate way?" Dora asked, after they had been riding in silence for a few minutes.

Butch wouldn't have been more surprised had she broken a branch off a passing tree and hit him over the head with it. Where he came from women didn't say things like that, not even married women, as far as he knew. He felt his face turning red. He looked straight ahead, avoiding her eyes.

He wasn't sure how to respond. He didn't want to hurt her feelings by saying where he came from women didn't say things like that. He didn't know why he was reluctant to tell the truth and let her know he had never been with a woman. He also felt uneasy about lying to her and telling her he had been with lots of women. His leather reins were getting

231

slippery in his wet hands. He began to feel angry at her for asking the question, and at himself for feeling so uncomfortable.

"Are you going to answer my question?" she asked. Whereas the first time her voice had been somewhat timid, it was now bold. "Have you ever been with a woman in an intimate way?"

"No," Butch said, trying to appear as calm as possible. She remained silent, waiting for him to say more. He didn't want to say any more on the subject, but his anger got the best of him.

"I have never been with a woman, or a sheep, or a cow, or anything else in an intimate way," he blurted out. She began to laugh. Butch hadn't tried to be funny, but Dora's laughter made his comment suddenly seem funny to him too. He laughed with her, but when they finally stopped, the subject of intimacy was not brought up again.

Dora did most of the talking, and Butch just listened. He was finally enjoying the ride with Dora. His hands were no longer sweating. The warm spring air felt good in his lungs. The smell of new grass and worm-turned earth smelled good. The powerful horse beneath him felt good against his thighs. Dora's words, mixed with the singing of birds and the humming of bees, were beautiful music to his ears. It was good to be alive. Butch was happy.

It was mid-afternoon when they reached the Boyd place. The house was similar to most on the rural frontier. What had started out as a one room log cabin when the land was settled, now had several rooms added on. While the original building was made of logs, the additions were made of rough-sawed lumber. Hand-split shingles covered the roof. Like the Stagner place, there were children running about. Dora said Mary was the second of six. For the second time in one day Butch was reminded of the home where he was raised.

"Maybe Mary isn't home," Dora said as they rode into the yard. "The wagon is gone." A ten-year-old girl, who came out of the house to greet them, said her parents had

Chapter 19

taken the wagon to Lander, but Mary was out back plowing the garden. Remaining on their horses, Butch and Dora rode around to the back of the house.

Across a small field they could see a woman walking behind a plow pulled by an ugly brown mule. She was a young woman, obviously the Mary they had come to visit. Her black hair fell loosely about her shoulders. She was wearing a light-colored cotton dress, too large for her. She had gathered the material above the back hem and pulled it between her legs and tied it to the gathered front hem, giving the appearance of pantaloons. There were perspiration stains under her sun-tanned arms and down the middle of her back. She was wearing a heavy pair of men's boots. Her gloved hands held firmly to the handles of the plow. The long leather rein was looped around her neck. She had been working hard and Butch noticed how the soiled dress was sticking to her perspiring body in the right places.

When Mary saw the approaching riders, recognizing one of them as her friend, Dora, she stopped the mule, removed the reins from around her neck and dropped them on the ground. The well-trained mule stayed in his place, while Mary trudged through the plowed ground towards the welcome visitors.

Realizing Dora had brought a male friend along, Mary's face broke into a broad smile. She invited her guests to join her for a cup of cold water on a bench under the cottonwood tree. Butch and Dora dismounted, handing the horses' reins to the children who were following them. Instead of tieing up the animals, the children crawled onto the horses' backs and began riding through the plowed ground.

Butch and Dora sat on the bench while Mary fetched a wooden bucket of water and a tin dipper. After politely offering the first drink to Dora, then to Butch, Mary gulped down three dippers of the cold spring water, drinking so quickly that some of the water spilled over her lips and onto the front of her dress. Then she sat down on the bench next to Butch. Using her teeth she pulled off the leather gloves and threw them on the ground, then she kicked off the big boots, and untied the big knot between her legs, letting her dress fall loosely over her strong thighs. Butch found himself staring at her bare feet. They were beautiful, even with black soil between her toes and under the nails. He blushed when the thought entered his mind that he woundn't mind kissing those feet. He found himself memorizing every detail of Mary's appearance, keenly noticing everything she did or said, while Dora prattled on about how she and Butch had sneaked off on the horses so Emery and Alice could be alone, and how they were getting very serious about each other.

Butch hardly heard a word she said, his attention silently riveted on Mary. He knew young women her age who would have been embarrassed almost to tears to have a young man come into the yard while they were plowing in men's boots and a dirty, sweat-stained dress. Mary didn't seem to be bothered at all. She was glad to see Dora, and delighted Butch had come along.

"It's time we started back," Dora said, standing up. It seemed to Butch they had just arrived. He didn't want to go.

"But you just got here," Mary said, sharing Butch's sentiments. "Please stay for supper."

"We'll be riding in the dark as it is, but there will be a moon," Dora said, putting special emphasis on the words dark and moon, like she was bragging to her friend about riding in the moonlight with her young man.

"Why don't you ride back without me. I'll just stay for supper, then head back to Horse Creek from here," Butch wanted to say, but the words didn't come out.

When the children brought the horses over, Butch tossed them a dollar, at the same time thanking them for watching the animals. From the way the children squealed with delight he could tell they didn't see cash money very often.

As he stepped into the saddle, Butch looked down at Mary just as she looked up at him. Emery's comment came back to him. Eyes like deep pools in a clear mountain stream, that if a man dared look, he could fall in and get lost forever.

Chapter 19

Butch could feel the blood rushing through his head and heart. He wondered if he was blushing again, but didn't care. For the first time he thought he understood what Emery had been trying to say.

During the ride back to the Stagner place, Butch kept mostly to himself, his mind filled with memories of Mary Boyd. He knew he would never forget the first time he saw her, standing behind a plow, wearing boots and gloves, her soiled cotton dress tied between her legs, her black hair hanging loosely over her shoulders. He would never forget how she had dropped the reins and walked towards him through the freshly plowed ground--the way she moved, her warm smile, her gentle voice, and when he got on his horse to leave, looking into her eyes. He remembered every detail and went over them again and again in his mind, missing most of Dora's persistent attempts at conversation.

When they finally reached the Stagner home the children ran out to greet them, bubbling over with important news. Alice and Emery were getting married in June. While everyone was so busy talking about the wedding, Butch was lost in his own thoughts about Mary.

On the midnight ride back to Emery's place, the big German talked the entire way about his upcoming wedding and all the things he had to do to get ready, including building an addition on his house. He could hardly wait to get Alice heavy with child. She would bear him strong, healthy sons and daughters.

The next day Butch checked on his cattle, returning in the evening to his cabin on Horse Creek. Al was gone. Butch assumed his partner had gone into Lander. Having been in the saddle all day, Butch thought he should feel tired and hungry, but he did not. All he had to do was close his eyes and see Mary behind that plow and he felt like he could do another day's work.

He fried up some steak and potatoes, normally a meal he would wolf down with relish, but found himself toying with his food, his appetite mostly gone. When he finally crawled into bed, he found himself tossing and turning, unable to sleep. It seemed he could do nothing but think of Mary Boyd. He tried to tell himself he was foolish, that he barely knew the woman, that she probably didn't have similar feelings towards him. For a minute or two he was angry with himself for letting thoughts of a woman so completely overwhelm him. But thoughts of Mary made him feel so good. How could he do anything else?

The next morning, after a mostly sleepless night, and having little interest in breakfast, Butch decided that since he could neither eat, sleep, or concentrate on his work, he might as well pay Mary a visit. He washed his face, put on a clean shirt and his best spurs, then saddled his horse and headed for the Boyd place.

When he arrived there was a man out front sawing up a fallen tree. When the man saw Butch he let go of the saw, straightened up, removed a handkerchief from his pocket and wiped the sweat from his forehead. Butch got off his horse.

"Hello, I'm George Cassidy. Some of my friends call me Butch. Is Mary home?"

"I'm Bill Boyd. What do you want with my daughter?"

The question caught Butch by surprise. He wasn't about to tell the man he had to see his daughter because thoughts of her had taken away his desire to eat and sleep.

"Thought she might need some help with the plowing," Butch said. He laughed, but Mr. Boyd didn't.

"You didn't bring your mule," Boyd said.

"Is Mary home?" Butch asked.

"Yes," Boyd said, grinning at Butch, obviously enjoying making it tough for the young man to see his daughter.

"Can I see her?"

"If you'll help me get this log out of the way so I can get the wagon turned around." Butch tied his horse to a bush and helped Boyd move the log. It felt good to do something besides talk. It was hard to get to know a man by just talking, but tackle a job together and soon you were friends.

When they were finished, the front door to the cabin opened and Mary stepped outside. She looked different than before. She wore a clean, short-sleeved dress with no dirt or perspiration stains. Her hair was neatly brushed behind her shoulders. She was just as beautiful as Butch remembered her, perhaps more so.

"You have a visitor, Mary," Bill said. "Wouldn't say why he wanted to see you."

"Pa, stop teasing," she scolded. "Ain't polite."

Bill Boyd went back to work cutting wood while Butch and Mary started walking towards the road. Because there were no children around to take care of his horse, and not daring to ask Bill Boyd to do it, Butch untied the animal and led it behind him.

"Dora said you've never had a steady girlfriend," Mary said, when they were far enough from the house that her father couldn't hear what she was saying. It was a nice day for a walk. There were a few clouds in the sky, and a soft breeze. They were not wearing coats.

"I don't remember telling her that," Butch said, amazed at how fast women got together and talked about things. "She asked if I had ever been with a woman in an intimate way. I told her I hadn't. That was all that was said."

"I guess I misunderstood what Dora was trying to tell me," Mary said, blushing slightly. She hadn't intended to start their conversation on such an intimate subject. Butch liked the way she talked. He thought the sound of her voice was as beautiful as her face.

"But Dora was right," he continued. "I never had a steady girl. Last time I touched a woman was when I gave my Ma a hug the day I left home, not counting a little square dancing at Brown's Hole."

"Would you like to touch me?" she asked.

Butch didn't know what to think. This woman had been foremost in his thoughts since the first moment he saw her. But he hardly knew her. This Mary Boyd couldn't be like the women Cap Brown had visited in Telluride. There had to be innocence in her comment. He would find out.

"Yes," he said. They stopped walking, turning to look at each other. Neither noticed the sun had started shining through the clouds. Neither noticed the breeze had stopped. Neither noticed the nearby scolding of two magpies who had been busily engaged in building a nest.

Cautiously, Mary extended her hand towards Butch, palm down.

"You may touch it," she said. By now both were looking down at her hand. Butch couldn't be sure, but it appeared the hand was trembling, as were his own.

Cautiously, he reached forward, placing his palm on the back of her hand, stroking gently, as if he were petting the head of a small kitten. Neither looked up, both feeling that something wonderful was passing between them where their hands touched, but neither had the words to describe the energy, warmth, passion, and love that was not flowing, but gushing through their touching hands. They knew something very strong and very wonderful was passing between them. Butch was the first to speak.

"Are you cold?" he asked, not looking up from the touching hands.

"That's a strange thing to ask," she said. "Coldness is something I am not feeling right now."

"But there are goose bumps all over your arm," he said.

"I am not cold," she uttered, quietly fighting to control her voice as her emotions boiled. Silence followed.

His hand slipped under her palm, tightening as he took her by the hand. She did not resist. He led her to the side of the road, asking her if she would like to sit down. She said she would. Both of them felt a weakness in their knees that made standing uncomfortable. Quickly, he tied the horse to a small tree.

Using his hand, Butch swept some dry leaves from the top of a flattopped boulder. They sat down, side by side, continuing to hold hands. Butch thought he could hear the sound of rushing water coming from a nearby stream, but he couldn't be sure, wondering if what he was hearing was his blood rushing through his head. Neither said anything for a long time. Mary was the first to speak.

"What are you thinking?"

"That I'm so much in love with you I can hardly stand it," he blurted out before thought or caution had a chance to shackle his tongue.

They looked into each others' eyes. She didn't pull away as he leaned forward and kissed her on the lips, a hungry, but careful, gentle, lingering kiss. Eventually she pushed him away.

"You shouldn't have done that," she said, still holding his hand.

"Why not?" he asked, genuinely concerned she found something objectionable in what he thought had been the most fantastic moment of his life.

"Pa would be angry. This is our first time alone together. You should not have given me a kiss."

"Then I will take it back," he said, leaning over and kissing her again. This time she did not push him away, but leaned into his kiss, letting go of his hand and reaching around his neck with both arms.

Chapter 20

One afternoon while Butch and Al were helping Emery lift the rafters into place for the new addition on his house, three men leading three unsaddled horses rode into the yard and asked for something to eat. Since it was almost time for the noon meal everyone went inside while Emery stoked up the stove and started cooking some meat and biscuits.

One of the strangers introduced himself as Billy Nutcher. Butch had heard the name before in connection with Jack Bliss, an outlaw who at one time had terrorized the country east of Hole-in-the-Wall. Nutcher said the three horses he and his friends were leading had strayed from his home ranch in Johnson County, and it had taken all summer to find them. He was sure they would run off again if he took them home, and wanted to know if Butch was interested in buying them.

Butch went outside with Nutcher and his two companions, who said their names were Green and Willis, to look at the animals--a brown mare, a sorrel gelding and a gray gelding.

Chapter 20

A few minutes later Butch went inside to tell Al he was going to buy the horses even though Nutcher didn't have a bill of sale. Nutcher said he had traded some cattle for the horses a year or two earlier. Butch figured he would brand the animals with the double E, and as soon as the brand had healed, the horses would be easy to sell. He knew he could sell the animals for at least double and probably triple what Nutcher was asking for them.

The men shook hands on the deal. Butch gave Nutcher the money, and took possession of the three horses, which he turned loose in the corral behind the house. The men went back inside to enjoy the huge platter of biscuits and fried beef Emery had just placed on the big table.

When not helping Emery, or looking out for his livestock, Butch was usually at Mary Boyd's place. He was a frequent guest at the Boyd supper table, and a frequent playmate for the Boyd children. This was sometimes a sore spot with Mary, seeing her brothers and sisters using up those precious moments which Butch otherwise would have been spending with her.

In addition to spending time with the children, Butch often found himself helping Mr. Boyd with various tasks requiring strength and cowboy skills. In an effort to spend time alone with Mary, Butch often took her with him on long rides to check his cattle and horse interests. Sometimes they rode on the wagon seat with Emery on his mail route. They talked, laughed, and even sang together when they were alone.

On one of these outings, Mary gave Butch the only piece of valuable jewelry she owned, a gold chain with a cross on it. They began to talk about marriage. When he told her how much money he had hidden away, she begged him to give up the double E brand and buy a legitimate cattle ranch where they could settle down and raise a family. She wanted to have lots of children.

Butch hesitated, not because he didn't want to settle down with Mary, and not because he wanted to stay on the

241

wrong side of the law. He was on the blacklist of the Wyoming Cattlemen's Association, and didn't want to involve Mary in that. He was sure he was still wanted for the Telluride bank robbery. Sooner or later someone would figure out Roy Parker had changed his name to George or Butch Cassidy. He didn't want to burden Mary with that either.

When he expressed these concerns to Mary, she said she understood, and wanted to marry him anyway. She was willing to take her chances with the Wyoming Cattlemen's Association and the Telluride authorities. Still, Butch was reluctant, though he wanted Mary more than anything in the world. He didn't want to hurt her.

As Butch thought about settling down with Mary he thought he would want to stay in the Lander area. In addition to Emery, who was now married to Alice and settled on the Mail Camp Road in his newly remodeled home, Butch was making a lot of new friends, people he liked. His nearest neighbors, Gene Amoretti Jr. and John Simpson, were constantly inviting Butch and Al to join them for dinner, especially on Sundays and holidays. Butch went out of his way to help the Simpsons and Amorettis with branding and roping chores whenever he saw an opportunity to be helpful.

Gene Amoretti took pride in being the first baby born at South Pass. He had started his thriving ranch at the age of 16, and was now in the process of opening a bank in Lander.

While worrying about being wanted for the Telluride robbery, and being on the blacklist of the Wyoming Cattlemen's Association, Butch's suddenly found himself in a new kind of trouble, over a simple transaction involving three horses.

One morning as Butch was preparing to ride over to Mary's place, Gene Amoretti galloped up on a lathered horse with the news that Otto Franc of the association and a neighbor by the name of John Chapman had ridden into Lander the previous afternoon and sworn out a complaint against Butch and Al for stealing a sorrel horse. The sheriff was making preparations to ride out to Horse Creek and arrest

Chapter 20

Butch and Al.

Thinking it over, Butch guessed the horse in question had to be the sorrel he had bought from Billy Nutcher. Butch wanted to kick himself for not insisting on a bill of sale. He had no idea where he could find Nutcher or the two men who were with him when he sold the horses to Butch. He remembered their names, Green and Willis. The fact that the sheriff hadn't come out to talk to him before charges were filed, and the warrant issued, made Butch very nervous. Though he had honestly purchased the horse in question, he wasn't about to trust the legal system which had treated him unfairly so many times before. There was no reason to believe he would receive fair treatment this time.

Butch and Al packed up their personal belongings and headed for Star Valley, the same place Tom McCarty and Matt Warner had gone after splitting up with Butch following the Telluride holdup.

Star Valley was a remote valley surrounded by mountains, located on the Wyoming-Idaho border south of Jackson Hole. Settled by the Mormons a few decades earlier, it became a sanctuary for many Utah Mormons running from the law during the anti-polygamy persecutions of the 1880's. During winter months, roads and trails leading to the valley were often closed, giving a safe feeling to those hiding there. Star Valley had provided safe sanctuary for Matt and Tom, so Butch thought he might as well go there too.

He and Al rode to Auburn, a small community on the west side of Star Valley, a short distance northwest of Afton. They rented a cabin, and began to settle in for what both guessed would be a long wait.

Butch had left the Lander area without saying goodby to Mary, so the first thing he did, once they were moved into the cabin, was sit down and write a long letter to her. He said he was sorry to have left in such a hurry, but would return as soon as it was safe.

As soon as he had finished the note to Mary, he wrote a second letter to Douglas Preston, the attorney whose life he

Cassidy

had saved in Rock Springs. Butch explained how he had
bought the three horses from Billy Nutcher, and was now
accused of stealing the horses. He explained how he had
neglected to get a bill of sale for the animals. He asked
Preston if he should go back and stand trial, and if Preston
would represent him. Butch advised Mary and Preston to send
return mail to general delivery in Afton.

He gave a dollar to a neighbor girl who was riding a
horse past their cabin, asking her to take the letters to town
and mail them. Her name was Kate Davis, and she was
delighted at the opportunity to earn some cash money.
Shoving the letters down her shirt, she headed for Afton at a
full gallop, disappearing in a cloud of dust.

Butch already knew that hiding out was the most boring
occupation there was. To help pass the time while waiting for
Preston's reply, he lashed a couple of cow skulls to a log in
the front yard and practiced throwing loops. Al joined him.
To make it interesting they began wagering against each other.
At first they bet on who could make the most catches in a
hundred throws. Butch won. Then they wagered on who could
make the most long-range catches from behind a 30-foot line.
Butch won again. Al was soon broke, and wandered off to
land a job at the local sawmill.

Now that he was alone, Butch spent his time roping,
eating, sleeping and reading books which he borrowed from
neighbors. After a couple of weeks had passed, he thought he
might be receiving mail any day from either Mary or Preston.
He told Kate Davis he would give her a dollar for every letter
she brought him from the Afton post office. Kate began
making daily visits to the post office.

What Butch didn't know was that John Chapman, owner
of one of the stolen Nutcher horses, had gone to Evanston and
joined forces with Deputy Bob Calverly to track down and
arrest Butch Cassidy and Al Hainer. It didn't take the officers
long, snooping about the Lander area, to find the trail of the
wanted men leading to Star Valley.

One cloudy, rain-drenched afternoon when Kate arrived

244

at the post office in Afton to check for mail, she was confronted by the two lawmen. Their badges were out of sight in their pockets. They told Kate they had urgent news for Cassidy and Hainer. She sensed something was wrong, but having been taught from an early age not to be disrespectful towards adults, she agreed to lead them to the sawmill, then to the cabin.

The officers had no trouble arresting Hainer. After handcuffing him to a tree they proceeded to the cabin where the girl said Butch would be.

Butch had left the door open to listen to the rain. He was stretched out on his bed, his gun belt hanging on the arm of a nearby chair.

Without any advance warning to Butch, Chapman entered the cabin, Calverly close behind. "We have a warrant for your arrest," Calverly said as Butch leaped out of bed.

"Well, get to shooting then," Butch said as he grabbed for his .44.

Reaching around Chapman, who now seemed paralyzed, Calverly was the first to pull the trigger. His pistol was pointed at Butch's stomach. The hammer clicked forward, but the bullet did not go off. As Butch jerked his pistol from the holster, Chapman suddenly reached forward and grabbed it, forcing the barrel to point ineffectively towards the wall.

Calverly pulled his trigger a second time. Again, all he got was a click.

Unable to jerk his pistol out of Chapman's grasp, Butch lowered his head and pushed into his two assailants, shoving them towards the door, at the same time trying to wrestle his pistol free so he could use it.

The third time Calverly pulled the trigger the gun fired, but he was off balance, the pistol barrel pointing up and to the side. The bullet didn't entirely miss its mark, however, creasing the top of Butch's head, knocking him unconscious.

The officers took their captives to Evanston. Fremont County Sheriff Charlie Stough transported them from the Uinta County jail in Evanston to the Fremont County jail in

Lander, to be tried for horse stealing before Judge Jesse Knight. Butch and Al pleaded not guilty and their bail was set at $400 each.

Butch hadn't heard from Douglas Preston before leaving Afton, so he sent a second letter to the Rock Springs attorney, asking Preston to defend him.

It took Butch a few weeks to rustle up his bail. Al had his in a matter of days, and it wasn't clear to Butch where Al's money came from. Things started getting clearer when Emery visited the jail one afternoon, reporting he had seen Al in company with Otto Franc.

Butch knew the association had a lot of money. He also knew it wasn't above bribery and murder to achieve its ends. Still, he found it hard to believe a good friend of several years had joined forces with the Wyoming Cattlemen's Association to help send Butch Cassidy to jail.

No sooner had Butch raised his bail and got out of jail than Preston appeared at his doorstep with some good news. He said through confidential sources he had learned that John Chapman, the key witness against Butch, the only man who could positively identify the sorrel mare Butch was accused of stealing, was visiting a certain Lander woman in the middle of the night while he was staying in town waiting for the trial to begin. When Preston approached Chapman with this information, suggesting the defense would use it during the trial in an attempt to discredit the witness, Chapman saddled his horse and left town. Before doing so he assured Preston he would not be present for the trial, assuming of course the information about the woman was not made public. When the judge found out the key witness had disappeared, he was not willing to drop the charges against Butch and Al, but he agreed to postpone the trial date until the following summer.

In the meantime, Butch was free to do as he pleased, as long as he showed up for trial the next June.

"What will we do then?" Butch asked Preston.

"More witnesses will probably turn up missing, and we'll petition the judge for another delay," Preston explained.

Chapter 20

"With enough delays, we can win without ever going to trial."

"But I didn't steal the horses," Butch said. "Can't we win this thing fair and square, and just get it over with?"

"If only the law were that simple," Preston sighed. "Otto Franc is a powerful man with a lot of money and influential people on his side. He's determined to see you behind bars. We won the first round, and if you keep your nose clean while we're waiting for trial, I think we can win the second round. No more mavericking for you this winter. Understand?" Butch agreed to keep his nose clean.

"You might be glad to know," Preston added, "Franc is as mad as a hornet that I am defending you. He wants you in prison in the worst way."

Riding out of town that afternoon, Butch felt about as low as he had ever felt in his life. With a possible prison sentence still hanging over his head he didn't dare marry the woman he loved. He still had the nagging feeling he had been betrayed by his friend, Al Hainer. And if he wanted to keep from getting into deeper trouble, he knew he had better stop mavericking and branding cattle and horses with his double E brand.

After stopping by the Simpsons and Amorettis, asking them to keep an eye on his livestock, and a long visit with Mary, Butch headed north into Montana. He wanted to be alone, to think things through. He wanted to stay away from men like Otto Franc who might push him too far. He guessed seeking revenge would only get him in deeper trouble.

After falling in love with Mary, Butch really wanted to settle down. Mary tried to convince him that if he would just do it, everything would work out. He wasn't sure she was right. Maybe he had already gone too far, and he ought to quit worrying and just be an outright, honest-to-goodness outlaw.

He spent the fall and winter working on a number of ranches in the Miles City and Billings area. He wrote frequent letters to Mary. Though her English skills were not very good, she always wrote back, urging him to come home. In the spring he did, and they shared a few wonderful months together before he had to ride into Lander and stand trial.

As the trial date approached Preston petitioned Judge Knight for a postponement on the grounds that the two witnesses to the transaction between Cassidy and Nutcher, Green and Willis, could not be found. The judge denied the request.

John Chapman, the man who had lost the horse Butch was accused of stealing, could not be found either, so Preston was optimistic the prosecution would not have a solid case against Butch and Al. Not about to see this outlaw get off on a technicality, Otto Franc got Richard Ashworth, owner of the gray horse Butch had bought from Nutcher, to swear out additional charges concerning that animal. The original charges against Butch for stealing the sorrel horse were dropped, while a second trial began concerning the new charges. This time Judge Knight would not listen to any of Preston's arguments for a postponement.

After the testimony and arguments on both sides were presented, Knight informed the jury that stealing horses was punishable with up to ten years in prison, also buying and selling horses known to be stolen. After a two-hour deliberation the jury returned with the verdict of guilty. Judge Knight didn't waste any time sentencing Butch to two years of hard labor at the state prison in Laramie. Al Hainer was given 30 days in the county jail.

Butch couldn't believe it. He couldn't complain if he had gone to jail for robbing the Telluride bank, or for the cattle and horses he had stolen. But he was going to jail for innocently buying three horses someone else had stolen. It wasn't right, and it wasn't fair, but it had happened.

Fremont County Sheriff Charlie Stough, along with several deputies, was given the job of transporting Butch and five other prisoners to Laramie.

They hadn't been on the trail more than a few hours when the sheriff rode alongside, asking Butch if he would like his handcuffs removed. Of course, Butch said he would.

"On one condition," the sheriff said. "Give me your word that you won't try to escape."

"Come on, Charlie," Butch said, "Just take them off."

"Not until you give me your word that you won't try to get away."

Butch finally promised he would not escape, and the sheriff removed the handcuffs. The sheriff refused repeated requests by the other prisoners to have their shackles removed too.

When they arrived in Laramie, Warden W. H. Adams marched into the prison yard to check in his new prisoners. He was a dignified man, wearing a black suit, and carrying a handful of official-looking papers. One by one he checked off five names on his list.

"Where's the sixth man?" he asked. "Where's George Cassidy?"

"Here," Butch said, brightly.

The warden looked at Butch, then at the sheriff. "Is this Cassidy?" he asked the sheriff.

"That's him, warden," Stough responded.

"Where are his handcuffs?" the warden asked, making sure guards were posted in the event this unshackled prisoner tried to escape.

"Right here," the sheriff said, removing a pair of handcuffs from his pocket.

"Why are they not on the prisoner?" the warden demanded.

"Gave me his word he wouldn't escape," the sheriff said, calmly.

"And you believed him?"

"He's here, ain't he?"

"Wouldn't have believed it if I hadn't seen it with my own eyes."

"Honor among thieves," Butch said, smiling. It was the last smile to cross his face for many days. A few minutes later he was ushered into a room with four stone walls and no windows, and ordered to strip naked in front of three guards. One of them examined every inch of his naked body, while the second asked questions about his past. The third guard kept notes.

When asked where he was born and raised, Butch said New York City. He didn't want anyone figuring out he was Robert LeRoy Parker of Circleville, Utah, one of the men who had robbed the Telluride bank. When he was allowed to dress he was ushered into another room where his picture was taken. An hour later the steel door to his solitary prison cell was locked tightly behind him. That same day, July 15, 1894, the following entry was made in the prison's Bertillon book:

> Wyoming State Prison number 187; George "Butch" Cassidy; Received 7-15-94; Age, 27; Nativity, New York City; Occupation, cowboy; Height, 5'9"; Complexion, light; Hair, dark flaxen; Eyes, blue; Wife, no; Parents, not known; Children, no; Religion, none; habits of life, intemperate; Education, common school; Relations address, not known; Weight, 165 pounds; Marks scars: features regular, small deep set eyes, 2 cut scars on back of head, small red scar under left eye, red mark on left side of back, small brown mole on calf of left leg, good build.

Chapter 21

Butch took some of his money with him to prison. With it he bought things to make his stay more pleasant--books, candy, newspapers, even new silk Manilla ropes which the guards let him throw at a longhorn bull skull in the exercise yard. Butch and some of the other inmates engaged in roping contests, sometimes accompanied by lively wagering.

There were 170 inmates in the prison, about half of whom had gone to jail for stealing cattle or horses. There was only one rapist, but quite a few guilty of manslaughter and murder. There were three black men, three Orientals, and one woman.

Butch was surprised to see some familiar faces, including Tom Osborn, a rancher he had stayed with on his first trip to the Hole-in-the-Wall country. Tom became angry just telling Butch what he had done to get sent to prison.

Tom explained what had happened. One afternoon as he was busy getting drunk on the proceeds from the sale of a saddle, the stranger who had bought the saddle presented him with a bill of sale to sign, supposedly for the saddle. Tom signed the document and went back to drinking.

The next day the stranger informed Tom he had signed a bill of sale, transferring title to Tom's Bad Water Ranch to the stranger. The stranger drew a gun and forced Tom off his own ranch at gunpoint.

Instead of turning to the law to get his property back, Tom followed the stranger into town and killed the man. Now he was in prison while his friends were petitioning the governor for an early release.

At first Butch received frequent letters from Mary, telling him how much she missed him. He longed to see her. Compared to prison life, thoughts of settling down with Mary on a little ranch somewhere and raising a family were almost too wonderful to imagine. He answered her letters, telling her about his new friends at the prison, the books he was reading, and that he missed her too, so much that he wished he could break out of the prison and come to her.

Butch became concerned when one of her letters described a conversation with Otto Franc, who told her the Wyoming Cattlemen's Association was in the process of putting together additional charges against Cassidy. They planned to add a lot more time to his two-year sentence.

In the last letter she wrote to Butch, Mary mentioned a young man by the name of Ol E. Rhodes who had come courting, from the Dubois area. A month or so later Butch received a letter from Emery with the news that Mary had married Rhodes.

He wasn't angry at Mary. He didn't blame her for losing hope. He did blame Otto Franc and the Wyoming Cattlemen's Association. He also blamed a court system that allowed him to go to prison for a crime he didn't commit, the same system that sent Tom Osborn to prison for killing the thief who stole his ranch.   Butch was angry, not openly, but quietly, and thoughts of revenge seemed to keep the feelings of anger and bitterness from dragging him down to despair.

While some of the prisoners talked about escape from the prison, Butch devoted his time to becoming a model

Chapter 21

Chapter 21

prisoner. Had his sentence been a long one, the idea of escape might have been more appealing, but he was in for only two years, and hoped his good behavior might shorten that. His biggest concern was that some enterprising lawman might figure out he was Robert LeRoy Parker, one of the Telluride bank robbers, and if that happened while he was behind bars there would be no getting away.

One winter morning, after Butch had been in jail about 18 months, he was informed Governor W. A. Richards was in the prison office, and would like to see him.

As Butch entered the office he was surprised at how friendly the governor was, even walking across the room to shake Butch's hand. When they were alone the chief executive congratulated Butch on being a model prisoner. He said he had an important matter to discuss with Butch.

"I've got until next July, so go ahead," Butch said, hoping the governor wasn't going to bring up the Telluride robbery.

"A young man with your talents and abilities shouldn't be behind bars," the governor began. Butch was wary. Why would the governor be showering him with compliments? What did the man want of him? Powerful men with important connections and property didn't talk to cowboy outlaws that way unless they wanted something.

"I'd like to let you go," the governor said. "I have a pardon here with your name on it. All I have to do is sign it and you are out of here."

"Sign it," Butch said.

"Well, I've got a problem," the governor said. Butch smiled. Now he was going to find out the real reason for the meeting with the governor. He waited for Richards to continue.

"The Wyoming Cattlemen's Association and some very influential people don't want you free. They control a lot of votes, and they think you are a threat to them. It isn't your rustling skills they fear as much as your ability to gather other men around you. You are a natural leader."

253

"You can't keep me in jail for that," Butch said, wishing the governor would get to the point.

"I am prepared to pardon you today, if you will give me your word that from this day forth you will keep out of trouble."

"How can I promise that?" Butch asked.

"I don't understand."

"Best I can figure, I was sent to this place for buying three horses in a square deal. It wasn't my business that Nutcher had stolen the horses earlier, but I went to prison for it. I didn't do anything wrong. How can I promise to stay out of that kind of trouble?"

"Just give me your word that you will not break the law in the future."

"I can't promise that," Butch said.

"Do you want to get out of prison?" the governor asked, more than a little annoyed this prisoner wasn't like most others, willing to promise anything to get out of jail.

"More than anything," Butch answered.

"Help me keep peace with the association then by promising that you won't do any more rustling."

"Rustling is a tough way to make any money, too slow," Butch said. "If I gave up rustling, I could get rich by going where the money is."

"Where's that?"

"The banks. Robbing banks is a lot easier than stealing cattle."

"Young man," the governor said, getting a little angry. "You start trying to rob banks and you'll be in serious trouble. We throw the key away for that kind of thing. What about giving me your word you'll give up rustling if I sign your pardon today?"

Butch was amused. Apparently the governor hadn't taken his comment about robbing banks seriously. Good. It was just as well the governor didn't know he was talking to a bank robber as well as a rustler. The truth was, while Butch was sitting behind bars, he had given a lot of thought to robbing more banks, expecially if the authorities and association pushed him in that direction.

"I'll give you my word of honor I will not steal any more cattle in Wyoming," Butch said, carefully picking his words. "My promise does not include horses, or livestock of any kind in Colorado, Utah, Montana, and anywhere else. Just cattle in Wyoming."

"Doesn't sound like you intend to give up the outlaw life," the governor said, disappointment in his voice.

"I didn't say that," Butch said. "I just have to keep some options open in case men like Otto Franc won't let me live a decent life. But you can tell the Wyoming Cattlemen's Association Butch Cassidy won't be stealing any more of their cattle. They should be happy with that. And they'll all vote for you in the next election."

Butch held out his hand to the governor. The two men shook on their deal.

"That's good enough for me," the governor said, walking over to the desk and signing the pardon. Butch was a free man. It was January 19, 1896.

As he rode back to Lander, Butch wondered if he should look up Mary, now that she was married. Emery said she had moved to town. Butch wasn't angry with her for marrying someone else. He couldn't be angry with her for believing Otto Franc about the association intending to keep Butch in prison for a long time. Butch just wanted to talk to her. He missed her terribly. But things would be different now. She was another man's wife.

He wondered if he should look up Al Hainer, and confront his old friend on possible involvement with Franc in getting Butch sent to prison. He decided that would do no good, other than stir up angry feelings. He decided he would leave Al alone, but never give him a chance to do anything like that again.

Butch was surprised at the warm welcome he received in Lander. People still remembered him. They wanted to buy him drinks, and talk to him about his plans. There didn't seem to be a stigma attached to being a convict. The people who liked Butch Cassidy before prison, still liked Butch Cassidy.

It felt good to be free. He felt reluctance about doing anything that might get him sent back to prison. He knew with spring just around the corner, the big ranches would be hiring new hands. He decided to get a job on one of the ranches and do some cowboy work. It would be good to be back in the saddle, roping, branding, breaking in a few broncs, sleeping under the stars with other cowboys, and eating good food after a hard day's work.

Before leaving town he found out where Ol and Mary Rhodes lived. He decided to ride by the house on the way out of town. Maybe he would stop, and maybe he wouldn't. When he saw the house, knowing Mary might be inside, he couldn't just ride by. He had to stop. He had to see her. He got off his horse, walked up to the front door, and knocked. She answered the door. Never had she looked so good to him.

At first Mary couldn't believe her eyes when she opened the door and saw Butch standing there. No one had told her he was back in town. The grin on his face told her he was not angry with her for not waiting.

"Mr. Franc said you wouldn't be getting out for many years," she cried.

"He was wrong," Butch said.

"I'm married now, I don't know what to do. I can't get a divorce, or maybe I can..."

"Don't do that," Butch said. "Not now. I don't know where I'm headed, not just yet."

"Do you still love me?" she asked.

"I'll always love you, Mary. I fell in love with you the first time I saw you behind that plow. You came walking across the plowed ground wearing your father's boots and gloves. Then you took a deep drink of cold spring water, letting it spill down the front of your dress. I'll never forget that. I loved you then. I love you now. I'll always love you."

"But not enough to settle down with me," she said, abruptly.

Chapter 21

"I don't know if they will let me," he said, wondering why being in love had to be so hard, and so complicated. He told her he couldn't stay, but that he would visit her next time he came to town.

Feeling more than a little sad and frustrated, Butch got back on his horse and headed east. The next few days he stopped at several ranches he knew would be hiring. Nobody had any openings, at least not for him. He began to suspect that the association still had a blacklist, and he was on it. He was a good cowboy, as good as there was, and nobody would hire him.

As he continued his search for work, his suspicions were confirmed. It seemed funny. By putting his name on their list, and keeping him from getting honest cowboy work, the association was pushing him back into the outlaw life, the very thing that had caused him to get on the list in the first place. Wyoming cattlemen weren't very smart, he concluded. If they had any brains they would see that men like Butch were given good jobs, and were kept too busy, and saddled with too much responsibility to get involved in rustling. But that was not the case.

And Butch was not alone. There were lots of unemployed cowboys wandering along the same trails Butch followed. One night he rode into a camp, where from a distance, he could see two cowboys standing by a blazing campfire, preparing a meager evening meal. As Butch drew near and began to dismount, the taller of the two men turned towards him.

"If it ain't Butch Cassidy, boss of The Wild Bunch," the stranger said in a familiar voice. Taking a closer look, Butch recognized his old friend from Brown's Hole, Elzy Lay, the young cowboy who had helped drive the cattle into the Rock Springs saloon.

After exchanging warm greetings, Elzy introduced Butch to his companion, Henry Wilbur Meeks, who answered to the nickname of Bub. He was about the same age as Butch, about the same height, weight and build. He had been raised a Mormon just like Butch had, except in the Wallsburg area east of Provo, Utah. At 18 he ran away to Wyoming to be a cowboy.

Butch unsaddled his horse, removed what food he had from his saddle bags, and spent the night with Bub and Elzy. The next morning they continued their journey together, stopping at ranches along the way looking for work, and finding none. Eventually they left the Powder River country and began heading west into the Big Horn Basin.

A few days later, about midday, they saw a rider approaching from behind. The man was riding hard, and as soon as he thought the three cowboys saw him, he began waving at them to stop. The man didn't look like a deputy, or an officer for the Wyoming Cattlemen's Association, so the three cowboys pulled up their horses and waited for the stranger to catch them.

As it turned out, the rider wasn't a stranger at all, but Butch's old friend, Emery Burnaugh. The fact that he was pushing his horse so hard indicated something was wrong.

"Otto Franc has sworn out another complaint against you," Emery puffed, as he pulled his weary horse to a halt. "This time for stealing 50 horses, five or six years back, I think."

"Where did he file the charges?" Butch asked, amazed at Franc's relentless persecution. "In Lander, day before yesterday. They're forming a posse to come looking for you."

Butch knew Emery wouldn't make up such a story. Otto Franc and the Wyoming Cattlemen's Association had finally pushed him too far. If they insisted on treating him like an outlaw, then he damned well wouldn't disappoint them. He'd be the toughest, smartest, and best outlaw they had ever seen. He'd rustle and rob until they didn't have anything left. Nothing would be safe anymore, except cattle in Wyoming. He would honor his promise to the governor.

After feeding the tired Emery his supper and staking his horse out to graze, Butch asked Elzy and Bub if they wanted to ride with him in the newly organized Wild Bunch.

Chapter 21

"What'll we do?" Elzy asked.

"The first item of business is to steal all of Franc's horses. As long as he continues to file horse stealing charges against me, I might as well give him something legitimate to complain about. I'm going to run off his horses, and I'm inviting you two to come along."

"I haf not hurt any-ting," Emery said, helping himself to a second plate of beans.

Several nights later, under the light of a three-quarter moon, Butch, Elzy and Bub rode through Franc's Pitchfork Ranch on the Greybull River and drove off 60 horses. Butch set a blistering pace, driving the horses south towards the Colorado border. All the horses carried Franc's brand. This time there would be no lost bills of sale, or tales of mavericking by mistake, or any other excuses. They had stolen a herd of horses, clear and simple. Butch was no longer operating in the gray area of the law. He was an outright horse thief, and proud of it.

They pushed the horses south across southern Wyoming's Red Desert to Baggs on the Colorado border. Every time they came near a hill one of the outlaws would ride to the top and look back to see if they were being followed. There was no sign of pursuit. After four or five days they began building fires at night, roasting fresh antelope. The animals were in such abundance the men had no trouble shooting their evening meal just before making camp each evening.

After entering Colorado they continued south, eventually crossing the Colorado River and heading west through some of the same remote country Butch had ridden across after the Telluride robbery.

One morning, as they were breaking camp, somewhere east of Monticello, Utah, Butch suggested they head north through some of the Utah communities, looking for some excitement. When Elzy and Bub began to round up the horses, Butch stopped them, explaining that Franc was too important of a man not to find out if horses carrying his brand began

259

showing up in the Utah horse market. Butch didn't want Franc filing any more charges against him. He told his friends to just let the horses go.

At first Elzy and Bub were reluctant. The 60 Franc horses were worth thousands of dollars. They had worked very hard driving the horses out of Wyoming. It didn't seem right to just let them go. Butch explained that the persistent Franc would send notices to every police department and sheriff's office in the western states. Every law officer in seven or eight states would be on the lookout for horses carrying Franc's brand. Franc would certainly offer a handsome reward for information leading to the arrest of the horse thieves. Butch finally convinced his companions to let the horses go.

"Then why did we steal them?" Elzy asked, bewildered.

"Revenge, for sending me to prison, and trying to send me back. That's all," Butch said.

The discussion was over. They left the horses behind, free to join the wild mustang herds of southern Utah. The outlaws headed north to Vernal, where Butch thought the bank might need a little help getting rid of some of its money.

Chapter 22

No sooner had The Wild Bunch reached Vernal than they forgot all about the bank. The town was in an uproar. A mob of angry men, armed with guns and clubs, was milling about in the middle of the main street. Some of the men were shouting and cursing towards the town jail.

There was a log barricade in front of the jail, and more men behind it, pointing guns at the mob. Asking one of the men on the street what was going on, Butch learned Sheriff John Pope, his four brothers and 80-year-old father were defending three prisoners who had killed two local men and wounded a third in a fight over a mining claim. Folks were angry that two of their friends had been killed, and were determined to see the guilty parties lynched.

"Sounds like a good plan to me," Butch said, not about to take the side of the law in any dispute. "Maybe we'll give you a hand, but first we got to wash down some trail dust."

As they entered the nearest saloon, Butch was surprised to see a familiar face. Behind the bar was Charlie Crouse, the horse rancher from Brown's Hole. He had moved to Vernal and was now in the saloon business.

After a brief greeting, Charlie added some startling details about the conflict in the street. One of the men the sheriff was determined to protect from the mob was Matt Warner.

Butch's old friend had been hired by a Salt Lake City mine developer, Henry Coleman, to scare off three local men who were trying to follow Coleman to a newly discovered copper deposit in the Uinta Mountains. A gunfight started, and Warner killed two of the men, Dave Milton and Dick Staunton. The third man, Ike Staunton, was seriously wounded.

Butch headed into the street and marched over to the jail. The sheriff pointed a cocked Winchester over the top of the log barricade at Butch, ordering him to stop. Butch raised his hands high over his head. He said his name was Butch Cassidy, that he was a friend of Matt Warner's. Cautiously, Pope lowered his rifle and invited Butch to come behind the barricade.

When Butch asked to talk to Matt, the sheriff said he would let him, on one condition, that he would stick around for a few days and help protect the prisoners from the mob. Butch quickly agreed, though it felt strange to be on the side of the law for possibly the first time in his life.

Pope led Butch to the cell where Matt was locked up. Both went inside. While the sheriff was glad to have Butch's help protecting the prisoner, he was not about to leave the two alone.

Matt could hardly believe his eyes when Butch walked into the cell. Not only did they shake hands, but they threw their arms around each other and hugged. But Matt's joy at seeing his old friend quickly evaporated. He walked to the far wall and sat on the edge of his bed. Butch sat beside him as Matt described his troubles.

After getting out of the Ellensburg jail in Oregon, Matt had moved back to Diamond Mountain, the same place where he had ran horses before he and Butch first met in Telluride.

Chapter 22

Matt made a serious effort to leave the outlaw life behind.

While on a trip to Rock Springs he ran into his father-in-law, David Morgan, who had come down from Star Valley to work in the mine. Morgan told his son-in-law that Rose, and Matt's daughter, Hayda, were in Boise. Matt gave Morgan his address, asking him to send it to Rose. Morgan said he would.

Rose had left Matt while he was in jail at Ellensburg. The officers had in part turned her against him, telling her Matt had been seeing other women. Matt thought he had lost her for good.

About a month after his visit with Morgan, Matt received a letter from Rose. She still loved him, and felt very bad about what had happened in Ellensburg. He wrote back, sending train tickets and travel money for her and Hayda.

Reunited with his family on Diamond Mountain, Matt was more determined than ever to go straight. The last time he had seen Hayda she was a baby. Now she could walk, talk, play, and tease. He loved to play with her. He told Butch that year on Diamond Mountain, after Rose's return, was the happiest of his life.

Then Rose developed a cancer on her knee. By the time Matt got her to the doctor in Vernal, it was so far along that the leg had to be amputated. He was in Vernal, so Rose could be near her doctor, when the present trouble turned his life upside down.

One day he was in Charlie's saloon, killing time with his gambler friend, Bill Wall, when the mine developer, Henry Coleman, came in and offered Matt a hundred dollars to move his prospecting camp from the Uinta Mountains to Diamond Mountain. As Matt found out later, Coleman wasn't as much interested in moving his camp, as he was in bringing a famous outlaw and gunfighter back with him in the hopes of frightening off three men from Vernal who had been following him, obviously intending to jump the claim he was headed to.

With a pile of medical bills to worry about, Matt accepted the job. Seeing an opportunity for adventure, Wall asked to ride with them. They left right away, but Coleman lost the trail in Dry Canyon north of Vernal, and they were forced to spend the night on the trial. Early the next morning they were back on the trail, and within a few hours were getting close to the camp.

When Matt saw smoke coming from a wagon canvas draped across a log, he turned to ask Coleman if that was his camp. Coleman had apparently fallen behind, and could not be seen. Matt didn't think anything of it.

As he turned to look at the camp again, three shots shattered the still morning air. His horse screamed like a man, mortally wounded. As his mount crumbled beneath him, Matt's instincts took over. His left hand reached for his Marlin repeating rifle in the scabbard, while his right hand grabbed his .44 from the holster on his belt. Kicking his boots from the stirrups he landed on his feet, cocking his pistol. Seeing a shoulder above the edge of a log, Matt fired three shots, each bullet striking Dave Milton's shoulder in a grouping no larger than the palm of a hand. Because Milton was crouched forward, the bullets didn't pass through the shoulder, but penetrated deep into his body.

"God almighty, I'm done for," Milton gasped. Nothing else was heard from him during the fight.

While Matt was filling Milton with lead, Bill Wall, who had been a short distance behind Matt, spurred his horse forward, pointing his pistol at the pile of logs and firing as fast as he could pull the trigger. This distracted the Staunton brothers enough to allow Matt to jump for cover behind a large aspen tree, about 15 inches in diameter.

Ike Staunton, in an effort to get a better angle to shoot at Matt, left the barricade and raced to a nearby tree. About this time Wall, his pistol empty, reached Matt. About a hundred feet from the Stauntons, he was an easy target, but before they could shoot, Matt jerked Wall from his horse. Now both were seeking cover behind the big quakie.

The Staunton brothers began pumping lead into the soft, green tree. Ike continued to shoot at the same spot, each bullet

Chapter 22

pushing further and further into the same hole. It was just a matter of time until the hole was pushed all the way through the tree, allowing well-placed bullets to pass through.

Peeking around the edge of the tree, Matt saw Dick raise above the log barricade, in an effor to take a more exact aim at the tree. Seeing Dick's shoulder and part of his neck, Matt whipped the Marlin to his hip and fired. There was no time to aim through the sights, but having had plenty of practice shooting from the hip, Matt hit his target.

At first Matt wasn't sure he had hit Staunton. Dick continued to squat there, as if nothing had happened. Then his Winchester, still cocked, rolled over the front of the log barricade onto the ground. Still, Dick continued to squat in the original position, too paralyzed to fall.

Matt looked over to where Ike was hiding in the trees. At first he could see no sign of Ike. Then he saw a knee, extending just a few inches beyond the edge of one of the trees. Shooting again from the hip, Matt hit the knee. Staunton screamed, but the fight wasn't over yet. Ike swung his rifle around the tree and fired another shot into the same hole where he had been shooting earlier. This bullet pushed almost all the way through, bulging the bark by Matt's chest. Matt knew the next bullet would be deadly. Matt and Wall both fired at the same time, one of the bullets striking the bridge of Ike's nose, splashing blood all over the front of his face. He fell forward on the ground. It appeared the fight was over.

The first thing Matt and Wall did was to inspect themselves for injuries. Wall didn't have a mark on him, but there were several creases across the front of Matt's chest where bullets had passed close enough to tear his shirt. There was still no sign of Coleman who had been absent during the fight.

"You're through, Matt. You got'm all," a voice yelled from the timber. It was coming from the wrong direction to be Coleman. Matt raised his rifle, ready to fire again.

"Who the hell are you?" Matt yelled.

"Bob Swift," the voice said. Matt knew Bob Swift. He

had been hired by Coleman to pack his things. When Coleman had come to town to hire Matt, Swift had stayed behind to keep an eye on the camp.

"Come out where I can see you," Matt said, keeping his gun ready. Bob stepped out of the trees where he had been watching the fight, his hands high over his head. Matt told him to gather up all the guns from the wounded men.

None of the men were dead. Milton was crying because he thought he was going to die. Dick Staunton wasn't able to move or talk. Ike was talkative and cooperative, in spite of a shattered knee and face. All of the men were bleeding. Matt removed his shirt and begin tearing it up in pieces to plug up the bleeding wounds. While he was doing this, Coleman arrived.

"Jimminy, Matt," he said, trying to conceal his delight. "You killed'em all." For the first time, Matt realized why he had been hired by Coleman, not to move the camp, but to get in a fight and kill these men. Things had turned out just like Coleman had planned. Matt was furious, calling Coleman a low-down cur. Bill said some mean things too. They wanted to rip Coleman's hide off for what he had caused to happen, but there had been enough bloodshed already.

While Matt continued to dress the wounds, Bill hurried to Vernal to get help. It didn't occur to Matt and Bill they could get in trouble for shooting the three men in self defense.

Bill returned the next morning with a wagon half full of hay to make the ride as comfortable as possible for the injured men. The wounded were loaded in the wagon and carried back to Vernal.

Dick Staunton died the next day, Milton a few days after that. Ike Staunton lived, but nursed a crippled knee the rest of his life.

After Milton and Staunton died, Matt, Bill and Coleman were arrested and bound over for trial by the justice of the peace and lodged in the Vernal jail.

Staunton and Milton had a lot of friends in the Uinta Basin. It didn't seem to matter that Staunton and Milton had fired first, shooting Matt's horse out from under him. All the friends of the dead men seemed to care about was that an outlaw gunfighter by the name of Matt Warner had killed two of their friends, and was alive and well in the Vernal jail. Angry men gathered, drank whiskey, and discussed plans for taking care of Matt Warner. While this was going on, Sheriff Pope built the log barricade in front of the jail, and gathered his brothers and father around to help defend the prisoners.

Public sentiment was running so high that a coroner's jury returned a verdict of murder in the first degree against Bill and Matt. But the mob wasn't satisfied. Friends of the dead men talked openly of organizing a vigilante committee to take Bill and Matt from the jail and hang them.

Butch wanted to ask Matt about a possible jail break, but with Sheriff Pope listening to every word, it was impossible to bring up a subject like that. Instead, Butch told Matt he knew the best lawyer in Wyoming, Douglas Preston of Rock Springs. He suggested Matt retain Preston's services for the upcoming trial.

Matt said he didn't have but a few dollars. Most of the money he had received from Coleman had been spent on medical bills, except for $21 he had given his wife. He said the straight life didn't pay as well as the outlaw life.

Butch said his personal funds had pretty much been spent while he was in prison, but he knew where he could get some new money right quick. Butch said he would take care of Preston's fee.

A few days later it was announced the prisoners had received a change of venue and were to be moved to Ogden, Utah to stand trial. When Butch offered his services to help escort the prisoners to Ogden, Sheriff Pope was openly suspicious. On the one hand he knew the mob might try to intercept the prisoners, not wanting them to leave the Uinta Basin alive. On the other hand, the sheriff was just as concerned that Matt's outlaw friends might interfere too, in an attempt to free their friend.

Of course, the sheriff was right on both counts. While

the mob was preparing to ambush the sheriff on his way to Ogden, Butch and his men were discussing similar plans.

Sheriff Pope surprised both sides. After announcing that he intended to transfer the prisoners to Ogden in about a week, he headed out the next morning at 4 a.m. His prisoners were mounted on mules, their handcuffed hands tied to saddle horns, their feet tied together under the mules' bellies.

By the time the town woke up and realized what had happened, the sheriff and his prisoners were halfway over the Uinta Mountains, following an abandoned army trail Pope had discovered when he was prospecting the area. After crossing the mountains, he headed west to Evanston, then down Echo Canyon to Ogden. Pope had been too fast, and too smart for both the mob and the outlaw gang.

With Matt in Ogden, awaiting trial, Butch devoted his attention to getting money to hire Preston's services. Since getting out of prison, Butch had talked a lot about robbing banks. But he had been procrastinating. He remembered the intense efforts on the part of the Colorado authorities to run down and catch him, Matt and Tom after the Telluride robbery. It was nice, after getting out of prison, to be able to go wherever he pleased without fear of someone trying to arrest him. All that would change once he robbed another bank. Rewards would be offered for his arrest. His picture would be on wanted posters. Every lawman and bounty hunter in the west would be looking for him. Even if his raids were successful, it would be hard to spend the money.

But now Butch had more than his own selfish interest at stake. His friend, Matt, was in trouble and could end up with a long prison sentence, or even the gallows, if he didn't have a good lawyer, and good lawyers were expensive.

Leaving Elzy and Bub at Brown's Hole, Butch headed north into Idaho, looking for the right bank to rob. He guessed the authorities in Colorado were still looking for him for the Telluride robbery, so he didn't want to go back there. Utah was his home state where he had a lot of friends, so he didn't want all the law officers there on his trail. As for

Chapter 22

Wyoming, the governor had let him out of prison early on a promise of good behavior. He didn't want to break that promise, at least not at the present. Idaho seemed like the best place to find a fat bank with money to pay Preston.

Butch rode through Pocatello, Blackfoot and Idaho Falls, thinking any of the banks in those towns might serve his purpose. From Idaho Falls, he headed southeast through Soda Springs, then to Montpelier. He liked this little town at the north end of Bear Lake near both the Wyoming and Utah borders. Mounted bank robbers could be out of town into open country in less than a minute. There was plenty of remote country east of Montpelier which would provide an excellent escape route into southwest Wyoming, country Butch was already very familiar with. Montpelier served a large area consisting of many farms and ranches, indicating the assets in the bank would probably be substantial.

As Butch scouted the town, he noticed a sign in the window of a jewelry store asking for ranch help. He went inside and talked to the owner of the store, Mr. Emelle, who said jobs for ranch hands were available at his ranch about eight miles north of Cokeville, Wyoming. He agreed to hire Butch and two of his pals, provided they would show up at the ranch in less than a week. Butch said they'd be on time. They were to report to Emelle's wife, who was living at the ranch. Butch figured the ranch would be the perfect base of operations while getting ready to rob the Montpelier bank.

As Butch was turning to leave, he couldn't help but notice some of the beautiful rings on the counter. One was particularly beautiful. He asked Mr. Emelle what kind of ring it was. The jeweler explained it was a Mexican Fire Opal ring and very valuable. Butch bought it, and waited while Emelle engraved "Geo C to Mary B" on the inside of the band.

Ever since Mary had given him the gold chain with the cross he had wanted to give her something in return. It didn't matter that she had married another another man. Butch made it a point to have the initial of her maiden name and not her married name engraved in the ring. He wasn't trying to take

269

her away from Rhodes. He was too much of an outlaw, and didn't think he could afford the luxury of a wife. But the fact remained, he still loved Mary, and wanted her to have the ring, if she would accept it.

Butch hurried back to Brown's Hole to get Elzy and Bub. It took some talking to explain why it was necessary to work at the Emelle Ranch while preparing to rob the bank.

"What do we need to prepare for?" Bub asked. "Don't we just walk into the bank, tell everyone to stick-m up, put the money in a sack, then ride like hell. How much do you need to prepare to do that?"

"More than you think," Butch said, patiently. "By working with people who use the bank we can learn a lot of helpful things. We need to know when the bank is busy, and when it is empty, when the most money is there, which of the clerks might be fighters, and which ones will lay down. I want to know where the sheriff eats his lunch every day if we are going to do it at noon."

"Then you got to get your horses ready," Butch continued. "Not just the one you are riding when you hit the bank, but the relay mounts too. They've got to be fast, in condition for a long run, and full of grain so they won't quit before the posse horses. Takes time. They've got to be freshly shod so you won't throw a shoe. If there's a big river to cross, you've got to know where to do it and get your horse used to doing it. Your horse has to be trained to stand still with lots of shooting and excitement going on. Otherwise, you might not get mounted if the shooting starts while you're running out of the bank. You've got to study the escape route, knowing where the telegraph lines run, where the railroad tracks and big ranches are. There can't be a way for the people ahead of you to know you're coming, and you don't want people to see you, people who can later tell a posse which way to go. We can get our horses conditioned and trained, and do our planning from the Emelle Ranch."

Early in the morning, August 13, 1896, Butch, Elzy and Bub picketed their relay horses in a quakie grove at the top of

Chapter 22

Montpelier Canyon about 15 miles east of the town of Montpelier. They had quit their jobs and collected their pay at the Emelle Ranch the day before. There was plenty of grass and shade in the quakie grove, so the horses would be rested and full of feed when the men returned late in the day.

Remembering the heavy money belts which wore sores on his sides after the Telluride robbery, Butch brought along a palomino mare carrying a pack saddle with panniers containing nothing but empty gunny sacks. The men had wrapped some sandwiches up in their slickers which were tied behind their saddles.

As they headed down the trail towards Montpelier, Butch wasn't leading the pack mare, just letting her follow behind. He had used the same mare to carry his camp when he had made the loop through Idaho, scouting the other towns, and by now his confidence in her ability to stay with him, without the benefit of a lead rope, was so complete that he had decided to let her carry the loot. Even a hundred pounds of money wouldn't slow her down. With a pack horse available to carry the money, they would be able to take all the gold and silver coins, in addition to the paper money. And since the mare didn't need to be led with a rope, she would not slow them down.

Both Elzy and Bub expressed some doubts in trusting the money to the whims of an untetherd horse. But Butch insisted the mare be given a chance to prove herself. Her name was Ginger.

It was noon when the men reached town. The August sun had brought the temperatures into the 90's. The streets of Montpelier were hot and dusty. Few people were outside.

Before entering the town, Butch and Elzy each shoved a gunny sack under his shirt. They were the ones who were going to enter the bank and get the money while Bub tended the horses. The men rode directly to the bank, leaving the horses with Bub across the street from the front door.

Butch and Elzy didn't waste any time getting inside the bank. There were several customers conducting business with a clerk named Gray, and an assistant cashier by the name of MacIntosh.

Pulling their bandannas over their noses, Butch and Elzy drew their guns at the same time, quickly forcing the customers and clerk Gray against the wall, backs to the outlaws, hands up. Butch then jumped behind the cage and forced MacIntosh to start filling the gunny sacks, first with all the currency in the bank, then the gold. After they had gathered up the money in the cage, they went into the vault. Glancing out the window, Butch could see Bub, looking very nervous, with the horses across the street. He couldn't see anyone else.

When all the money in sight was in the bags, Butch pushed MacIntosh ahead of him out from behind the cage to join Gray and the other customers. Butch ordered them all to get down on the floor, face down. A little boy with one of the men was already on the floor.

"There's a man with a rifle on the roof across the street," Butch warned. "His job is to make sure we have a peaceful departure from this town. He'll shoot to kill anyone who leaves this bank in the next ten minutes."

Butch led the way out the door, carrying the two gunny sacks with the money. Elzy followed, keeping an eye on the people in the bank until he had closed the door.

Looking up and down the street, Butch could see a lot of horses tied to hitching rails, but very few people. He couldn't see anyone looking towards the bank. He and Elzy removed their bandannas from their faces, returned their guns to the holsters, and instead of running, walked quickly across the street to the horses. They knew MacIntosh and Gray wouldn't be quiet for long, but they didn't want to call attention to what they were doing any sooner than was necessary. While Elzy was getting on his horse Butch put one of the gunny sacks in the palomino's left pannier, and the other in her right pannier, then got on his horse. Bub led the way as they began cantering up the street. They hadn't gone more than a hundred yards when they heard someone yelling,

Chapter 22

"Robbers, they have robbed the bank."

The outlaws urged their horses into a full gallop, leaving town without a shot being fired. But not five minutes later, a posse consisting of a couple of deputies and a dozen cowboys was thundering after them.

By the time the outlaws reached the top of Montpelier Canyon, they knew the posse was close, but after changing to fresh horses they left it far behind, heading eastward into Wyoming. While each man was now riding a fresh horse, the palomino mare was still carrying the money. Since the two bags of money didn't weigh more than 50 pounds, she had no trouble staying up with the fresh horses the men were riding.

A few days later the gang reached Rock Springs where Butch called on Douglas Preston and gave the attorney a $3,000 advance to defend Matt Warner. The next morning, Preston packed his things and headed for Ogden.

Traveling at night, and hiding out during the day, Butch and his little gang went up to Lander, where he arranged for Alice to ask Mary to meet him in a quakie grove a short distance from town.

When Mary arrived Butch didn't waste any time giving her the ring. There were tears in her eyes when she started to put it on. Her beautiful eyes were asking him what he wanted her to do now.

"Remember the gold chain with the cross?" he asked, but did not wait for her to answer. "When I run it through my fingers I think of the wonderful times we had together. I want you to have something to help you remember those good times too. So I give you this ring. That's all. I'm an outlaw now. I can't give you anything more, unless you want some money."

They both laughed. But the tears were still in her eyes. When he helped slide the ring on her finger, holding her hand in his, he noticed the goose bumps on her arm. This time he did not ask if she was cold. He knew she was not.

When they said goodby that afternoon there were no promises. The path he had chosen to follow did not have a place for her, not yet. She knew it. He knew it. Still, there

Cassidy

were tears in her eyes as she rode back to town.

Chapter 23

With Preston on his way to Ogden, and having delivered the Mexican Fire Opal ring to Mary, Butch decided to go back to Brown's Hole. Before leaving Lander he picked up a newspaper with an article on the Montpelier holdup. Butch was amused to read Tom McCarty had been blamed for the robbery. He was surprised the bank reported just $7,165 taken in the holdup. Each of the three outlaws had over $4,000, after giving the $3,000 advance to Preston. Butch guessed the bank reported a low figure in an effort to maintain customer confidence in the bank's financial strength.

Upon reaching Brown's Hole, Butch was surprised to see a dramatic increase in population since his last visit. It seemed a good portion of the outlaws, horse thieves and unemployed cowboys from the Hole-in-the-Wall country had come to Brown's Hole. The Wyoming Cattlemen's Association, with Bob Divine leading a virtual army of Texas gunslingers, was driving every unemployed cowboy out of eastern Wyoming. Many had fled to Brown's Hole.

Butch recognized some of the new residents, including George Curry, Tom O'Day, Walt Punteney, Harvey Logan, and Ben Killpatrick who had quit the association. One of the unfamiliar faces was a tall, good looking, well dressed, hot tempered young man named Harry Longbaugh. His friends called him Sundance, or Sundance Kid. He had picked up the nickname after serving time in the Sundance, Wyoming jail for rustling.

Even though Charlie Crouse had gone to Vernal to open a saloon, his ranch in Brown's Hole was still the gathering place. Butch, Elzy and Bub quickly became the center of attention as they began telling how they had robbed the Montpelier bank to get lawyer money for Matt Warner. Invariably, as they talked about the Montpelier robbery, one of them would say how easy it had been. No shots had been fired. In fact. the posse had never gotten within rifle range. There had been no trouble with any of the horses, not even the palomino mare that had been allowed to run free, carrying the loot.

One evening, after Butch had finished telling the story for the fifth or sixth time, making it sound like robbing banks was the most glamorous and exciting thing a man could do, four young cowboys approached him about joining his gang. Their names were George Harris, George Bain, Joe Rolls, and Dennis Shirley. None of them were over 20 years old.

Butch told them to come and see him in a couple of years, after they had learned to shave, and had a little experience. This wasn't good enough. The boys wanted to join The Wild Bunch now. Butch remained firm. He didn't want to be followed around by a bunch of kids.

The next thing Butch knew, the four young men had formed their own junior version of The Wild Bunch, and had left the Hole with the intention of robbing a bank on their own. They wanted to show Butch they were ready to be members of his gang.

The young gang headed east, their target the bank in the little town of Meeker, Colorado, about 75 miles from Brown's Hole. All of the boys had been to Meeker. They were familiar with the town, the bank, and the surrounding countryside.

Chapter 23

They had little trouble figuring out an escape route. Each was leading a second horse so they could have a relay of fresh horses, just like Butch Cassidy would have done.

On the morning of October 13, 1896, they left Joe Rolls with the relay horses several miles from town. The other three, with gunny sacks tucked inside their shirts, headed into town.

The Bank of Meeker was small, operated in conjunction with a general store. The two businesses were under the same roof, connected by an open doorway. The bank had only one employee, a cashier. The teller window was visible from the general store through the open doorway. The young cowboys were familiar with the setup, having been there many times before.

Two of the boys entered the store, ordering the clerks and customers to put their hands up. The third entered the bank and got the drop on the cashier. The young outlaw shoved a bag through the teller window and ordered the frightened cashier to fill the bag with money.

It appeared to the outlaw that the cashier was moving too slow. If this was indeed the case, or if it just seemed so to the nervous robber, no one will ever know. In any event, the outlaw fired a warning shot into the ceiling to let the slow-moving cashier know he meant business. The startled man didn't know what to make of this unusual tactic. He sort of froze in his tracks. In frustration, the outlaw fired a second shot into the ceiling. Finally getting the message, the cashier quickly filled the bag.

Dragging their bag full of money across the wooden floor, the three outlaws herded their hostages out the front door, then headed for the back door where their horses were waiting.

Unfortunately for the outlaws, the two shots fired harmlessly into the ceiling had alerted the entire town. Word spread quickly that the bank was being robbed and dozens of men--after grabbing their rifles, pistols and shotguns--were scurrying into ambush positions around the bank as the three young outlaws charged out the back door.

The shooting started before they could reach their horses. The brave young men returned the fire, wounding five or six citizens. Over a hundred shots were fired before the three young outlaws lay wounded and dying in the street. Shirley and Bain were killed almost instantly. Harris lived about two hours.

When his friends failed to return for their relay mounts, Joe Rolls panicked, jumped on his horse and hurried back to Brown's Hole, leaving the three relay horses tied to a fallen tree in the event the young outlaws eventually came along. When the horses were found a week later, they were still tied to the tree, almost dead from lack of feed and water. They had stripped the fallen tree of all the bark they could reach.

The bodies of the three young men were on display in Meeker for several days. A photograph was taken, and later hung in a local hotel, a warning to young cowboys to behave themselves in Meeker.

Upon returning to Brown's Hole, Rolls broke the bad news to relatives of the young bank robbers.

When Butch heard what had happened he felt horrible, and partly responsible. In the future, he decided, he would never again brag about how easy it is to rob a bank.

Butch began to feel uneasy about staying in Brown's Hole. As news of the attempted robbery in Meeker spread, there would be increased attention focused where the young outlaws came from, Brown's Hole. There were too many men there anyway, and some were wanted by the law. It was just a matter of time until a posse decided to check out the Hole. When that happened, Butch hoped to be far away. He decided to return to the remote Robbers' Roost country where there were more good hiding places than anywhere in the world.

Elzy had no problem with the move. He agreed with Butch that it was too risky to stay in the Hole any longer.

On the other hand, while Bub agreed that Brown's Hole might not be the best place to hide, he was strongly against the idea of spending the winter in the wild, desolate Robbers

Roost country. His pockets were full of gold, and he would darn well spend the winter where he could spend at least a portion of the most money he had ever had in his life. He decided to go east towards Cheyenne, alone.

When Butch announced he was leaving, he was surprised some of his friends, who weren't wanted by the law, wanted to come along. Not only Elzy, but also Ben Killpatrick, Walt Punteney, George Curry, and even his new friend, Sundance, wanted to go with him to Robbers' Roost. His gang was growing. He was glad to have the new fellows along. In the event law officers decided to invade the Roost, Butch would be able to field an army of resistance.

On the way to the Roost, Butch stopped in Vernal to visit Matt's wife, Rose. Efforts to get rid of the poor woman's cancer by cutting off her leg had not worked. The disease was spreading. In addition, she was pregnant. She gratefully accepted the money Butch offered her. But they both knew what she really needed was a husband to take care of her.

Butch decided to do something about the situation. He told his gang they were going to Ogden to bust Matt Warner out of jail. They headed north over the Uinta Mountains, then west on the main wagon road to Evanston. From there they intended to travel down Echo Canyon to Weber Canyon which would lead them to Ogden.

As they approached Evanston, the conversation turned to Bob Calverly, the Evanston deputy who had followed Butch into Star Valley, eventually making the arrest that resulted in Butch's conviction and prison sentence. While in prison, Butch had frequently wondered how he might get revenge on Calverly. He respected Calverly as a man for being able to arrest and bring in Butch Cassidy. Still, he felt the deputy should pay for all the trouble and inconvenience he had brought into Butch's life.

As they passed Evanston, Butch sent Ben Killpatrick into town with instructions to look up Calverly and tell him Butch Cassidy and his Wild Bunch were hiding in the nearby mountains preparing to rob A. C. Beckwith's Bank and

Mercantile in Evanston. Since Ben had been an employee of the association, Butch thought Calverly would believe the story.

Ben returned the next day with news the entire town of Evanston was in an uproar. Barricades were being built. Horses were being shod. Everybody was having meetings. Wagon loads of people and valuables were being shipped to Rock Springs for safekeeping. The entire town of Evanston was making preparations against the invasion of The Wild Bunch. Butch laughed until his sides hurt as they dropped into Echo Canyon, continuing their journey to Ogden.

After setting up camp in some thick willows at the mouth of Weber Canyon, Butch rode into town alone. He wasn't sure how he was going to do it, but he had to find a way to communicate with Matt.

In a saloon near the jail he had the good fortune of running into Bob Swift, Matt's friend from Vernal who had been working for Coleman at the time of the gunfight between Matt and the two men he had killed. Swift was scheduled to be a witness in the trial. Butch gave Swift a note to deliver to Matt. It read:

Dear Matt: The boys are here. If you
say the word we'll come and take you out.

As Swift was entering the jail, Chief of Police Davenport decided to search the visitor. He found the note. He gave it back to Swift with instructions to deliver it to Warner, then bring back Matt's reply. Swift was warned that he would find himself behind bars if he told Warner the chief knew about the note, or if he didn't cooperate.

Fifteen minutes later Swift gave Matt's written reply to the police chief. It read:

Dear Butch: Don't do it. The boys
here have been mighty good to us, and I
wouldn't want them to get hurt. Preston says

Chapter 23

*they can't convict us. If they do, we'll be
out in a couple of years. Don't take the
chance. Thanks anyway.*

Davenport instructed Swift to deliver Matt's note to
Cassidy, which he did. Honoring Matt's request The Wild
Bunch packed up and headed up the canyon.

As they approached Evanston, Butch sneaked into town
under cover of darkness to see for himself Calverly's
fortifications. Dozens of armed men were doing nothing but
waiting for Butch and his gang to come into town. When he
returned to camp he sent Ben into town to chat with Calverly.
When Ben returned he brought a note from the deputy. It
read:

*Butch: I've heard what you propose
to do. Beckwith will not stand for it and
neither will I. We will be waiting for you
with every man in Evanston at our side. You
can't hope to succeed and I hope you will
reconsider what you propose to do. Let me
know if you will talk it out. I will listen to
what you have to say and will promise you
no one will lay a hand on you if you come
in alone. But if you come in armed and with
friends we will be ready.*
Bob Calverly

After Butch and his men had a good laugh, Butch wrote
his reply.

*Dear Bob: I got your note all okay.
Had to see for myself. I have been in town
had a drink and seen your defenses. You are
a man of your word. But I had to see for
myself. You have my promise that I won't
bother your town again. But you have got to*

281

be more careful. I had my sights on you three times last night. Bob, if I would have been any other man you would have been a dead man this morning.
Butch Cassidy

Butch and his gang returned to Vernal where Butch visited Rose again and told her what he had learned from Matt. A week later he and his gang were in Robbers' Roost, the same spot where he had hidden out with Matt and Tom after the Telluride robbery. Not long after they had settled in for the winter they received word that Matt, and his friend Wall, had been found guilty and sentenced to five years each in the Utah State Prison at Sugarhouse near Salt Lake City.

With nothing to do but shoot, rope, race horses and gamble, some of the men became restless after a few weeks. The weather had been wonderful, no snow or cold winds to inhibit travel.

One morning Elzy announced he was heading back to Vernal. He said he would be glad to check in on Rose and let Butch know how she was getting along. His main reason for going to Vernal, however, was to see another woman whom he had met earlier in the year. Her name was Maud Davis.

As Elzy was washing his face, putting on a clean shirt, and polishing his best spurs, Sundance announced he was going to Springville. His mission was similar to Elzy's. There was a young woman, a school teacher, who needed visiting.

Had he not just robbed the Montpelier bank, Butch probably would have headed up to Lander to see Mary, but his better judgement told him he'd better stay out of Idaho and Wyoming for a while. He decided to head over to Huntington, Utah. Bub had a cousin there, Joe Meeks, who had some fine horses. Butch thought he might buy a new horse or two to break during the long winter months.

Chapter 24

Butch stayed in Huntington longer than he expected. The local ranchers were bringing in their herds to brand the calves born the previous spring, and there weren't enough cowboys around to do the work. The Huntington ranchers had plenty of jobs for cowboys, even those with suspicious backgrounds. Butch would work a few days at one ranch, then move to another.

He met Joe Meeks who had a herd of fine horses. Butch immediately took a liking to a tall gray gelding. Meeks, however refused to sell Butch the horse, but said he could use it whenever he wanted.

Butch learned why there was such a shortage of cowboys in the area. When the Denver-Rio Grande & Western Railroad had laid its first tracks through Price Canyon in 1869, the workers uncovered a number of huge coal deposits, which eventually were developed into working coal mines. The largest was the Pleasant Valley Coal Mine at Castle Gate, a few miles up the canyon from Helper. A cowboy could earn twice as much digging coal as he could roping cows; therefore

283

most of the men who worked the cows ended up in the mines, leaving the ranchers without enough help.

As Butch observed the situation, and listened to the complaining of the ranchers, it occurred to him that the larger mines, with hundreds of workers on their payrolls, would handle lots of cash. Security at a mine probably wouldn't be as tight as at a bank. Maybe that payroll cash would be easy to pick up.

As the cowboy work around Huntington wound down, Butch packed up and headed towards Price, then to Helper, eventually winding up at Castle Gate, where the Pleasant Valley Coal Company had its offices.

Hanging out at saloons frequented by miners, Butch began gathering information. He learned the mine employed nearly 150 workers who received their pay twice a month. The payroll money came from Salt Lake City on the D&RGW passenger train which arrived every day about noon, but no one knew which day the money would arrive each payday. Aware that outlaws were in the area, the management deliberately brought the money in at irregular intervals, making it impossible for an outlaw to know when the money would be there.

Each payday when the train with the money approached Castle Gate, the mine would sound a whistle letting the miners know it was time to come and collect their wages. Within an hour of receiving the payroll money, the mine would disperse most of it to the workers, thus reducing the window of opportunity for being robbed to less than an hour, twice a month, and supposedly no one outside of company management knew when that hour of vulnerability would be.

Instead of getting discouraged, Butch became excited. Stealing the payroll from the Pleasant Valley Coal Company would be a challenge, and he was eager to see if he was man enough to meet that challenge. He found the mine office, where the workers received their money, was in an upstairs room above the Wasatch Company Store, with an outside staircase, about a hundred yards from the train station.

Chapter 24

Butch stayed in Castle Gate long enough to watch one of the payroll shipments arrive. Some quick math helped him conclude the payroll was about $10,000 each pay period.

The whistle announcing payday sounded just before the train arrived. The steam-powered locomotive ground to a halt, puffing steam, smoke and cinders. A few minutes later the mail car was opened. Forty or fifty men were already moving towards the mine office to get their pay. Butch watched closely as four men, two of them armed, carried sacks of money from the train to the stairway leading to the mine office. One of them was E. L. Carpenter, the paymaster.

Butch continued to watch as over a hundred men climbed the wooden stairs to the mine office to collect their money. He could hardly wait to get back to the Roost and tell the rest of the men what their next job would be.

When Butch arrived at the Roost, the men were not interested in talking about the Pleasant Valley Coal Company. Two recent developments had taken their minds off the business of being outlaws. Both reasons were wearing skirts.

Elzy had gone to Vernal to visit a young woman named Maud Davis. Things went so well that he married the girl and brought her back to the Roost with him. When Butch arrived, Elzy was happily constructing a crude shelter to house his new bride.

The men were even more stirred up over the Springville school teacher Sundance brought back with him. Her name was Etta Place, and some of the men were saying she was the most beautiful woman they had ever seen. She had class and style. She looked like a New York fashion model, women whose likenesses appeared in periodicals. Sundance had brought back a canvas tent to keep her in.

Butch's first thought was that maybe he should run up to Lander and fetch Mary. He had always assumed an outlaw camp was no place for a woman. Robbers' Roost was a dangerous place. It was just a matter of time until posses and bounty hunters would get up the courage to come in after the men they knew were hiding there. These women could find themselves in the middle of a gun battle.

It also occurred to Butch that the men around him, while his friends, were outlaws, men who didn't keep the rules of society, when it came to money, or women. He wasn't sure how safe these women would be from other members of his gang. He guessed that jealousies, or outright conflicts might be stirred up by having two attractive women in camp. He could already see the men were more interested in the doings of these two women than in Butch's brilliant plan to rob the Pleasant Valley Coal Company.

Sundance, on the one hand, was quick with his temper, and quicker with his gun. Butch guessed the men wouldn't dare get too familiar with this beautiful Place woman. On the other hand, Elzy was happy, easy going and trusting. Some of the men in camp might try to take advantage of Elzy's trusting nature, especially when Elzy was gone.

At first Butch thought he should tell Sundance and Elzy the women had to go, but as he watched the women about camp, helping with the cooking and dish washing chores, pleasantly cooperating with the men who wanted to teach them to ride, rope or shoot, he gradually changed his mind.

The presence of women was changing some of the unpleasant things in camp. Butch noticed a dramatic drop in the use of abusive and vulgar language. The men seemed more cheerful, more considerate of others, more polite and kind. There was more cleanliness in camp. The men washed their faces, cleaned their dishes and changed their shirts more often.

Still, Butch was concerned. The Place woman was too beautiful. He guessed it was just a matter of time until one of the men fell in love with her, and got in a fight with Sundance.

Rather than tell Sundance and Elzy to get rid of the women, Butch came up with another solution to the problem. If the presence of only two women brought about such a pleasant change in camp atmosphere, why not bring in a whole wagonload of women? Then every man would have his

Chapter 24

own. The chance of fighting would be minimized because there would be plenty of female companionship to spread around.

Butch knew some women who worked in saloons in Price whom he thought would come, if the price was right. He guessed they probably had friends who could be persuaded to join them. The next morning, Butch packed up his gear, filled his pockets with gold and headed for Price. When one of the men asked him where he was going, he said he was going to town to get their Christmas presents. At the last minute Harvey Logan and Ben Killpatrick decided to tag along.

Butch found the woman he was looking for at the Bridger Saloon. Her name was Ella Butler, and yes, she would love to take a winter vacation to Robbers' Roost. She introduced Butch to two of her friends, Millie Nelson and Maggie Blackburn, both from Loa. They expressed enthusiasm at coming along too. Before the evening was through one of their friends agreed to join the party.

Butch was surprised at how easy it had been to persuade the women to come to his camp. On the way to Price he thought the gold in his pockets would be the main incentive, but it seemed the women were just like the young members of his gang, eager to participate in a great adventure, whether or not they would end up any richer when it was all over.

Butch's next challenge was to get four women out of town, with all their luggage, and not be noticed or recognized. He told Ella the women were allowed one carpet bag and one bedroll each. He would pick them up at the train station the next morning.

Butch noticed a good team of horses hitched to a large wagon in front of the saloon. Checking around he found the owner of the wagon, Jim Wiscombe from Mapleton, a little farming community near Springville. Wiscombe had been hauling supplies and gravel for the railroad, but work had slowed down for the winter, and he was wondering whether to wait for another job or two, or just head back home. He said he would be glad to haul a load of women, if he could wear his ear muffs, an obvious reference to all the talking he thought he would have to listen to. Butch liked this Wiscombe fellow.

The next morning Butch and Jim picked up 75 boxes of ammunition, two cases of whiskey, a box of canned peaches, and three canvas tents before heading to the train station. It seemed to Butch like he was forgetting something he had wanted to pick up in town, but for the life of him he couldn't think what it was. As they went from store to store, Jim kept running into people he knew who would ask where he was headed. After consulting with Butch, he told them Nine Mile Canyon. In the event someone decided to follow, Butch wanted them looking in Nine Mile Canyon which was over a hundred miles to the north of where they would really be.

After loading the women, along with their baggage and bedding in the back of the wagon, Butch instructed them to keep low, behind the sides of the wagon until they were out of town. He told them there would be no talking either, until they were in open country. The women were enthusiastic in their compliance. Butch was beginning to think the women were more excited about going to Robbers' Roost than his men would be to have them there.

With the arrival of the women Butch felt the winter hideout for The Wild Bunch was finally complete. What more could a man want? They raced horses and had shooting contests during the day, sharpening their riding and shooting skills. There was a poker game nearly every night, plus whiskey and women. Butch guessed about the only thing to make it better would be to have Mary there, and not to have to worry all the time about which lawmen might be planning a raid on the Roost. He also began to worry about his money. The Montpelier loot was almost gone.

A few weeks after the women arrived, Butch finally remembered what he had forgotten to buy in Price. A new shovel. There wasn't a shovel in camp. With all the people, there was a desperate need for an outhouse, especially now there were women in camp. Everytime he tried to get someone to dig a hole for an outhouse, the person would complain because there was no shovel.

One morning Butch called the men around and in no uncertain terms said he wanted an outhouse hole dug if they had to do it with their fingers. He said the camp was beginning to smell, no matter which way the wind was blowing. With winter setting in, no one wanted to wander a half a mile away to take care of body functions. As far as Butch was concerned, the only solution to the problem was to build an outhouse, and now was the time to do it.

George Curry was the only one to disagree. He said he had lived in a number of Indian camps. Indian villages, even large ones with a hundred Indians, did not smell of human waste, and Indians did not build outhouses. He said the reason Indians didn't have problems with human waste was because they had dogs to clean it up.

Some of the men hooted and hollered. They didn't believe what Curry was telling them.

"I've got fifty bucks that says I'm right," Curry said, calmly throwing out his challenge. "And I can prove it. Put up or shut up."

Not about to be bluffed, the other five put up ten dollars each to finalize the bet.

"How are you going to prove it?" Sundance asked.

"Guess I'll just have to find me an Indian camp and buy a dog," Curry said. He saddled his horse and left that same day. Some of the men placed additional bets with each other on whether or not Curry would return. Against Butch's objections, the outhouse project was postponed until George's return.

One thing Butch did notice about having women in camp, there were a lot more trips to Green River and to Gibbons' store in Hanksville for items that previously hadn't seemed very necessary--like soap, factory cloth, needles and thread, butter, even lipstick and stockings.

Butch and Elzy were paying the bills, and the money

was almost gone. They began discussing in earnest the Pleasant Valley Coal Company payroll. All the men seemed enthusiastic, except Sundance. Assuming Butch's figures were correct, he argued that a maximum of $10,000 split five ways wouldn't go very far. As long as they were going to risk going to prison, they might as well find a job big enough to make it worth their while.

When Butch asked him what he had in mind, Sundance suggested the bank in Belle Fourche, South Dakota. The town was small, which would make the robbery and getaway easier, but it was also the nearest bank for all the ranches and farms in the northwest part of South Dakota. It would have a lot of moeny, and it was far away. The gang could return to Robbers' Roost. South Dakota posses wouldn't come this far.

Butch liked the idea, but explained that by spring they wouldn't have enough money left to buy supplies for the ride over to Belle Fourche. If they got the Pleasant Valley payroll in the spring they would have the operating capital to finance the Belle Fourche job later in the summer. This explanation made sense to Sundance. Everyone went to work planning the payroll robbery.

One reservation Butch kept to himself was the fact that he had never done a job with Sundance. The Castle Gate robbery, if successful, would give him a chance to watch Sundance in action, to see if his new friend could follow orders and keep a cool head in a real robbery.

A few days later Curry returned. At the end of a long rope he was leading the ugliest animal Butch had ever seen. It was a large brown and white dog, obviously a mixture of many breeds. One ear was missing, the other torn to shreds, probably from fights with other dogs. It was a male, with one eye blue and the other brown. It looked half starved, every one of its ribs clearly visible from top to bottom. From the row of pointed bumps along the top of its back it appeared that if the dog took a deep breath his backbone would push through his thin skin.

As everyone gathered around to see the new arrival,

Chapter 24

Curry explained he had bought the dog from some Paiutes for a dollar. He said in order for the dog to get into his desired eating routine, it was important it not be given table scraps. All agreed.

"What's his name?" Sundance asked.

"Shed," Curry responded, matter-of-factly.

"Doesn't sound like an Indian name to me," Killpatrick said.

"Picked the name myself," Curry said. "The Injuns didn't have a name for him. Shed is short for shit-eating-dog."

Everyone agreed the dog would have to earn his name before Curry collected the $50 they had bet against the dog doing his assigned task. Curry dismounted and turned the dog loose. Two days later there were no objections when Curry collected his $50.

News on the grapevine traveled quickly. It seemed every outlaw, and would-be outlaw, upon hearing about the setup at Robbers' Roost wanted to join The Wild Bunch. If you were a bad man, or just wanted to be one, Robbers' Roost was the place to be. There was gambling, horse racing, whiskey and women, every day. When money ran low you picked up some more at a bank, and when you returned to the Roost the law was afraid to follow. From the outside, life looked awful good for those belonging to The Wild Bunch.

Keeping five men supplied with women, whiskey, bullets, and food was already more than Butch could afford. He didn't need any more recruits, but they kept riding in, wanting to prove themselves, wanting to be initiated into the gang.

The usual procedure was to feed the newcomer a hot meal and send him on his way. Butch usually avoided such visitors, worried that one day a gutsy bounty hunter or lawman, his badge in his pocket, might attempt to get into camp disguised as an outlaw.

One afternoon, a handsome young man from Price, calling himself Gunplay Maxwell, refused to leave after his

Cassidy

hot meal. He insisted on an interview with Butch. When the
men told him Butch wasn't in camp, he still refused to leave.
He insisted on showing the men how fast he was with a gun.
He mentioned a bank in Provo that needed robbing, and
described in detail how he would do it. He talked, and talked,
and talked, refusing to leave.

It was Tom O'Day who finally decided to do something
about the situation.

"We can't just let anyone ride in here and see Butch,"
Tom explained. "Don't know who might be a bounty hunter,
or a spy for the law."

"You can trust me," Maxwell said.

"There's one thing we've learned around here," Tom
continued. "While it's hard for a man to accurately judge
another man's character the first time they meet, a dog is
never wrong."

"I've heard that," Maxwell said, trying to be
agreeable. "Dogs are good judges of character."

"If you can win the trust of our dog, Shed, we'll let
you talk to Butch."

"How do I do that?" Maxwell asked, beaming at this
new opportunity to prove himself.

"All you have to do is get him to lick your face," Tom
said, almost choking on his words. Some of the men had to
turn away, not wanting Maxwell to see their faces. Tom called
for the dog.

Shed trotted up, his tail between his legs, his nose to the
ground. He looked better than when he first arrived. Living
on the fringes of a camp with ten people, he was prospering,
and gaining weight.

"Does he bite?" Maxwell asked.

"Never," Ben said.

Pulling a piece of beef jerky from his pocket, Maxwell
dropped to his knees. He called to the dog. "Here, Shed.
Come here, boy." By this time everyone in camp had
gathered around Maxwell and the dog.

The dog was reluctant. Because of the nature of his

Chapter 24

business, he was not accustomed to being petted.

Maxwell wasn't about to fail his test. He licked the jerky and rubbed it over his face. Then on his hands and knees he crawled slowly towards the dog. Shed was suspicious, but he could smell the jerky. He didn't run away.

By the time Maxwell was face to face with the dog, Shed couldn't resist the smell of the jerky any longer. He reached out with his long, red tongue and licked Maxwell's face. The dog's tail began to wag as he licked all the jerky flavor from Maxwell's face.

The men and women of the camp cheered until Maxwell commented on how bad the dog's breath smelled. The cheering turned to laughter. Etta called Tom downright disgusting, and marched back to her tent.

Butch who had been watching the proceedings from between the flaps of another tent, stepped outside and shook Maxwell's hand. He thanked Maxwell for coming so far, but was sorry to report The Wild Bunch was filled up with outlaws. He said they were going to California soon to do some bank jobs. When they were through some of the men would be so rich they probably wouldn't want to come back to the Roost, thereby creating some openings for new members. He told Maxwell to report back in the fall or the next spring, but in the meantime to practice his shooting.

Promising he would return in the fall, Maxwell got on his horse and left, his face cleaner than when he arrived. He was still wondering why his comment about the dog having bad breath was so funny.

From that day forward every stranger who rode into camp asking to see Butch had to pass the see-if-you-can-get-the-dog-to-lick-your-face test. Etta and some of the women thought it was a vulgar thing to do and tried to convince the men not to do it, but Tom, especially, was having too much fun to stop. Eventually Shed lost his shyness, and was ready and eager to lick the face of any stranger who would bend over and call to the dog.

By the first part of April, everything was in place to

relieve the Pleasant Valley Coal Company of its payroll.

About mid morning on April 15, Butch rode up to the Castle Saloon in Castle Gate, dismounted from the tall gray gelding he had borrowed from Joe Meeks in Huntington a few days earlier, and went inside. Butch was wearing a five gallon hat, chaps, jingling Mexican spurs, high-heeled boots and a red bandanna. He asked the bartender if any of the local ranches were hiring. The man said things were slow as far as cowboy work was concerned, but if Butch stuck around a few days something might turn up. On the other hand, for someone who didn't mind getting his hands dirty shoveling coal, there was plenty of work.

"No thanks," Butch said. "I'd rather work under the open sky than in a hole like a muskrat."

About noon the train rolled in from Salt Lake. Butch got on his horse and rode over to the train station. The gray had never been close to a train before, and began rearing and lunging, providing an entertaining show for the people gathered at the station. Butch kept his seat, talking quietly to the frightened animal, touching its sides with his spurs as he coaxed it closer and closer to the puffing, belching black steam engine.

All the time he was working with his horse, Butch was keeping a close eye on the express car. Other than a bag of mail, nothing of value was unloaded. When the train resumed its journey, Butch returned to the saloon.

The next day Butch was hanging out at the saloon again. About noon, when the train from Salt Lake City came rolling out of the canyon, he got on the gray horse and once again rode over to the train station. The horse was somewhat calmer, and Butch was able to get close to the engine. Again, nothing of interest was removed from the express car.

Butch followed the same routine for three more days. The bartender was beginning to feel sorry for the poor cowboy who couldn't find a job, and was trying a little harder each day to get Butch to put his horse out to pasture and get a good job in one of the mines. Butch ignored such talk,

Chapter 24

commenting on how good his horse was getting around the train, how it would now stand perfectly still next to the puffing engine.

On Monday, April 19, Etta Place, in her finest dress, one with a low neckline, walked into the constable's office at Castle Gate. She said she had come from Denver looking for her lost brother. The last the family had heard from him, he was going prospecting at a place called Bristle Cone in the mountains near Castle Gate. She asked the constable, a middle-aged man named Black, if he thought it was safe for her to ride up there alone. He said he didn't think it advisable for a woman to ride anywhere alone in this country, but if she wanted to go up on Tuesday or Thursday, he'd be glad to ride with her. Wednesday he couldn't because he was supposed to be on guard at the train station when a shipment of gold arrived from Salt Lake City. She said she would let him know the next morning.

Butch was pleased when he met with Etta and the rest of the gang that evening. If the information from the constable was correct, Wednesday, April 21, was the day the payroll would arrive.

Tuesday, late in the morning, when it was too late to begin a ride to Bristle Cone, Etta dropped by the constable's office, announcing some urgent news received from home made it necessary for her to return to Denver on Thursday. She had to go to Bristle Cone on Wednesday. If the constable wouldn't accompany her, she would have to go alone. She asked if he could loan her a horse.

After scratching his head for a few minutes, Black said he thought he might be able to find someone else to guard the gold, that he might be able to ride with her on Wednesday after all. Squealing with delight, Etta threw her arms around the blushing constable and kissed him on the cheek. They decided he would pick her up at her hotel at 8 a.m. sharp. She agreed to prepare a picnic lunch, including a bottle of wine she had brought with her from Denver.

The next morning while Constable Black was happily

showing Etta the way up the Bristle Cone Mountain, Sundance was inspecting the telegraph wires a short distance downstream from Castle Gate. He had a pair of wire cutters in his pocket. Tom O'Day and Harvey Logan were hanging out like a pair of loafing cowboys near the train station, stretched out on the new spring grass, holding the reins to their horses which nibbled at the grass.

Butch was at his usual place behind the bar in the Castle Saloon. Elzy was in a poker game at one of the tables. Both of their horses were tied out front.

About mid morning, Tom O'Day sauntered into the saloon and ordered a drink. Butch started talking to him as if he were a casual acquaintance. Tom said a lot of miners were showing up near the train station and mine office, apparently to get their pay. It appeared the mine management wasn't very good at keeping secret the arrival time of the payroll. The money's arrival time was supposed to be a secret, but it seemed half the town knew when the payroll would arrive.

By this time Butch had gotten on such good terms with the bartender that he asked if he could have credit for four bottles of whiskey. He promised he would pay for them when he got a job. The bartender handed over four full bottles. Butch gave them to Tom with instructions to take them back to the train station and pass them around. Butch knew there was nothing like good whiskey to slow down a man's thinking and reaction time.

Shortly before noon everyone heard the distant whistle of a train coming down the canyon, the D&RGW passenger train #2 from Salt Lake City.

"Here comes my train," Butch said, falling into his regular daily routine of getting on his horse and riding down to the train station. Elzy excused himself from the poker game and followed.

As Butch approached the train station, he could see why Tom had come for more whiskey. There were two or three times as many people gathered around as on any of the previous days. It seemed the mine management had become

Chapter 24

lax in keeping secret the time of the payroll arrival. As far as Butch was concerned, there was no turning back now, even if a thousand people showed up.

Half a mile down the track, Sundance heard the whistle too. He climbed to the top of a telegraph pole and cut the line. High on the mountain, among the bristle cone pines, Etta heard the train whistle while she was pouring a cup of wine for Constable Black. Down by the track the bottles of whiskey were passed around one last time.

Instead of riding over to the train like he had done on previous days, Butch turned his horse towards the mine office. Elzy followed.

Butch dismounted, handing the reins to Elzy, who remained in the saddle, leading Butch's gray horse just beyond the stairs leading up the side of the building. Beside the building, just beyond the bottom of the stairs, was an empty box. Butch walked over to the box and sat on it, elbows on his knees. He looked towards the train as it chugged to a halt.

People filed out of the passenger cars and went about their business. Some were greeted by friends and relatives. Railroad employees loaded sacks of mail, baggage and freight from the express car onto carts which they wheeled into the baggage room at the train station.

A minute later Butch spotted Paymaster E. L. Carpenter coming out of the train station carrying a heavy bag, bulging with coins. His two assistants, Phelps and Lewis, were carrying similar loads. The three men were carrying the Pleasant Valley Coal Mine payroll. All three were walking quickly towards the mine office. Butch couldn't see any guards.

Butch stood up and stretched, acting as nonchalant as possible. His .44 was still in the holster. Elzy moved the horses closer to the stairs.

By the time Carpenter and his two assistants reached the stairs, Phelps was in the lead. Butch stepped in front of the man, shoving his pistol into Phelps' ribs, telling him to hand over his bag. Phelps took one quick, startled look at Butch, then began to push his way past the outlaw to get onto the stairs. It occurred to Butch the man did not realize a cocked .44 was pushing against his ribs.

Butch had never killed a man, and didn't want to do so now. He could feel the cold steel of the trigger against his finger. He had checked the cylinder a few minutes earlier and knew the gun was ready to fire. It appeared Phelps was determined to continue up the stairs. There was no time to lose. It was time to pull the trigger.

It was not necessary. As Butch stepped up to Phelps, Elzy rode his horse along side the stairway, his pistol in hand, and struck Phelps on the side of the head with his pistol barrel. The man fell to the ground, his head coming to rest on the bottom step.

While pointing his pistol at the other two men, Butch grabbed Phelps' money bag with his free hand and tossed it up to Elzy. Carpenter handed his money bag to Butch without argument. Lewis dropped his bag to the ground, then dove through an open doorway into the store.

Butch tossed Lewis' bag up to Elzy, then started to get on the gray horse with Carpenter's bag, the heaviest of the three, in his hand. Just then a man named Frank Caffe, who was in the store when Lewis dove through the open doorway, stepped outside to see what was the matter. He startled Butch's horse, which began to pull away before Butch could get his foot in the stirrup.

Elzy pointed his pistol at Caffe, and said. "Get back in there you SOB, or I'll fill your belly full of hot lead." Caffe quickly complied.

A number of people could see what was happening. They began shouting: "Holdup!" "Robbers!" "They're stealing the payroll!" "Somebody get the sheriff!"

Butch was wondering what good it was to have the fastest horse in Central Utah if he couldn't get on its back. Amidst all the excitement, Butch spoke calmly, yet firmly to the excited animal. Finally, he got his foot in the stirrup. He could hear the gold jingling in the bag as he swung into the saddle. All around him, the place was exploding with excitement. Expecting guns to start going off at any moment, Butch and Elzy urged their horses into full gallops, racing south towards Price. Tom and Harvey, who had mounted their horses a few moments earlier, fell in behind.

The holdup had happened so quickly, that no one had been able to respond effectively. Before the bandits were out of sight, a clerk came out of the store, aimed an ancient black powder rifle at the fleeing bandits and pulled the trigger. Nothing happened. When the outlaws were nearly half a mile away, someone fired a shotgun which had an effective rang of less than 50 yards.

Finally getting his wits about him, Carpenter ran over to the train station to call the sheriff in Price. The outlaws were headed that way. The line was dead.

Sundance joined Butch and the others as they galloped by. There was still no sign of a posse, and with Constable Black up on the mountain with Etta, they didn't think there would be, at least not from Castle Gate.

Carpenter, not about to watch his money disappear without doing something, requisitioned the train to chase the outlaws down the canyon to Price. He invited men with guns to join him. As soon as a dozen or so men were hanging onto the side of the train, pistols and rifles in their free hands, the train whistle sounded, and the locomotive began chugging down the track to Price. One of the posse members, David Kramer, fell off and was injured.

When the outlaws heard the train coming down the canyon, they reined their horses into some thick junipers, dismounted, and held the horses still as the train chugged by.

When the train was out of sight they continued their journey towards Price, turning east up Spring Creek, making a wide circle around the town before stopping at the Niebauer farm where George Curry was waiting with fresh horses. From there they headed straight south to the Roost.

When Carpenter reached Price, he telegraphed ahead to Castle Dale, Huntington, and Cleveland, ordering the little communities to send out posses to cut off the retreat of the outlaws.

When Carpenter told Sheriff Donant, of Price, he hadn't seen the robbers while coming down the canyon from Castle Gate, the sheriff led his posse up the canyon. While the sheriff was heading north to the scene of the crime, the outlaws were heading south from Price to Robbers' Roost.

When the little town of Huntington organized its posse, Joe Meeks was chosen to lead it. Having loaned his best horse to Butch Cassidy a few days earlier, Joe was forced to ride one of his mules. He led his posse down Buckhorn Wash, thinking that might be a good place to intercept outlaws. When he discovered a bunch of men riding hard, he ordered his men to open fire. The targets returned the fire, wounding Joe in the leg. It turned out they were fighting members of the Castle Gate posse out looking for outlaws too. Joe returned home, deciding it was too dangerous to chase outlaws.

The gang changed horses a second time at Cedar Mountain south of Cleveland, then hurried on to Buckhorn Flat. They reached the San Rafael River before dark and camped there. They did not light a fire.

Upon counting their money, they had $8,700 in gold, which divided five ways was not much to brag about. Elzy had dropped a small bag containing silver money.

The next morning while Butch and the men headed south to the Roost, Sundance rode over to Green River to meet the afternoon train from Price. When the train arrived Etta stepped off. She said she was tired and sore. She and Constable Black had spent the entire day on the Bristle Cone Mountain and had found no sign of her lost brother. They both laughed. An hour later Sundance and Etta were headed south to the Roost, on horseback.

As they were riding along, Sundance asked Etta how she liked being an accomplice in a big time holdup.

"I hated it," she said, without hesitation.

Sundance was surprised by her answer. He asked her to explain. She said the day on the Bristle Cone Mountain was

Chapter 24

the longest and most miserable day of her life. Sundance, was suddenly angry, thinking Constable Black was the cause of the misery, and perhaps had taken unfair advantage of Etta, having her alone with him on the mountain top.

"That wasn't it at all," she explained. "Constable Black was totally proper in his behavior."

"Then why were you so miserable?" Sundance asked.

"I was afraid I would come back to Castle Gate and find you dead," she said, her voice becoming strained with emotion. "The ride back to Castle Gate was the longest of my life."

"I love you so much," she continued. "I'll follow you anywhere, even if I don't like where you are going, even if I have to be a bandit. But I would rather live like normal people, if you would do it too."

Sundance edged his horse close to Etta's. He reached out with his arm and pulled her close, kissing her on the mouth.

"I love you too," he said. "Someday we'll quit this life. I promise."

Chapter 25

As soon as Butch and his gang divided up the Castle Gate loot, they began preparations in earnest to rob the Butte County Bank in Belle Fourche, South Dakota.

One of the first things Butch did was get word to his teamster friend, Jim Wiscombe, to meet him up Nine Mile Canyon. Wiscombe had returned to Price for another season of work with the railroad. It was Butch's intent to take all the women in camp to Nine Mile Canyon on horseback so Wiscombe could take them from there into Price. Having been in the outlaw camp all winter and spring, the women seemed happy with this plan. It would be nice to get back to civilization.

Except Etta Place. She had played a valuable role in the Castle Gate holdup, and was willing to do it again at Belle Fourche. She wanted to go with Sundance to South Dakota. But Butch wouldn't be persuaded. He remembered the long, hard chase following the Telluride robbery. Women didn't have the physical stamina and strength for rides like that, he thought. Plus he guessed he was a little old fashioned in not

Chapter 25

wanting to expose a beautiful woman like Etta to possible posse gunfire. No, she would have to say goodby to Sundance and the gang when they departed for Belle Fourche.

Everyone left the Roost together. The plan was to drop the women off at Nine Mile Canyon then head for Belle Fourche. Because no one stayed behind, the camp dog, Shed, decided to trail along, not wanting to be left in camp alone. Butch didn't want a dog tagging along on a bank robbery, and none of the women wanted to take the ugly, stinking dog back to civilization.

As they were crossing the San Rafael desert north of the Roost, Butch spotted a sheep camp consisting of a canvas-topped wagon, one herder, two or three dogs, a horse and about four or five hundred sheep. Butch had grown up with his own cattleman prejudices against the flocks of so-called prairie maggots, but after watching the abuse the sheep men took in Wyoming, Butch had taken a new liking to the down trodden sheep men. They were common people like him. He saw himself increasingly as their protector, sometimes the only one standing between them and financial disaster, and sometimes death.

Tying a rope around Shed's neck, Butch led him to the sheep camp. The herder was a short, thin man with black hair and a dark complexion, perhaps Spanish or Italian. He said his name was Tony Ponderosa. He invited Butch for supper, saying he was the best open fire cook in these parts. Butch said he didn't have time for supper, but would come back another time. He asked Tony to watch his dog until he returned in a month or so.

Tony was glad to do it. He took the rope from Butch and tied it to one of the wheels on his wagon. Shed started to whine, realizing he was going to be left behind, but quickly forgot about that when Tony threw him a piece of mutton, welcome fare compared to what the dog was used to.

The gang split up for the ride across Wyoming, not wanting to call attention to themselves, especially around the Hole-in-the-Wall country where the association with CY

303

foreman Bob Divine was still active in hunting down and killing suspected rustlers.

The gang re-grouped at the head of Rye Grass Creek east of the Powder River. On Sunday, June 27, they camped about 15 miles west of Belle Fourche. The next morning, after leaving their relay horses at camp, they headed for town, eventually hiding out in some cottonwood trees a mile or two from town.

Tom O'Day rode into Belle Fourche alone, a couple of hours ahead of the proposed mid-day robbery. His job was to check out the town in general, find out if the sheriff was on duty, and how many deputies there were, if any. He was supposed to look at the inside of the bank, take note of the general layout, and count the number of employees. When he had done all this he was to report back to Butch.

As Tom entered the town he noticed there were more men than usual on the streets. The town was just winding down from a weekend Veterans' celebration, and some of the participants were still drinking.

As Tom rode by the Sebastian Saloon, a couple of men from the Powder River country recognized him and insisted he come in for a drink. Tom was never one to turn down a free drink from a friend. Besides, declining such an invitation might call undue attention to himself. His friends would start wondering what business was important enough to keep Tom from having a drink with them.

One drink led to two, then three, four and five. Tom lost track of time.

About noon, Butch began to worry. Tom had not returned and it was time for the gang to ride into town. Ready and mounted, Butch and his men waited an hour. The noon hour was generally the time when banks had the fewest number of customers. Some of the employees were out to lunch. Valuable time was being lost. Still no Tom.

A few minutes after 1 p.m., Butch decided to ride into town, look for Tom, and if everything was all right, go ahead with the robbery.

304

Chapter 25

As they rode down Main Street they could hear the laughter of drunken men coming through the open doors of the Sebastian Saloon. Harvey Logan went inside and brought out Tom. From Tom's slurred speech it was obvious to Butch he was not an effective lookout or anything else. He ordered Tom to stay with Walt, who was going to hold the horses outside the bank. Without protest, Tom said he would.

Butch debated whether or not to postpone the robbery until the next day, but a number of people had seen Tom in town, and now there was a good chance other members of his gang might have been recognized. The longer they waited, the better the chance the authorities might get suspicious of the new men in town. He decided to go ahead with the robbery, even without the information Tom was supposed to have gotten.

It was 1:30 p.m. when they tied their horses across the street from the bank. Walt and Tom stayed with the mounts while Butch, George and Harvey entered the bank. Sundance was busy cutting telegraph wires south of town.

George and Harvey herded the customers against the wall, while Butch rounded up the bank employees. There was a lot of money in the teller cage and vault. Butch had done this enough to know the take was substantial.

When the bags were full, Butch and his men pushed the customers and bank employees into a back room and locked the door. The outlaws didn't make it halfway across the street before people began shouting, "Bank robbers!" "Holdup!"

Still feeling the effects of the liquor, Tom had gotten off his horse and was talking to a man on the wooden sidewalk. As Butch and the men were throwing money bags over saddle horns and getting mounted, several shots were fired. Hundreds of people, it seemed, were hurrying from businesses and homes into the streets. There was no time to lose.

"Get on your horse," Butch yelled, when he saw Tom was the only one not mounted. Looking back and forth in confusion, the drunken Tom, suddenly let go of his horse's reins and ducked into an open doorway, as if he wanted to

305

hide from the mob.

Tom stepped back into the street just in time to see his companions race up the street, his horse running with them. Looking for a place to hide, Tom ran behind a nearby saloon and locked himself inside an outhouse where he was later captured.

The town blacksmith, Joe Miller, upon seeing the bandits in the street, grabbed his new .30-.40 Winchester, and leaped on one of his horses, bareback, and started after the outlaws. The flour mill owner, Frank Bennet, thinking Miller was one of the outlaws, shot the blacksmith's horse out from under him.

The town jail had burned down a short time before. All that was left in a pile of black ashes was the steel cage that formerly had been the prisoners' cell. They locked Tom in the cage, with no walls or ceiling to protect him from the weather. A few days later he was transferred to the jail at Deadwood.

The rest of the gang pushed their horses hard until they reached their fresh mounts at the previous night's camping place, then they continued westward into Wyoming, eventually ending up at an old cabin hideout at the head of the Big Horn River.

After filling their bellies with beans, bacon and biscuits, they counted the money. No one was disappointed. They had just under $30,000.

As they began dividing it up the question came up as to whether or not Tom should get a share, and if so, what they should do with it. Sundance argued that since Tom got drunk instead of doing his assigned work, he wasn't entitled to any of the money. He added that by failing to do his assigned task and by letting himself get caught, Tom had increased the risk for the rest of the men. The men should be compensated for that additional risk by dividing up Tom's share of the money.

Sundance's arguments had merit, but it was Butch who had the final say. He thought a few minutes before speaking.

"Tom let us down in Belle Fourche. Still, I think we

should put his money in a lawyer fund. Sooner or later some of us will get caught too. If and when that time comes it will be nice to know there's money available to hire the best lawyers.''

There was no sign of pursuit, and because the little valley had plenty of feed and water, and received no visitors, not even Indians, the outlaws stayed there for the rest of the summer.

Finally, in September, Harvey Logan, Walt Punteney and Sundance decided to ride up into Montana to the town of Red Lodge to find out what the rest of the world had been doing during the summer. Plus they wanted to spend some of the Belle Fourche money. While they were doing this Butch decided to ride over to Lander and see how Mary was getting along.

The first thing the three men in Montana learned was that Bub Meeks had been arrested earlier in the summer in Evanston after returning from Cheyenne. Authorities thought he might have been involved in a train robbery in Wyoming about a year earlier. When Meeks' testimony placed him in southeastern Idaho at the time of the robbery, deputy Bob Calverly, the same officer who had arrested Butch in Star Valley, wondered if Meeks might have been involved in the Montpelier robbery.

Calverly sent to Montpelier for A. N. MacIntosh, the teller who had been in the bank at the time of the holdup. When MacIntosh arrived he said Meeks was the man who had held the horses for the Montpelier bank robbers. MacIntosh said he saw Meeks through the window.

Meeks was shipped back to Montpelier. After a hasty trial, he was sentenced to 35 years in the state prison at Boise.

While the boys were enjoying the comforts of civilization at Red Lodge, they were recognized by a local deputy. A posse was quietly rounded up, and one evening as the boys were returning to camp, not far from town, they were surrounded by deputies and captured. Harvey Logan received a nasty bullet hole in his right wrist when he tried to hide behind his horse to shoot at the deputies. The horse was killed by the returning gun fire, and Logan was wounded. The prisoners were shipped off to South Dakota to join Tom O'Day in the Deadwood jail.

It was mid October before all of them were charged with first degree robbery. When the authorities pushed Sundance to tell them his real name he told them it was Tom Jones.

When Butch found out four members of his gang were in the Deadwood jail, he headed back over to South Dakota. It was evening, October 31, when Butch entered Deadwood. With his hat drawn low over his face, he tried to look like a weary cowboy riding into town for a glass of whiskey.

As he was wondering how he would get close to the jail, without drawing suspicion, he noticed children going from house to house asking for candy. It was Halloween. The younger children were accompanied by adults while the older children were going from house to house alone or in small groups. Noticing some of the children were dressed like cowboys, Butch had an idea he thought might get him access to the prisoners.

He dismounted, tied his horse to a hitching post, and retrieved a leather pouch from his saddle bag. After writing a note on a small piece of paper, he folded it up and clamped it under the hammer of a loaded pistol which he placed in the leather pouch.

After pulling his bandanna over his nose and mouth, just as he had done in the Belle Fourche holdup, he walked up to the front door of the jail and knocked. He was surprised when a woman answered the door. She was a tall, stern woman.

"Trick or treat," Butch said, trying to make his voice sound as youthful and immature as possible.

The woman gave him an annoyed look, mumbled something about how older children shouldn't be allowed to go out on Halloween, then turned away, leaving the door open. Butch waited until the woman returned with a piece of candy. She shut the door as he was thanking her.

Butch turned away from the door and walked until he came to the barred window to the jail cell. "Trick or treat," he said in a normal, quiet voice.

"Sorry kid, they won't let us have candy in here," a voice said from behind the bars. Butch recognized the voice. It belonged to Walt Punteney.

"Then reach through the bars and take some of mine," Butch said. "Hurry up."

Butch held up the bag. A hand reached through the bars, and took not only the loaded gun, but also the piece of candy the woman had given him. Butch walked back to his horse.

The prisoners found the note under the pistol's hammer. It said there were four saddled horses waiting for them in the mouth of Spearfish Canyon a short distance from town.

Butch returned to the saddled horses and waited for his friends. Sometime after midnight Sundance and Harvey Logan found the horses. Sundance said he and Logan had separated from Punteney and O'Day in town, thinking four men traveling in a group would be more likely to attract attention. He guessed Punteney and O'Day would be along shortly.

Sundance said they had gotten the drop on the jailer with the pistol Butch had given them, let themselves out of the cell, tied up the jailer, then headed for the front office. He said when the jailer's wife saw them come out of the cell block, she started screaming. Sundance pointed the pistol at her and ordered her to be silent, and to move away from the door. She refused to obey him on both counts.

"What did you do?" Butch asked, when Sundance hesitated, obviously not eager to tell what happened next.

"He punched her in the stomach, and knocked the wind out of her," Logan said. "She dropped to the floor like a beef hit in the head with a sledge hammer. Her mouth was still moving, no sound coming out, like when you jerk a fish out of the water."

They waited for Punteney and O'Day for nearly an

hour. Butch remembered the day of the Belle Fourche robbery when they waited all morning for Tom who was in the Sebastian Saloon getting drunk.

Butch began to wonder if maybe Tom had found another saloon, or even worse, if he and Punteney had been caught. In either case, Butch wasn't about to wait any longer. Leaving two horses in the event Tom and Walt eventually came along, Butch, Sundance and Harvey headed back to Wyoming.

They later learned that Walt and Tom got their directions mixed up and headed out of town in the wrong direction. When it became light the next morning, they were still looking for Spearfish Canyon. A farm boy out hunting rabbits fired a shot into some brush and flushed them out. A short time later a posse ran them down and brought them back to jail.

It was a week later, near Thermopolis, Wyoming, when Butch found out Tom and Walt had been captured. Not about to go back himself and risk getting caught a second time, Butch got an old friend, Bob McCoy to do his work. McCoy knew how to keep his mouth shut, was not known in South Dakota, and could be trusted. In addition to knowing Butch, Bob was a good friend to Tom O'Day.

Butch gave McCoy $3,000 with instructions to go to Deadwood and hire the services of Temple and McLaughlin, the two best lawyers in the area. He instructed McCoy to give the lawyers a thousand up front to take the case, and promise them a second thousand if they succeeded in winning the case for Walt and Tom. The third thousand was for expense money, and to make life as comfortable as possible for the prisoners.

When Walt and Tom came to trial, the lawyers lined up a row of witnesses, including Bob McCoy, who claimed he had contact with the defendants three hundred miles away in central Wyoming at the time of the robbery. One of the witnesses was an old woman who said she had cooked supper and heated bath water for them on the day of the robbery near Lander. The prosecution didn't come up with anything to

Chapter 25

discredit or challenge the witnesses. As a result Walt and Tom were acquitted.

On the way back to the Roost, Butch and Sundance, seeing Tony Ponderosa's sheep camp off in the distance, decided to ride over and see how old Shed was getting along. Tony seemed more happy than the dog to see them, and insisted they stay for supper. The two were glad to oblige, having not enjoyed a hot meal since leaving the McPhearson Ranch north of Green River. In their travels they were carefully avoiding towns and public restaurants where they might be recognized. They weren't so much worried about being identified as the Belle Fourche bank robbers as they were the Castle Gate bandits. While Belle Fourche was about 600 miles distant, Castle Gate was less than a hundred miles away.

There were no ranches in this part of the San Rafael Desert where they could stop in for supper so they were grateful to receive a dinner invitation from the sheepherder.

Tony didn't want any help with the meal. He insisted his two dinner guests sit in the shade drinking whiskey from tin cups while he prepared the food. This was fine with Butch and Sundance. They would have shown the same hospitality to Tony had he visited their camp. Besides, their unspoken rule of the trail was to tip generously, even if the food was not as good as Tony claimed it would be. Butch and Sundance both had nearly $6,000 in gold in their money belts from the Belle Fourche holdup, and there was a lot more buried under the sand near the Roost. Butch had argued with Sundance at some length on whether or not to be generous with their gold when they were flush. Butch argued that if they were generous with their money when times were good, the recipients of that money would be generous with them when times were not so good. Besides, people on the receiving end of outlaw gold were less likely to talk to authorities.

When supper was finally served, it was well worth the wait--fried lamb steaks, Dutch oven potatoes with onions, sour dough biscuits with butter made from ewes' milk, strawberry jam out of a can, coffee and whiskey. The food was served on tin plates. For a table they used a pine plank, one end resting on two wooden boxes, the other on the tail gate of the wagon. Two of the men sat on boxes, the third on a water keg. While Butch and Sundance managed to the three steaks each, but they could not finish off the potatoes and biscuits.

When the meal was finished, the men sat on the ground, leaning against boxes and kegs, their feet stretched out in front of them, while they whittled away at rabbit brush sticks to use in picking their teeth.

The sun was low in the western sky, slowly disappearing behind the Boulder Mountains. A cool breeze was blowing in from the Henry Mountains. With their money belts full of gold and their bellies full of tasty food, life seemed about good as it could be, until Sundance said he sure missed Etta. He guessed she had returned to Springville. He said he hoped to pay her a visit as soon as possible.

Butch was the first to get up. He picked up the tin plates and asked Tony where he kept the wash pan. When Tony asked what for, Butch said he was going to wash the dishes.

Tony said that wouldn't be necessary, that he already had a dishwasher. Butch wasn't sure what Tony was trying to say. There was no one else in camp, only the three men who had just finished eating.

Seeing Butch's hesitation, Tony told him to just spread the plates out on the ground, dirty side up. Butch complied, wondering what kind of game Tony was up to.

When the plates were on the ground, Tony whistled. Shed charged from his hiding place beneath the wagon and began licking the plates.

Butch and Sundance began to laugh, realizing they had been eating on plates licked clean by Shed, the cleanup dog. They no longer felt sorry for Maxwell and others who had had their faces licked by the dog, now they had eaten off plates licked clean by Shed. They laughed until their sides hurt. When they finally stopped, Tony, not knowing what was so funny, tried to get them to clean up the last of the potatoes so Shed could clean the Dutch oven. This only started them laughing again.

Chapter 26

After the Castle Gate and Belle Fourche holdups Butch decided to move his winter camp from Roost Springs to Horseshoe Canyon, about eight miles to the east. Roost Springs had been the traditional hideout for cattle and horse rustlers mainly because it was a good place to keep cattle and horses. The spring was the only source of water for many miles, making it necessary for the animals to stay close, even without fences. Plus there was plenty of good feed in the area.

Butch was no longer a rustler, though. He did not need grazing for hundreds of animals. The rolling hills to the north and east of the Roost made it easy to get to, for posses as well as outlaws. A lot of people knew the exact location of the Roost, and some, for a price, would give directions to any posse willing to go there.

There were a lot of other places, if one didn't have large herds of cattle and horses to care for, better suited for hiding and defending. One such place was Horseshoe Canyon. Winding for dozens of miles through the barren desert, there were only a few places where mounted riders could gain access to the canyon. A few lookouts at strategic locations could easily spot any unwanted visitors. A handful of men with Winchesters could defend the access points against an army of deputies. Besides, few people were familiar with the canyon and its secret access trails.

Once inside the canyon, one found himself in a peaceful sanctuary with plenty of feed and water for the horses, and frequent overhangs offering shade from the summer sun and warm, dry places to cook and sleep while winter storms raged above the sheer canyon walls.

Dropping into the canyon from the north rim, about eight miles east of Roost Springs, the outlaws carried their tents and supplies up the canyon a mile or so to a wide grassy spot. There were ancient Indian drawings on the north canyon wall indicating the ancient ones had favored the same location.

At the spot where the trail dropped into the canyon the outlaws had found much of the ground surface littered with flint and obsidian chips, and broken pieces of pottery, the litter of ancient civilizations.

The men went to work setting up the tents and digging latrines, which Butch had finally decided would be permanent fixtures in camp, whether the men liked it or not. While the men were doing this, Butch arranged for Ella Butler and Margaret Blackburn to buy supplies in Price, and Etta Place and Millie Nelson to do the same in Green River. By now Butch figured people knew these women frequented his camp. When they started buying large quantities of supplies, Butch was sure local authorities would pay close attention. He told Etta and Millie to go into Malcolm Politano's Green River store and buy every round of ammunition in the place. Butch knew the news of two women buying thousands of rounds of ammunition would spread quickly. He instructed Ella and Margaret to do the same in Price.

Butch wanted the authorities to think an army of outlaws was quartered at the Roost, and that the outlaws had enough ammunition and fire power to fight the United States Army. He was counting on the free-spending women to get this message across.

Since Tom Fares had been sent home without his pants, the only officer to enter the area with any degree of success was U.S. Deputy Marshall Joe Bush out of Salt Lake City had led eight deputies into the Roost from Loa. They surrounded the Granite Ranch, and arrested a small time cattle thief named Blue John--a foul-smelling fellow with one eye blue and the other brown. He spoke with an English accent and never buttoned his shirt above the navel, even in winter.

Joe Bush and his posse took the prisoner back to Loa to stand trial. Throughout the proceedings, Blue John insisted he was only a cowhand at the Granite Ranch. There was no hard evidence he had rustled cattle so the judge had no choice but to set him free.

The efforts to catch Blue John and bring him to jail were not totally futile. Even though the prisoner was released, Joe Bush had shown it was possible for a posse to enter the Roost and bring out a prisoner, safely. Butch wondered how long it would be until Joe Bush or someone else would try to catch a more formidable thief, namely Butch Cassidy. Moving his camp to Horseshoe Canyon, and buying all the ammunition in Price and Green River, were moves on his part to postpone the inevitable.

Butch figured his gang would be safe at the Roost for another winter. Whereas the previous winter money had been scarce, this winter, after Castle Gate and Belle Fourche, there was plenty of gold to buy whatever a man wanted.

After moving his camp, Butch was amazed at how news of the new location got around. He had a problem the previous winter of would-be bad men wanting to join his gang. It was worse now. Pulling off the Castle Gate and Belle Fourche holdups had elevated Butch to new levels of esteem and admiration among bad men and those who would become such. Everyone seemed to think riding with Butch would bring adventure, fame and easy money.

Every few days someone new would show up. While most could be talked into leaving after a meal and a cup of

316

whiskey, there were three who refused to accept the invitation to leave. They were Joe Walker, John Herring and the bad man from Price, Gunplay Maxwell, the same young man who had persuaded Shed to lick his face the previous winter.

Maxwell insisted he could make a significant contribution to the gang, namely through his brother, Tom, who had a butcher shop in Price. It was a perfect outlet for stolen beef. Maxwell seemed offended when Butch said he was not interested in supplying stolen beef to Maxwell's brother. Butch said he did not rustle cattle anymore, and didn't have any rustled cattle to send to a butcher shop.

"You think you're so smart," Maxwell exploded. "I'll show you. I'll start my own gang. Someday your best men will want to ride with me."

"They're free to ride with you right now," Butch said. There were no volunteers for Maxwell's new gang. The enraged bad man left the Roost alone.

Joe Walker tried to buy his way into the gang by presenting Butch with a beautiful sorrel mare, carrying a new bridle and saddle. Walker had been leading the mare when he entered the camp.

Butch asked Walker if he had brought the mare all the way from Price. The bad man bragged about taking the horse from a boy who was herding cattle on the San Rafael Desert. Butch refused the gift, without offering an explanation. Walker continued to hang around the camp.

John Herring, unlike Maxwell and Walker, didn't seem interested in joining the gang. He just wanted to play poker with the outlaws. He was about the same age as Butch, similar in build, with the same color hair and blue eyes. With all the gold around camp, he guessed the poker games would get very exciting. He had brought about $1,000 with him to buy his way into the poker action.

There had been some exciting poker games the previous winter, and with all the new money in camp, Butch guessed they would be even better this winter. Undoubtedly some of the outlaws would lose a lot of money while others would

317

double or triple their wealth, and fortunes could change dramatically in a single night. Generally before beginning a game, the players set a time when the game would end, usually at daylight the next morning. Invariably those who were winning or losing big did not want to stop, and became angry with those who did. By setting a time limit ahead of time, there were fewer arguments and fights at the end of a game.

The best poker games were in the winter when there was nothing else to do, when there were fewer distractions. Butch told Herring he was welcome to play poker with the boys, but if he wanted to be in one of the big games, he would have to wait until winter. Herring was friendly and seemed to get along with everyone, and he didn't seem to be a professional gambler.

Once the camp in Horseshoe Canyon was in place--tents up, latrines dug, supplies stashed away for the winter, the men became restless. Winter had not yet set in. Travel was easy, and the abundance of gold from the two robberies was begging to be spent.

Butch felt the same way, but he knew better than to show his face in any public place in Utah. After the Castle Gate robbery, wanted posters seemed to be showing up everywhere.

He decided to ride up past Vernal to Brown's Hole, visit his friends there, then ride over to Dixon and Baggs, small border towns with thriving saloons, far from the reach of the law. Nine men rode with him, including Joe Walker.

They were a short distance north of the Roost on the San Rafael Desert when they came upon a herd of cows. Butch rode right into the cow camp, seeing no reason to make a detour around it. The lone herder was not anyone Butch had met before, but a Mormon boy who stood scowling at the outlaws, offering no greeting. Butch thought this strange. People out alone with cattle or sheep usually welcomed visitors.

"Aren't you going to invite us for supper?" Butch

318

asked.

"Horse thieves aren't welcome in my camp," the boy said, speaking for the first time, his voice high and breaking. He was obviously frightened by the ten riders, but still willing to speak his mind. Butch admired the boy's courage. The boy was not carrying a gun.

"We're not horse thieves," Butch said in an attempt to calm the boy.

"Hell you're not," the boy responded. "Where do you think that sorrel mare came from?" He was pointing at the horse Joe Walker was riding, the same one the bad man had tried to give to Butch a short time earlier.

"Is this the boy you took the horse from?" Butch asked, looking at Walker.

"Damn right," Walker responded. "Looks like he's got another one tied to the wagon. Think I'll take that one too."

Walker started to ride towards the wagon where a bay gelding was tied. The boy stepped in Walker's path, but the outlaw did not stop. The boy's dog started barking, sensing its master was in danger.

When Butch drew his .44 everyone thought he was going to shoot the dog. Instead he pointed it at Walker, ordering the outlaw to halt. Butch cocked back the hammer. He wanted Walker to know he meant business.

"Get off your horse," Butch barked at Walker.

Walker looked confused, wondering if Butch was playing some kind of joke on him.

"Get off the horse," Butch repeated, his pistol still pointing at Walker.

"I don't understand," Walker whined.

"Where I come from a man doesn't steal from kids, or from neighbors," Butch explained. "Get off the horse and give it back to the boy."

Slowly, Walker dismounted and handed the reins to the boy.

"Start walking," Butch ordered.

"All the way back to camp?" Walker asked.

"No. To Green River. Never want to see you in my camp again. Understand?"

Walker didn't say anything more as he began walking towards Green River. Butch made sure one of the men kept an eye on Walker, from a distance, for the remainder of the day, to make sure the outlaw didn't return to the boy's camp.

Upon reaching Vernal, Butch thought about riding into town while Elzy was visiting in-laws, but decided against it. Butch stayed in camp while some of the men went in for supplies.

Later that night the men returned with news that Gunplay Maxwell was in one of the bars bragging the town wasn't big enough for himself and Butch Cassidy, and that was why Cassidy was camped outside the town, afraid to come in. Butch was amazed at how fast news traveled. He thought his movements were unknown outside his gang, but it seemed apparent someone had told Maxwell the gang was near Vernal.

Butch didn't want to fight Maxwell, but he was not afraid of the man either. It seemed men who talked as much as Maxwell were more bark than bite anyway. But it would be nice to shut that big mouth. Butch asked Sundance to return to Vernal and invite Maxwell back to camp, thinking such an invitation might cause the bad man to back down and shut his mouth.

Such was not the case. An hour later Maxwell rode into camp wearing two loaded pistols.

"Never killed a man before," Butch said, walking up to Maxwell as the bad man dismounted. "Never hated a man enough to send him out of this world." Maxwell stood his ground, looking at Butch. To everyone's surprise he didn't say anything.

"There's two things I hate," Butch continued. "A man who talks too much, and a man who brags about himself. Put both together and I guess that's a man I could kill. Maxwell, how would you like to be responsible for the first notch on my gun handle?"

Chapter 26

Still, Maxwell said nothing. His guns were in his holsters, ready to be used. So were Butch's.

"I'm going to count to five," Butch continued. "Real slow. If you're still around when I get to five I'm going to kill you." Butch's voice was calm and firm. His blue-gray eyes were cold steel, unblinking, looking Maxwell square in the face.

"One," Butch said, moving his hand closer to his gun handle. Maxwell looked at Butch's gun, then at the other men. Nobody moved. Nobody made a sound.

"Two."

Maxwell turned and swung into the saddle. He said nothing as he galloped into the night. Butch hoped this was the last he would see of the man.

The outlaws moved on to Brown's Hole, then to Dixon where they consumed every drop of liquor in town, and when that was gone shot out half the windows, which were promptly paid for with Castle Gate gold.

The next stop was Jack Ryan's Bull Dog Saloon in Baggs. When the town constable saw the gang riding into town he suddenly had urgent business elsewhere. During the next few days, everyone who entered the Bull Dog Saloon enjoyed free drinks, courtesy of The Wild Bunch. The boys talked freely of Castle Gate, Belle Fourche, and future jobs they intended to pull off. In addition to drinking and swapping stories, they played poker, arm wrestled, even raced horses up and down the main street of Baggs.

Everyone seemed happy until some of the boys began shooting holes in Ryan's new mahogany bar. The saloon owner protested vigorously until Butch agreed to pay him a dollar for every bullet hole. When the boys ran out of ammunition, it was Ryan who placed a new box of bullets on the bar. When it was all over, Ryan had enough money in his pocket to move to Rawlins and open the biggest saloon in that railroad town.

Upon returning to the Roost the poker games began in ernest, almost every night, lasting until the sun came up.

Butch insisted the men in the game be unarmed. With all the gold in camp, the games were intense. Sometimes a single bet would go as high as $1,000 when a man had a particularly good hand, or if he was trying to follow up on a bluff and drive the rest of the players to fold. More than once, Butch and other players would disappear into the dark to get more gold from hidden caches.

The new arrival in camp, John Herring, was an enthusiastic poker player, though he never seemed to win or lose very much. He folded most of the time, conserving his stake. Butch wondered why a man who played so cautiously was always so eager to be in the next game. High stakes poker was not a game for timid souls. Butch guessed that Herring was waiting for an unbeatable hand that would win him a lot of money. Then he would leave.

No one guessed the real game Herring was up to until he showed his cards. One night when the betting seemed to be more vigorous than usual, with some of the pots containing upwards to two and three thousand dollars, Herring, after folding as usual, suddenly excused himself from the table to relieve his bladder. The game was being played around a plank table in Butch's tent. Seven men were receiving cards.

When Herring returned, he stepped inside the tent flap, waving a double-barreled shotgun. Almost before anyone realized what was happening he tossed a gunny sack onto the table and ordered the men to put all the money in it. The shotgun was cocked. Some of the players swore in protest, but they obeyed.

Butch was amused, realizing this was no impulsive act on the part of Herring. It all fit together--Herring's intense interest in the poker games, his conservative style, his cheerfulness when he lost. He had come to the outlaw camp with the intent of holding up a poker game, and now he was doing it.

"You can't do this, not now," Curry whined.

"Hurry up and fill the bag," Herring growled.

"But I haven't played my hand," Curry complained.

Chapter 26

"Everybody put their cards on the table," Herring said.

The men obeyed. Curry had the best hand with four jacks.

"Congratulations Curry. You win. Now fill the bag," Herring said. Curry grumbled, but obeyed. Reluctantly, he handed the bag to Herring.

"The first man to step outside the tent gets blasted," Herring said as he began to step outside. "If someone blows out the lamp the tent gets both barrels," he added. He seemed deadly serious. No one moved.

The best Butch could figure, Herring was getting away with nearly $8,000 in gold, an amount nearly equal to the Castle Gate holdup. No one dared step outside the tent until they heard the hoofbeats of Herring's departing horse.

With no moon it was too dark to follow the horse's trail. The chase would have to wait until daylight. The men were furious at having been robbed by a man they thought was a friend. Butch was still amused. He was impressed at Herring's imagination in thinking up such a plan, and his courage in pulling it off. The man had brains and balls. Too bad he couldn't be trusted.

Butch was further amused to see his men organizing a posse to chase Herring. It gave one a funny feeling to be on the other side of the fence, to be the robbed instead of the robber. Butch watched as the men by lantern light nailed shoes on horses, cleaned weapons, and packed supplies.

Curry and Killpatrick were emerging as leaders of the posse. Most of the money Herring had taken had been theirs. Butch had already lost everything he had brought to the poker game that night. Herring had nothing of his, so Butch decided not to ride with the posse when it departed at first light. Butch went back to bed.

The posse returned the next day without the gold. Herring's trail had been easy to pick up and follow, but just like Butch would have done in robbing a bank, the outlaw had stationed two relays of horses along his escape route. By the time the posse reached the second relay point they realized

Herring could be in Idaho before the posse reached Price. They finally admitted the clever outlaw had beaten them at their own game. The bandit had robbed the bandits and gotten away.

After the Herring episode the camp settled down for the winter. For the most part the men kept themselves amused with poker, horse racing, whiskey and women. Gradually the days became warmer, and the grass on the south side of the sandy hills began to turn green.

One afternoon a rider on a lathered horse arrived from Green River with the news Butch Cassidy had been killed by Joe Bush. Joe Walker had been killed in the same gun battle and both bodies were on display in front of the sheriff's office in Price.

"It's in all the newspapers," the man said. The outlaws who were gathered around his horse were not taking his news very seriously.

"Where did Butch get shot?" Butch asked, stepping out of his tent.

"Upper chest, just below the collarbone," the man said, not recognizing the outlaw leader.

"Can't feel anything," Butch said, rubbing his fingers across his upper chest, just below the collarbone. Everyone began to laugh, including the rider who by now realized to whom he had been talking.

The rider handed Butch a newspaper clipping describing how Butch Cassidy had been killed. The men gathered around while Butch read the news.

According to the written account, Butch and Joe Walker had severely beaten two cowboys near Sunnyside, a little community south of Price, then stole their victims' cattle and horses.

U.S. Deputy Marshall Joe Bush happened to be in Price when news of the beating and robbery reached town. He didn't waste any time putting together a posse.

After picking up the outlaws' trail, the posse followed them eastward to the head of Range Creek, then downstream until they reached the Green River. After crossing the river where it split into two channels just above the mouth of Range Creek, the posse followed the trail up the east side of the river to the Joe McPherson Ranch at the mouth of Florence Creek where they spent the night.

Before daylight the next morning Bush led his men upstream to Chandler Canyon where the posse turned east, winding its way to the top of the Book Cliffs, eventually coming upon the outlaw camp on the south edge of Moonwater Point overlooking Florence Canyon. Finding themselves surrounded by a posse, the outlaws rolled out of their blankets, guns blazing. But the pistols in the bedrolls were no match for the posse's Winchesters. Joe Walker, and the man the newspaper reported to be Butch Cassidy, were killed instantly.

The victorious Joe Bush lashed the dead men to their horses for the trip back to Price. The ride down Range Creek and up the Green River to the top of Moonwater Point had been so hard that Joe and his men decided to take a different route back to Price. They headed south along the top of the Book Cliffs, eventually dropping down to Thompson Springs where they caught the train back to Price. They made the journey from Moonwater Point to Thompson Springs, a distance of nearly 40 miles through some of the most rugged country in North America, in one day. They had to stop frequently to adjust the dead men, who were continually slipping to one side to the other on their horses. By the time the posse reached Thompson Springs, men and horses were so weary they could hardly stand.

When the train rolled into Price the next day the bodies were carried to the sheriff's office, nailed to eight foot, two-by-twelve boards, and leaned against the wall for everyone to see. Covered with trail dust and drilled with bullets, the bodies were not a pretty sight.

During the next two days, all the mothers in Price made sure their little boys saw the bodies, so the boys would grow up with unforgettable memories of what happened to rustlers and outlaws.

When Butch finished reading the clipping he said he wasn't about to miss his own funeral. He saddled his horse and headed for Price, five or six of his men tagging along.

When word reached Wyoming that Butch Cassidy's body was on display in Price, Douglas Preston and Mary Rhodes caught the first train to Utah. Mary was on the verge of shedding tears most of the way, finding little comfort in reassuring words from the lawyer.

They arrived in Price on the noon train from Salt Lake City and went straight to the sheriff's office where the bodies were on display.

Mary took Preston's arm in hers as they approached the group gathered in front of the porch where the mounted bodies were leaning unceremoniously against a wall. A deputy was standing on the wooden sidewalk next to the bodies.

The dead outlaws were not pretty. The eyes were covered with dust turned to mud. The faces were distorted in death, showing little resemblance to the living, breathing beings of a few days earlier. To add to the distortion, the bodies were beginning to bloat from the warm spring weather. They were beginning to smell too. The time had passed when they should have been buried under the ground.

The shirt on the one they called Butch Cassidy was unbuttoned at the neck allowing viewers to see the bullet hole below the collarbone.

Mary glanced at the body they called Butch, then looked away, fighting to control her emotions. She hadn't expected it to look so terrible, so dirty and ugly. She forced herself to take a second, more detached look. The emotion that had wrenched her heart during the train ride began to soften. This body was not the Butch Cassidy she knew and loved.

She still wasn't sure if the body belonged to another man, or if it was the shell formerly occupied by the warm, glowing, friendly, passionate spirit of the man she loved. But she knew how to find out, once and for all.

"Take his pants off," she said to Preston.

Chapter 26

Preston didn't move. He thought perhaps his ears were playing tricks on him. Mary wouldn't say something like that.

Getting no response from Preston, Mary let go of his arm and walked up to the deputy.

"Take his pants off," she said, her voice firm and confident, "if you would like a positive identification on whether or not this is Butch Cassidy."

"There seems to be some question as to whether or not Bush shot the real Cassidy," the deputy said, thoughtfully. "But how do I know you can offer a positive identification?"

"I am an attorney from Wyoming," Preston said. "And believe me, if anyone can positively identify the real Butch Cassidy this woman can."

"Pleased to oblige," the deputy said, grinning from ear to ear. Before anyone could offer any more thoughts on the subject, the deputy bent over, unbuttoned the trousers on the dead man and jerked them down. The boots had already been removed, allowing the deputy to remove the trousers.

Several mothers with sons quickly retreated against the protests of the curious boys. Mary walked up to the body and asked the deputy to lift the left leg. When he did so, she took a careful look at the calf muscle, then turned to Preston.

"George had a mole on the left calf. This poor man has no mark at all. This is not Butch Cassidy," she said.

The deputy didn't seem surprised with Mary's claim. He said a number of other people had come by claiming the body was not Butch Cassidy's, in spite of E. L. Carpenter's claim that the man was unquestionably the same one who had robbed the Pleasant Valley Coal Company. The deputy said Sheriff Ward from Evanston was expected on the next train. Ward had checked Cassidy into the Evanston jail a few years earlier and would be able to settle the matter once and for all. Mary and Preston caught the next train back to Wyoming, just missing a visitor they both would have been glad to see.

Later in the day, Jim Sprouse of Price, drove his canvas-topped wagon by the sheriff's office. A saddle horse was tied to the back of the wagon. Sprouse pulled the wagon

327

to a halt directly behind the group of people gathered to look at the outlaws' bodies. No one seemed to notice a slight movement as the canvas parted to allow Butch Cassidy a view of what was supposed to be his own remains. A minute later the wagon lumbered ahead. Now Butch knew what had become of John Herring, the poker thief. He had joined up with Joe Walker. The two had been killed by Joe Bush. Butch wondered what had happened to the poker winnings Herring had stolen.

At the edge of town, Butch hopped out of the wagon, brushed away the straw, thanked Jim for the ride, got on his horse and headed back to the Roost.

The next day Sheriff Ward arrived from Evanston, confirming what the young lady from Wyoming had claimed, that the body next to Joe Walker was not Butch Cassidy. Once it was determined Cassidy had not been killed, it didn't take long to identify the man as John Herring. No one was more disappointed than Joe Bush, unless it was E. L. Carpenter. There was no reward on John Herring's head.

The next piece of big news to reach the Roost, kept the boys laughing for a week. It concerned Gunplay Maxwell who had finally got his own gang together and went to Provo to rob Senator Reed Smoot's bank. One of the men who had ridden with Maxwell brought a firsthand account of what had happened back to the Roost.

The newly-organized Maxwell gang had set up camp in a grove of cottonwood trees at the mouth of Provo Canyon. As the outlaws studied the location of the bank and various escape routes, the whereabouts of this rough-looking group of men was soon common knowledge in the area. Not only were there houses and farms nearby where people noticed the strangers coming and going, but every day boys were venturing out from Provo and Orem to fish in the Provo River, and farmers were working on various irrigation projects in the area.

On the morning of the fourth day, when Maxwell thought he had everything figured out, a rider who identified himself as a deputy to Sheriff George Storrs rode into their camp carrying a letter for the leader. Maxwell was more than a little surprised when he realized the letter was from Senator Reed Smoot, owner of the Provo bank. In the note, Smoot said he was aware of the gang's interest in his bank and had shipped the greater part of the bank's deposits to Salt Lake City for safekeeping. There wasn't enough money left in the bank to make it a worthwhile target for even the most modest of bank robbers, especially now that the local sheriff was posting armed guards around the bank.

Maxwell was embarrassed to think his movements in and around Provo had been so closely observed. He counted his blessings. Instead of sending a warning to the outlaws, the bank could have set up an ambush for Maxwell's fledgling gang.

Figuring he had learned an important lesson, Maxwell decided the next time he tried to rob a bank he would be much more careful in disguising his scouting activities.

Leaving his gang at the mouth of Provo Canyon, Maxwell and one of his men, who went by the name of Porter, rode into Provo and rented a horse and buggy. They drove to Springville, a sleepy little town about five miles to the south. Maxwell figured no one in a dozy town like Springville would be suspicious of two men in a buggy. In fact, the town appeared so dead to him, Maxwell guessed it would be two or three days before most people realized their bank had been robbed. Maxwell and Porter spent the afternoon and evening scouting the bank and an escape route leading out of town to the south towards Spanish Fork, then to the east along the Mapleton bench to the mouth of Hobble Creek Canyon. Maxwell figured he could make his getaway to the head of Hobble Creek, across the Strawberry Valley to Vernal, then to Brown's Hole. That evening he sent word to the rest of his gang still camped in Provo Canyon, to bring the relay horses to the mouth of Hobble Creek Canyon. Maxwell and Porter planned to rob the Springville bank at 3 p.m. the next afternoon. That night Maxwell and Porter rented a room in a Springville hotel.

Maxwell's plan was simple. He and Porter would enter the bank at 3 p.m., scoop up the gold, drive their buggy to the mouth of Hobble Creek, get on the fresh horses, and disappear into the mountains before the sleepy little town realized what had happened. It seemed so easy, Maxwell wondered why more people didn't take up bank robbing.

Their simple little plan ran into its first snag the next morning while the two outlaws were eating breakfast in a Springville cafe. A constable from Provo entered the room, asking who belonged to the horse and buggy tied to the hitching post out front. Acting as nonchalant as possible, Maxwell acknowledged the buggy was his.

In a very matter-of-fact manner the constable explained the rental agreement for the buggy had expired the previous evening, and the liveryman had already filed a complaint with the constable's office.

"Are you going to arrest me?" Maxwell asked, dumbfounded.

"Heavens no," the constable said. "Just return the buggy before noon and the whole matter will be forgotten."

"I will, I will," Maxwell promised.

After the constable left, Maxwell and Porter did some quick figuring. They guessed the rest of their gang had received the message about robbing the Springville bank the previous evening, and would be riding to Hobble Creek while Maxwell and Porter were eating breakfast, arriving mid morning. To avoid further problems with the constable, Maxwell decided to move the robbery time up to 10 a.m. By the time the constable returned to look for the buggy the outlaws would he halfway to Strawberry Valley.

"But what if our relay horses aren't at the mouth of Hobble Creek?" Porter asked.

"They'll be there," Maxwell said.

"But what if a posse comes after us. Won't it be hard to outrun them in a buggy?" Porter asked.

"It's only a few miles to the relay horses at Hobble

Creek," Maxwell explained. "Besides you don't understand how these sleepy little Mormon towns work. After we take the money, the banker will run to the bishop and ask what to do. The bishop will run to the stake president who will have to find the boy who is supposed to ring the bell to call out the militia. When the people hear the bell they will go looking for the guns and ammunition, saddle their horses, and ride to the bank where the stake president will give a speech and the bishop will say a prayer. Have you ever heard of a Mormon bishop saying a prayer lasting less than 10 or 15 minutes? By the time all this happens we'll be in a Vernal saloon spending our gold."

At 10:05, Maxwell and Porter tied their buggy horse in front of the Springville bank.

"What will we put the money in?" Porter asked as they were getting out of the carriage.

"Banks have money sacks all over the place," Maxwell said, defensively, after a moment of thought. He didn't want Porter to think he hadn't made preparations for carrying the gold. He hadn't seen money sacks in a bank before, but he was sure they had such things, out of sight in the cage or the vault, perhaps.

As they entered the bank Maxwell congratulated himself on his timing. Except for some boys on bicycles, the streets were practically deserted, and there were no customers in the bank, only one clerk, a young man. The name plate in front of his window said "Al Packard."

Maxwell didn't waste any time walking up to the window and handing Packard a bank draft for $100, signed by C. H. Carter.

As Packard began to explain that C.H. Carter had no money on deposit, Maxwell and Porter drew their guns and ordered Packard to put up his hands. Maxwell leaped into the cage and began scooping up $20 gold pieces.

"Where are the money sacks?" Maxwell demanded.

"Little banks like this don't have money sacks," Packard said. Maxwell didn't notice as Packard stepped on a

331

button setting off an alarm in the H. T. Reynolds Hardware Store across the street. The alarm had just recently been installed, so when Mr. Reynolds heard it ring he figured someone in the bank was fiddling with the new alarm again. To make sure this was the case, and to get after Packard for sending false alarms, Reynolds picked up the telephone and rang the bank.

By this time Maxwell and Porter had removed red bandannas from around their necks and were busy tieing up $3,020 worth of gold coins in the bandannas. When the phone started ringing Maxwell told Packard not to answer it.

When Reynolds couldn't get anyone to answer his call, he decided to go over to the bank. His assistant, Joseph Storrs, was out back loading coal, and not available to watch the store. But Reynolds didn't figure he would be gone long enough for any harm to come to his store.

Just as Reynolds stepped out the front door he saw Maxwell and Porter climbing into their carriage with heavy red bundles in their hands. Reynolds wasn't sure the two men were outlaws until Maxwell whipped the buggy horse into a gallop.

"Bank robbers," Reynolds screamed before running back into his store and opening the glass door of a cabinet containing three rifles and several boxes of bullets. Grabbing the rifles and bullets he returned to the street. By this time Packard had emerged from the bank, and was sounding the alarm too.

Suddenly the sleepy little town was alive. Men seemed to be running everywhere. The number of boys on bicycles tripled.

A short distance down the street Reynolds saw a wagon hitched to a team. A boy was on the wagon seat holding the reins. Reynolds and five or six other men piled into the back of the wagon, shouting orders at the boy to head south after the robbers. Reynolds passed out the rifles and bullets as the boy whipped the team into a gallop.

No sooner had the wagon started moving than it was

joined by a dozen boys on bicycles. William Roylance, one of the first men in the street, had ordered the boys to ride down the streets calling for men to join the posse, but most of the boys decided it would be more exciting to join Reynolds and follow the outlaws.

From behind Reynolds' store, Joseph Storrs heard the commotion in the street. He removed the big black gloves he was using to handle the lumps of coal and hurried into the store. When he saw the glass door to the gun case was open, and the rifles gone, he knew there was trouble. He stepped into the street just in time to see the wagon, surrounded by boys on bicycles, disappearing in a cloud of dust down south main.

"Joseph, get a horse at the livery," someone shouted. It was Dr. Dunn, standing on the porch in front of the bank. He was holding a Winchester. "I'll give you my rifle as you ride by."

Joseph didn't waste any time running to the livery stable and borrowing a white horse he knew could outrun anything in Springville. Storrs was an excellent rider, having participated in plenty of bareback horse races. He didn't take the time to saddle the mare. He just slipped on a bridle, leaped upon her back and headed up the street. Dr. Dunn handed him the Winchester as he galloped by. The little mare didn't need any coaxing to extend her stride to a full gallop.

Before he had gone a mile, Storrs passed the posse in the wagon and the boys on the bicycles. Ahead of him he could see the outlaws had stopped to buy a horse from Thomas Snelson who said his horse wasn't for sale. They took the horse at gunpoint, and after throwing $46 on the ground to pay for the animal, hurried on their way, making a sharp left turn at the Barlow place at the edge of the Mapleton bench. Now the outlaws were headed east towards Hobble Creek Canyon.

Storrs was within a hundred rods now, and began to worry that he would be all by himself when he caught up with the outlaws. He raised his Winchester and fired in the

Cassidy

direction of the fleeing bandits.

The shot worried the outlaws sufficiently to cause Maxwell to leap from the carriage onto Snelson's horse. This lightened the load for the carriage horse, allowing it to travel faster. Maxwell showed no intention of leaving behind the carriage carrying his gold.

Storrs continued to close in on the bandits, his shots fired from the back of the galloping mare, getting closer and closer.

Upon reaching the mouth of the canyon, the bandits surprised Storrs by deserting their horse and carriage and scampering on foot up the steep sidehill overlooking the creek.

Maxwell hoped his relay horses and the rest of the men would be waiting for him at the mouth of the canyon. When he could see no sign of them, he decided to go up the steep sidehill on foot, figuring that by getting a better view of the canyon, he would be able to see his men and relay horses. What Maxwell didn't know was that the rest of his gang, figuring they didn't need to reach Hobble Creek until 3 p.m., had taken their time in breaking camp that morning, and were only halfway to Springville when Maxwell robbed the bank.

Seeing no sign of the gang or the relay horses, Maxwell and Porter eventually worked their way off the steep hillside into the thick brush bordering the stream. Storrs decided that rather than follow the two outlaws on foot it would be more prudent to wait for reinforcements. He didn't have long to wait. Within ten minutes he was joined by the posse in the wagon, a dozen boys on bicycles, and another dozen men on horseback.

While half the men followed the trail of the outlaws along the hillside, the rest, led by Joseph Allen, the Springville blacksmith, headed directly into the river bottom.

Those on the hill had no trouble following the outlaws' trail. In addition to boot tracks they found pieces of gold scattered on the ground. Folded bandannas were not a good way to carry over $3,000 in gold. It seemed for a short time the posse members were more engrossed in looking for gold

334

coins than for outlaws.

Eventually Allen's men in the bottoms discovered Porter hiding under some brush. When Allen ordered the outlaw to surrender, Porter responded by firing his gun. The bullet struck Allen in the leg, knocking him to the ground. Rolling over in pain, Allen brought his Winchester to the shoulder. He fired into the brush, killing Porter instantly.

While some of the men helped tend the wounded Allen, others continued the search for Maxwell, first finding his guns, then the grinning outlaw who gave up without a fight. He still had over $2,000 in gold in his bandanna. As they took him to town Maxwell said his big mistake was trying to make a getaway in a buggy.

Utah was offering a $500 reward for Maxwell's arrest for the trouble he was causing as a cattle rustler in the Price area. When it was realized Allen would lose his leg as a result of the bullet wound, the posse voted to give all the reward money to Allen.

All but $300 of the $3,020 taken from the bank was recovered by the posse, but over the next few weeks Springville merchants reported a large number of purchases by 12-year-old boys on bicycles with $20 gold pieces in their pockets. Maxwell was sentenced to 18 years in the state prison at Sugarhouse.

Cassidy

Chapter 27

It was obvious to Butch why Maxwell failed in his attempt to rob the Springville bank. While the outlaw succeeded in stealing the money and getting safely out of town, he had been unable to outdistance a makeshift posse of farmers and school boys. Robbing the bank from a horse and buggy was a clever disguise, and would have worked had the outlaws had saddle horses stationed at the edge of town. Having half the town of Springville after them in a matter of minutes wouldn't have mattered had the outlaws been mounted on fast horses. Even the speedy white mare Joseph Storrs had been riding couldn't have kept up with the bandits after the first relay change. No posse in the world could keep up with a bandit with one or two relays of fresh horses.

Of course, with the money wrapped up in red bandannas, most of it probably would have been spilled during the relay changes. Still, there was only $3,020 to lose, hardly enough to risk losing one's life and freedom over. There was no large industry and not very many large farms and ranches with payrolls in the Springville banking area, making it necessary for the bank to keep large quantities of cash on hand. Maxwell should have known that. Still, Maxwell would have succeeded if he had only taken the time to set up some relays of fresh, fast horses.

The problem associated with using relays of fresh horses after a holdup, as Butch saw it, was that in each holdup the bandit had to leave behind his best horses, forcing him to find and train new mounts before the next holdup. The most critical point in any getaway was that first minute after taking the money. First you had to get safely out of the bank. No telling when a bank employee would go for a hidden shotgun and start blasting away. The next critical point was getting mounted. Sometimes in the commotion, like at Castle Gate, horses became frightened and pulled away. Shooting, yelling, running, jingling sacks of gold, were all things that could frighten a horse and make it difficult to mount. The first horse in the getaway had to be the best trained, the calmest, and also the fastest--not an easy combination to find in horses.

The process of finding, training and conditioning fast, calm, dependable getaway horses was a never ending project for Butch and his men, a project that began anew after each holdup.

The hard part for Butch was that he got attached to the best behaved and fastest horses, the ones used for the first leg of the getaway, the ones always left behind. After what was sometimes months of training and conditioning, it was like deserting an old friend.

One evening as Butch was returning to Horseshoe Canyon after picking up two new horses in Richfield, he decided to ride over to a ranch house, hoping for a hot meal and a place to spend the night. He had gone to Richfield with the intent to buy half a dozen horses, but had found only two he liked. The fall sky was dark and threatening. Rain was likely. It would be nice to spend the night in a dry barn.

Butch had been to the ranch before. It was a small, modest place, running about 40 cows. It belonged to Fred Noyes and his wife. Butch didn't know the woman's name, only that everyone called her Mrs. Noyes. She was friendly, and a good cook. The Noyes were poor, honest people. Even though they didn't have money, they would not turn a man in for a reward. Butch knew he would be safe at their place.

Mrs. Noyes answered the door. She reminded Butch of his mother, a middle-aged woman accustomed to hard work. Her hands were red and calloused. She was not heavy, nor was she thin. Her brown hair, some of which was turning gray, was tied straight back in a bunn behind her head.

Upon recognizing Butch, she forced a smile. Butch wondered if something was wrong, or if the woman was just tired after a long day. He hesitated about asking her for something to eat, not wanting to add to her burdens.

He asked if Fred was home. She said her husband had gone to Salina to sell some cattle, that he should have returned several days ago. She didn't know why he had been gone so long.

As she talked, she looked like she was about to cry. The red around her eyes indicated she had been crying. If the Noyes had had children Butch would have guessed that maybe one of them had been injured or killed. But he couldn't ever remember seeing any children on the place. He couldn't imagine her being upset just because her husband was a few days late returning from a cattle selling trip.

"Looks like it's going to rain," Butch said, deciding not to ask about the food. "Could I put my horses in your corral and sleep in your barn tonight?"

"Of course," she said. "And after you've tended to your horses come back to the house. I'll rustle up a hot meal for you."

"That isn't necessary," Butch said. "I've got plenty of stuff in my saddle bags."

"My guests don't eat cold food in the barn," the woman said, proudly. "Put up your horses and come back to the house." Not giving Butch a chance to offer any further objections, she turned towards the stove. Butch headed to the

339

barn to take care of his horses.

Butch put his horses away, hid his saddlebags with his money under some hay, washed his hands and face in a watering trough, then returned to the house. When he entered the kitchen, Mrs. Noyes had a place set for him at the table, which was covered with a freshly ironed blue and white checkered tablecloth. There was a place setting for him, but not for her.

"Aren't you going to eat with me?" Butch asked. He expected her to say she had already eaten, but instead her only comment was that she was not hungry.

A minute later she placed a plate of fried pork and potatoes before Butch. On a little plate beside the big one were fresh radishes and green onions from the garden. She brought him some homemade bread with desert holly preserves, bottled cherries and hot coffee. The woman sat down across from Butch as he began to eat, sipping on her own cup of coffee.

Butch was hungry after a long day on the trail. Except for some small talk about the weather and crops, little was said while he wolfed down his food.

"Want to tell me what's bothering you?" Butch asked, when she returned to the stove to get him more potatoes and meat. She didn't say anything until she had returned with the food and sat back down on her chair.

"This little ranch is all we have in the world," she said, fighting back the tears. "We have no close relatives, not even children. We've worked 20 years building up this place. It doesn't make us a good living by some people's standards, but we have enough to eat."

Butch told her how much he was enjoying his meal. His comments were sincere. He waited for her to continue.

"Last year we went to a bank in Price and borrowed $500 to buy grain seed and more farm equipment. Hard frost and summer rains ruined the crop. We couldn't make our payment to the bank. Now we are losing our place." She burst into tears, burying her face in a dish towel.

Chapter 27

Butch's first thought was that maybe he and his men should rob the bank in Price.

"Won't the bank let you make a partial payment?" he asked.

"When we borrowed the money we thought we could pay it all back with income from the grain crop. The whole note was due six months ago. Fred's trying to sell some cattle so we can offer a partial payment tomorrow when the banker comes. The last time Fred went to Price the bank said they wouldn't take a partial payment, that the note was due in full. I don't know why. I think we are going to lose our place tomorrow. I know we will if Fred doesn't get back from Salina with some money." Raising the dish towel to her face, she began to cry again.

"You say the banker is coming tomorrow?" Butch asked.

"Sent us a note a few weeks ago. Said he would be here tomorrow about noon, either to collect the money or serve us with foreclosure papers. I just don't know what I will do if Fred isn't home by then."

"I know what you can do," Butch said, suddenly getting up from the table. The woman looked at him in surprise. Neither said anything as he disappeared out the door.

A minute later he returned with his saddle bags. Without a word he counted out 25 $20 gold pieces and stacked them neatly on the table.

"How much interest do you owe?" he asked.

"I don't know, maybe $40," she said, not sure what Butch was doing. He took two more $20 gold pieces out of his bags, and set these on the table.

"Now you can pay off the loan and the interest," Butch said, grinning.

"You're giving us that money?" she asked, hardly able to speak.

"It's yours," he said.

"We couldn't pay the bank back," she said. "What

341

makes you think we can pay you back?''

"You don't have to pay it back."

"We can't just let you give us your hard-earned money," she said.

"I wouldn't call it hard-earned money," Butch said. "A bank in South Dakota gave it to me, so I'm giving some of it to you. As for the interest, how about a hot meal and a dry place to sleep when I'm passing through?"

Mrs. Noyes suddenly got up from the table, hurried around to where Butch was sitting, and threw her arms around his neck. She kissed him on top of his head, on the cheek, and the top of his shoulder.

"What does this banker look like?" Butch asked, when she had returned to her chair.

"He has narrow shoulders, a belly that covers his saddle horn, and a squat red face that reminds me of a baboon I saw at the St. Louis Zoo when I was a little girl. He wears a tall, black hat, and usually is chewing on a big cigar. His name is Brown, Mr. Brown. He never told us his first name."

"How will he come?" Butch asked.

"He rides a big, brown mule with eyes like a grasshopper. He'll come down the Green River trail, the one you'll be leaving on, if you're going back to the Roost."

"If you want to meet him, just stick around," she said. "He'll be here at noon."

"I'd like to meet him, all right," Butch said. "May need some money sometime."

"Don't let him get his teeth into you too," she said.

Butch excused himself for the night, after reminding Mrs. Noyes to be sure and get a signed receipt and a release on the ranch when she gave Brown the money. She promised she would, thanking Butch again for his generosity.

The next morning when Mrs. Noyes went out to the barn to check on Butch, he and his horses were gone. The banker, Brown, showed up at noon, as he had promised in his note. He seemed more than a little surprised when Mrs. Noyes paid the note in full, plus the interest. Though she invited him inside the house, she did not offer him lunch or coffee. She didn't show him to the door until he had given her a receipt and a release document.

Later that afternoon, while riding along a deserted wash on the way back to Price, Brown met an armed bandit wearing a red bandanna over his face. When the banker said he didn't have any money, the doubting bandit searched the banker's pockets until he found the $500 plus interest the man had collected from Mrs. Noyes. When Brown protested, the bandit told him to shut up, that the money didn't belong to the Price bank in the first place, but to a bank in South Dakota.

Chapter 28

On February 15, 1898, the U.S. Battleship Maine was blown up in Havana Harbor. Americans began talking about war with Spain. Outlaws were Americans too, and nowhere was interest in shooting Spaniards higher than at Robbers' Roost, Brown's Hole and Hole-in-the-Wall. Interest soared even higher when news reached the outlaw hideouts that Congress had approved three regiments of volunteer cavalry, one headed by Colonel J. Torrey of Wyoming's Embar Ranch. This regiment was to be called the Torrey Rough Riders, and was to be given the job of driving the Spaniards out of Cuba.

When Torrey announced he was recruiting the best horsemen and marksmen in Wyoming, Montana, Colorado and Utah, the outlaws were ready to enlist, especially the young, impulsive ones. The more cool heads entertained a few lingering questions. Would they be arrested for their outlaw crimes when they tried to enlist? If not, what guarantees would they have that they would not be arrested when their enlistment was finished? The outlaws decided to hold a big rendezvous at Steamboat Springs to discuss the matter.

Butch was more enthusiastic about the meeting than anyone. Not only was he patriotic and eager to fight the Spaniards, but he saw in the Spanish American War an opportunity to put the outlaw life behind, to turn a new leaf, to settle down and live a normal life with a wife and children on a ranch. He wanted that.

He had seen enough to know the outlaw life would eventually come to an end. It was just a matter of time until he was killed or sent to prison again, if something like the war with Spain didn't offer a way out.

There had been a strong cattle market for over a year, with fat cattle bringing as much as $35 a head. Rustling activities had increased dramatically. The Wyoming Cattlemen's Association was holding meetings to increase their efforts to rid the state of rustlers. There were rumors the association had hired a ruthless scout from the Apache wars in Arizona and New Mexico, Tom Horn, to wage war on Wyoming rustlers.

Recent killings of a boy named Willie Strang and Valentine Hoy in Brown's Hole had unified ranchers there in an effort to rid that country of outlaws. A letter to a Denver newspaper from J. S. Hoy, brother of one of the murdered men, called for a $1,000 reward to be placed on the head of all Brown's Hole outlaws. Some of the boys drove off Hoy's cows a week after the letter was printed.

In the meantime in Utah, Governor Heber Wells was offering $500 rewards for every two-bit outlaw in the Roost, including Silver Tip, Blue John, Jack Moore, Pete Neilson, Charley Lee, Tom Dilly and even Mrs. Jack Moore. With the average salary of a Utah sheriff only $500 a year, Butch knew the rewards would bring droves of lawmen and bounty hunters to the Roost. In a matter of weeks, the Roost would no longer be a sanctuary for outlaws. It was time to leave.

Butch led his men to Steamboat Springs with the hope The Wild Bunch could win clemency by killing Spaniards in

Cuba. Other men trailed in from Hole-in-the-Wall, more from Brown's Hole. Some of the younger rustlers were eager to hurry up and enlist while there were still openings, trusting the government would give clemency to those willing to fight for their country. The more seasoned outlaws, and those with more serious crimes to their credit, generally thought it would be best to work out a deal with the government before turning themselves over for service.

Since the governors of the western states were planning to meet in Salt Lake City in mid-March to solve the outlaw problem, Butch agreed to establish contact with the governors during their meeting, and offer them a solution. Butch and his Wild Bunch would abandon the outlaw trail and go to Cuba to fight the Spaniards, if the charges against them were dropped, allowing them to return to normal living after the war with Spain was won.

Butch established contact with his old acquaintance, Sheriff John Ward of Evanston, who was going to accompany Governor Richards of Wyoming to the Salt Lake City meeting of governors. Butch explained his proposal to Ward. The sheriff couldn't say whether or not the governors would be interested in any such arrangement. Butch and Ward agreed to meet again, after the governors had had a chance to discuss the offer. They agreed to meet on a given night at Soldier Summit at the head of Spanish Fork Canyon.

Soldier Summit was an isolated, out-of-the-way spot where the trains stopped to refuel and check their brakes. There was no town within 20 miles. At 8,000 feet elevation there was snow on the ground, or at least north sloping drifts, eight to ten months of the year.

On the designated day, Ward arrived by train, waited until evening, then wandered off into the darkness along the ridge to the north, until he came to the clearing Butch had described to him. He sat on a log and waited.

The sheriff didn't have to wait long. Butch stepped out of the nearby woods. He knew he was taking a chance, a wanted man agreeing to meet a sheriff. But he also thought

Chapter 28

Ward could be trusted. Butch felt there was too much at stake here not to take a chance.

Ward stood up to greet Butch. The two men shook hands and exchanged small talk, about men and times they had known in the past. Finally they got around to talking about the governors' response to Butch's proposal.

Ward said governors Robert Smith from Montana and Frank Steunenberg of Idaho did not come to the meeting, and therefore were not represented in the decision. But Governor Richards of Wyoming, Heber Wells of Utah and Alva Adams of Colorado were not willing to make any deals with The Wild Bunch. They said there had been too many cattle stolen, too many banks robbed, too many people hurt for any pardons to be granted. Richards suggested it would be a sign of weakness and political suicide to pardon the outlaws. The governors did not intend to enter into any deal that would make them look weak, defeated, or afraid.

On the other hand, the governors wanted Butch to know they would not tolerate continued rustling and robbing. From this moment on they were determined to increase efforts and use every means available to them to catch and punish outlaws, and would continue to increase their efforts until the outlaws were forced to stop their criminal activity.

"I was looking forward to fighting the Spaniards," Butch said in a tired voice. "I was looking forward to leaving the outlaw life. But I guess they won't let me."

"That's the way it looks," Ward said. "What will you do now?"

"I suppose there's a lot of banks that need robbing," Butch grinned. "Might as well get all I can before they get me. But don't worry, the Evanston bank is safe, especially with Bob Calverly around."

"Bob won't be around long," Ward said. "He's joining the Rough Riders under Teddy Roosevelt. He'll be fighting the Spanish for you. He's back at the train stop, waiting for me. We came together. He'd like to see you."

"Is this some kind of trap?" Butch asked.

"If I were setting a trap," Ward said, "I'd have told you the governors wanted to meet with you to work out the details. This is no trap."

Butch believed Ward. Together they walked back to the train stop where Ward called to Calverly to step outside the caretaker's shack. Butch knew Calverly well. It was Calverly who had arrested Butch in Star Valley and brought him back to Evanston to stand trial for stealing Otto Franc's horses, the trial that resulted in Butch going to prison. Normally a man would hate the man who made the arrest that resulted in a prison sentence, but not so with Bob Calverly. Butch respected the man's courage, competence, and straight shooting. In arresting Butch, Calverly had only been doing his job. Of all the lawmen looking for Butch, Calverly was the only one ever able to catch the leader of The Wild Bunch.

Calverly was both surprised and glad to see Butch. It had been a long time since the two had talked. Both remembered well the ride from Star Valley to the Evanston jail after the arrest. They talked about it. They laughed about the exchange of notes when Butch was threatening to rob the Evanston bank. They passed around a bottle Bob had brought with him from the shack.

"Sorry the govs wouldn't go for your deal," Calverly said. "Wonder if the Spanish will ever know how close they came to having to fight The Wild Bunch in Cuba."

"Hell, if I'd known you was joining Teddy's Rough Riders, I wouldn't have offered the deal to the governors in the first place," Butch said.

"Why's that?" Bob asked.

"With you off to Cuba and not on my trail any longer, I won't worry half as much about getting caught," Butch laughed. The two officers laughed with him. But underneath their laughter was sadness, knowing Butch was trapped in his outlaw life, and sooner or later would be caught or killed.

Chapter 29

With the Roost and Brown's Hole no longer safe, Butch headed back to Wyoming. At least for the time being, The Wild Bunch was dispersed. Butch needed time to think about what he wanted to do now.

Winter storms had begun to close some of the mountain passes. After visiting Mary in Lander, Butch decided to head for a cabin on Green Mountain at the head of Willow Creek Valley above the Jesse Johnson Ranch. The cabin was located in a mixed stand of aspen and lodge pole pine overlooking a series of beaver ponds, one above the other, like stair steps leading to the valley below. He knew the south-facing slopes above the beaver ponds would provide plenty of feed for his horse, even in winter.

Butch looked forward to having a few months alone in a remote place where he wouldn't have to worry about the law, where he would have plenty of time to think, even read a few books.

After the Belle Fourche holdup he and Elzy had buried

some of their gold in the Wind River country at the head of Muskrat Creek. Before heading to Green Mountain, Butch decided to get some of the gold.

By the time he reached the mouth of Muskrat Creek Butch's face had been numbed by a cold north wind. White snowflakes were beginning to fall from the gray winter sky. There were four Shoshone lodges in the open meadow next to the creek.

One of the lodges belonged to Lone Bear whom Butch had known for years. Sometimes the two men traded horses, always with the unspoken agreement that neither asked questions about brands and origins.

Bracing themselves against the cold wind the two looked over four or five animals, Butch eventually buying a buckskin gelding. After Butch paid for the animal, Lone Bear warned him not to let the horse out to graze without a tether rope. The animal had strong homing instincts and if given its freedom, would return to the ranch near Lander where it was raised.

Lone Bear urged Butch to come inside until the storm had spent its fury. Butch declined, realizing there was enough daylight remaining to make it to the buried gold before dark. He did, however, let the chief give him a leather pouch full of jerked venison.

The wind continued to blow and the snow was still falling as Butch hurried along the well worn trail leading to the head of Muskrat Creek. He came upon a sheep camp, where he could see smoke blowing from a rusty chimney poking through a hole in the top of a white canvas tent. He was tempted to stop for a cup of coffee, but decided against it, not wanting to get caught short of his destination before nightfall.

He planned to spend the night in the same camp where he and Elzy had stayed when they had buried the gold. It was in a thick patch of tall sagebrush which would provide adequate protection from the wind.

Several miles past the sheep camp, as he came around

Chapter 29

a sharp bend in the trail, where the creek had cut away the side of the mountain, Butch spotted a lone rider approaching from upstream. The stranger was only about 50 yards away, but apparently hadn't noticed that Butch was ahead of him in the trail. The rider's hat was pulled down to protect his face from the bitter wind. Butch pulled his horse to a stop, cautiously placing his hand on the butt of his revolver.

The rider might not have noticed Butch at all, had his horse not shied to one side at the sight of Butch and his horse. The stranger looked up, and upon seeing another man, started talking. Though the rider was only about 20 feet away, Butch couldn't understand a word. At first he thought the howling wind made the stranger's words hard to understand, but as the man grew closer, Butch realized the words were slurred and poorly articulated, not from strong drink, but from the cold. The man was half frozen.

Continuing to look at the approaching rider, Butch realized he was little more than a boy, maybe 17 or 18 years old. Butch removed his hand from the revolver and urged his horse forward.

As the two horses reached each other and stopped, the young man somehow communicated to Butch that he was lost, and feared he was freezing to death. Realizing there was no time for idle conversation, Butch told the boy to follow him up the trail. He would lead him to a camp where they could build a fire and thaw out. The stranger nodded for Butch to lead the way.

Butch hoped for the boy's sake the camp in the tall sagebrush wasn't very far. He had been there only once, and guessed they could be there in 10 or 15 minutes.

Butch urged his horse into a trot. At first the boy's horse didn't want to turn around and go back, but soon resolved itself to following Butch's horses. After what seemed an eternity they reached the tall sagebrush. It was almost dark.

Butch swung down from his horse, at the same time asking the boy to help him gather wood for a fire. The boy's only response was to slump forward and fall to the ground.

After tying up the horses, Butch dragged the boy behind a bank that had been cut away by the stream during high water. With the boy out of the wind, Butch went to work gathering sage for a fire. He also retrieved a coffee can he had left under a log. Soon he had a blazing fire going, and snow melting in the can.

Butch left the saddles on the horses in an effort to protect the animals as much as possible from the freezing wind.

When the coffee can was about half full of melted snow water, and beginning to steam and bubble, Butch tossed in a handful of ground coffee. By the time the coffee began to boil, Butch had retrieved Lone Bear's venison jerky and some old bread from his saddle bag.

The boy was shivering badly. There was no feeling in his shaking hands. When Butch tried to hand him the can of steaming coffee, the boy was unable to hold onto it. Butch held the can to the boy's lips as the lad gulped down the hot liquid. By now it was dark. Steam was hissing from their damp clothes.

When the coffee was gone, both of them sat with their backs against the dirt bank, looking into the fire, munching contentedly on old bread and dried venison.

"What's your name?" Butch asked.

"Buck Ashworth," the boy responded.

Butch felt the hair on his neck raise at the mention of the Ashworth name. It was Richard Ashworth, who with Otto Franc, had filed the horse stealing charges that resulted in Butch going to prison. At the time Butch had vowed to get even with Ashworth, but had never done anything. He knew one other Ashworth, Bill, the owner of the Fremont Saloon in Rock Springs.

"Are you related to Richard or Bill Ashworth?" Butch asked, cautiously.

"Yes, Richard is my father," the boy responded, obviously pleased the stranger, who had saved his life, knew his father.

352

Chapter 29

"What's your name?" the boy asked.

"George. George Parker." Butch wasn't about to tell the boy who he really was.

The boy said he had left Haily that morning, headed for Wind River. He said he had traveled that way before, but must have lost the trail in the storm.

"You sure did get lost," Butch said. "Do you have any idea where you are?"

"No."

"You're at the head of Muskrat Creek, at least 25 miles from the trail to Wind River."

The boy didn't have a blanket with him, so Butch covered both of them with his own. It wasn't a big enough blanket to keep them warm, so they spent the night huddled in front of the fire, occasionally replenishing it with fuel, catching a brief nap from time to time. The wind continued to howl. Nothing more was said about the boy's relation to Richard Ashworth. It didn't occur to Butch that he now had an opportunity to get even with the man who had helped send him to prison.

When morning arrived Butch brewed up another can of coffee which they gulped down as they ate the last of the bread. The wind was still blowing when they got on their gaunt horses and headed down the trail. Butch told the boy he would lead him out of the mountains to the wagon road so he would not get lost again. The cold wind was still blowing, but the snow had stopped.

Several times during the morning ride Butch asked himself why he was going out of his way to help the nephew of an enemy who was responsible for bringing so much misery into his life. The only answer he had was that his feelings about the uncle had nothing to do with the boy. Butch had saved Buck from certain freezing the night before. He wasn't about to let the boy get in a similar fix again today. The weather showed no signs of softening.

As they followed Muskrat Creek towards the valley, not only did the wind seem to be getting stronger, but colder too.

More snow began to fall. Butch thought it might be better to stop and make camp, rather than try to travel in the storm. Each time he asked Buck if he wanted to stop, the boy said it would be all right to go a little further. Butch knew the boy's hands and feet were numb, and knew at a certain point frostbite would set in. Butch admired the boy's courage, and willingness to suffer, but didn't want to push him too far.

Just when Butch figured they could go no further he saw the same sheep camp he had seen the day before. As on the previous day, smoke was coming from the rusty chimney poking through the top of the tent.

Today, instead of passing quietly by, Butch reined his horse straight for the tent, the boy following close behind. The wind was blowing harder than ever.

"Anybody home?" Butch called, as they dismounted and tied their horses to a cottonwood tree. They hurried towards the inviting tent, and were almost there when one of the flaps was suddenly pushed back revealing the sour face of a thin weasel of a man. From the gray handlebar mustache, receding hairline, and weathered face, Butch guessed the man to be in his late fifties or sixties.

"What do you want?" the stranger asked, coldly. He did not invite Butch and Buck into the warm tent.

"Had to spend the night on the mountain. Need some hot food. Our horses need some hay and grain. We'll gladly pay," Butch explained, trying hard to maintain his usual friendly countenance. He thought his offer to pay for food would help the old man feel more welcome towards them.

"No food to spare, so be on with you."

Butch couldn't believe what he was hearing. Nobody in this country turned a man away in this kind of weather. Most people he knew would be offended if a stranger tried to pay for a meal offered in time of need.

"We're pretty cold," Butch said, his voice still friendly. "Mind if we come in and warm up a bit?"

"I said be on with you," the old man repeated.

Butch had always figured that somewhere down the

354

Chapter 29

outlaw trail he would have to kill a man. He didn't know when, but sooner or later that day would come. Why not now? For a second he felt like the man in front of him deserved killing, even more than Richard Ashworth.

"Maybe we better move on," Buck said, seeming to sense the growing animosity between the two older men.

"Maybe so," Butch said, taking a step back. The old man glared at him, sensing victory over the two strangers.

"Suppose I could go another couple of hours with nothing to eat," Butch continued. "Suppose my toes would just hurt if I thawed them out." He paused.

Butch noticed a bucket of oats beside the opening to the tent. He looked directly at the grain. He reached down and picked up the bucket.

"Our horses haven't had anything to eat in two days," Butch said, still looking into the bucket. He handed it to Buck with orders to feed the horses.

"Put them oats down," the old man growled, stepping from behind the tent flap for the first time. He held a 30-30 Winchester in his hand. He pushed down the lever to pump a cartridge into the barrel, but before he could pull the lever home, Butch's .44 was pushing against his ribs.

Butch jerked the rifle out of the hands of the startled sheepherder. Holding the rifle by the barrel, Butch swung it once, twice, three times around his head in a wide, sweeping arc, then let go. The rifle disappeared out of sight 50 or 60 feet behind the tent.

Butch returned the .44 to its holster. Smiling again, he told Buck to give all the oats to the horses, then find some hay for them. He told the boy to give them all they could eat.

"I'll have the law after you for this," the old man whined. Butch wanted to tell the oldtimer the law was already after him, and that it had been after him for a considerable length of time without success. Instead he asked if there were any more guns around.

"No," the man responded.

"Then stoke up the fire. I'm getting something to eat

355

and damn quick. And if you try anything funny, something will happen to you damn quick." Butch pushed the herder ahead of him into the tent. As soon as the little stove was shaking and rattling with a roaring blaze, Butch told the man to lay down on one of the beds while he fixed the food.

Butch threw a couple of wedges of bacon into a black fry pan which he placed on the fire. After getting a pot of coffee started, he threw four thick red lamb steaks into the now-greasy skillet. The old timer said nothing more, but maintained a surly look on his face.

Butch found some potatoes and biscuits left over from breakfast. When he turned the steaks he put the potatoes and biscuits on top of the meat so everything would be hot at once. When Buck came in the tent, announcing the horses were taken care of, Butch told him to stretch out on the other bed and get some rest.

The herder couldn't hold his tongue any longer.

"You're going to be mighty sorry for this," he threatened.

"What's your name?" Butch asked.

"J. P. McDougal. This is my sheep camp, and I order you to get out of here."

"Oh, so that's how you feel about it," Butch said. "You're damned lucky to get off this easy. It would serve you right if I took everything you have. Where in hell are you from? You haven't been in this country long or you would know better than to turn a stranger out in the cold with nothing to eat. You're a damn fool, and the only sheepherder I ever met who wouldn't be insulted if someone offered to pay for a meal. Now shut up while we enjoy our supper." Butch didn't invite the herder to join them at the little table.

Nothing more was said as Butch and Buck wolfed down the partly rare meat with potatoes and biscuits. Each gulped down a half a quart of boiling coffee flavored with two or three tablespoons of brown sugar. While they were eating, Butch put a pan of snow on the stove to melt for dishwater. For dessert they divided a can of peaches.

Chapter 29

No sooner had they finished than another man showed up at the door of the tent. It was soon apparent the new arrival was McDougal's hired man who had been out with the sheep when Butch and Buck arrived. The new man offered a friendly greeting to Butch and the boy, apparently not paying any attention to McDougal's scowling face.

Buck traded places with Butch, and began working on the dishes while the herder, who called himself Cal, put the pan back on the stove to cook himself some supper. He assumed all the rest had eaten, so he just cooked for himself. McDougal went without supper.

When Buck had finished cleaning up, Butch checked outside to see how the weather was for traveling. Not only was the wind still blowing, but snow had begun to fall again.

"Looks like the storm is worse," he said. "Guess we'll have to spend the night." As he spoke he looked at McDougal and smiled.

A little while later McDougal finally got up and fixed himself something to eat--the last lamb steak and some warmed over potatoes. At first Cal tried to be friendly with the strangers, until he noticed the animosity his boss had towards Butch. From then on Cal remained mostly silent. Butch and Buck did all the talking.

"Do we dare go to sleep with McDougal waiting to get the drop on us?" Buck asked, when it was time to go to bed. "And where are we all going to sleep?" he added. "There are only two beds."

Butch told Buck to get in bed with Cal. As soon as that was accomplished, Butch slipped his boots off and crawled under the blankets in the other bed. He ordered McDougal to turn out the lantern.

"Where am I supposed to sleep?" McDougal whined.

"Guess you could curl up on the ground by the stove," Butch responded, trying to suppress a yawn.

"I'm not sleeping on the ground," McDougal said.

"You're welcome to crawl in bed with me," Butch said.

357

"I'd freeze to death before I'd share a bed with the likes of you."

"Suite yourself," Butch said. "Now turn the lamp out."

An hour later, a shivering McDougal crawled under the blanket next to Butch.

"Just remember, my revolver is cocked," Butch said before he closed his eyes and went back to sleep. McDougal didn't sleep very much, and he was very careful to hold perfectly still, all night.

The next morning the sky was blue, and the wind had stopped. While Buck fed the horses more oats and hay, Butch cooked a hearty breakfast of bacon, eggs, and hot cakes. He cooked enough for everyone, including McDougal.

After a good night's sleep Butch was in good spirits. When breakfast was finished, Butch tossed a $10 gold piece at McDougal's feet. Buck was outside feeding the horses.

"Never had to pay for my food in a sheep camp before," Butch said. "But I wouldn't want the meanest man in Wyoming saying Butch Cassidy stole his food."

Neither McDougal or the man named Cal said anything in response, but both of their jaws dropped as they realized they had just spent the night with the most notorious outlaw in the West. Butch turned and walked out of the tent.

A few hours later, at the mouth of Muskrat Creek, Butch revealed his real identity to Buck. The boy didn't seem very surprised. He just grinned at the outlaw who had saved his life.

"Tell your uncle when you see him," Butch said, "that I'm not sore at him anymore for sending me to prison. As I think about it, I think I really did steal some of his horses."

"I'll tell him," Buck said. "I'll also tell him how you saved my life. Thanks."

Butch nodded to the boy, pulled his horse around, and headed back up Muskrat Creek. This time he hoped there wouldn't be any distractions to keep him from finding the gold, buying supplies and heading over to Green Mountain.

Chapter 29

This time he intended to make a wide circle around the sheep camp. He had no desire to spend any more time in the company of the meanest man in Wyoming.

Chapter 30

It was December. Butch was enjoying his stay alone on Green Mountain, with occasional trips to Lander to see Mary. One day he received a message from Elzy and Harvey inviting him to join them after Christmas in Santa Fe. It seemed like a good idea to leave the country where every law officer and bounty hunter was looking for him. It would be good to see some new country where he wasn't wanted by the law. Perhaps in New Mexico he would find it easier to relax and enjoy life. At least he would be leaving the Wyoming winter behind.

Butch decided to ride the new buckskin gelding he had purchased from Lone Bear. He was heading towards Lander to say goodby to Mary when the storm hit.

When he left Green Mountain the weather had been unseasonably warm, but cloudy. The second day of his journey it began to rain, a drizzle at first, but eventually turning to a downpour. Hoping to make Lander before nightfall he didn't seek shelter. For Wyoming in December, it was an unusually warm rain, so he didn't worry about getting wet.

During the latter part of the afternoon the wind suddenly changed, bearing down hard from the north, bringing with it much colder air. The rain changed to sleet, then to snow. The wind blew harder, and colder. Butch urged his horse into a trot. His teeth began to chatter from the cold.

It was soon dark. Butch's frozen clothes were hard like rawhide, but he had no choice but to push on, thinking he would soon be in Lander. When he reached the top of the last hill, thinking he would see the lights of the little frontier town ahead of him, there were none.

Earlier the clouds had obscured the tops of the mountains. Apparently he had made a false calculation as to where he was. Now it was too dark to see ten feet in any direction. Because the lights were not where they should have been, he knew he was lost.

The matches in his coat pocket were wet and frozen. His feet were numb, already partly frozen, and his fingers, still hurting from the cold, would soon be numb too.

It occurred to Butch that he might be on his last ride. The most notorious bank robber and horse thief in the country was about to freeze to death in a blizzard--unless he found shelter and warmth very soon. The problem was that he didn't know which way to go. He couldn't see. If he picked the wrong direction, he might ride for miles, or he might ride in circles all night, or at least until he froze to death.

For the first time in his life Butch began to feel panic. Unless he became very smart, or very lucky, very fast, he would soon be dead.

Butch remembered something Lone Bear had told him when he had purchased the buckskin, that the animal had a keen homing instinct, that if it ever got loose, it would head straight home to the ranch where it was raised. Lone Bear had said the horse had been raised somewhere in the Lander area. Butch couldn't remember anything more.

"I don't know where you were raised old boy," he said to the horse, "but take me there as fast as you can." Butch tied a knot in the reins and dropped them on the animal's neck. Folding his arms and hands across his chest, he nudged the horse with his heels to hurry it along.

In the blackness of the storm Butch had no idea whether the animal was going north, south, east or west. He knew only that it moved with confidence, not seeming to hesitate as to which way it should go.

Butch was surprised when he began to feel drowsy. The pain in his hands and feet began to subside. Then he could hear singing, beautiful music. It reminded him of when he was a boy, and his mother used to play the pump organ with the children standing around singing together.

For a minute he thought he was home again, with everything just fine. He wasn't cold anymore. He felt happier than he had felt in a long time.

Then suddenly he was in agony again. The pain in his hands and feet was excruciating. His chest hurt too, like big nails were being pounded into his heart whenever he tried to breathe. For a minute he felt hot. Then he was cold again, his teeth chattering.

He didn't notice when the horse stopped in front of a gate. He didn't hear the dog barking, or the voice calling to him from a partly opened cabin door. He didn't remember being pulled from the horse and dragged inside.

The first thing he remembered was a man, a woman and two small children standing around him, rubbing his frozen extremities with snow which they fetched a handful at a time out of a wooden tub. To get at one of his frozen feet the boot had to be cut away with a knife.

Butch groaned in pain. Every inch of his body hurt. Because of the continuing pain in his chest, the man and woman concluded he had pneumonia. After the woman and children went to bed the man stayed up all night putting hot aspen branches over Butch's chest and under his arms. Butch had never heard of such a cure for pneumonia, but with time the pain in his chest began to subside. Breathing became easier.

Chapter 30

In the dim light of the lantern he could see that he was not in a cabin, but a shack made of rough sawn boards. The walls were not very tight when it came to keeping out the cold north wind. The lamp flickered from the movement of air through the shack. The wood stove had to be full all the time to keep the room from getting cold. If the fire went out he was certain the temperature would drop below freezing very quickly.

The man said his name was Billy Hancock. He was a young, strong man with a thick neck and broad shoulders. He didn't talk much. Butch didn't feel much up to talking either, so the two got along just fine. As the night passed, Butch wondered why this Hancock man was trying so hard to save a half-frozen stranger.

Butch was even more surprised when Hancock said he had raised and trained the buckskin gelding Butch had been riding, but that it had been stolen from him the previous spring. Butch wondered why the man had brought him out of the cold, probably thinking Butch was the man who had stolen his horse.

"Bought him from an Indian," Butch said, "and that's the absolute truth."

"I believe you," Hancock said, a simple sincerity in his voice. He believed the frozen stranger.

Looking around the inside of the dimly lighted shack left no doubt in Butch's mind about how poor the Hancocks were. The cupboards were nothing more than upright apple boxes. The dishes consisted of tin plates and cups. There was no glass in the windows, just oil cloth. The children slept in an old wagon box resting on blocks of wood. The door had no doorknob, just a wire latch.

Butch's observations were confirmed when Mrs. Hancock got up to fix breakfast. The fare consisted of fried corncakes and salt pork, nothing more, not even coffee. There was no butter, syrup or honey for the corncakes. When Butch asked for a glass of milk to wash down his food, all she could give him was cold water.

363

Mr. Hancock said the cow had died a month earlier, and that as soon as he could find time to go mavericking he planned to get another. He had worked in the mines for a while, and was trying to homestead some land to get a start as a farmer.

Mrs. Hancock was a thin, tired woman. Butch guessed she was younger than she looked. The frontier life, along with bearing children, had taken a hard toll on her. Watching the Hancocks in their seemingly hopeless poverty made Butch feel grateful to be an outlaw.

As Mr. Hancock had been eager to care for Butch during the night, Mrs. Hancock was eager to please at breakfast. Her first name was Myrtle. She was a pale woman, her skin as white as beef tallow, except her hands which were red from hard work. An army blanket was draped around her frail shoulders to shield her against the cold air pushing through the thin walls. She apologized for not having coffee, sugar, syrup and butter.

Every time Butch finished a corncake, or a piece of pork, she was quick to place another on his plate. When he told them his name was George Parker they appeared to believe him.

While the adults were eating, the children finally woke up and crawled out of their wagon box. The boy, Jimmy, was six or seven, and the girl, Loretta, appeared to be about five. Both of them were friendly like their parents, and didn't waste any time crowding around Butch.

"Do you believe in Santa Claus?" Jimmy asked.

Butch began to laugh. The children had caught him by surprise. He was so used to handling questions about bandits, outlaws and Butch Cassidy, that he hadn't been ready for anything like this. Of course, it was December, just before Christmas, time for children to start thinking about Santa. He remembered his own childhood in Circle Valley and how excited the children had been before Christmas.

"Sure, I believe in Santa," Butch said. He leaned forward, placing one of the children on each knee.

364

Chapter 30

"Do you want me to let you in on a little secret?" he asked. Their eyes were wide with excitement, their heads bobbing up and down.

"I've been to the North Pole," Butch whispered.

"You have not," Jimmy challenged.

"You saw how frozen I was when your Pa brought me in last night," Butch explained. "Traveling from the North Pole does that to a man."

"Did you see Santa?" Loretta asked, her blue eyes bright with excitement.

"Yes, I did." Butch said. "And I saw his workshop and all the toys he is making."

"Did he get our letter?" Jimmy asked. "We mailed it from Lander about two weeks ago." Butch looked at the parents. Both looked surprised.

"There were so many letters," Butch said, "I'm not sure if I saw yours, or not. What did it say?"

"We asked for new boots for Ma so she wouldn't have to borrow Pa's when she goes to the outhouse," Loretta said.

"I asked for a new saddle, and a doll for Loretta," Jimmy said.

"I asked for an orange," Loretta added. "I've never tasted one before. Have you?"

Butch looked at the parents. Neither one of them looked very happy. It was obvious they were too poor to buy the things the children were asking for.

"Santa said he got more letters than usual this year," Butch said, his voice very serious. "He was worried he might not have enough presents to give all the boys and girls everything they ask for."

"We never get what we ask for," Jimmy said. "Last year we didn't get anything we wanted. That's why I wrote to Santa himself this year."

Billy Hancock didn't want to hear any more. He put on his coat and went outside to do the chores. Myrtle started cleaning up the breakfast dishes. Butch was surprised that even after a filling breakfast he still felt very weak. The cold had drained his strength. He needed time to recover.

He spent the remainder of the day in the shack. Some of the time he slept. When the children were beside him he told them about his own boyhood, and his brothers and sisters. Such talk made him homesick, but the children were so eager to hear what he had to say that he continued. Myrtle seemed to enjoy the children finding someone else to pester with their incessant chatter and questions. Butch liked the children.

Butch spent another day with the Hancocks before announcing it was time for him to leave. When they refused to accept payment for taking care of him, he insisted they take two $20 gold pieces for the stolen horse. Billy agreed to do that. He said he would use it to buy seed for the spring planting. He thanked God Butch had come along with money. Now there would be a summer crop. If the weather cooperated they would make it through another year.

Two days later, after borrowing another horse and a wagon at a nearby ranch, Butch drove up to the hitching post behind the general store in Lander. He had entered town through a back alley, not wanting to drive down the main street. With so many warrants out for his arrest, the fewer people who saw him the better, especially in Lander where so many knew what he looked like.

He knew the store owner, Gus Sweeny, wouldn't turn him in. Butch was a frequent customer at the store, always paying with gold. Sweeny wasn't about to ruin a relationship with one of his best customers. It didn't matter that the man was wanted by the law.

The first thing Butch picked out was a sweater for Myrtle. Then a pair of boots. He asked the merchant to wrap them up. Then he picked out a saddle for Jimmy, a doll for Loretta, and a new coat for Billy. He asked Sweeney to throw in a ten pound bag of sugar, some butter, honey, coffee, a blue and white checkered tablecloth, and four big oranges from California. After paying Sweeny and having the merchant wrap the doll too, Butch threw everything in the back of the wagon and slipped quietly out of town, heading

Chapter 30

straight for the Hancock place.

Butch didn't think anyone had seen him enter or leave Lander, but just before reaching the turnoff to the Hancock's farm he noticed two men riding parallel to him on a nearby ridge. As he watched them, not only did they seem to be watching him too, but they were pacing their horses in order to remain parallel with him.

Butch's first thought was to stop the wagon, unhitch and saddle the buckskin, and head for the woods as fast as the horse could run. It occurred to him that might be a foolish thing to do in the event the two riders didn't mean any harm.

He decided to do nothing, at least not until he was absolutely sure the riders were following him. When he reached the turnoff to the Hancock place, he left the main road, acting like he hadn't noticed the two riders.

For a minute they disappeared behind the ridge, Butch hoping he would never see them again. But as he approached the shack he saw the riders again, this time much closer. They came over the top of a hill directly above him and were riding straight for the shack too. There was no way he could outrun them in the wagon, and there was not enough time to saddle the buckskin. He didn't want to shoot it out with the two strangers.

Even though Butch had been an outlaw for some time and had stolen countless numbers of cattle and horses, and robbed banks and trains, he still had not killed a man, and had no stomach for it. It was one thing to take money from the rich and powerful, but shedding a man's blood was something he wanted no part of. Years on the outlaw trail had not hardened him that much.

Destiny had seemed to bring him to the Hancocks. He wondered why. It didn't seem right that they save his life just so he could go back to prison. Perhaps his life had been spared so he could provide a happy Christmas for the Hancocks.

At any rate he intended to finish what he had set out to do. He pulled the team to a halt in front of the shack.

367

Cassidy

Myrtle was the first one out the door, the old army blanket wrapped around her shoulders.

"Merry Christmas," Butch said, tossing her the sweater and boots, still wrapped in clean white paper. Soon the children were scampering from the house, and Billy was walking up from the barn. Butch handed down all the presents.

"You'll never believe this," Butch explained, "but I ran into Santa up the road a bit. And boy was he mad."

"Why?" Loretta asked, concern on her little face.

"The runner on his sleigh was broken," Butch explained, a serious expression on his face. He noticed the two men he had seen on the hill were directly in front of the team. He ignored them.

"He said the broken runner was going to make him late getting around to all the boys and girls on Christmas Eve," Butch continued, "so he asked me to help him out by running some things over to the Hancocks. Told him I'd be glad to do it."

By this time Loretta had torn the wrapping off the doll and was hugging it tightly. Jimmy had thrown his new saddle over the hitching rail and was climbing aboard.

"You didn't need to do all this," Billy said as Butch handed him the sugar, oranges and other food stuffs.

"You saved my life," Butch said, simply.

"You shouldn't have," Myrtle said.

"My way of saying thanks," Butch said, pulling the team to the right so they could pull the wagon alongside the two strangers. He noticed one of them was wearing a badge on his coat.

"Sorry, Santa didn't give me anything for you fellers," Butch said in a happy voice, pulling the horses to a halt.

"Maybe he did," the marshall said, his voice deep and strong. "All I want for Christmas is to catch an outlaw. I have a warrant for the arrest of Butch Cassidy. Far as I can tell, there's about $1,500 on his head right now. That kind of money would come in real handy at Christmas time."

368

Chapter 30

Butch was surprised the marshall hadn't reached for his gun. The man beside him hadn't either. It seemed they were stalling for time, but why? Were reinforcements on the way? Did they think two against one was not good enough odds, if the one was Butch Cassidy? Butch guessed he could probably beat them both, if he went for his gun first. He had checked the cylinder before going into town for the presents. He knew his gun was ready to fire. Even if he wasn't fast enough to get both of them, it would be better to die than to return to prison.

"Should have brought a bigger posse, if it's Butch Cassidy you're after," Butch said, stalling for time, still not sure what he was going to do.

"Marshall, would you like to come in for a cup of coffee," Myrtle called from the doorway to the shack.

"Thank you, in a minute," the marshall said, not taking his eyes off Butch.

Billy walked up to the marshall. Loretta was in her father's arms, holding tightly to her new doll.

"Marshall," Billy said, "I think I know where Cassidy's camp is. I'll take you there after we have a cup of coffee." It was obvious to Butch that Billy and the marshall already knew each other. What Butch didn't know was if Billy knew whom he had really saved from the cold.

"Do you know where Cassidy's camp is?" the marshall asked, still looking at Butch.

"I sure do," Butch said. "Right where Billy intends to take you. But I can't go with you. If I don't get this wagon home by dark, there's a farmer up the road who'll swear out a warrant for my arrest."

Butch decided to take a chance. He tapped the reins on the horses' backs. They started forward, pulling the wagon in a wide circle. At first, he had thought the lawmen were afraid to attempt an arrest. Now he knew differently. After seeing what he had done for the Hancocks, they didn't want to arrest him, at least not at Christmas time.

"Hope you get your man," Butch called back to the

369

marshall as his team trotted back towards the main road.

Butch felt happier than he had felt in a long time, realizing the gifts he had bought for the Hancocks were nothing compared to the gift he had received from the two lawmen. He hoped they had a happy Christmas too.

"Me too," the officer responded.

"Coffee's ready," Myrtle called from the shack.

Chapter 31

There were too many deputy sheriffs and marshalls in Santa Fe to suit Butch--too many wanted posters, too many people who might recognize him, Elzy or Harvey. After a few days they wandered south through the Rio Grande Valley, not sure where they were going; they only knew they were moving away from Colorado, Utah and Wyoming.

Eventually they found themselves in Silver City, a small mining town southwest of Albuquerque, near the Arizona border. Butch felt like he was a long way from his old haunts, and about as safe as he could be. There was no reason for the authorities to look for him here. But even Silver City had a marshall, a jail and telegraph office. Butch decided to make it even harder for the authorities to find him by finding work on one of the outlying ranches where he felt he could literally disappear.

Asking around Silver City for possible employment opportunities on ranches, Butch was directed to Colonel William French, an Irishman who was running the WS Outfit

371

for an absentee Englishman named Wilson. The WS was the largest ranch in the area with headquarters near the little town of Alma, about a day's ride to the northwest near the San Francisco Mountains.

As Butch was preparing to head up to Alma, he learned Colonel French had come to Silver City for supplies, and was in the Carson Saloon.

By the time Butch found French, the Irishman was polishing off his fourth glass of whiskey, and was soundly cursing the ranching business in New Mexico, loud enough for everyone in the saloon to hear.

"Understand you might be looking for some new hands," Butch said, edging up to the Irishman.

"Are you good with numbers," the Irishman asked, without looking away from his glass. Usually ranchers looking for hands wanted to know how good a man was with a rope and a horse. The question about numbers caught Butch by surprise.

His first thought was to tell the rancher he could count $30,000 in stolen gold and divide it into fractions faster than any man alive, but decided against a reckless answer like that.

"Got a college education in figuring and numbers," Butch said.

"Where did you get your degree?" French asked, finally looking up from his glass at the blue-eyed cowboy. Butch was smiling, exposing a row of white teeth.

"College of horse and cattle trading," Butch said. "Learned a lot every time I got burned."

"Since you're so smart," French said. "See if you can figure this out."

"Shoot."

"I got 1,100 brood cows with 50 or 60 bulls. How come I only have 200 to 300 yearlings to take to market at Fort Worth every winter?"

"You got problems," Butch said.

"The bulls don't seem to have lost interest in breeding the cows, and we've shot or poisoned almost all the wolves and lions. That leaves the hired hands, the Mormons, or the Holomans responsible for my lost cattle."

"Didn't think the Mormons were this far south," Butch said.

"Mormons everywhere," the Irishman said. "Want to run the whole country. One of them, Brother Coats, named our little town, Alma, after one of the prophets in their Book of Mormon, and the rest of us can't change it."

"Who are the Holomans?" Butch asked, changing the subject.

"Neighbors," French said. "Run five of six hundred cows, but always seem to have six or seven hundred yearlings to run to market."

"Sounds like they are the thieves, not the Mormons or your hired hands."

"Except the hands never catch the Holomons running off cattle," French said, gulping down the last of the whiskey in his glass.

"That kind of problem's easy to fix," Butch said.

"How's that?" French asked.

"Hire me and my two friends." Butch pointed out Elzy and Harvey to the rancher. "The petty larceny crowd will disappear. I guarantee it."

"What's your name?" French asked.

"Jim Lowe," Butch said, without hesitating. Elzy and Harvey walked up to French and introduced themselves as William McGinnis and Tom Capeheart.

"I'm tempted to hire you men," French said.

"If you got any horses that need breaking, Elzy--I mean Bill--is the best hand with horses you'll probably ever see," Butch boasted. "We'll work for free the first day just to show you we're top hands with stock."

"Sounds like you men ought to go to work for the WS," French said.

"Before you hire me," Butch cautioned the rancher, "There's something in my past you ought to know."

Elzy and Harvey were amazed at Butch's comment.

373

Surely he wasn't going to tell French they were bank robbers.

"Let me guess," French said, good naturedly. "You killed the last rancher you worked for, ran off his cattle and raped his wife."

Butch let the suspense with his companions build before responding.

"I'm a Mormon, born and raised with the Mormons in southern Utah," Butch said.

Elzy and Harvey were obviously relieved at Butch's confession. French was surprised, but undaunted in his willingness to hire the three men.

Two days later, during one of the infrequent rain storms that passed over the area, Butch, Harvey and Elzy arrived at the WS Ranch. They were leading a single pack horse, carrying their belongings.

In order to get out of the rain, French didn't waste any time showing his new men to the bunk house. They had to wade through a big puddle to get to the front steps. As they entered, they saw four men at a round table, playing poker. There was a fire in the wood stove in one corner.

The poker game didn't look very exciting to Butch, there being little piles of pennies, nickels and dimes around the table. This was obviously cowboy poker, not outlaw poker.

Without bothering with introductions, French showed the new men which bunks they would be using.

"Wait a minute," one of the men at the table said, when he saw Harvey throw his bedroll on a bunk. "No greaser is sleeping in my bunk."

"That's not your bunk, not any more," French said. "All of you are fired as of right now."

"Better apologize to my friend," Butch said, his voice calm, but firm. Harvey was the toughest man Butch had ever met. He had a body of steel, but his feelings were easily hurt. He never forgot an insult, and those who crossed him usually lived to regret it. He feared no one, and unlike Butch, he didn't mind killing those he perceived as enemies. Normally a loner, Harvey had taken an unusual liking to Butch, and Butch was the only man alive who had any degree of control over Harvey.

"I don't apologize to greasers," the cowboy said.

"He's not a Mexican," Elzy explained, hoping to keep the lid on a situation that was rapidly getting very dangerous. "He's part Indian."

Harvey was standing by the bunk looking at the stranger, not about to say anything. When he spoke it would be with his Colt .44.

"Injuns is lower than greasers. I don't apologize to either," the cowboy said.

Butch was surprised when Harvey bent over and began rolling up the cowboy's bedroll, keeping a careful eye on the cowboy through the corner of his eye.

"You ain't going to be needing this where you're going," Harvey said, when he finished. Picking up the bedroll in both hands, Harvey tossed it through the open doorway into the big puddle at the bottom of the steps. Butch and Elzy knew Harvey was trying to get the cowboy to go for his gun so Harvey could kill him in self-defense.

But the cowboy had no intention of pulling a gun on Harvey. He was four inches taller and 30 pounds heavier than the man who had thrown his bedroll into the puddle, and figured he could whip Harvey with his bare hands. The cowboy rolled out of his chair and charged--but came to a grinding halt when he realized Harvey's cocked pistol was pointed at his chest. Looking into Harvey's cold, hard, unblinking eyes, the cowboy's resolve melted.

Harvey backed his victim over to the open door.

"Don't start shooting," Butch warned. "In this little bunk house, you'll break everybody's eardrums." He didn't want Harvey to kill the man.

Harvey had fully intended to shoot the cowboy, but Butch's argument made him hesitate.

Elzy, who had been standing by the door, and also realizing it was not in the best interests of the outlaws to kill this stupid cowboy, saw an opportunity to change the situation. He dropped to his knees behind the startled cowboy. This was a que for Harvey to step forward and shove his cocked gun in the cowboy's chest. As he did so the man instinctively stepped back, away from the pistol, falling backwards over Elzy, onto the porch, rolling down the steps into the puddle next to his soggy bedroll.

Harvey turned towards the other three men, still at the table. "You heard Mr. French," Harvey hissed. "You're all fired. You've got 30 seconds to grab your bedrolls and get out of here."

The men hurried to their bunks and began gathering their things. While several of them complained, it was obvious the desire to fight was gone. They were on the run, their tails between their legs.

"Hold it," Butch said, as the men were about to go out the door. "Now the three of us are working for Mr. French, we're going to become very attached to every cow and horse on this place. Better not be any rustling, or there's going to be hell to pay. Understand?" The three men nodded, then hurried down the steps, across the puddle, and to the barn to get their horses.

"Anybody for poker?" Butch asked, walking over to the table and sitting down.

During the coming weeks, word spread throughout the area that French had hired three Panhandle gunfighters. The rustling of WS cattle stopped.

French's concerns that he had hired gunfighters instead of cowboys were quickly put to rest. As soon as the rain stopped, Elzy went to work breaking horses while Butch and Harvey took care of the cattle.

In a matter of days they had a herd ready to trail to the Fort Worth cattle market. When it was time to start the drive, friends of the three new men showed up, ready to hire on. Still going by the name of Jim Lowe, Butch was the undisputed leader. The men were well-behaved by cowboy standards.

Chapter 31

When the cattle drive was over, and Butch brought home the statement and check from the cattle market, French could hardly believe that during a 300-mile cattle drive not a single animal had been lost. Actually, a few had been lost, but Butch's men had brought along a running iron, and had little trouble picking up replacement cattle along the way.

French couldn't have been more pleased with Jim Lowe and the new hands. For the first time the WS cattle operation was running smoothly, without interference from rustlers, though two of the men who were fired went immediately to work for the neighboring Holomans, and were seen on several occasions scouting WS herds. The branding, castrating, and doctoring was accomplished punctually without problems. The horses were broke, shod and ready when needed. The fences and sheds were in good repair.

While the new men were well armed, they were also well-behaved. When any of them went to town to visit a saloon or attend a dance, there were never problems. Jim Lowe had a lot of friends who were constantly coming and going. There was always plenty of help for whatever job needed doing, even though there was a lot of turnover among the help. It seemed Lowe's men were constantly coming up with urgent business that made it necessary for them to leave for a while, but others always showed up to take their places.

One afternoon while Elzy was in Alma picking up some supplies, he ran into two more Mormon boys from west central Utah who had gone astray. Their names were Tom and Sam Ketchum. Tom used the alias, Black Jack. After leaving their Snake Valley ranch west of Milford, Utah they had wandered south into Arizona. What started out as mavericking soon turned to outright rustling. Then they graduated to robbing stores, post offices and were now hiding out at a local ranch after a spectacular train robbery.

The Ketchums recognized Elzy first. They had seen his face on a wanted poster and knew all about The Wild Bunch. After a few drinks, Elzy agreed to take Tom and Sam out to the WS to meet the notorious Butch Cassidy.

At first Butch wasn't very pleased with Elzy bringing strangers out to meet him. He certainly didn't need to recruit any more followers. The fewer people who knew about the WS hideout, the better. Still, it was fun to meet two boys from Utah with backgrounds similar to his own. They talked until late into the night.

"Ought to do a train sometime," Black Jack said. "More fun than banks, a lot safer too."

"How's that?" Butch asked.

"Banks are in towns. Lots of people around, including sheriffs, deputies and other people with guns. Look what happened to the McCartys in Delta." He was referring to Tom and Bill McCarty, and Bill's son, Fred, trying to rob the Farmers and Merchants Bank in Delta, Colorado, just before Butch went to prison in Wyoming.

When one of the bank employees refused to cooperate with the outlaws, Fred fired a warning shot into the bank ceiling, which had the desired effect on the bank employee, but also alerted the local townspeople who grabbed their guns and surrounded the bank. While trying to escape Bill and Fred were gunned down by hardware merchant, Ray Simpson. Tom was the only one who escaped.

"You can pick the spot where you want to hit a train," Black Jack continued. "I always pick a nice, out-of-the way place where there are no people."

"How do you get the train stopped?" Butch asked.

"Three ways," Black Jack said. He was speaking with authority and experience. Butch knew the man had robbed at least one train, maybe two or three. "First and easiest way is to have one or two of your men buy a ticket at the last stop and be riding on the train. As they near the place where the rest of the men are waiting with horses and dynamite, they crawl up into the engine, hold a gun to the engineer's head, and turn off the steam."

"The second way is to just hop on the train while it is going slow near the top of a steep climb, but it's risky stopping on a hill. Things can get rolling away from you if

378

you're not careful.''

"The third way is to put something across the tracks to get the train to stop, like a log, a flock of sheep. Next time we thought we would get a wagon and write 'School Bus' on the side of it and stop it on the tracks. That'd stop'm for sure.''

All the time Black Jack was talking, Butch's mind was churning. He was thinking of several remote spots in Wyoming that he thought might be perfect for holding up a train.

"What's the dynamite for?" Butch asked.

"The money, gold and other valuables are carried in the express car which is usually locked, sometimes from the inside by a guard who feels pretty safe as long as the door is shut. You can open any door with a stick of dynamite. Then there's a safe in the express car. Dynamite opens safes too. Then if you don't want a posse on your tail, you blast the tracks in front of the train, so it can't just run to the next town to notify the authorities.

"When you hit a bank the local sheriff knows about it in minutes at most," Black Jack continued. "When you hit a train, it might be a whole day before the closest sheriff knows about it. By then you're a hundred miles away.''

That settled it. Butch decided it was time to rob a train.

"How do you know which trains are carrying the money, and which ones are not?" Butch asked.

"Don't know," Black Jack said. "Guess that's part of the excitement. Never know how much will be in the safe. But I'll tell you this much. I never seen an empty safe in an express car. Sometimes there's so much gold being shipped, an express car will have two or three safes.''

It didn't take Butch long to decide where to pull off his first train robbery. During his travels he had frequently followed railroad tracks. He remembered a remote stretch of track in Wyoming between Rock Creek Station and Medicine Bow which he thought would be perfect for a holdup. There was plenty of rough, rugged country for a getaway, either north to the Hole-in-the-Wall country or south into Colorado. Furthermore, he knew exactly how he would stop the train.

With the spring sun beginning to melt the snow in the mountains, the rivers would be high with runoff water. The engineers would approach each river or stream crossing with caution, wondering if there might have been a washout since the last train. Butch or one of his men would stand at one of the river crossings in the middle of the night waving a red lantern. The train would have to stop.

Butch did not discuss what he was thinking with the Ketchum brothers. It wasn't that he didn't trust them. It was just that he had plenty of good men already and there was no sense in taking chances with newcomers. The only thing he and his men didn't have experience with was dynamite. Blowing open express cars and safes was new to him and his gang. They would have to experiment, perhaps make a few mistakes.

At 2 a.m. on the morning of June 2, 1899, Butch and George Curry were standing on the Union Pacific track between Wilcox and LeRoy, Wyoming, waiting for the Overland Flyer coming west from Rock Creek Station. They were standing in front of a trestle or bridge crossing a small tributary to the North Platte River. All the rivers in the area were swollen with brown run-off water. The sky was covered with heavy, black, clouds blocking the light from the moon and stars.

Butch was holding a kerosine lantern with red glass in it. When they heard the approaching train, George struck a wooden match and lit the lantern. They pulled their bandannas over their faces.

Elzy, Harvey, Sundance and Bill Carver were waiting about a mile further west, on the other side of the gully. Standing between the two tracks, Butch began waving the lantern, the distress signal, indicating problems on the tracks ahead.

Going slower than normal because of the uphill climb, and having seen the lantern a good half a mile away, the train had plenty of time to stop before reaching the trestle.

In the darkness, the engineer couldn't see the trestle or the outlaws, only the swinging red lantern. He couldn't ignore such a signal, especially when all the streams were running high, increasing the chances of bridge or trestle washouts.

When the train had come to a complete halt, the conductor, a man named Storey, walked ahead to see what the problem was.

Butch had agreed ahead of time to let George do the talking, even though the tough outlaw wasn't known for his ability with words or his tactfulness.

"Better do exactly as we say or the whole damn train will get blowed off the tracks," were George's first words to the startled conductor, who did an immediate about face and headed back to the train, Butch and George close on his heels.

The express, baggage, and mail cars were behind the engine, with passenger cars following. The lights had been turned out to let the passengers sleep.

After forcing the conductor at gunpoint to disconnect the passenger cars from the mail car. Butch and George climbed into the engine, getting the drop on the engineer and fireman. The engineer hesitated when Butch ordered him to move the engine across the trestle. George promptly slapped the engineer on the side of the head with his pistol barrel. When the man continued to hesitate, George cocked back the hammer on his pistol.

"Don't want any killing here," Butch said, reaching out and pushing the pistol barrel to one side. "Please get this train moving."

Rubbing the side of his head where he had been struck with the pistol, the engineer looked first at Butch, then at George. Somehow he seemed to know that Butch was all that was standing between him the George's gun. The engineer finally decided to do as he was told. He reached out and pulled the handle that diverted a burst of steam into the drive cylinders. The train began to move forward.

When the train had crossed the trestle and stopped,

George jumped to the ground and ran back up the track to light three sticks of dynamite he and Butch had planted between two of the large timbers holding up the trestle. The train moved ahead as soon as Curry was back aboard. The explosion from the trestle was loud, but no one went back to see how much damage was done. Butch had never used dynamite before, and was just guessing on how much to use.

About a mile up the track the engineer was ordered to stop the train a second time. Harvey, Elzy, Sundance, and Carver were waiting. At their feet were two heavy sacks of dynamite. The getaway horses were tied in the nearby trees. The robbery was going as planned.

Converging upon the train, the outlaws began banging on the express car, ordering the guard stationed inside to open the door. His response was to turn out the light, lock the door even tighter and inform the outlaws he had a shotgun and intended to blow away the first outlaw to attempt entry into his car.

"We'll fix him," Sundance said, dragging one of the sacks of dynamite up to the car and shoving it underneath.

"Do we need that much?" Butch asked as Sundance began attaching a fuse to one of the red sticks.

"Hell, I don't know," Sundance said. "The man's got a shotgun. Want to be sure to knock it out of his hand."

"Let's start with one stick on the edge of the door," Butch suggested. "If that doesn't do the job, we'll use a little more the second time." Reluctantly, Sundance pulled the sack of dynamite from under the car.

In the meantime the engineer and fireman walked back to the express car to try and persuade the guard to open up.

"Open the door, Woodcock," the engineer shouted. "Or they'll blow up the whole train. No use getting hurt."

Woodcock refused. He said he had taken an oath to guard the contents of the car, and that's exactly what he intended to do.

Butch nodded to Sundance to light the fuse to the stick of dynamite resting on the sill of the door. Butch didn't intend

382

to stand around half the night arguing with this Woodcock, not when he had two gunny sacks of dynamite at his command.

Everyone hurried to get out of the way, and when the dynamite finally exploded, Butch was sure glad he had stopped Sundance from lighting the whole sack. There was a flash of blinding light and a deafening explosion which shook the ground. When the outlaws approached the train, there was no longer a door on the express car. When they called to Woodcock, he did not respond.

When Butch placed the lantern inside the car his first thought was that they had blown poor Woodcock to bits. Blood was splattered on the walls and ceiling of the car. Closer inspection, however, revealed the red ooze wasn't Woodcock's blood, but the remains of a shipment of fresh raspberries that had been stacked by the door. Woodcock was on the floor by the safe, unconscious, but not bleeding.

Butch threw some water on the guard's face, ordering him to get up and open the combination lock on the safe. Woodcock began to stir, mumbling some incoherent gibberish about his determination to protect the money in the safe. Repeated efforts to get him to unlock the safe failed. Butch couldn't be sure if Woodcock had really forgotten the combination, a result of the explosion and being knocked out, or if the guard was faking his forgetfulness.

"Get the dynamite," Butch yelled to Sundance, hoping the threat of more explosions might jog Woodcock's memory. It didn't.

Butch offered no objections when Sundance piled half a dozen sticks of dynamite on the safe. He agreed with Sundance that opening the safe would be much harder than opening the express car. When everyone had moved a safe distance from the express car, Sundance lit the fuse.

The explosion was deafening. The ground moved. Tree limbs rattled against each other. As the cheering outlaws raced up to the car, the air was filled with floating pieces of paper-- unsigned bank notes, thousands of them. The safe no longer had a top on it.

The outlaws spent the next ten minutes gathering up the bank notes and some gold coins from the bottom of the safe. As they were gathering up the last of the notes, one of the men asked Butch what he intended to do with the unsigned notes.

"Sign'm and spend'm," Butch replied.

As Butch was getting on his horse, it was beginning to rain. He noticed Sundance dragging the two bags of unused dynamite towards the engine.

"What are you doing?" Butch asked.

"Want to see how high this old engine will blow," Sundance said as he began to shove the bags between two of the big wheels.

"Forget it," Butch said. "Let's get out of here. Blowing up the engine isn't part of the plan." He was concerned that Sundance was more engrossed in setting off dynamite than pulling off a successful robbery. The rain was falling hard.

"If we don't blow it up," Sundance argued, "what's to stop the engineer from running into Medicine Bow and bringing back a posse?"

Sundance's argument made sense. While Butch didn't like the idea of senselessly destroying a perfectly good steam engine, the thought of delaying pursuit by a posse another six to ten hours made a lot of sense. He told Sundance to go ahead and get the fuse ready while he and the rest of the men rode up the tracks to get out of the way. He told Sundance to make the fuse plenty long, then to catch up with them as soon as it was burning.

Butch and the men put a good half a mile between them and the engine before stopping to wait for Sundance. They didn't expect to wait more than a few minutes for the explosion, but they found themselves waiting a good half an hour. The dynamite didn't go off. They began to wonder if something had happened to Sundance. Perhaps the engineer or Woodcock had got the drop on him. Butch thought about

Chapter 31

sending several of the men back to look for Sundance, but with a couple of gunny sacks full of dynamite under the engine he hesitated. The rain continued to fall. Minutes seemed like hours.

Finally Sundance came stumbling up the tracks, cursing his bad luck. Water had soaked his matches. In the pouring rain he had been unable to light the fuse. It was too late to go back and try again. It was time to get away with the loot. Elzy, Bill and Sundance headed south, back to New Mexico. Butch, George and Harvey headed north, hoping to disappear into the Hole-in-the-Wall country, ride over the Big Horn Mountains then back to the Wind River Mountains. With heavy rains to wash away tracks, the outlaws anticipated an easy getaway.

As night turned to day the rain continued. Though the outlaws were soaked and cold, there was solace in knowing their tracks were washing away. About mid afternoon the following day, Butch and his two companions reached the outskirts of Casper. During the holdup they had worn bandannas to cover their faces, so they thought if they split up they would not raise suspicion passing through town. Even though they could use some supplies, the reason they were entering Casper was to cross the bridge on the north end of town. The North Platte River was swollen with run-off waters from the snow melt and the recent rains, making fording the river on horseback too dangerous, if not impossible. Butch thought the main bridge in Casper, with lots of people going back and forth, would be the safest place to make the crossing.

As they rode through town they did not ride together, but kept each other in sight. With the town peaceful and quiet, Butch decided to go into a saloon and see what news he could pick up on the robbery. He went in first, followed a few minutes later by Harvey and George. They did not drink together.

When he had been sipping on his drink for a few minutes, Butch asked the bartender if anything exciting had been going on in Casper.

"You haven't heard about the holdup?" the bartender asked.

"Been out on the range for a couple of weeks. Was it the bank?"

"No, the Overland Flyer, at Wilcox, just out of Rock Creek Station. They blew the timbers out from under the trestle, blasted the door off the express car and the top off the safe, and if the rain hadn't got their matches wet they'd have set off 50 pounds of dynamite under the engine. Dynamite fools, them outlaws."

"Has a posse gone after them?" Butch asked, shoving his glass towards the bartender for a refill.

"Three posses after them. One from Casper, one from Medicine Bow, and another from Dana. Over a hundred men out looking for them outlaws right now. A special train carrying bloodhounds, railroad detectives and sheriffs should be rolling in from Omaha any minute. The Cattlemen's Association is sending in stock detective Joe LeFors, greatest man hunter since Porter Rockwell. The Union Pacific has already offered a $1,000 reward for each of the robbers. Biggest man hunt in the history of Wyoming."

"Who are the outlaws?" Butch asked.

"They think one was a Hole-in-the-Wall rustler known as George Curry. Not sure on the others," the bartender explained.

"What does this Curry look like?" Butch asked, making sure his voice was loud enough for George, who was at the other end of the bar, to hear.

"Hell if I know, but here comes somebody who will know, Sheriff Josiah Hazen of Converse County. He and Oscar Hiestand of Natrona County are in charge of the search.

Butch turned slowly towards the door and watched the sheriff enter. Then he looked at Curry and Logan, hoping to convey through his eyes the message that they ought to remain calm and nonchalant, while maintaining readiness for anything that might happen.

386

Chapter 31

"Sheriff, how would I recognize this Curry fellow if I saw him?" the bartender asked the sheriff, a middle-aged fellow with too much paunch hanging over his belt buckle.

"Part Injun," the sheriff responded. "Looks like someone hit him in the face with an iron skillet. Not much of a nose. Some call him Flat Nose. Quick temper, mean. Wanted to kill the engineer but the other outlaw stopped him."

"Thought there were six," the bartender said.

"Just two stopped the train," the sheriff explained. "The rest joined them further up the track, after they had uncoupled the passenger cars and blown up the trestle."

"The posses having any luck?" Butch asked.

"Rain's washed out most of the trail, but we think three of them is headed this way," the sheriff said. "They'll need to cross the Platte. Looking for some men to guard the bridges."

"The name's Jim Lowe," Butch said, reaching out to shake the sheriff's hand. "Glad to help out until you can get some regular guards. I could ride over to the town bridge right now, if you like." Butch wanted to ask more questions about the robbery, but didn't want to risk seeming too curious.

"Your services are appreciated," the sheriff said. "Now if I can get one more man to go with you, the Casper bridge will be covered tonight."

"My name's Tom Capeheart," Harvey said, walking up to the sheriff. "Overheard your conversation. I could take a shift at the bridge tonight." A few minutes later Butch and Harvey were riding towards the Casper bridge to guard it for Sheriff Hazen. Curry was following about 50 yards behind. Even with the sheriff's description, neither the bartender or the sheriff had paid any attention to George.

On the way to the bridge, Butch stopped at a dry goods store to get more ammunition. With so many posses running about, he thought it might be wise for each man to carry several hundred rounds.

387

As he was standing at the counter waiting for the clerk to get his bullets, he noticed a poster advertising smokeless gunpowder which was supposed to provide more thrust than conventional powder. Butch had heard of the new powder before, but had never tried it. When the clerk finally came over to wait on him, Butch bought all the smokeless .44 caliber ammunition on the shelf, several hundred rounds. As he left the store the rain was beginning to fall again.

While Butch and Harvey stayed at the bridge to watch for outlaws, George went ahead to a deserted cabin on Casper Creek about six miles northwest of town. Butch and Harvey agreed to meet him there later.

About midnight, when they figured Sheriff Hazen was in bed, Butch and Harvey, in pouring rain, abandoned their post and hurried to the cabin where George had a pan of warm grub waiting for them on the stove. They didn't go to bed until they had spread wet bank notes all over the cabin to dry. After the robbery, Butch had divided the money in what seemed like two equal parts. He had brought one bundle with him, while giving the other to Elzy to take back to New Mexico.

The next morning, as they were finishing counting the unsigned bank notes, a little over $20,000, they suddenly noticed a lone rider approaching the cabin. Harvey hurried outside to intercept the stranger while Butch and George gathered up the money.

The stranger introduced himself as Al Hudspeth and asked to come in out of the rain. Unable to think of a tactful way to turn the man down, Harvey just told him to get the hell down the road before he found the seat of his pants full of hot lead.

When they finished gathering up the money, and after a quick breakfast, the outlaws headed north towards Hole-in-the-Wall. The rain had finally stopped.

What they didn't know was that Hudspeth, after being sent away by Harvey, concluded he had stumbled onto the train robbers, and raced to Casper with the news. Within an

Chapter 31

hour, a posse headed by Sheriffs Hazen and Hiestand was headed towards to the cabin. When the posse reached the shack the outlaws were gone, but with the rain finally stopped, and the ground wet, and the trail was easy to follow.

Later that afternoon, while crossing a ridge, Butch looked back and saw the posse. There were eleven riders. Knowing his trail was easy to follow across the wet ground, Butch decided to ambush the posse, hoping to drive the officers and their deputies back to Casper for reinforcements, giving the outlaws time to get safely away.

"Looks like were going to find out how good this smokeless powder really is," Butch said as they hid themselves in some boulders overlooking a stretch of the trail about 500 yards long. "Shoot the horses, not the men," Butch cautioned.

When the posse came into sight, Butch fired the first shot, the bullet striking the ground in front of Sheriff Hiestand's horse. The sheriff was standing beside the horse, checking something on his rifle, the reins hanging loosely over his arm. Startled by the bullet, the horse pulled away, spun around and galloped back towards Casper. Hiestand set out after the horse on foot. Now there were only ten men to contend with.

The posse had stopped, the men looking up the trail for a puff of smoke which would tell them where the bullet had been fired from. There was no smoke to see.

Butch's next bullet struck one of the horses. Harvey and the Kid opened fire too. The men in the posse scrambled behind rocks and boulders.

After the initial exchange of gunfire the posse began to creep forward. They found courage in the knowledge that there were ten of them against only three outlaws. George asked Butch if he could start shooting at men instead of horses. Butch said no.

George was content to obey orders until he discovered Sheriff Hazen and one of his men, Dr. Leeper, sneaking up a draw no less than 50 yards from George's hiding place.

Hazen and Leeper had left their horses behind and were sneaking forward on foot.

George aimed at the sheriff and fired. The bullet struck Hazen near the navel and passed all the way through. Dr. Leeper began calling for help as he tried to administer aid to the wounded man. Suddenly, the efforts of the posse were focussed on rescuing their sheriff rather than catching outlaws. The posse retreated with their wounded sheriff back to Casper.

Butch didn't say anything to George about shooting the sheriff against Butch's orders. Wounding the sheriff had discouraged the posse, and possibly saved the outlaws' lives. But a bag full of unsigned bank notes wasn't worth taking the life of a man. Later, in a newspaper account of the holdup, Butch learned Hazen died two days later.

The outlaws headed north, crossing the flooding waters of the Powder River, then to the familiar Hole-in-the-Wall country.

Chapter 32

By the time Butch and his men reached Hole-in-the-Wall they found out veteran stock detective Joe LeFors was tracking them with a new posse. They also learned the amount of the reward for information leading to the capture of the train robbers had been increased to $18,000.

Guessing his men were better mounted than those riding with LeFors, and knowing that tracking was still easy in the damp soil following the rain, Butch decided the only practical thing to do was put as many miles as possible between him and the posse, and do it as quickly as possible.

They headed around the north end of E K Mountain, and on to the Billy Hill Ranch in the foothills of the Big Horn Mountains. After changing horses they headed west over the Big Horns, dropping into the Big Horn Basin on the No Water Drainage. From there they went straight west to Kirby Creek, then down the road to Thermopolis.

Making a wide sweep around Thermopolis, they climbed a well-hidden trail on the west side of the rugged Wind River Canyon to the top of the Owl Creek Range. From there they dropped into Wind River Basin by way of Mexican Pass, a saddle in the range.

Once over the mountains they made their way to the Muddy Creek Road Ranch recently established by Butch's old friend Emery Burnaugh on the Casper to Lander stage road. While the exhausted outlaws made themselves comfortable in a natural cave under a sandstone outcropping behind the Burnaugh ranch buildings, Alice made sandwiches which her two boys, Carl and Claude, carried to the cave in a lard pail.

There hadn't been any new rain to wash their trail away, so the outlaws knew their stay at the Burnaugh Ranch would be a short one. It was just a matter of time until LeFors and the posse followed their tracks to the cave.

They decided to split up, each outlaw heading in a different direction, forcing the posse to decide which trail to follow. The best way to lose a posse with good tracking skills was to ride through towns and along well-traveled roads, mixing tracks with others, hoping no one recognized you.

After speaking with Emery, Butch learned Mary had arrived in Lander a few days earlier to spend some time with her parents and brothers and sisters at the family farm at the mouth of Crow Creek.

Butch knew he couldn't stay in one place very long, but it would be good to see Mary again, even if the visit had to be short. With an $18,000 reward being offered, he knew there would be posses everywhere, some headed by law officers, others by bounty hunters.

Butch could not hide his disappointment when Mary's father said she had left the day before to return to Rock Springs. Under less pressing circumstances, Butch would have followed her, but not now.

He headed north over the Owl Creek Mountains. After a short rest at a secluded cabin in Cook Stove Basin, he crossed the Big Horn River continuing north through Pryor Gap into Montana. At Laurel, he sold his horse and saddle, and bought some fancy clothes. Dressed like a banker, he boarded the train to Seattle, Washington. It wasn't until he walked out of the train station and disappeared into busy downtown Seattle, that he began to relax. At last, he felt confident he had given the posse the slip. Still, he had no intention of waiting around for someone to figure out he had gotten on a train to the coast.

After spending the night in a cheap hotel, he walked down to the waterfront, hoping to land a job as a seaman on a ship traveling to some distant location. Before talking to anyone, he went into a seaside shop and bought some wool pants, a sweater and a cap, similar in appearance to what the sailors along the waterfront were wearing. He knew better than to apply for a job as a deck hand dressed like a banker.

Once he was wearing his new sailor outfit, he walked into the nearest waterfront tavern, which in many ways was similar to the saloons of the Rocky Mountains, but very different too. There was sawdust on the floor and the place smelled like stale fish. Instead of steaks and potatoes cooking in the kitchen, there was a steaming pot of fish chowder. In addition to Missouri corn whiskey and beer, the bar served rum, tequila, Sakai, vodka and wine--the drinks sailors had become accustomed to in their travels around the world. Like in many of the saloons of the west there was a painting of a nude fat lady above the bar.

Butch found himself a place beside some sailors at the bar and ordered a beer. After a while he asked the man next to him if he knew of any ships that might be taking on deck hands. He learned men were still going north in search of gold in Alaska. Three years had passed since gold was discovered at Klondike Creek in the Yukon Territory. Crewmen were still leaving their ships, especially in May and June, to head north in search of gold, leaving vacancies for new deck hands on southbound ships.

By nightfall Butch had landed a job as deck hand on the Elinor, a steamship headed for San Pedro Bay, south of Los Angeles. He guessed Los Angeles would be a safe place to get lost for a while. When the authorities began to forget about the Wilcox robbery, he could take the train east to New

Mexico to rejoin his companions.

Before reporting for work at the ship the next morning, Butch cashed in a few of the bank notes. He guessed the authorities would eventually trace the notes to Seattle, but he figured it would be better to cash them in Seattle than Los Angeles where he hoped to be able to stay for a while. With all the interest in Alaskan gold, he figured anyone tracing the money to Seattle would have good reason to believe he had gone north to Alaska, not the opposite direction to Los Angeles.

He had thought about going to Alaska. But he guessed the easy gold had already been claimed. Besides, he knew how to find gold without having to dig it out of the ground. Bank and railroad vaults held all the gold a man could ever want, and he knew how to get it.

The Elinor was a cargo ship returning to San Pedro Bay after unloading its northbound cargo of food supplies and mining equipment in Skagway, Alaska.

When Butch started work, the ship was taking on a load of cedar lumber. Butch spent the day stacking boards. In getting the job, he used the name, Jim Lowe. There were six men in the crew, and none seemed very talkative. After three or four days of shore leave, all seemed to be nursing sore heads from too much drinking, sore fists from too much fighting, and sore genitalia from over indulgence in other activities. Butch wasn't in the mood to do a lot of talking either. As far as he was concerned the less said the better.

Though the men dressed in seaman's clothing, Butch guessed they weren't much different than the typical bunch of men one would find in a Wyoming cow camp--tough talking, vulgar, hard working, critical of authority, some hard to get to know, some eager to tease or joke, one or two inclined to be the bully. Butch guessed there was some sort of pecking order among the seamen, and it wasn't a matter of if, but when he would be challenged. He didn't have long to wait.

As the Elinor pushed away from port into Puget Sound, the dinner bell sounded. The men filed into the galley to feast on fresh salmon steaks, fried potatoes and cabbage salad. After a hard day of loading lumber the men were looking forward to a big feed.

"Lowe, fetch me ein salmon steak."

Butch didn't move, nor did he look up from his plate. He knew who was speaking, a burley German sailor with a row of broken yellow teeth across the top of his mouth. His name was Wolfgang, and he had been the last to come aboard. Earlier, in the sleeping quarters, the big German had removed another sailor's blankets from one of the sleeping racks and thrown them on the deck. Without a word the other sailor had picked up his blankets and moved them to another rack. Having established his superiority over the sailor in the sleeping quarters, it appeared Wolfgang had now singled out the new man, the one they called Jim Lowe.

"Lowe, haf you got ears?" Wolfgang growled. "Fetch me ein salmon steak."

Butch didn't want to fight Wolfgang. He only wanted to be left alone. But he also knew if he fetched the salmon steak, additional orders would follow. Men like Wolfgang didn't leave those alone who allowed themselves to be bullied. Eventually, the big German would have to be challenged. The question was whether it would be best to do it now, or later.

Butch continued to look at his plate as he entertained these thoughts. He figured the German would give him one more chance to obey the order before starting a fight. Butch was wrong. Quietly the German had slipped from his chair, while Butch was still looking down at his plate. While Wolfgang appeared large and clumsy, his big paws were deceptively fast. Almost before Butch realized what was happening, one of the big hands had grabbed the hair on the top of his head, while the other hand held a knife under his chin.

"I say fetch me ein salmon steak," Wolfgang hissed, leaning over Butch's shoulder. Along with the words, he spit out pieces of salad. His breath smelled of fish and mildew.

Feeling the cold steel against his throat, Butch knew he

was in no position to argue. "Yes sir," he said, politely, carefully starting to get up from the table. "Would you like some potatoes and cabbage with it?"

"Dat's better," Wolfgang said, returning the knife to his belt and sitting back down in his chair, figuring he had just won the dominance battle with Jim Lowe.

Some of the other men weren't so sure. Even though none of them had ever heard of Jim Lowe before he came aboard the Elinor, there was something different about him. There had been no look of fear in the stranger's eyes when he found a knife at his throat. His voice had been calm, and even cheerful, when he offered to get the food. No fear. No panic. Only the calmness that came from strength. Here was a man with control, with strength, a man who had faced and handled situations tougher than this.

But none of this was noticed by Wolfgang who resumed shoving food into his huge mouth. The others continued to give the appearance of eating, but watching closely as Lowe walked over to the serving table and heaped a tin plate high with salmon, potatoes and salad. As he turned to bring the food to Wolfgang, Lowe began to whistle a tune none of the men recognized. They only knew a defeated man did not whistle a happy tune. Lowe was not defeated. Lowe was not afraid. Lowe was about to do something, and poor Wolfgang was busy stuffing food into his mouth, thinking he had already won the battle.

As Butch bent over to place the plate of food on the table in front of the big German, his right hand holding the heavy plate suddenly glided back around his right hip, stopped, then shot forward with the force of a prize fighter delivering a right hook. With a loud slap, Butch delivered the plate square into the face of the unsuspecting German. The force of the blow sent food flying in every direction, pieces of potato even sticking to the ceiling.

Before Wolfgang had a chance to respond, Butch's boot slammed down on the top of the German's foot. A moment later Butch's fist buried deep into Wolfgang's paunch, sending the German crashing over backwards onto the floor. As he fell, Butch's other hand snatched the knife from his opponent's belt. No sooner had Wolfgang landed on his back, gasping for air, his wind gone, than Butch cocked back his arm and threw the knife with all his might, the blade burying a full two inches into the deck between the German's partially spread thighs.

"Anything else I can fetch for you?" Butch asked, his voice as calm and controlled as it had been before. The German said nothing. Butch returned to his chair and resumed eating his meal.

As the Elinor left Puget Sound heading due west into the Straits of Juan de Fuca, a strong north wind began to rough up the sea, pushing huge white-capped waves against the starboard side of the ship.

As Butch was coming up from the hold to help the rest of the men lash down everything on deck against what the captain thought was an approaching storm, he heard someone yell, "Man overboard!"

Butch joined two men running towards the starboard side of the stern. One was carrying a life preserver. Someone else was running forward to shut off the engine. The Elinor had two masts, like the old sailing ships, but was powered by a coal-fired steam engine.

When Butch reached the railing, he could see a man thrashing about in the black, choppy water below. It was Wolfgang, and it was apparent by his helpless floundering that he didn't know how to swim.

When the sailor next to Butch tried to throw the life preserver towards the drowning man, the wind blew it back against the side of the ship. Repeated throws met with the same result, and there was no sign of the wind letting up soon. The momentum of the ship was carrying it further away from Wolfgang who was being carried by the churning sea directly behind the ship.

The life preserver was too light to throw against the wind, and no one seemed willing to leap into the churning sea to save their drowning companion.

Spotting a pile of rope, Butch quickly fashioned a loop and began swinging it over his head. The rope was thicker and heavier than the silk Manilla he was accustomed to, but it responded to his experienced hand. He fed some additional rope into the loop as he swung it faster around his head. He was ready to throw, but Wolfgang had disappeared below the surface of the water.

Butch continued to swing the rope, carefully watching the boiling surface of the water. The wind was blowing in his face, but Butch guessed throwing a rope into this ocean wind would be no more difficult than the wind he faced every time he urged his horse into a full gallop after a steer or cow.

"There he is," someone shouted. Looking to his right, Butch could see a single hand reaching out of the water, extending maybe a foot or so, grasping helplessly at the air.

When nothing else appeared, Butch let his loop fly. A hand was better than nothing at all. The loop shot forward and down, defying the wind, finally settling in a circle around the hand. Carefully, Butch pulled his slack, tightening the loop around the wrist just as it disappeared beneath the surface.

At first Butch didn't know if he had caught the hand or not. He fed out a little more slack, like a fisherman does when a fish first takes the bate. He was hoping to give the German a chance to get a good hold on the rope before the pulling began.

Butch began to pull on the rope. There was resistance, and tugging, like he had hooked a big fish.

"I got him," Butch yelled. Several men rushed to his side. They began to pull. A few seconds later Wolfgang's head and shoulders broke the surface of the water. He was gasping for air, but hanging onto the rope with both hands.

A few minutes later, with the help of all the hands, the gasping German was hoisted up the side of the ship and rolled onto the deck.

"Where did you learn to throw a rope like that?" one of the men asked.

Chapter 32

"Worked on a ranch in Wyoming. Used to catch cows that way," Butch said. From that moment on, the sailors no longer called him Jim Lowe. His new name was Cowboy.

The storm continued throughout the day, the sea becoming more and more choppy as the ship neared the west end of the strait and the Pacific Ocean.

When the dinner bell rang, Butch went to his bunk instead. He didn't feel well. He found the incessant rocking of the ship more and more annoying. He had to find a bucket to throw up in. By evening he was still throwing up, and felt sick enough to die.

He found little sympathy from the other men who said he was seasick, and ought to get over it in a week or two, or three. Butch curled up on his rack and prepared to die.

The next afternoon, as he awoke from a short, restless, nap, he noticed the smelly bucket he had been throwing up in, had been emptied and washed, and returned to its place beside his rack. Then he noticed a cup of warm, salty broth beside his rack. He hadn't eaten in two days, and his body craved nourishment. The sea was much calmer now, and he felt a little better. Sipping at the broth made him feel even better.

Later, when one of the sailors walked through the hatch to get something from his sea bag, Butch thanked him for cleaning the bucket and bringing him the broth.

"Wasn't me," the sailor said. "Wolfgang did it. He's up on deck washing your clothes right now."

As Butch stretched back on his bunk, letting the broth turn to strength, he pondered the interesting chain of events that turned a bully and enemy into a caring friend. It had never occurred to Butch, when Wolfgang was washed overboard, not to throw the rope thereby letting the bully drown. But neither had it occurred to him that saving the German would win the man's friendship and services as a nurse. He had thrown the rope because it was the thing that needed to be done at the time. That was all. Now he had a new and loyal friend. Sometimes life delivered pleasant surprises.

Butch wondered about Sheriff Hazen, the man who had died of the stomach wound following the Wilcox robbery. It was George Curry who had pulled the trigger on the sheriff, but Butch had planned and led the holdup, and felt at least partly responsible. Butch wondered if saving Wolfgang from drowning, had somehow evened the score, if saving a life had somehow justified the taking of a life.

Butch found himself wishing he could stop being an outlaw. He longed to settle down and raise a family. He wondered what it would be like not to be chased and hounded by the law. He wondered what was wrong with a government system that wouldn't let him stop being an outlaw.

Butch got over his sea sickness and did his share of the work, mainly shoveling coal into the belching, puffing steam engine. During the long afternoons on deck, he put on roping demonstrations at the request of the other men. In time he got out his .44 and did some fancy shooting for the men.

When the Elinor reached San Pedro Bay, Butch realized he had shown the men on ship too much to feel safe around them any longer. One of them might read a newspaper article about The Wild Bunch and get suspicious. Saying goodby to Wolfgang and the rest of the crew, Butch turned his back on the Elinor and disappeared.

He hired a carriage to take him north into Los Angeles. Since he was dressed in seaman's clothing he went to the waterfront and rented a room in an old hotel that provided rooms for sailors on shore leave. He picked up a month's supply of old newspapers, carried them to his room and began to read.

He was amused to find several accounts of holdups in Montana and Colorado, only a day or two apart. The Wild Bunch was given credit for both.

Then he read about a holdup of the Colorado Southern near Folsom, New Mexico on July 11. He didn't have to read very far to know Elzy, Harvey, and Sam Ketchum were the robbers. Like at Wilcox they had unhitched the passenger cars and driven the engine and express car up the track where they proceeded to blow up the latter with dynamite. When they finally got the safe open, there was nothing inside.

Empty-handed and frustrated, the bandits departed in the direction of Cimarron Canyon, and apparently thought they had avoided pursuit. Five days later while hiding out in a cabin in Turkey Canyon they were attacked by a posse. The outlaw the newspaper called William McGinnis received wounds in the shoulder and back. Sam Ketchum was shot in the arm. The newspaper said G. W. Franks escaped unscathed. Butch recognized G. W. Franks as an alias Harvey sometimes used. The bandits had killed two of the posse members, Sheriff Ed Farr of Huerfano County and a cowboy by the name of Love. Several others had been wounded.

Butch wondered if Elzy would be able to use the unsigned banknotes from the Wilcox robbery to hire a good lawyer. He was going to need one.

Every morning Butch bought a newspaper to check for news on Elzy's trial, and any other news about bank and train robberies in the Rocky Mountains. When finished with the newspapers he read books. Some he bought. Some he borrowed from a local library. Dickens, Melville and Twain were his favorites authors. He even indulged in a little Shakespeare.

One morning after he had purchased a newspaper, eaten his breakfast, and was walking back to his room, he was approached by a boy who wanted to sell him a newspaper.

"But I already have one," Butch said.

"You've got to buy another," the boy said. The lad appeared to be five or six years old. While his blond hair was neat and combed, he was dressed in rags. He was wearing no shoes. Butch realized the little fellow had taken on a formidable task in trying to sell a paper to someone who already had one.

"If I already have one why should I buy another?" Butch asked, doubting the boy could come up with a satisfactory response to his objection.

"Because my brother and sisters won't have any supper

if I don't sell 30 papers,'' the boy said, holding out his palm for Butch's money.

"How many papers do you have left?'' Butch asked.

"Nineteen.''

Butch reached into his pocket for a handful of coins and promptly counted out money to buy, not one, but all nineteen papers. He handed the money to the surprised boy.

Quickly the boy handed the papers to Butch, grabbed the money, turned and ran. It was as if he wanted to get out of reach before the foolish stranger changed his mind. Butch tossed the papers in a box by the side of the street and trotted after the little boy, trying to keep far enough back, and out of sight, so the boy would not know he was being followed.

Two blocks up the street the boy ducked into an alley, then into a doorway halfway down the alley. Butch walked up to the weathered door, but he didn't knock. He felt a little foolish meddling in the little boy's business. On the other hand, when a child had to sell papers so his brother and sisters could eat, something was wrong, that maybe needed looking into.

Through the door, Butch could hear a baby crying. He was about ready to knock when the door was suddenly opened from the inside. The same little boy he had been following was standing in front of him, a surprised look on the lad's dirty face, an empty milk pail in his hand.

"You can't have your money back,'' the boy cried, trying to slam the door. Butch's foot prevented it from closing. Somewhere through the partly opened door, Butch could hear a woman's voice, weak and frail. He couldn't make out the words.

"Is everything alright?'' Butch asked, his words directed more to the adult inside than the little boy in front of him. There was no response.

"Ma is sick,'' the boy said. "Real sick.''

"Maybe I better take a look at her,'' Butch said, his voice soft and friendly.

"You don't want your money back?'' the boy asked.

Chapter 32

"Heavens no," Butch responded. "If you have any more papers, I'll buy them too. Let me see your Ma."

Cautiously, the boy stepped back, letting the door swing open. Butch stepped into the darkness, leaving the door behind him open. It still took a minute or two for his eyes to adjust. The air was stale and damp, and heavy with human body smells. It was hard to breathe. Butch wanted to throw open windows and doors, letting in sunshine and fresh air.

As Butch's eyes became accustomed to the darkness, his eye caught the quick movement of a large gray rat scurrying across the floor and into a crack in one of the walls. Beside the wall was an iron bed.

There was a woman in the bed. She was trying to sit up, matted red hair covering half her face. Unable to do so, she fell back, her head finally coming to rest on a dirty pillow, her tired eyes staring at Butch. Behind her, on the bed, a naked baby, perhaps a year old, was sitting up, looking first at its mother, then at Butch, the corners of its mouth turned down in a quivering frown, like it was about to cry, not sure whether to be afraid or happy that this stranger had come to their room. Two more children were sitting in their underwear on a rumpled quilt on the floor in one corner of the room. Uncertainty was on their faces too.

"What's the matter?" Butch asked, sincere concern in his voice.

"Been sick for about a week," the woman whispered. "Don't know what's wrong."

"Where's your husband?"

"His ship didn't come back."

"I'll get a doctor," Butch said.

"No. We don't have any money."

"Don't worry about that. I won't be gone long. Everything is going to be fine."

As he was hurrying out the door, he tossed a silver dollar to the boy, telling him to get some cookies to go along with the milk.

Half an hour later Butch returned with a doctor, who

quickly diagnosed the woman as having appendicitis. Not wanting to waste any more time by calling an ambulance, he had Butch help him lift her into his carriage, then without any further conversation rushed her to the nearest hospital. Butch suddenly found himself alone with the four children.

He couldn't just leave them, and he wasn't about to hang around that filthy room with them. He threw open the door and window, hauled the dirty clothing and bedding to the nearest laundry, and scrubbed down the walls and floor with lye soap. The children helped, quickly warming up to Butch.

He filled the cupboard with food, and picked up a fresh block of ice for the ice box so milk, butter, and eggs would keep. The first three or four times he cooked a meal he could hardly believe how much the children ate.

Jess, the boy who had sold Butch the newspapers, was the oldest. He was seven. The two younger than Jess were girls, Vanessa, age four, and Susan, age two. The baby's name was Ben. While the mother had been sick, Jess had learned to change Ben's diapers. Butch let him continue with this duty.

Butch did his best to patch up numerous holes in the walls, but he could not keep the rats away, especially with the new food that was now in the room. That evening, about bedtime, the children cheered when Butch announced it was time to declare war on the rats.

With a lantern to provide plenty of light, Butch scattered pieces of dry bread along the back wall. He closed the window and door, hoping the noise from his six shooter wouldn't bother the neighbors. After settling the children down for the night on blankets along the front wall, he put balls of cotton in all their ears before checking the cylinder of his .44.

Butch blew the head off the first rat that tried to steal a piece of bread. The noise frightened little Ben and he started to cry, until he noticed the other children screaming with delight. He began to laugh.

Butch let the lantern burn all night. He made himself

comfortable on the floor beside the children, his .44 in his hand. By morning there were five dead rats that needed to be thrown outside, but not before careful inspection by the children.

Butch checked with the doctor later that morning and learned the mother was recovering from an appendicitis operation, but that it would be five or six days until she was well enough to return to the children. Later that afternoon Butch took the children to see their mother, but not before buying a lot of new clothing, including shoes for the three oldest.

The day the mother came home from the hospital the children were busy playing train and bank robbers with Butch. Jess was Butch Cassidy. Susan and Vanessa were Sundance and Harvey. Little Ben was Flat Nose George Curry. For loot, they had a bag of unsigned bank notes. Butch was using the alias, Jim Lowe. If the mother wondered why a sailor knew so much about The Wild Bunch she didn't say anything. To her this Jim Lowe was an angel sent from heaven.

But he left as quickly as he had come, giving no indication where he was headed. After he left, as the mother was going through her cupboards, which were well stocked for the first time, with food and staples, she found a hundred dollars in bank notes folded up neatly in the sugar bowl.

Butch returned to his rented room to catch up on his reading and get ready to head back to New Mexico where he promised to meet some of his gang members in the fall. He found a short article on Elzy, announcing that William McGinnis had been sentenced to life in The New Mexico State Prison at Santa Fe.

Butch went to the train station and made reservations for a compartment on the evening train to Albuquerque. His alias now was Mr. Jones. The train left Los Angeles early in the evening, leaving him undisturbed in his compartment until morning. After the porter made up his bed, Butch slipped the man a dollar, saying he didn't want to be disturbed the rest of the day.

Cassidy

Upon arriving in Albuquerque, Butch bought a horse and saddle and headed down to Alma, and the WS Outfit. Harvey, Sundance and Bill Carver were already there. Harvey had a lot to say about the Folsom robbery, including Elzy's capture and trial.

Ranch owner William French was glad to see Jim Lowe had returned. Not only did he offer Lowe his old job back, but asked Butch if he would become foreman of the WS. The other foreman had quit right after some horses had turned up missing. Harvey said he saw cowboys from the Holoman Outfit riding WS horses in Alma.

Butch was reluctant about accepting the foreman's job. He knew he was kidding himself to think he could settle down. He knew it was just a matter of time until his presence at the WS would be common knowledge to enough people that he would have to leave. Already, too many people knew the WS was headquarters for The Wild Bunch. Someday Captain French would find out too.

A week later Frank Murray, assistant superintendent of the Pinkerton Agency in Denver, rode into Alma where some unsigned bank notes had been passed. After asking a lot of questions at the local saloons he headed out to the WS where he showed Captain French a photograph of The Wild Bunch obtained from a photo studio in Price, Utah.

"That's Jim Lowe," French said, pointing to Butch in the photograph.

"You know this man?" Murray asked.

"Sure, he's over in the bunkhouse this very minute," French replied. Murray gulped.

"Is he alone?" Murray asked.

"Nope. Some of his friends work here too, including Tom Capeheart. He's in the bunkhouse too." He pointed at Harvey Logan in the photo. "Want to meet them?"

"Sure," Murray replied, hesitation in his voice.

As French led him to the bunkhouse, Murray decided there was no way he was going to try to arrest the entire Wild Bunch without an army to back him up.

Chapter 32

"Men, I want you to meet Frank Murray, assistant superintendent of the Pinkerton Agency in Denver," French boomed in a loud voice as they entered the bunkhouse.

French was the only one who seemed surprised when men began falling over the furniture and each other, scrambling for their weapons.

"Easy," Murray said, "I'm not here to arrest anyone. Not today."

Finally, everyone was still, none of the outlaws very far from their guns. All of them were looking at Murray who quietly removed the photo from his shirt.

"Mr. French was kind enough to identify several of you. Are any of the rest of you in this photo?"

"Are these men wanted for something?" French asked, still not sure what was going on.

"You might put it that way," Murray said. "The Pleasant Valley Coal Company in Price, Utah would sure like to talk to a couple of these men. So would the bank at Belle Fourche, South Dakota. The Union Pacific Railroad hired the Pinkerton Agency to find them. Seems to be a little misunderstanding over $42,000 in unsigned bank notes that turned up missing in Wilcox, Wyoming a short time ago."

"What are you saying?" French asked.

"Mr. French. The WS Outfit is headquarters for The Wild Bunch. Jim Lowe is Butch Cassidy."

"I'll be damned," French said, grinning from ear to ear. "No wonder the rustlers disappeared when Jim Lowe showed up."

"Are you going to try to arrest us?" Butch asked Murray.

"I'm not that foolish."

"What are you going to do?"

"Go back to Denver and report my findings."

"Maybe we'll stop you," Butch said. "There's half a dozen of us, and only one of you."

"My guess is you won't," Murray said. "Butch Cassidy has stolen lots of money, but doesn't seem to have the

407

stomach for hurting people. Our investigations indicate Butch Cassidy is a pretty decent human being.''

"Would you bet your life on that?" Butch asked.

"Looks like I already did when I stepped into this bunkhouse," Murray said.

Ten minutes later Murray was riding back to Alma. Butch and the rest of the men were packing their things. French hung around the bunkhouse complaining about losing the best bunch of men he ever had.

"Holomans, I suppose, will get real bold now," French said.

"You won't have to worry about the Holomans, at least not for a while," Butch said. He winked at French, but offered no further explanation.

Butch and his men were gone within the hour. Two days later the sheriff from Alma rode to the WS asking for Jim Lowe. The sheriff hadn't talked to Frank Murray, and knew nothing about The Wild Bunch using the WS as headquarters.

The sheriff explained how every horse on the Holoman place had been driven off early the previous morning. The rancher, Holoman, had to walk ten miles to find a horse to ride to town to report the theft. He claimed Jim Lowe was the responsible party.

Holoman claimed just before sunup, Lowe and four other men simply rode through his front gate and over to the big horse corral. They acted like they owned the place. Some of the Holoman hands had just gotten out of bed and were coming out of the bunkhouse. Lowe said good morning to them as he rode past them towards the gate. Lowe was so calm and collected in what he was doing, that the hands figured he had made some kind of deal with Mr. Holoman to buy some of the horses. The hands just stood by the bunkhouse and watched as Lowe and his companions drove all the horses out of the corral, out the front gate and down the road. They didn't know the horses had been stolen until Mr. Holoman got out of bed a half hour later.

Chapter 32

"It must have been Lowe, alright," French said, knowing there was no need to cover for Butch now. "Lowe drew his pay and left here two days ago. Have no idea where he went, or if he'll return. But it sounds like he's got plenty of horses to take him wherever he decides to go."

After leaving the WS Outfit, The Wild Bunch went to San Antonio, except for Butch, who returned to Utah. He had an idea that might enable him to quit the outlaw trail.

Chapter 33

Harvey Logan, Bill Carver and Kid Curry headed for Fanny Porter's sporting house at 505 South San Saba Street in San Antonio. Butch agreed to meet them there later. He worked his way up to Salt Lake City, hoping to arrange a private meeting with an influential judge named O. W. Powers, who before becoming a judge had been one of the most widely known criminal lawyers in the West.

With Elzy serving a life prison sentence, Butch was thinking more and more how he would like to quit the outlaw life, and settle down. His appeal to the western governors to win clemency for The Wild Bunch by enlisting in the Spanish American War had fallen on deaf ears. Maybe they would listen now. More banks and trains had been robbed, and all efforts by the authorities to catch him had failed. He didn't think Governor Richards of Wyoming would be sympathetic to his request, mainly because of pressure from Butch's old enemies in the Wyoming Cattlemen's Association.

Governor Heber Wells of Utah, however, Butch thought

would lend a listening ear. Butch guessed he could contact Wells through Judge Powers.

After riding into Salt Lake City and checking into a hotel room under the alias Jim Lowe, Butch went to the courthouse and hid himself behind the door in Powers' office while the judge was in court.

Near the end of the day, when the judge entered his office, Butch kicked the door shut. Powers appeared to be in his fifties, with gray hair, and the body of a man who spent too much time sitting in a chair. Powers didn't recognize the face of the man who had kicked the door shut. The judge looked worried, wondering which of all the men he had sent to jail had come back to get revenge. He couldn't believe he could forget the face of a man he had sent to prison.

"Who are you?" the judge asked. "Do I know you?"

"Never was in your court," Butch said, guessing what the judge was thinking. "But there's a lot of people who would like to get me there."

"Are you an outlaw?"

"Most people call me Butch Cassidy. My real name is Robert LeRoy Parker, Mormon boy from Circleville."

Suddenly the judge was grinning. His earlier concerns had vanished. He was no longer concerned for his safety. On the one hand, this Cassidy was a notorious outlaw who should have been behind bars a long time ago. But according to the official record, Cassidy had never shot anyone. The judge smiled, obviously pleased at meeting the most notorious outlaw on the American continent.

"What can I do for you, Mr. Cassidy?" the judge asked, sitting in his chair behind the desk, reaching for a cigar. He offered one to Butch, but the outlaw refused.

Taking a chair opposite the judge, Butch carefully began the presentation he had been practicing in his mind for weeks.

"The Wild Bunch is laying plans to hit another half a dozen banks and trains over the next two years," Butch said, then waited for the import of what he said to sink in.

"Based on your past successes," Powers said,

carefully, "I don't doubt it. But why are you telling me this?"

"Every time I ride by a little farm and see children playing in an irrigation ditch, a young mother hanging freshly washed clothes on a line, the father mending a gate, or driving a team in front of a plow, I feel like maybe the best things in life are passing me by." Butch stopped, quietly savoring the image he had just created, thinking what to say next.

"Maybe they are," the judge said, softly, waiting for the outlaw to continue.

"You see," Butch continued. "I don't want to be an outlaw anymore. I don't want to rob any more banks and trains."

"Then stop," the judge smiled.

"I can't. Law officers and bounty hunters are carrying loaded guns, hoping to get a crack at me. The Pinkertons are on my trail night and day. Four states are offering rewards for my capture. They won't let me rest. They won't let me stop. If I relax, even for a minute, I fear a bullet in the back, or worse, a life prison sentence."

"What do you want me to do?"

"I would like you to approach Governor Wells for me. In exchange for amnesty I will agree to go straight. I will dissolve The Wild Bunch and cancel all plans for future robberies."

"There is no precedent for this kind of arrangement," the judge said, thoughtfully.

"I'm offering the Governor a way to stop a lot of robberies before they happen. You don't think he would be interested in that? Maybe I should go to The Salt Lake Tribune."

"A newspaper has no power to grant clemency, only stir up more trouble for those who can. I wouldn't recommend going public with your proposal, not yet. I'll present your offer to the governor."

Butch met with Judge Powers again, two days later. It appeared to Butch the judge and the governor had spent considerable time discussing his proposal.

Chapter 33

Powers started with the bad news, saying the governor had no power to pardon Butch for crimes committed in other states, especially crimes for which the outlaw had not been tried. On the other hand the governor said if Butch could get the Union Pacific Railroad to drop charges for a promise from Butch to cease robbing trains, Wells would use his influence as governor to help Butch get a fresh start. He wanted to know if Butch would be willing to work for the Union Pacific as a railway express guard in an effort to demonstrate his good intentions and to discourage other outlaw bands from picking up where The Wild Bunch left off. Butch said he would do this, at least for a year or two.

With Governor Wells on his side, Butch headed to Wyoming, where he hoped Douglas Preston would help set up a meeting with Union Pacific officials. Concerned the railroad people might attempt a double cross, Butch instructed Preston to bring them to the Lost Soldier stage station at the base of the Green Mountains in Wyoming. Preston promised to be there on the designated day with the U.P. officials.

Butch could hardly sleep the night before the proposed meeting. He decided as soon as he had made the deal with Union Pacific he would ride to Lander and tell Mary.

He was camped on a hilltop overlooking the abandoned stage station. His horse was hidden in some trees below the crest of the hill. When morning came he saddled the horse so he would be ready for a fast getaway in the event the U.P. tried to double cross him. But he guessed, with Preston serving as the middle man, there would be no double cross. As soon as the sun came up Butch began looking for the approaching delegation of railroad dignitaries. He was curious to see how many would venture forth to face the enemy.

Because of the distance involved in traveling to the abandoned stage station, he didn't expect them to arrive early in the day, but when noon arrived, he guessed it was time. He was wearing clean clothes and a new hat. During the morning hours he had washed and shaved. He hoped he would make a favorable impression on his new employer.

413

By mid-afternoon Butch was growing restless, and angry. Preston was usually punctual. For an important meeting like this, men should make extra efforts to be on time. But the railroad officials were not on time. Perhaps this meeting wasn't important to them. After all it wasn't their money that was being stolen from the express cars. Maybe the railroad was making so much money that the little bit taken by outlaws from time to time wasn't worth worrying about. But then why did they hire the Pinkerton Agency and offer such big rewards?

When the sun went down, there was still no sign of Preston and the railroad delegation. Butch waited until dark before getting on his horse. He rode down to the abandoned stage station, and tacked a note to the door. It read:

> "Damn you, Preston. You double-crossed
> me. I waited all day but you didn't show up.
> Tell the U.P. to go to Hell. And you can go
> with them."

Butch rode south that night, feeling more like riding than sleeping, wondering what to do next. The only thing that sounded good to him was another robbery of the Union Pacific Railroad. That'd show those railroad hot shots a thing or two. Maybe they would show up for their next meeting with Butch Cassidy. But there probably wouldn't be a next meeting. That was all right with Butch. What he didn't know was that Preston and his railroad delegation did show up at the Lost Soldier stage station, about an hour after Butch had left.

While Preston and his companions were mulling over Butch's angry note, wondering how they might schedule another meeting, Butch was a day's ride to the southeast watching a Union Pacific engine chugging up a hill west of Rawlins. At the top of the hill the train stopped at a coal re-fueling station called Tipton.

The surrounding country was remote and wild, a perfect place for a holdup. The Red Desert to the south provided an

414

excellent escape route leading to the remote Green River country of Utah.

Butch's feelings were hurt. If the Union Pacific didn't have enough respect for him to show up for a scheduled meeting, maybe another robbery at Tipton might get their attention.

But Butch had no intention of setting up another meeting. He was entertaining a new solution to his problems. Maybe he would just leave the country, and get a fresh start somewhere else, perhaps in one of the mostly unsettled countries of South America, far from the reach of the Pinkertons. Mike Cassidy had gone to Argentina. Butch thought he might go there too. But if he started over, he wanted to do so as a landowner, a person people respected with huge land holdings, stocked with numerous cattle and horses. To start out that way in a new country would take money. He knew where to get the money. Perhaps two or three holdups would be enough, starting with the Union Pacific Railroad at Tipton.

"Say fellows, I hear the Union Pacific is looking for more trouble," Butch remarked to Bill Carver and Harvey Logan when he found them at Fanny Porter's in San Antonio a week later. "What do you say we give them a little something to think about?"

"Count me in," Logan said, "but there damn well better be something in the safe. That was no fun at Folsom, when the safe was empty."

They located Sundance who was staying at a more reputable place on the other side of town, with Etta Place. He wanted in too. So did George Curry. Two days later, after picking up a sack of dynamite, they began the 300-mile journey to Tipton, Wyoming.

They headed north, crossing the Union Pacific tracks, on their way to the Sweet Water country where each man picked up two additional horses. They decided to change horses twice during their getaway, which would enable them to cover a hundred miles the first 12 hours. Butch had heard about a special posse the Pinkerton Agency and the Union Pacific had put together for the express purpose of chasing down train robbers. With an engine, and an express car remodeled to carry horses, the posse was ready to go anywhere along the U.P. rail course with only a few minutes notice. Butch hoped to be a long way away from Tipton when the special posse arrived.

After getting their relay horses, they headed south across a high desert, over the railroad tracks to a low range of hills 15 to 20 miles beyond the tracks. Here, in a fenced meadow, they left one string of relay horses. They continued southwest another 20 miles where they made camp on a small stream flowing out of the hills. The next morning they carefully staked out the second string of relay animals, making sure each horse had enough rope to get to both water and feed. They tied the rope to the front foot of each horse to reduce the risk of the animal getting tangled in its tether rope. The gang then returned to the first relay horses which were grazing contentedly in the meadow. The men made camp, spending the next morning carefully going over their plans. Some of the men thought Butch spent too much time reviewing and rehearsing the upcoming robbery. It was August 29, 1900.

They finally broke camp about 5 p.m. and headed for Tipton, arriving at the coal station about 1:30 a.m. The expected arrival of the train was about 2:30 a.m.

After watering the horses, Harvey led them west along the track about a mile. After tieing the mounts to bushes, a short distance from the track, he built a sagebrush fire next to the track, so Butch would know where to stop after hijacking the engine and express car. Harvey continued to feed the fire as he waited and listened for the chugging steam engine. He was careful to keep plenty of distance between the sack of dynamite and the fire.

The train arrived at Tipton on time, about 2:30. As soon as it stopped, Butch and Goerge jumped into the engine, pointing guns at the engineer and fireman. George forced the fireman to the ground, then to the rear of the express car to do the uncoupling. As soon as George was back in the cab, Butch ordered the engineer to pull ahead to Harvey's sagebrush fire.

At the sound of the approaching train, Sundance cut the telegraph wires which ran parallel to the train track.

As soon as the engine stopped beside the fire, Butch uncoupled the engine from the express car and ordered the engineer to drive the engine a mile up the track, and not to come back for the express car and the rest of the train for at least half an hour. The engineer seemed glad to go, leaving the express car alone with the bandits and their sack of dynamite.

The door to the express car was locked from the inside as the outlaws had anticipated. Butch called to the agent inside to open the door immediately. Butch was not surprised when the agent refused to do it. Butch did not ask again. Even though the agent's voice was strangely familiar, Butch placed two sticks of dynamite on the door sill and lit the fuse.

The resulting explosion left a huge hole in the side of the car. Once again Butch ordered the agent to come out. There was no response. Butch thought the agent might be unconscious. On the other hand, the guard might be sitting at one end of the car with a loaded shotgun waiting for the bandits to enter.

Butch wasn't about to take any chances. He lit a stick of dynamite, and reaching into the hole that was once a door, flipped the charge to the back of the car. After the explosion, Butch ordered the guard to come out. Again there was no response. Butch lit another stick of dynamite and tossed it into the front of the car.

Suddenly there was noise in the car, the sound of overturning crates, shuffling footsteps. The guard dove through the opening just as the charge exploded.

As the guard attempted to get his footing, Butch shone a lantern on him to make sure he was alright. The face was familiar too. It was Earnest Woodcock, the same guard who

417

had refused to open the express car at Wilcox. Butch shook his head and grinned, asking Sundance to keep an eye on the guard while he and George entered the car and began blasting away at the safe.

After two or three well-placed shots, the top came off. The safe was full of currency and gold, enough to fill all the saddlebags. When the bandits finally got around to counting it the next day they had over $45,000.

As they were getting ready to leave, Woodcock began complaining of a headache.

"Express guards who resists bandits should have cotton in their ears," Butch advised, "and should show a little more respect for dynamite."

Without a word, or even a smile, Woodcock just stared at Butch.

"Hope to see you again, Woodcock, at our next holdup," were Butch's last words as he galloped into the night.

Chapter 34

By nightfall Butch and his men had put a hundred miles between them and Tipton. They had crossed the Red Desert into Colorado. Here they split up. Harvey and the Kid returned to Texas, while Butch, Sundance and Bill Carver headed west into Utah. Three days later they finally indulged in a day's rest, camped above a thick juniper forest on a mountain a short distance southwest of Lehi, Utah.

Butch guessed that in addition to the posse attempting to follow his trail from Tipton, others would be searching for him at Hole-in-the-Wall and Robbers' Roost. The Pinkerton Agency now knew about the WS hideout in Alma, New Mexico. They would be sure to check there. He guessed the last place they would think to look for him was Nevada. The Wild Bunch had never pulled a job in Nevada. Butch had never worked there, only passed through on horseback a time or two.

The next day they headed west along the old stagecoach road towards Nevada. They passed the old Porter Rockwell Ranch at Government Creek, circled Fish Springs at the south end of the salt flats, they headed south of Haystack Peak past Trout Creek towards Ely. From there they continued east towards the remote mining town of Eureka, then north into the Diamond Mountains, finding a cabin where they felt it would be safe to rest, letting their saddle sores and aching hips and knees heal. In less than a week they had put over 500 miles between them and Tipton. Posses were looking for them all over Wyoming, Utah, Idaho, Colorado and New Mexico. No one would think to look for them in Nevada.

After a week of rest, Butch headed north into Huntington Valley, hoping to get supplies and news at one of the ranches. He met a rancher named Hammit who had just returned from Winnemucca with a pile of newspapers, the usual month's reading for him and his men. All the recent newspapers contained an account of the Tipton robbery. There was a quote from a Pinkerton official saying the posse was hot on the trail of the outlaws and capture was certain. One of the papers quoted a Union Pacific official who said the outlaws had taken only $54 in the holdup. Another paper quoted express guard Earnest Woodcock who said the outlaws had taken $55,000 from the blown-up safe.

"Money's not safe anywhere anymore," Hammit said, "Except maybe at the First National Bank in Winnemucca."

"Why's it any safer there than anywhere else?" Butch asked.

"Nobody thinks there's any money in a little cow town like Winnemucca, not even the outlaws," Hammit said.

"Maybe they're right," Butch said. "No reason for a little bank to have very much money on hand."

"That's where you're dead wrong," Hammit said. "When I opened my account last year, Mr. Nixon himself, the bank president, told me he had over $40,000 in the safe. Said he needed a lot of cash on hand so the big ranches could pay the help, first during the hay season, then during roundup. I was flabbergasted that a bank in a little town in this part of the country could have that much money."

"Me too," Butch said, thoughtfully, the wheels in his

Chapter 34

head beginning to turn.

Butch bought a lot of stuff from Hammit, including food, whiskey, a deck of cards, some of the newspapers carrying accounts of the Tipton robbery, and three horses, including a magnificent white gelding named Patsy. Hammit claimed it was the fastest horse in Nevada. By the time Butch was through, he had given the grinning Hammit nearly $2,000.

As Butch rode back to the hideout, he felt great. The Tipton robbery had been a runaway success. Not only had they gotten a lot of money, but no one had been hurt, and The Wild Bunch had completely outwitted the special posse and everyone else, so it seemed. One or two more robberies like that and Butch could buy about any ranch he wanted in South America.

"Are you boys ready to pull another holdup?" Butch asked as he rode up to the cabin.

"Might be a little soon," Sundance said. He was sitting on a chair on the front porch, leaning back against the log wall. "Too many posses combing the countryside right now."

"Nobody's looking for us in Nevada," Butch said.

"Went into Eureka," Bill said. "You're right. Lots of talk about the Tipton holdup, but no posse talk. Hasn't seemed to occur to anybody that we could be hiding out in this country."

"The U. P. would die if we hit'm here," Sundance said. "All the Pinkerton agents and special posses are over in Wyoming. We'd catch'm with their pants down, for sure."

"I wasn't thinking of holding up the Union Pacific," Butch said. "But the First National Bank in Winnemucca."

"I don't know if a little bank like that would have much cash," Sundance said. Butch told his two partners what Hammit had said about the president of the bank, Mr. Nixon, telling him there was $40,000 in the safe.

The next morning the three headed northwest towards Winnemucca, crossing the Sonoma Mountains, west of Golconda, and finding a camp site about four miles

421

downstream from the CS Ranch on the Humboldt River. It was a comfortable camp, next to a haystack in some cottonwood trees. A nearby spring provided plenty of fresh water. It was early September with warm days and cool nights, a wonderful time to be getting ready for a big holdup, Butch thought.

The first thing they did was ride into town for needed supplies. They purchased food, bullets, grain, even paper and pencils. Butch, in his efforts to make meticulous plans, was beginning to sketch out robbery and escape plans. He felt putting things on paper helped reduce the chance of error.

Butch cashed a legal bank note at the First National Bank. A clerk by the name of Fanny Harp waited on him, a stern-looking Mr. Lee looking over her shoulder. The door to Mr. Nixon's office was closed. Butch noticed the location of a back door leading to the ally behind the bank. After walking out the front door with his money, he strolled around back to see if there was a good place to secure getaway horses by the back door. There was a good hitching post there.

After the supplies were in camp, the outlaws visited local ranches, looking for horses. As soon as they had nine animals, three each, they settled in to get ready for the robbery.

Most of their time was spent training and conditioning the nine horses. Each horse had to be in condition for a long run. Hard runs every other day, and lots of oats took care of this. Each horse also had to be trained to stand still while being mounted, even when the rider approached at a run, even if there was yelling and shooting going on. The horses also had to learn to stand still while sacks of gold were thrown over their backs. The outlaws used bags of rocks for this purpose.

They were several days into their training routine when they noticed a lone rider approaching their camp. Each outlaw quickly checked the gun on his belt to make sure it was ready for action. Each also knew which horse he would run to in the event this was some kind of trap. They spread out, Sundance

Chapter 34

next to the haystack, Bill checking a pot of coffee on the fire, and Butch began saddling the white horse.

They soon realized their precautions were unnecessary. The approaching rider was only a boy, maybe ten years old. Having seen the riders running their horses, the boy had ridden down from the CS Outfit to see what was going on.

"What's your name, son?" Butch asked as the boy rode into their camp. The lad was well mounted, on a bay gelding. The horse was well broke, but spirited. It looked like it could run. The boy was confident in the saddle.

"Vic Button," the boy said. "This is my father's ranch. What are you men doing here?"

"Just camping for a few days," Butch said. "Training these horses so we can sell them."

"My father owns the CS Outfit, and you don't have his permission to be here," the boy said. For a ten-year-old he seemed very confident.

"Since your father owns the CS, why don't you give us permission to camp here?" Butch asked, catching the boy by surprise.

"I might," the boy said, trying to maintain his advantage.

"I'll race you for it," Butch said. Then he explained. "My white horse against your bay, half a mile. If I win you'll give us permission to camp. If you win, I'll pay you $20 to camp here." Butch reached in his pocket and pulled out a $20 gold piece. He flipped it in the air, caught it, then held it up so the boy could see it was a real gold coin.

"A deal," the boy blurted out, eager to accept the challenge. Obviously he thought his bay could outrun Butch's white horse.

Butch returned the coin to his pocket and turned back to his horse to tighten the cinch. When he finished he pointed to a cottonwood tree up the road towards the CS ranch.

"See that tree?" Butch asked. The boy nodded. "It's about a half a mile away. We'll start here. The first one to the tree wins."

"Fine with me," the boy beamed. He was pleased the horses would be running towards the home corral, instead of away from home. He knew his horse would run faster thinking it was going home, though it might be harder to stop the horse once the race was over.

After tightening his cinch Butch got on the white gelding and galloped it in circles for a minute to warm it up. When he was finished, Butch and the boy began riding their horses at a walk towards the cottonwood tree. When their horses were exactly even, Bill fired his gun, the signal for the race to begin.

Even though the big bay was carrying less weight, and was headed home, it was no match for the white gelding which won by half a dozen lengths.

When Vic finally got his horse stopped, he rode back to Butch. By the frown on the boy's face, Butch knew he didn't like being the loser in a horse race.

"I guess we can camp here for free now," Butch said.

"Just tonight," Vic said.

"Wait a minute," Butch said. "My understanding was if I won we could camp here as long as we wanted."

"No, just one night," Vic insisted.

"Should I jerk the little bugger off his horse and teach him some respect for his elders," Sundance said, finally entering the conversation. Butch waved him away.

"We need to stay a few more nights," Butch said.

"If you want to stay tomorrow night, you'll have to beat me again tomorrow," Vic said. "If you lose it'll be twenty bucks."

"That's good enough for me," Butch said, grinning. "But you better bring a faster horse. Patsy didn't have much of a contest today." Without another word the boy left, but he was back again the next day, this time mounted on a tall, black mare.

Patsy won again, but by a narrower margin. This time the boy didn't seem to take his loss so hard, and hung around for a while asking question, and getting to know the outlaws who in turn asked Vic questions about Winnemucca. In time the outlaws slipped in questions about the bank, when the ranchers made their deposits and withdrawals, when the employees went to lunch, who the sheriff was and did he have good horses ready to chase outlaws. They asked about a little-known trail over Soldier Pass into Clover Valley.

Nearly everyday the boy brought a different horse, and every time Patsy won. No one else visited the camp with Vic. The hands and his father were busy with the fall roundup, leaving the boy to entertain himself the last few days before school started.

One day Vic asked Butch if he would be willing to sell Patsy, and how much he would take. Vic thought his father would be willing to buy the horse for him.

"Patsy's not for sale," Butch said. "I need him." Seeing the look of disappointment on the boy's face, Butch said. "But I'll make you a promise. I'll give him to you, but I can't do it now. Just be patient. Someday he'll be yours."

Vic started to ask a lot of questions which Butch did not answer. "I promised to give him to you. That's all you need to know."

By the time Vic started school in Golconda, the outlaws were ready to rob the bank. They left their camp for two days taking their third string of relay horses further to the east. They staked the horses out so they could reach both feed and water. The outlaws poured a pile of oats on the ground near each horse.

Since their camp was less than 15 miles east of Winnemucca, they placed the second relay of horses in a wire correl at their camp, again pouring plenty of oats on the ground. Early the next morning, September 19, 1900, they headed for town, Butch riding Patsy. They had enough food in their saddle bags to last several days.

They decided to enter the bank at noon when they thought it would be least crowded, and most of the employees would be out to lunch. As they approached the outskirts of town, Butch tried something he hadn't done before. He asked

Bill to get off his horse and walk across the fields to town, carrying his Winchester wrapped up in a sleeping blanket. The plan called for Bill to enter the bank first, all alone, and as nonchalant as possible, take a chair at the back of the bank, hopefully where he would not be noticed. From this position of semi-concealment he would wait for Butch and Sundance to enter the bank. If something went wrong, no one would connect Bill with the other two, leaving him in position to get in the way of anyone trying to interfere with the robbery. When the robbery was finished, he would ride away with Butch and Sundance.

As Bill was walking across a big hayfield towards town, just as he jumped over a ditch, he saw his foot coming down on a skunk. Bill tried to dodge out of the way, but before he could do so, the polecat sprayed the front of his trousers.

Butch and Sundance were riding along the main road into town, and there was no way Bill could get word to them that he needed to do something with his pants. He didn't have any clean pants with him. There wasn't time to go into a store and buy a new pair, and change. Besides, that would attract attention, considering the way he smelled. Bill decided there was nothing to do but go ahead with the original plan.

Bill tried to ignore the stares of curiosity, and disgust, when he walked into the bank smelling like a skunk. There were more people than he thought there would be, maybe half a dozen customers and three clerks. One lady removed a handkerchief from her purse and held it over her nose and mouth while she conducted her business. Bill found himself a chair and made himself comfortable. With his skunk smell having already permeated every corner of the bank, he made no attempts to be inconspicuous.

When the lady with the handkerchief left, it seemed the other customers followed. Since it was almost noon, and all the customers were gone, two of the three clerks decided to take an early lunch, and disappeared out the back door. Bill was surprised no one asked him to leave, or wanted to know why he was sitting in the bank, smelling the way he did. No one seemed to want to come near him.

Bill and the clerk were the only ones in the bank now, unless Mr. Nixon was in his office. The door to the office was closed. Conditions were perfect for the holdup, thanks to the skunk. Bill reached under the blanker and felt the hammer and trigger on his Winchester. Everything was ready. He hoped Butch and Sundance would hurry up.

Bill didn't have to wait long. Sundance and Butch came strolling in like a couple of lost cowboys who needed some money, so they could extend their stay at the saloon across the street. There was a neatly folded bundle of canvas bags tucked under Butch's arm.

"Damnedest smelling bank I ever been in," Sundance said, wandering towards Bill. Butch slipped a note into the teller window as if he were going to cash a check. When the teller saw nothing was on the paper, he looked up in surprise, into the barrel of Butch's cocked Colt revolver.

Just as Butch got the drop on the clerk, two customers walked in through the front door. Sundance didn't waste any time covering them. By this time the bandits had pulled their bandannas over their noses and mouths.

Bill opened the door to Mr. Nixon's office, getting the drop on the bank president and Fanny Harp, one of the cashiers. Bill herded them into the lobby of the bank with the others. Everyone was made to lie face down on the floor. While Bill and Sundance kept them covered, Butch jumped into the cage and began filling his canvas sacks. When he was finished there, he then cleaned out the vault. Filling the bags didn't take more than a minute or two.

When Butch was about finished gathering up the money, Sundance stepped out the back door to make sure the horses were still there, and ready for a fast getaway. Bill continued to point his Winchester at the prone hostages. So far everything was progressing according to plan, except for the skunk smell.

Bill kept his gun on the hostages while Butch carried the sacks of money outside to the horses. Sundance was already mounted. Butch handed him two of the sacks, then mounted himself. When all was ready, he whistled to Bill who charged out the door and leaped on his horse. They headed towards the east end of town at a gallop, but hadn't gone more than 50 yards when Butch dropped one of the bags containing gold coins. There being no pursuit, he reined in his horse and returned for the gold.

Suddenly the front door of the bank burst open, and Nixon and Lee charged onto the porch, shouting the bank had been robbed. Each was armed with a shotgun. Knowing he was out of range of the scatter guns, Butch guided his horse alongside the bag of gold and reached down to get it.

As he did so Nixon and Lee opened fire. When Butch heard the blasts of the shotguns he thought maybe there would be a sprinkling of lead shot that might spook his white gelding. But such was not the case. Not only had the bankers miscalculated in their choice of weapons, but their aim was bad too. As the shotguns went off, the big front window in the saloon on the side of the street between Butch and the bankers, shattered into a thousand pieces. The white gelding remembered his intensive training, neither shying or bolting, but standing still as Butch leaned over in the saddle and reached for the gold. Smiling in relief at the horse's good behavior and the bankers' bad aim, Butch pulled the bag of gold into the saddle, then urged his horse into a full gallop after his fleeing companions.

Several miles south of town Butch rode to the crest of a little hill and looked back. To his surprise, a posse was already on their trail, and it appeared from the size of the cloud of dust being stirred up, that the posse was large and well mounted. Butch raced back to his companions with the news. It was time to push their horses to the limit. After weeks of conditioning and graining, the animals were as ready as they would ever be for a ten-mile race with a posse.

The outlaws were well ahead of the posse when they reached the fenced enclosure with the first three relay horses. But in the distance they could see the dust from the

Chapter 34

approaching posse, which was now down to three men, the the horses of the other posse members being unable to maintain such a blistering pace. There was little time to lose.

Tieing their spent horses to the fence, the men rushed inside to catch the fresh animals. Quickly, they switched saddles, bridles, and bags of money.

As they swung into their saddles, they could see the three-man posse was about a quarter of a mile away and almost within rifle range. Without fresh horses, the posse would soon be far behind.

"Hold up," Butch shouted as Bill and Sundance began to turn their new horses away from the fence to resume their flight from the posse. Butch had pulled a piece of paper from his front shirt pocket and was writing something on it.

"Just remembering a promise," Butch said, when Bill and Sundance asked what he was doing. When he finished writing on the piece of paper he spurred his horse alongside Patsy who was standing quietly beside the fence, winded and dripping with sweat. As Butch folded up the paper and began to tie it to Patsy's mane, Bill and Sundance drew their Winchesters and began aiming at the approaching three-man posse. Realizing the danger they were in, the men in the posse pulled their horses up. Because they were not yet within pistol range they pulled out their Winchesters too.

"Don't shoot," Butch cautioned as he finished tieing the paper to the mane.

"I can get all three if I start shooting now," Sundance said.

"No," Butch insisted. Then to the posse, he yelled. "Put your rifles away and no one will get hurt."

"I'm going to start shooting," Sundance said, not believing the posse would respond to Butch's request.

"Put up your rifles," Butch yelled. "Now!"

Shaking his head in amazement, Sundance slowly lowered his rifle from the shoulder as he watched the three possemen return their rifles to their scabbards.

"Now put your rifles away," Butch said to Sundance

and Bill, who obeyed, realizing their lives were no longer in danger, at least not for the moment.

"Now let's get out of here," Butch said. spinning his new horse to the east and spurring it into a full gallop. Bill and Sundance were close behind.

Realizing the outlaws were on fresh horses, the posse gave up any hopes of pursuit, but before heading back to town to report their failure in catching the outlaws, they figured they might as well get the three good, but tired horses the bandits had left behind, especially the beautiful white horse, the one the leader of the bandits had been riding.

The three men in the posse were Burns Colwell, Shorty Johnson and Jim McVey. As McVey was untying the white horse, he noticed the folded piece of paper tangled up in the long mane. Carefully, he loosened the mane and removed the paper. Unfolding the note, he read, "Return this white horse to Vic Button, the kid at the CS Outfit." After telling his two companions what the note said, McVey rumpled up the paper and threw it on the ground.

Later that day, as the posse was riding through Golconda, leading the three outlaw horses, the Golconda school was just letting out. McVey recognized one of the children.

"Hey Button," he called. "Get over here."

Cautiously, the boy approached the three men and the six spent horses. He recognized one of the horses. It was Patsy.

"Does this white horse belong to you?" McVey asked.

Vic didn't answer right away. In spite of his young age, he sensed that his answer was important. He didn't know why these men were asking him about Patsy. Where was Jim Lowe? Vic remembered how Jim had promised to someday give him Patsy, but had refused to say where and when.

"Do you know this white horse? Is he yours?" McVey asked, growing impatient with the boy's reluctance to answer his question.

"His name is Patsy," Vic said. "I guess he's mine."

Chapter 34

"You're not sure," McVey asked.

"I am sure. He's mine," Vic said.

"Can you prove it?" McVey asked, thinking he ought to make the boy produce a bill of sale, especially since the lad had hesitated in claiming the horse.

"Let me ride him," Vic said. "I'll show you Patsy is mine."

Not sure what the boy could prove by riding the horse, but curious to find out, McVey stepped out of the saddle and gave the boy a boost onto the white horse. Then he handed Vic the end of the halter rope and stepped back. The boy showed no concern at having no bit in the horse's mouth.

Vic looked across the school yard. Beyond a willow fence was a creek. Guessing his horse was thirsty after a hard run, he urged the horse into a gallop, heading straight for the willow fence. Neither the boy, nor the horse hesitated. His ears straight forward, Patsy continued to increase his speed and he galloped across the school yard. Surprised children jumped out of the way. Patsy leaped into the air, clearing the fence easily. Two or three strides later he stopped, dropped his head, and drank deeply from the creek.

When Patsy was finished drinking, Vic pulled his head around and headed back towards the fence. There was not enough space between the creek and the fence for the horse to build up speed. Still Patsy had no trouble clearing the fence for the second time. Vic galloped back across the school yard to the three men, having satisfied their doubts about who the horse belonged to.

"One of the bandits left a note tied to the mane, asking us to return the horse," McVey said.

"Thank you," the boy said, as the three tired deputies turned their weary horses towards Winnemucca.

As Vic Button rode home from school that evening on his new horse, he concluded, after much thought, that bank robbers were what his mother would call decent folks.

While Vic was entertaining this kind thought, Butch Cassity, Bill Carver and The Sundance Kid were busy

431

dividing up $31,000 in twenty-dollar gold pieces, $1,200 in five and ten-dollar gold coins, and a pile of currency including one fifty-dollar bill.

Chapter 35

After dividing up the money, Sundance said he was heading back to Texas where Etta was making plans for the trip to South America. He gave Butch an address where he could be reached. Butch decided to head north and then east, hoping to visit Mary in Wyoming. He guessed things had settled down sufficiently after the Tipton robbery to make travel safe. Bill decided to go with Sundance to Texas.

Butch headed north into Idaho then east towards Wyoming. As he was following the Snake River upstream from Idaho Falls, he came across a stagecoach with a broken wheel. While the driver was repairing the wheel, a man in a black coat and hat was pacing back and forth on one side of the coach. When Butch stopped to see if there was anything he could do to help, he recognized the man in the black coat as Bishop Ethelbert Talbot. Butch had met the bishop when he had first come to Wyoming after the Telluride robbery. With Mary, Butch had attended several of the bishop's services. Butch had also been present at several weddings performed by the cleric.

The bishop recognized Butch too, but was careful not to do anything that might focus the driver's attention on the famous outlaw.

"Hello, old friend," the bishop said. "Well, well, you of all people are the last one I ever expected to see."

Butch dismounted and started walking up the road with the bishop. The driver continued to work on the wheel, ignoring Butch's arrival.

"I never thought you would turn out to be a bandit," the bishop said. "Something must have happened to you to put you outside the law. You had such a wonderful character. Why do you rob banks?"

"Because that's where the money is," Butch said. "But I will tell you this much. I am not a common thief. I was sent to prison for a crime I didn't commit. I was framed by Otto Franc and he is lower than a snake's belly. I am getting even. The money I steal comes from men like him."

"I don't mind being chased," Butch continued. "I like outsmarting posses. Just think of the thousands of people who are looking for me all the time. It's good sport to outwit them. No, bishop, I would rather go right into a bank and get my money at the point of a gun than get it the way men like Franc do. Many people have been left homeless by their doings. You feel men should obey the law, but in my heart there is only one law, the one of the almighty God, and God did not order that families should be put out of their homes and go hungry so their bank can grow fatter. An animal will leave a carcass after he gets a belly full, but a banker is never satisfied, no matter how much misery he brings on people. A banker is a loan shark. They all look alike to me."

"You believe all bankers are this way?" Talbot asked.

"I know only three. There may be others who are different, but I never met one."

"So you think its alright to kill a man for his money?"

"I never killed a man for his money. I wouldn't take a man's life for a million dollars."

"Several men have been killed in your holdups. How

do you reconcile yourself to that?''

"If men are fool enough to chase me to get a reward, and to get the other fellow's money back, it may become a matter of his life or mine, in which case I hope it is his. I have never taken a man's life yet, and hope I will never have to do it.''

"I can't say I agree with your way of life,'' Talbot said, "but I do know many people who have suffered from the greediness of bankers and money lenders, but they are not all alike.''

"I don't expect you to agree with me, Bishop, but I think your almighty God furnished sufficient food on this old earth of ours to feed every human alike, and I don't think God has extended any special privileges to any man or group of men to keep the fullness of the earth from those it was intended for.''

"You are a socialist, then,'' Talbot remarked.

"No. I just think people unfortunate enough to have lost everything they have through no fault of their own ought to be provided with food, shelter and clothing.''

"I have tried on several occasions to turn around and live the straight life,'' Butch continued, "but they won't let me. They let me out of prison early so they could get me back on something more serious, and keep me there a long time. They'll never catch me again, if I can help it.''

The driver called to the bishop, announcing the wheel was finally repaired. As Talbot departed, he said he hoped they would meet again.

Butch continued his journey into Wyoming where he learned Mary was on an extended trip to Missouri to visit her father's relatives. Disappointed, Butch rode to his old hideout in the Green Mountains--the log cabin in the mixed stand of aspen and lodge pole pines overlooking the beaver ponds extending down the Willow Creek Valley to the Jesse Johnson Ranch.

Butch hadn't had time to hardly settle in for the winter when he was surprised by a visitor. It was Harvey Logan, who had been wandering around Montana since the Tipton holdup.

After bringing each other up-to-date on what had been going on, Harvey began describing what he thought would be a perfect place for a holdup in northern Montana, near Malta. Just west of the regular fuel and water stop at Wagner was a siding called Exeter were bandits, after relieving the train of its money, could cross the Milk River and disappear into the sparsely populated cow country to the south. Harvey said he had recruited Ben Killpatrick and Camillo Hanks to help with the job. They had located a hideout cabin near Miles City. From there they would ride north to do the job, as soon as the spring runoff in the rivers had dropped sufficiently to allow the rivers to be crossed on horseback. Before Harvey left, Butch agreed to meet him at the Miles City hideout in the spring. He guessed the move to South America would probably cost more than anticipated. A little extra cash would help. He liked the idea of one more train job before leaving the United States.

After a quiet winter, spent mostly at the Green Mountain cabin, Butch started north to meet Harvey at his hideout near Miles City. It was early April.

He passed through the familiar Hole-in-the-Wall country, down Goose Creek, over to the Rosebud, then east across the Tongue and Pumpkin Rivers to the Powder River. Near the mouth of Lame Deer Creek he stopped to spend the night with an old acquaintance by the name of Nathan Pressy. The next morning as Cassidy was getting ready to leave, Pressy gave him a note to deliver to a neighbor at the head of Rye Grass Creek, since Butch would be heading in that general direction. Butch was happy to do it.

After delivering the note, Butch stopped at a spring to drink and wash his face. After quenching his thirst, he removed his shirt and unbuckled his gun belt, hanging both on a nearby tree limb. Then he dropped to his knees and began splashing the cool water over his face and upper body.

Thinking he heard a thud, he began to straighten up.

Chapter 35

"I want you," a deep male voice said. Suddenly Butch could feel the cold steel of a pistol barrel pushing against his side.

"I guess you got me," Butch said, looking into the face of Deputy Sheriff Matt Morgan who had stepped between Butch and his gun. Butch quickly concluded that if he wanted to make a break, now was not the time. It would be best to submit, looking for a better opportunity to get away later.

Somehow, Morgan had gotten onto Butch's trail at Sheridan, and had been following him for nearly a hundred miles, waiting for the perfect opportunity to get the drop on the outlaw.

And now that he had his prisoner, Morgan wasn't about to take any chances. He ordered Butch to put on his shirt and get on his horse. As soon as this was accomplished, Morgan handcuffed Butch's hands behind his back, and tied his feet together under the horse. Morgan removed the bullets from Butch's six-shooter and placed it in his saddle bags. He rolled up the gun belt and holster and placed it in the other side of the saddle bag.

Confident his prisoner was secure, Morgan began leading Butch's horse back to Sheridan. Morgan was a quiet, careful man. There was little conversation between the two. Butch guessed Morgan was dreaming about how he was going to spend all the reward money he was going to collect for bringing in Butch Cassidy.

Butch decided to be as agreeable and pleasant as possible, hoping such behavior might increase the chances of Morgan allowing an escape opportunity.

The first day's ride took them as far as the OD Outfit on the Rosebud. When they were invited to share the evening meal and sleep in the Thompson home, Morgan removed the ropes from Butch's feet, but left the handcuffs in place. When it was time to eat, Morgan allowed Butch to have his hands handcuffed in front.

When it was bedtime, Morgan unlocked one of the cuffs and secured it to his own wrist. Chained together, Morgan and Butch climbed into bed. Butch could think of other people he would rather be chained in bed with. Still, Butch tried hard to maintain his cheerfulness.

The next morning, when Butch was mounted, Morgan handcuffed Butch's hands in front, and didn't bother to tie the prisoner's feet together under the horse. Butch decided his friendly, cooperative attitude was beginning to pay off.

At the head of the Rosebud they entered a stretch of country where there were no ranch houses or cabins for about 30 miles. Morgan seemed to relax, perhaps thinking there would be little chance of running into any of Butch's friends during this portion of the journey.

The weather began to turn cold, a brisk northerly wind blowing out of Canada. With his hands handcuffed together, Butch was unable to put them in his pockets. He did not have gloves. He complained to Morgan that his hands were freezing.

At first Morgan seemed to ignore the complaint, but as his own hands became cold, he apparently began to feel sorry for his prisoner. He removed Butch's handcuffs, ordering the outlaw to ride ahead so the deputy could keep an eye on him.

About ten miles further up the trail, they decided to water the horses at a place called Big Spring.

Though they had been on the trail for nearly 30 miles, Morgan's horse refused to drink. Butch could hardly believe a horse would not be thirsty after so long a ride. Morgan explained that sometimes his horse would not drink with a bit in its mouth. He didn't know why, only that the animal could be very stubborn about this. Not sure how far it was to the next spring, Morgan dismounted to remove the bridle so the horse would drink.

As the deputy leaned forward to unbuckle the throat strap, Butch edged his horse closer to the deputy's horse. Earlier, while putting his hands in his coat pockets for warmth, Butch had discovered two cartridges Morgan had overlooked in his search. Reaching to the side, Butch removed his pistol from Morgan's saddlebags, at the same time removing the two cartridges from his own pocket. Quietly, he slipped the cartridges into the cylinder, then cocked back the hammer.

Hearing the click, Morgan spun around, but he was too late, Butch had the drop on him.

"Stick'm up," Butch said, "You're too slow this time. Now toss your six-shooter into the spring." Slowly, the startled, and angry, Morgan removed his pistol from his belt, and realizing he was dealing with a desperate outlaw, tossed the gun in the water.

"Now, lie down on your belly," Butch ordered. "And if you have any interest in returning to Sheridan, don't make a move. It's my inning now."

Morgan didn't move as Butch got off his horse, obtained a small piece of rope from his saddle bag and began to tie the deputy's hands behind his back. Quickly, Butch checked Morgan's pockets for weapons. Except for a pocket knife, there were none.

Butch removed his gun belt from Morgan's saddle bag and buckled it around his waist. Then he unsaddled Morgan's horse. After removing the bridle he gave the animal a hard slap on the rump, sending it at a gallop down the trail towards Rye Grass Creek.

Butch went over to Morgan and untied the deputy's hands, at the same time telling him not to move. After Butch climbed into the saddle, he told Morgan to get up.

"Morgan, the shortest way to Sheridan is right across them hills," Butch said. He knew Morgan would run into a ranch, owned by a man by the name of Prairie Dog Wilson, about four miles up the trail, so it did not concern Butch that he was leaving the deputy in wild country without a horse or gun. Morgan picked up his saddle and bridle, and started walking. Butch headed back the way they had come, driving Morgan's horse ahead of him for a few miles, eventually letting it wander off to one side as he rode by.

Eventually Butch found the outlaw hideout in the hills near Miles City. It felt good to be with Harvey and Ben

Killpatrick, planning another job. Camillo Hanks had been let out of prison at Deer Lodge, Montana earlier that spring where he had been serving time for holding up a Union Pacific train near Reed's Point in 1893. Because he was deaf in one ear he had a habit of tilting his head to one side when someone was talking to him. He had sandy hair and blue eyes.

In late June the four outlaws headed towards Wagner. They went north to the Musselshell River, then crossed the Missouri River to the Milk River country. They camped for a few days near Chinook where they made final plans for the holdup.

Harvey boarded the westbound Great Northern Coast Flyer when it pulled into Malta on July 3, for a water stop. He hid himself in the baggage car. As soon as the train pulled out of the station, he crawled over the coal car and dropped to the engine platform, pulling out his six-shooter and pointing it at the engineer, Tom Jones, and his fireman, Mike O'Neil.

A few miles down the track, at the Exeter switch, Harvey ordered the engineer to stop the train near a bridge where the Milk River ran close to the tracks.

Ben and Camillo covered the train from the express car to the caboose with their Winchesters while Butch started making preparations to blow up the safe. Harvey kept an eye on the engineer and fireman. There were a number of passenger cars in the train, and curious travelers began to stick their heads through windows and doors to see what was happening. Ben and Camillo began firing their Winchesters at the passengers, causing them to scramble away from the windows and doors. From the clamor coming from inside the passenger cars, it seemed some of their bullets had ricocheted inside the cars, wounding several people.

Not wanting a shootout with angry passengers, Butch ordered the coach cars disconnected so the engine could pull the express car three or four hundred yards further up the track. With the passengers at a safe distance, Butch proceeded to blow up the safe. He realized he was getting better at this kind of thing. He didn't need to try two or three times. The first charge was just right to take the top off. He quickly filled his money bags with $17,000 in gold and $40,000 in unsigned bank notes. After thanking the engineer and fireman for their cooperation, Butch and his men got on their horses. They dropped over the bank and crossed the Milk River, heading south to Wyoming.

Posses were quickly formed, combing and crisscrossing the country from the Milk River south to the Missouri Breaks, but no sign of the outlaws could be found.

Several days after the robbery an eastern Montana rancher by the name of Morton tried to cash some of the stolen notes in Miles City. When questioned by authorities he said four men had given him a hundred dollars worth of bank notes for trading four of his best horses for their four tired horses. By now the trail was too old to follow. The outlaws had vanished.

After dividing up the money, Butch bid a final farewell to his friends. He invited them to visit him in a few years, in South America.

"That's a big place," Harvey said. "How will I find you?"

"When I get settled, I'll write to Mrs. Davis, Elzy's mother-in-law in Vernal. There's a lady who can keep a secret. Check with her before you head south."

Butch hurried south through Wyoming, checking one more time in Lander to see if Mary had returned from Missouri. She hadn't. He had hoped that maybe she would want to go with him to South America. But he couldn't wait. There were too many rewards, too many posses, too many people looking for him.

Sundance and Etta were waiting for him in Texas. It was time to leave the country. He would have to write to Mary later.

Chapter 36

When Butch arrived in San Antonio, Sundance and Etta were already in New York City. They left him a note with an address where he could find them. A week later Butch walked up the steps to Mrs. Taylor's boarding house, 234 East 12th Street. When Mrs. Taylor answered the door, Butch asked for Mr. Harry and Etta Place.

Butch hardly recognized his old friends. Sundance looked like a candidate for the presidency of the United States, dressed in what looked like the most expensive black suit Butch had ever seen on a man. His white shirt was freshly starched and he wore a silk tie. Butch could see his face in Sundance's new shoes, polished to perfection. Sundance carried a silk hat in his hand. His hair was neatly trimmed, greased with something that smelled like women's perfume, and parted in the middle.

When Etta entered the room she was dressed to complement Sundance. There wasn't a wrinkle in her floor-length black satin dress. Borders of rich lace circled the hem, the waist, the wrists and elbows. A yellow silk scarf fluffed from the front of the dress, from the collar to the waist. On her left breast hung a gold watch attached to a short gold chain pinned to her dress with a diamond stud pin. Her chestnut hair was bundled above her head in shapely twists and curls, several loose curls hanging in front of her ears. Everything seemed to enhance Etta's natural beauty. Butch had never seen a more elegant woman, unless it was the first time he saw Mary Boyd, her sweat-stained dress tied between her legs, as she guided a plow behind her father's mule.

Etta and Sundance looked more like they were about to embark on a trip to Paris or London, than the remote back country of South America. Butch had expected to find them dressed in leather boots and coveralls, pouring over maps of remote mountains, unnamed rivers and endless jungles. But such was not the case. Butch hoped Sundance's resolve to leave the country wasn't softening.

As for Etta, Butch wouldn't mind if she decided at the last minute not to go with them. It wasn't that he didn't like her, or objected to Sundance's relationship with her, he just didn't know if he wanted a woman along when they entered the unchartered back country--full of bandits, Indians, and the strange wild animals he had heard about, including alligators, giant lizards, jungle cats, little fishes that eat cows, and snakes as big as Ponderosa pine trees.

"I don't think she should come with us," Butch said, when Etta left the room to get some fresh orange juice.

"Why not?" Sundance asked, his voice sounding more than a little defensive.

Butch explained his concerns, suggesting that it might be better to leave her behind, then send for her once they were settled.

"If she doesn't go, I'm not going," Sundance said.

"What about the unsigned bank notes?" Butch asked, deciding to change the subject. "Do you think they'll be of any value outside the country?"

"Don't need to worry about that," Sundance said, suddenly grinning. "Found a place right here in New York City where I can get eighty-five cents on the dollar for them.

443

Already exchanged mine. We can do yours tomorrow.''

"Good," Butch said as Etta entered the room with three tall glasses of orange juice on a tray.

While they were sipping the juice, Sundance guided Butch over to a table to look at some photographs he and Etta had collected.

"I've ordered some more of these from John Swartz in Fort Worth," Sundance said, pointing to one with Sundance, Bill Carver, Harvey Logan, Ben Killpatrick and Butch taken about a year earlier at Swartz's studio in Fort Worth. The five outlaws had dressed in suits and new derby hats for the photo. There was another picture of nineteen of their outlaw friends taken in 1896 in Price, Utah. The photo Sundance liked best was a recent one of him and Etta taken the day he bought her the gold pin-on watch. There were two of the Fort Worth photos, so Sundance gave one of them to Butch.

"I have half a mind to send this with a thank-you note to Nixon, that banker in Winnemucca," Butch said. "Never seen a man so upset at having his money stolen."

"If you do," Sundance cautioned, "better clip Swartz's address off the back. The Pinkertons would be on our trail in a minute if a banker got hold of that photo."

The next morning as Butch and Sundance were walking back to the apartment, after exchanging Butch's unsigned bank notes, Butch resumed his arguments on why Etta should not go with them to South America.

"Etta and I talked about it last night," Sundance said, his voice calm. "We're going to stay here. We like New York. You go to South America without us."

Since Butch had walked into Sundance and Etta's apartment, he had been worrying something like this might happen.

"I thought we were best friends," Butch said.

"We are."

"All the planning, the dreaming, the work, risking our lives...you're just going to turn your back on all that?"

"You don't want Etta to go with us," Sundance said.

444

Chapter 36

"She's a woman."

"Now you're getting to the heart of things," Sundance said. "You and I are best friends, but Etta's a woman. I love her, and she loves me. When you've spent so many years by yourself--with loneliness gnawing at your insides like a hungry hog, night and day--then suddenly a woman like Etta comes into your life, even your best friends have to take a back seat. Understand?"

Butch had never seen Sundance so emotional, and it showed in the moistness in his eyes, and the fervor in his voice.

"Then maybe Etta ought to go with us," Butch said, starting to bend.

"Did you know she speaks Spanish?" Sundance asked.

"I guess that settles it. She's coming with us."

"We decided last night to stay here," Sundance said. "I can't go back on that without talking to her. Thinking you don't want her along, she doesn't want to go to South America any more. I don't know if we can talk her into going. Besides, she loves New York."

"I can change her mind," Butch said, a gleam in his eye as he walked over to one of the new iron boxes where people deposited mail. Butch removed a brown over-sized envelope from inside his coat and slipped it through the slot into the iron box.

"What are you doing?" Sundance asked.

"Mailing that photo to Nixon in Winnemucca, along with a note thanking him for the $32,000 we are having so much fun spending."

"Did you clip off Swartz's address in Fort Worth?"

"No."

"But the Pinkerton's..."

"The envelope has a return address too, 234 East 12th Street, New York City."

"The Pinkertons will be at my door in a week."

"You think you were lonely before. Try going to jail for a year or two, or for the rest of your life. You and Etta

445

better go with me to South America.''

"I guess that settles it,'' Sundance said. "When do we leave?''

Figuring the Pinkerton Agency would probably trace the photo, and possibly some of the unsigned bank notes, to New York City, they decided to make their trails to South America as difficult to trace as possible. After deciding to meet in Montevideo, Uruguay, Butch took a train north to Montreal, Canada, where he hired on as a deck hand on a cattle boat headed for Liverpool, England. From there he booked passage on a boat for Pernambuco, a port in Brazil. It was a long trip, the ship stopping first in the Canary Islands, then the Cape Verde Islands. After arriving in Pernambuco, Butch booked passage to Montevideo with one long layover in Rio de Janeiro.

Sundance and Etta had not yet checked in at the hotel where they were supposed to meet, so Butch booked a room and waited. When Sundance and Etta finally arrived, the three boarded a boat to Buenos Aires. Upon arriving in the Argentine capital, Butch breathed easier, guessing there was little chance the Pinkertons would be able to follow them this far.

After booking rooms in the Hotel Europa, they deposited their money in the London and River Platte Bank, using the names, Harry Place, and Jim Ryan. Next they went to the Registry of the Colonial Land Department and began inquiring about land available for settlement.

After considerable discussion, with Etta doing most of the translating, they discovered almost all of the good land near railroads and seaports had already been claimed. The only land still available in large pieces was that located hundreds of miles from seaports, roads and rail lines. The workers in the registry seemed very apologetic for this situation.

Butch and Sundance did not complain. They wanted to settle hundreds of miles from civilization. They didn't want to be by any of the big cities or seaports. As soon as the workers in the registry realized this, they began showing Butch and Sundance maps and pieces of maps describing the kind of land they were looking for. The outlaws began making a list of blocks of land they wanted to look over.

Then Etta translated a piece of information that focussed Butch's attention on the western edge of the Chubut Province, near the town of Cholila, about 1600 miles southwest of Buenos Aires. Cholila was a remote town on the east slope of the Andes Mountains about five hundred miles inland from the nearest seaport and railroad. Being so far from transportation to markets, the area around Cholila hadn't been heavily settled, and there was still plenty of free land one could have just for settling on it. Hundreds of square miles of land was still available, and according to the workers in the registry, all of it was ideal for raising cattle.

The news that caught Butch's attention was a recent announcement by the Chilean Government to build a road over the Andes Mountains near Cholila. Looking at the maps, it didn't take Butch long to figure out that from Cholila a herd of cattle could be driven to Puerto Montt, Chile in a matter of days. Butch also learned that beef cattle brought higher prices in Chile than in Argentina. It would take the Chilean Government several years to complete the road, just enough time for Butch and Sundance to build up a ranch to the point where hundreds of cattle would be ready to ship to market every year. The fugitives were confident they could earn a comfortable living raising beef for Chile markets.

Before leaving the registry office they had their names on four square leagues, about 13,000 acres of government land in the province of Chubut, district 16th of II October near Cholila.

From Buenos Aires they sailed south to Rawson City, at the mouth of the Chubut River, then up the river to a small village called Gaiman. Here they purchased horses, saddles and pack mules to carry themselves and their belongings upriver to their new home.

It felt good to be in the saddle again. It felt good not to

447

have to look over the shoulder to see who might be chasing them. It felt good to Butch to be starting a new life in which he wouldn't have to steal, or hide from the law. He was confident the long arm of the Pinkerton Agency would never reach him in Cholila.

Butch, however, had some concerns about Sundance's commitment to live a law-abiding life. One afternoon when Etta attempted to teach Sundance some Spanish, he said he already knew all the Spanish he would ever need in Argentina. This comment didn't set well with either Etta or Butch, both knowing Sundance hardly knew enough Spanish to order a meal in a cafe.

"You don't know enough Spanish to ask directions to a public restroom," Butch said.

"Maybe not," Sundance said, but I still know enough to get by just fine."

"And what exactly is that?" Etta asked, disgusted at Sundance's lack of desire to learn Spanish.

"Manos arriba," Sundance said.

"What does that mean?" Butch asked.

"Hands up," Etta said, offering to translate.

"Todos al suelo," Sundance added.

"Everybody down on the floor," Etta translated.

"Ponga el dinero en el saco," Sundance said.

"Put the money in the bag," Etta translated.

"That's all a man in my profession needs to know to get along in a place like this," Sundance said.

"Wait a minute," Butch said. "I thought we came down here to get away from the outlaw life."

"We did," Sundance said. "And I hope we make a fortune trailing cattle over the mountains into Chile. But dreams don't always work out the way you think they will. If something goes wrong. If our hiding place is discovered, we have something to fall back on, and I know enough Spanish to get by should that happen."

Butch sincerely hoped Sundance was wrong. Butch had wanted to quit the outlaw trail for some time, and now that he was finally doing it, he hoped the change was permanent. Unlike Sundance, he was not worried about being discovered in such a remote place. And after two weeks of following the Chubut River west towards the Andes Mountains, he was more convinced than ever that neither the Pinkertons nor anyone else would ever trail them to this remote corner of the earth.

If they strayed very far from the river they found themselves in arid desert lands, which became more and more lush as they approached the mountains. Butch thought he had never seen better grassland for cattle. Plus, the country seemed mostly unsettled, very few cattle growing fat on the lush grass. Butch, Sundance, and Etta began to get excited about the prospects of becoming successful and wealthy in a legitimate cattle venture.

As they neared Cholila, at the base of the mountains, they found crops of grain and vegetables that didn't need irrigating. It was late summer and the weather was mild, not as hot as Utah. When they quizzed people about year-around weather conditions they were told there was much rain in the winter, but little snow. What snow there was didn't last long.

The streams were clear, cold and full of fish. It was a rich, mild land, much like northern California, Butch thought.

Worries they had expressed earlier, that the officials in Buenos Aires might have talked the *gringos* into taking a worthless piece of ground, were soon forgotten. Their land had plenty of grass, water and trees. Butch found it hard to believe the government was giving them such a good piece of land. While the United States Government wanted to throw him in jail, the Argentine Government wanted to give him thousands of acres of prime land.

Butch's only regret was that he hadn't brought a woman along to share his dreams with him. Sundance and Etta got along so well, and enjoyed being together so much, that Butch often felt like an intruder. He envied the relationship they shared. They seemed to have everything a couple could want-- land, money and each other.

Cassidy

While Sundance and Etta assembled materials and supervised the construction of a four-bedroom home, a barn, stable and chicken house, Butch went looking for livestock. Most of the cattle he found on the open range were not branded, and he was tempted to do a little mavericking, but decided against doing anything that might put him on the outside of the law.

Before Sundance and Etta finished the house, Butch had driven home 300 head of cattle, 1500 sheep, and 28 good saddle horses. He thought he had made good purchases, in spite of his limited use of the language. When the local ranchers saw his gold, they had been eager to sell him their animals. After hiring two men, Roberto and Pedro, to help with the stock, Butch felt it was finally time to settle down and become a gentleman rancher. For the first time in his adult life, he would know what it would be like to a respectable, law-abiding citizen.

Chapter 37

Upon arriving in Cholila, near the towns of Esquel and Leleque, Butch and Sundance decided, since they were no longer outlaws, to use their real names. At first it felt strange to Butch to introduce himself as Robert LeRoy Parker. The hired men and neighbors called him Roy, a name he hadn't used in many years. He liked being called by his real name, though he thought Sundance still preferred The Sundance Kid over Harry Longabaugh. Everybody called Etta, Señorita Longabaugh.

The first few months everyone was busy--building, digging, planting, branding, and buying the many things needed to start a ranch from scratch. Their money was disappearing quickly, but they didn't mind, knowing they were establishing a ranch they hoped would support them in comfort for many years.

Etta did her share of the work. She could castrate a bull, or saddle a green colt better than most men. When she was working she dressed in men's clothing--cotton trousers, cowhide boots and denim shirts. By the end of the day she was as dirty and tired as Butch and Sundance. What impressed Butch was how she could go day after day, never complaining.

At least this is the way she was at first. But in time, she began to slow down--sleeping longer in the mornings, skipping occasional meals, complaining about not feeling good.

"Looks like Etta's losing some of her enthusiasm for this place," Butch said to Sundance when they were alone one evening.

"I don't think so," Sundance said.

"She's not working as long or as hard as she used to, and she doesn't seem as happy," Butch said, not wanting to start an argument, but not willing to accept Sundance's statement.

"She's not feeling good," Sundance said.

"She's sick?"

"No, she's going to have a baby."

"That's great."

"She's worried. Her mother and grandmother died in childbirth. Etta thinks she's inherited the same narrow hips that brought so many troubles for the women folk in her family."

"What are you going to do about it?"

"Maybe start going to church."

"Is there a good doctor around?"

"The hired men say there's one in Leleque. Don't know how good he is."

The next Sunday Etta made Sundance and Butch take her to church in Esquel, a Catholic mass. Butch had never been in a Catholic church before, and found it very different from the Mormon meeting houses he visited as a child. It didn't matter to him that much of the ceremony was in Latin. He didn't understand enough Spanish for any of it to make sense anyway, especially when the priests used religious words he had never heard before.

What surprised Butch most was that few men attended

the mass. For the most part the congregation consisted of women and children, mostly older women wearing black hoods. After an elaborate ceremony in which Butch understood nothing, the priests served wafers and wine. Butch figured this was sacrament, similar to the bread and water served in Mormon worship services. He didn't know if the holy water the women splashed on their foreheads was part of the sacrament, or not. When a silver plate was passed through the congregation, Butch and Sundance each placed a $20 gold piece on it.

After the meeting, Butch and Sundance waited outside, while Etta went to confession, after receiving strict orders from Sundance not to confess their outlaw past. As they were sitting on the edge of a stone slab waiting for her, they watched the women and children leave the church. The outlaws offered friendly greetings to those who looked at them.

After a while it seemed to Butch the young, more attractive women, seemed friendlier than anywhere else he had been in Argentina. They seemed to maintain longer eye contact when he looked into their faces. They seemed less shy, even eager to meet him, but some strange reason less eager to meet Sundance. Butch had always thought Sundance to be more handsome, and it seemed wherever they traveled, especially if Etta was not along, attractive women always seemed more attracted to Sundance than to Butch. But here in Cholila the tables were turned. Butch was pleased with the change, though he had no idea why it had happened.

As they were riding home Sundance asked Etta if she had told the priest taking her confession anything about her past.

"I told him I had stolen some money," she said.

"What did he say?" Sundance asked.

"He said I was forgiven, but that I should not do it again."

"That's all?"

"He said some other things."

"Like what?"

"Strange things you wouldn't expect from a priest at confession."

"Like what?"

"He said I was like the Virgin Mary," she said. Butch and Sundance started laughing.

"What's funny?" she asked in an annoyed voice.

"Nothing," Sundance said. "All I know is that the priest who took your confession doesn't know you as well as I do."

"He said there was a place for me on the right hand of God, right next to the Holy Mother, provided I did certain things."

"Like what?" Sundance asked.

"He said it was a holy secret, that I wasn't supposed to tell anybody."

"Not even your husband?"

"Not anybody."

"Did you promise not to tell?" Sundance asked.

"No."

"Then you can tell us."

"But it doesn't make sense."

"Just tell us what the priest said."

"He said Jesus had blue eyes."

"What does that have to do with you having a place on the right hand of God?" Sundance asked.

"I don't know."

"How would he know if Jesus had blue eyes?" Butch asked. "The Bible doesn't say Jesus had blue eyes."

"This priest thinks he did," she said.

"What does all this have to do with you, Etta?" Sundance asked.

"Mary had a blue-eyed baby, and if I have a blue-eyed baby I'll have a place in heaven beside her."

"This is the dumbest thing I ever heard," Sundance said. "I have half a mind to tell that priest a thing or two."

"Neither one of you have blue eyes," Butch observed.

454

Chapter 37

"So there is no way your baby will have blue eyes. I guess Etta has lost her place in heaven."

"Your eyes are blue, at least blue-gray," Sundance said to Butch. "If Etta has a blue-eyed baby I'll know it was fathered by someone other than me, and though Etta may be earning a place in heaven, I'll be sending you straight to hell with a belly full of hot lead."

They laughed, even though Butch and Etta knew Sundance was not joking. They also knew they had done nothing to invoke Sundance's wrath, and he knew it too.

The mystery of the blue eyes concerned them for a few days, but unable to come up with any reasonable explanation, they stopped worrying about it. Besides they were busy with the fall roundup, and the accompanying doctoring and branding. With cattle prices so low, they sold few cattle, deciding they would be better off waiting for completion of the road over the mountains into Chile. Besides, they still had a good portion of the money they had brought with them.

As busy as they were, Etta continued to worry about the upcoming baby. One day, without warning, Sundance announced he was taking her back to New York City to have the baby in a good hospital, attended by the best physicians. Butch couldn't leave the ranch unattended to go with them. Considering the history of complications during childbirth in Etta's family, he thought they were probably doing the best thing. A week later Sundance and Etta headed down the Chubut River to Rawson where they booked passage on a northbound steamer.

With Sundance and Etta gone, Butch became very lonely, very quickly. With his broken Spanish he didn't find his two hired hands, Roberto and Pedro, very good company. Neither had ever been more than 50 miles from Cholila, and seemed to have little to talk about. Besides, there was a lot of work to keep them busy.

With lonliness gnawing away at him, Butch decided to attend mass again. Like before, the congregation was mostly women and children. Like before, Butch dropped a $20 gold piece on the collection plate. Like before, when he went outside after the service, some of the more attractive women seemed more than a little friendly, even forward.

That evening as Butch was picking at a lonely supper of bread and milk, cheese, green onions and boiled eggs, a woman rode up to his door on a burro and dismounted. Butch stepped outside to greet her. She was one of the women he had seen at the church in Cholila earlier in the day. She was a pretty woman. She looked more Spanish than Indian, perhaps 25 years old. She was not fat, neither was she thin.

When he asked her what her name was, in broken Spanish, she seemed timid, almost shy. He concluded she wasn't a prostitute, at least not like the ones his men spent time with in San Antonio.

She said her name was Emma, and that she admired his blue eyes. She added that Jesus had blue eyes too.

Butch was puzzled. The mystery of the blue-eyed Jesus had surfaced again, and Butch had no idea why.

Looking down at her feet, Emma mumbled something Butch couldn't understand. Not only was he unfamiliar with some of the words, but he could hardly hear her. He asked her to say it again, louder and slower. The second time he understood a little more. He asked her to say it a third time.

The meaning was clear. She was telling him she wanted to have a baby with blue eyes. Butch looked down at her left hand. There was a wedding band on one of the fingers. He told her that if her husband had blue eyes, then it was possible for one of her babies to be born that way. She said her husband did not have blue eyes.

Butch was starting to feel very uncomfortable as the reason for the woman's visit became apparent. All he could think was what a strange place this Argentina was. Where he came from in the western United States, men still outnumbered women by a large percentage, and things like this did not happen. Where he came from, flirtation, courtship, and love preceded intimate contact between men and women. Apparently this was not so in Argentina, where

456

it appeared women were willing to pick total strangers to father children, as long as the eye color was correct. Butch guessed that even Jesus might have had a hard time with the celibate life in Argentina, especially if he really had blue eyes as the people in Cholila seemed to think.

Stalling for time, still unsure as to how to handle the situation, Butch offered Emma a glass of wine. She said she was thirsty. As Butch was removing the cork from the bottle, he heard approaching hoof beats.

A minute later a man jerked a sweaty black mare to a sliding halt beside the burro.

"Emma," the man yelled as he leaped from the saddle.

"Fernando," the woman answered.

Butch had been in Argentina long enough to know he was in trouble. He stepped onto the porch and held out the bottle of wine, a friendly gesture, offering the man a drink.

"No," the man shouted. There was anger, even rage in his voice. The man's left hand rested uneasily on the butt of a knife in a sheath on his belt.

Butch caught the man by surprise, suddenly cocking back his arm and throwing the wine bottle high into the air. Before the startled Fernando had time to guess what the gringo was doing, Butch drew his Colt .44 and fired at the bottle. The bullet struck the flask dead center, breaking it into two pieces. Butch fired a second time, shattering the top half, and a third time shattering the bottom half. By the time a hundred pieces of glass had tinkled to the ground Butch had slipped his pistol back in its holster.

Fernando was speechless. His left palm no longer rested on the butt of the knife. Without a word, he helped his wife onto the burro and pushed it towards the road. Without looking at Butch, he swung into the saddle and followed her down the road to Esquel.

Butch laid awake most of the night, pondering the mystery of the blue eyes, unable to come up with any reasonable explanation.

The next evening as Butch was sitting down to supper,

he heard the distant neighing of a horse. When he looked out through the open doorway he was amazed to see Emma returning, this time riding a sorrel horse. There was no sign of Fernando.

As Butch marched down the front walkway to turn the horse around and send it back to town, he realized the person on the horse was not Emma, but another women whom he had not met. Like Emma, she was beautiful, perhaps a little older.

"Buenos Noches," Butch said, having decided that if the woman said anything about blue eyes he would turn the horse around and send her back to Esquel without any further discussion.

"I bring fresh bread to the new neighbors," she said, her English quite good.

"You're the first person I've run into down here who speaks decent English," Butch said, unable to hide his surprise.

"Where I went to school in Sao Paulo they made us learn English."

The woman said her name was Rosa Molina. Her husband, Francisco, owned one of the nearby ranches. Butch invited her inside. He sliced the bread she had given him, spreading butter and honey on two slices, handing one to her. He poured her a glass of wine to go with the bread.

He kept asking her questions. It was good to listen to English again. Since Sundance and Etta had left, Butch had heard nothing but Spanish, most of which was difficult to understand.

Butch enjoyed being with Rosa. Not only was she pleasant to look at, but her conversation was warm and enthusiastic. Butch concluded very quickly that her husband was a very lucky man.

"Do you want to have a blue-eyed baby like all the other women around here?" Butch asked.

"Of course," she said, matter-of-factly.

"Why?"

"The Holy Mother had such a baby. His name was

458

Jesus.''

"How do you know Jesus had blue eyes?" Butch asked.

"Father Bruno said so."

"Did Father Bruno also tell you if you had a blue-eyed baby you would have a place in heaven with the Holy Mother?"

"Yes."

"Do you believe him?"

"Priests don't lie."

"I have blue eyes," Butch said, his voice suddenly very serious. "Perhaps I could help you have a baby with blue eyes."

Rosa looked down at her feet. She was uncomfortable. She was blushing. Butch wished he could take back what he had said.

"Thank you for the bread," he said. "Perhaps you should go now."

"Yes, I think so," she said, turning towards the door. He walked with her to her horse, and helped her into the saddle.

"I am glad you have come to Cholila," she said.

"I am glad too," he said. "Tell your husband we want to be good neighbors."

"I will," she said as she pulled her horse around and urged it into a gallop.

The next day Butch rode into Esquel to pick up some fresh fruits and vegetables at the market. While buying some apples and pears he found another woman who spoke good English. Her name was Ramona. She was a middle-aged woman, weighing at least 250 pounds. She was both friendly, and articulate.

"Oh, you have such pretty blue eyes," she said.

"Thank you," Butch said, not surprised at the comment. "And I suppose you would like to have a blue-eyed baby."

"Why would I want that?" she asked, surprise in her voice.

"Jesus had blue eyes," he said.

"No he didn't. He was Jewish. Jews don't have blue eyes."

"Do you go to mass?" Butch asked, wondering why this woman seemed to be outside the local mainstream of religious belief.

"Every Sunday," she said.

"And you have not been taught that Jesus had blue eyes?"

"I have never heard such talk, and I don't sleep in mass," she said. "Besides, do you think God cares about the color of eyes. It's what's in the heart that matters."

"You are right," Butch said, putting his fruit in a bag and tieing it to his saddle. As he rode back to the ranch, he was more confused than ever. He wondered if being alone so long was causing him to lose his mind.

That evening as Butch prepared his solitary supper, he kept looking out through the open doorway, wondering if another beautiful women would show up uninvited at his doorstep. None came, at least not while he was preparing and eating his meal. But just before dark he heard the bray of an approaching donkey.

This time his visitor was not a woman, but a brown-robed priest from the church in Esquel. Butch hurried down the walk to help the holy man secure his donkey to the hitching post. The sun was already behind the mountains. Soon it would be dark.

The priest introduced himself as Father Bruno. He spoke passable English. He thanked Butch for the generous donation at the last mass. Butch invited the priest to come inside for a glass of wine.

Because of the small windows it was nearly dark inside. He offered Father Bruno a chair. Butch grabbed a kerosine lantern and bottle of wine.

Father Bruno was a heavy man, perhaps in his middle years. He had large eyes, receding hair line, and sagging cheeks, red from either too much sun or too much wine.

460

Chapter 37

Butch wasn't sure which. The priest insisted on speaking English with Butch, even though his English was not very good.

Butch was glad the priest had come to visit. Perhaps the holy man could provide some answers to clear up the mystery of the blue eyes. After pouring a glass of wine for Father Bruno, Butch decided to fill the lantern with new oil before lighting it.

When the lantern was full, Butch removed the glass chimney, struck a wooden match with his thumb nail, and lit the wick. After adjusting the flow of oil into the wick, he returned the chimney to its place around the burning wick. He placed the lantern on the table and took a chair opposite the priest who had already finished his first glass of wine.

"Why did you come to this place?" Father Bruno asked.

"Free land. Good cattle country. When the road to Chile is finished our cattle will bring good prices," Butch explained. He was speaking the truth, just not the whole truth.

The priest asked something else, but Butch did not hear the question. His mind was racing, the pieces of a puzzle finally coming together and making sense. The mystery of the women wanting blue-eyed babies was solved.

In the bright light of the lantern Butch saw something that solved the riddle of the blue eyes. Father Bruno had blue eyes, and until Butch came along, the priest was probably the only man in Cholila with blue eyes.

Butch grinned, thinking this sly old stud of a priest ought to be whipped. In the private confines of the confession booth he had been teaching women he desired--like Etta, Emma and Rosa--that Jesus had blue eyes, and women who had babies with blue eyes received a special place in heaven. Women like Ramona at the market, who were not desirable to the priest, received none of this special instruction. Butch wondered how many good women Bruno had seduced with his blue-eyed nonsense.

"Are you Catholic?" the priest asked.

461

"No," Butch said. "Mormon, from Utah."

"Do you want to change?"

"No."

"I understand Joe Smith made a pact with the devil to get golden plates."

"That sure did happen, and part of that pact was that all good Mormons after Joseph Smith would be born with blue eyes."

"Are you serious?"

"Would I joke about a pact with the devil?"

"I don't know. Tell me why you are here."

Butch poured the priest another glass of wine. Father Bruno was visibly upset. His hand was shaking. There was perspiration on his forehead, but Butch wasn't through.

"I'm going to build a church, a Mormon church," Butch said. The priest gasped.

"This is the territory of the Roman Catholic Church. No one from Cholila will go to a Mormon church," the priest challenged.

"The beautiful women will," Butch said. "And if they go, the men will soon follow."

"Impossible," the priest groaned. "Why would the beautiful women want to go to your church."

"Because my eyes are bluer than yours," Butch said. "The women around here will do anything I want--and I mean anything--because I have blue eyes. They think Jesus had blue eyes, and if they have blue-eyed babies they will go to heaven. I have already sent a letter to Salt Lake City asking the church to send a hundred blue-eyed missionaries to Cholila."

"A hundred missionaries with blue eyes?" the bewildered priest asked.

"And a thousand more will follow, all with blue eyes. In ten years every family in Argentina will be reading the Book of Mormon, translated from Joe Smith's golden plates. The Catholic priests will have to pack up and go back to Spain."

Chapter 37

After gulping down the last of his wine, Father Bruno excused himself. He got on his donkey and headed back to Esquel. Butch hoped the priest would have a sleepless night worrying about what kind of sermon he could preach to turn the people against the blue-eyed Mormon menace from Utah.

Chapter 38

When Sundance and Etta returned, they did not bring a baby with them. It was a girl, but had been born dead, premature. But Etta seemed fine, perhaps a little subdued by the experience, but eager to get busy again at the ranch.

Sundance and Etta laughed when Butch explained how he solved the mystery of the blue eyes, and how he had tricked the priest into preaching a sermon against blue eyes.

"Did you send the letter to the Mormon Church asking for missionaries?" Sundance asked.

"No," Butch said. "The only letter I've mailed was one to Mrs. Davis in Vernal. I told her where we were in case any of the boys want to come down."

For the first time since leaving Circleville at age 18, life began to settle down for Butch. The only thing that prevented him from being totally happy was the nagging loneliness he felt for Mary. He still carried in a leather billfold the gold cross and chain she had given him. One cold, rainy afternoon he wrote her a letter. It made him feel better. She did not

Chapter 38

write back.

When Butch wasn't working with the cattle, horses and sheep, he roamed the local countryside. He always kept a supply of rock candy in his pockets for the children, especially the poor ones who never had any money. In the villages of Leleque and Esquel, crowds of children sometimes gathered around his horse. If his candy ran out, he bought more.

Frequently, he stopped by the Molina ranch to speak English with Rosa. Her enthusiastic conversation and fresh bread made him feel good. She became a good friend, but when he returned home, it was still Mary he saw in his dreams.

When longer trips were required to Buenos Aires or Rio de Janiero, Etta and Sundance were the ones to go, leaving Butch to keep an eye on the ranch. The herds and flocks prospered, the cattle and sheep nearly doubling in number in about three years. But while their wealth on the hoof was increasing, their bank accounts were rapidly decreasing to the point where Butch could no longer afford to buy candy for the children. It was just a matter of time until there would be no money at all. The new road over the mountains from Chile was behind schedule, and no one could guess when it would be open to herd cattle to Chile's markets.

Then one day a stranger, a *gringo*, rode a tired bay horse up the lane. As Butch watched through the open doorway as the man dismounted, he suddenly realized this was no stranger, but his old friend, accomplice and fellow outlaw, Harvey Logan. Butch ran outside and threw his arms around his old friend, the bravest man he had ever known.

Harvey looked a little older, perhaps a little thinner, but otherwise the same. As they shared supper together that evening, Harvey brought them up to date on the happenings in his life since the Wagner train robbery. Harvey had been captured and tried in Knox County, Tennessee, and sentenced to 20 years at hard labor in the Columbus, Ohio federal penitentiary. Before he could be transferred to the prison, he escaped from the Knox County Jail. He worked his way carefully back to his familiar hideouts in Wyoming and Utah, eventually stopping by the Davis place near Vernal. Mrs. Davis had received the letter from Butch just a month earlier.

From Vernal, Harvey headed south to San Antonio, then to Corpus Christi, where he landed a job on a tramp steamer, which eventually docked in Buenos Aires.

"I spent every penny I had getting here," Harvey said. "I hope you can give me a job."

"We've got plenty of work," Butch said.

"But we don't have any money to pay you," Etta added. There was a long silence. None dared say what they were all thinking.

"We are using our real names," Butch said. "We're law-abiding citizens. We haven't pulled off a single robbery or holdup the entire time we've been here." Again there was silence.

"Nor do we have any plans to return to the outlaw life," Etta added. None of the men seemed too excited or pleased with her comment.

"Look, I'm fat. I'm bored. I'm broke. I don't even have enough money to keep candy in my pockets for the children," Butch said. "And I don't have any idea when that blasted road over the mountains to Chile will be open. Why don't we take the old trail over to Puerto Montt and line up some buyers for our cattle. Then when the road is finished we'll have the jump on getting our critters sold."

"That's over a thousand miles," Etta said, trying to throw cold water on Butch's proposal. "We'd be gone for months."

"You could stay here and keep an eye on the ranch," Sundance suggested to Etta, cautiously. It was obvious the boys wanted to ride together again, and none of them seemed too excited to have a woman along. Etta got the message, and though her feelings were hurt, she agreed to stay home and keep and eye on things. She had no desire to ride over a thousand miles around the southern tip of the Andes Mountains up into central Chile and back again, just to have something to do.

A week later Butch, Sundance and Harvey were headed southwest towards the southern end of the Andes Mountains. None of them had been this way before. None of them had been in Chile before. They were leading two pack horses with enough supplies to last a month. It was exciting to be starting out on what they all thought would be a great adventure.

"There's only one thing I would like more than a trip to Chile," Harvey said, when they had been on the trail three or four days.

"A woman?" Sundance asked.

"No. Money in my pockets."

"We could hit a little bank or train a thousand kilometers from here and nobody could ever trace us back to Cholila," Sundance suggested, cautiously.

"We agreed to give up the outlaw life when we came here," Butch said.

"And we did," Sundance argued. "But we're out of money, and the only way I know how to get it is to rob banks and trains, and steal cattle and horses. And since the cattle and horses aren't worth anything around here, that leaves banks and trains."

"When the road is finished to Chile, we'll make a lot of money selling our cattle," Butch said.

"That damned road might not be finished for a hundred years," Sundance said. Butch could not argue with this. It seemed they had waited a hundred years already for the road. Maybe it would never be finished.

"Some of the hands on the ship that brought me to Rawson," Harvey explained, "told me about a town at the end of the world, the southern tip of Argentina, called Rio Gallegos. It's probably a thousand miles from Cholila. The town has a busy seaport, and several banks."

"Probably everyone traveling in and out of Rio Gallegos goes by sea. If we hit one of the banks and escaped inland on horses, they probably wouldn't know what to do."

"Wait a minute," Butch said. "I haven't agreed to hold

up any bank."

"Let's vote on it," Harvey said, knowing he and Sundance had Butch outnumbered.

"Everybody in favor of holding up a bank in Rio Gallegos raise his hand," Sundance said. He and Harvey each raised a hand high in the air.

"It would be nice to have some money again," Butch conceded.

"Then we go to Rio Gallegos instead of Chile," Sundance said. Butch could feel his heart pounding in his chest, and blood rushing through his head. They were no longer wanderers on a pleasure trip, but warriors heading into battle. Facilities that had been lying dormant deep within were coming to the surface. He found his eyes scanning the distant hillsides for the best hiding places, hidden feed pockets for horses, springs, ranches where fresh horses could be obtained, out-of-the-way buildings where men could seek refuge from storms without being noticed. He found himself committing every telegraph line, road, trail and railway to memory. It was time to begin training and conditioning horses and men for the rigors of the escape trail. Suddenly life was more exciting than it had been in years. He felt a rush of emotion, once again being in a situation that required courage, focus and discipline. Carelessness and lightmindedness had to be shelved.

Two weeks later, after crossing some of the most remote, uninhabited country on the South American continent, the three born-again outlaws rented a little cottage at the western edge of Rio Gallegos. Behind the cottage was a fenced enclosure for their horses.

Harvey and Sundance didn't see any sense in renting the cottage. They wanted to just wander into town, find and rob a bank, then ride like hell. But Butch insisted they first scout the town and the neighboring countryside, and become thoroughly familiar with both. He insisted they take the time to explore several escape routes, identify the best places to cross the Gallegos, Coug Coyle and Santa Cruz Rivers, and check out every bank to determine which would be easiest to hold up, and which had the most money. Besides, the outlaws needed time to train and condition the three new relay horses they had just picked up. Sundance and Logan both thought Butch was too obsessed with every little detail, that he spent too much time and energy worrying about every little thing that could go wrong. But Butch was the leader, so they endulged in his obsession for planning and preparing.

Every few days the outlaws rode into town to check out the banks, escape routes, and pick up supplies. The largest bank, which also appeared to be the most prosperous, was the Bank of Loudres and Tarapaca. The outlaws quickly decided this was the one they would rob.

One afternoon, after they had purchased some groceries and oats, and were tying the newly purchased supplies in gunny sacks to their saddles, Butch challenged his two companions to a race back to the cottage.

"But we don't want anybody to notice us," Sundance said. "If we race through town, everyone will watch, and wonder who we are. This is not a good idea."

"I think it's a great idea," Butch said. "Whoever comes in last has to shoe the new horses."

Harvey didn't need any more challenge than that. He jerked his horse around and spurred it into a full gallop. Butch followed. Not about to be left behind, Sundance galloped after them.

Everyone along the main street of Rio Gallegos stopped what they were doing to watch the three crazy Yankees race by. By the time the outlaws reached their cottage, everyone in town knew about the crazy Yankees.

"You are getting careless," Sundance said as they were removing the supplies from their winded horses. "By now everyone in Rio Gallegos is talking about us."

Butch just shrugged his shoulders as he carried some of the supplies into the cottage. He didn't seem concerned that half the town had seen their horse race.

Two days later, after riding into town to check out the

back of the bank and the roads leading away from it, Butch again challenged his companions to a race home.

"Why don't we just wear signs that say we are bank robbers?" Sundance asked, as he raced after his companions.

"We and our horses are getting used to the town, and the town is getting used to us," Butch answered. Sundance wasn't sure what Butch was getting at, only that the careful Butch Cassidy wouldn't do something to attract attention just before a robbery unless he had a very good reason to do it.

On February 11, 1905, the three bandits marched into the Loudres and Tarapaca Bank, drew their pistols, and shouted *"Todos al suelo."*

After scooping 20,000 *pesos* into their gunny sacks, the bandits leaped on their horses and raced out of town. No one in Rio Gallegos was surprised, or thought anything to be out of the ordinary, when the Yankees raced by. After all the Yankees engaged in this crazy horse racing every time they came to town.

By the time the people of Rio Gallegos realized their bank had been robbed, the outlaws had crossed the Gallegos River. A posse was finally organized to chase the outlaws, but stopped at the first relay point. Realizing the outlaws had changed to fresh horses, the posse gave up the chase and returned home empty handed.

Sundance asked Butch and Harvey not to tell Etta they had robbed a bank, but to let her believe their new money was an advance on the cattle they were going to drive to Chile as soon as the road was finished.

"If we were going to be regular outlaws again, we'd tell her," he explained. "But this is just a one-time job to keep money in our pockets until we can start selling cattle in Chile. It would be better if she didn't know."

During the first few months after arriving home, the outlaws watched closely for news of the Rio Gallegos robbery. There were no newspaper accounts. Neither was there any talk of the robbery, not even from travelers coming up the river from Trelew and Rawson. Butch even checked the post offices and police stations in Leleque and Esquel for wanted posters, possibly offering rewards for the Rio Gallegos bank robbers. There were none. In time, Butch decided the Rio Gallegos holdup had been a complete success. Once again he could afford to keep his pockets full of candy for the children.

One day news reached Cholila that a cattle buyer from the United States had arrived in Esquel to purchase 10,000 head of cattle from the local ranches. Butch hurried to town to meet the buyer.

Butch was in too big a hurry. By the time he recognized the buyer, Lloyd Apfield, a former Wyoming sheriff, Apfield had recognized Butch too.

They conversed with one another for a few minutes, Apfield saying he had already bought his cattle, but that he would remember Butch the next time he came to Esquel. The conversation was too nice, too formal. When Butch left, he was worried.

Two weeks later the local police commissar, a tubby fellow named Tasso, rode up to the ranch all by himself, announcing he had come to arrest Robert Parker and Harry Longabaugh. Butch and Sundance invited the commissar into the house, offered him a glass of whiskey, and started asking questions. They found Apfield had gone to the police station two weeks earlier claiming large rewards were offered for Parker and Longabaugh in the United States. Apfield told the commissar how to get in touch with the Pinkerton Detective Agency. After the commissar agreed to send half of any reward money to Apfield, the cattle buyer headed down river.

After Tasso had answered all their questions, they escorted him back to his horse, telling him they would not go with him. When Tasso said they were now his prisoners, and were required by law to go with him, Sundance threw two rocks into the air, drew his Colt .44, and shattered both rocks before they hit the ground. Tasso quietly withdrew without his prisoners.

Butch, Sundance, Harvey and Etta held a quick

meeting. They guessed Tasso would return, with reinforcements. They knew their cover was blown. Now, it was just a matter of time until the long arm of the Pinkerton Agency reached Cholila. Argentine authorities would cooperate with United States authorities. Perhaps someone would start wondering about the Rio Gallegos Robbery. Their days as peaceful ranchers in Cholila had come to an abrupt end. They had no choice but to return to the outlaw life. The only question was whether or not Etta would go with them. She didn't have any trouble deciding her place was with Sundance.

Knowing the road over the Andes from Chile was nearly finished, and not wanting to abandon nearly a thousand head of cattle, the outlaws joined their hired men, Pedro and Roberto, in a hasty roundup. While the men did this, Etta hurried into Esquel and bought a wagon full of supplies for the journey to Chile. Two days later the first cattle drive from Argentina to Puerto Montt, Chile had begun. The police offered no interference.

It was nearly a week later when Butch finally found the Chilean construction crew at the eastern end of the new road. Butch figured the going would be easy from this point on. He was wrong. As the hillsides, which the road had been cut across, became steeper and steeper, it became increasingly difficult to bring straying cattle back to the herd. And the cattle were constantly straying in search of something to eat. In time, Butch realized, that even with a road to follow, they would be lucky to get half their cattle to market in Puerto Montt.

After Butch rolled two horses to the bottom of steep gullies, both times breaking the horses' necks, he decided he had better find something better to ride. He wasn't sure if the roll to the bottom of the gully was as bad as carrying the saddle back up to the road.

After the second accident he threw his saddle on a white mule they had been using to pack supplies. The animal's name was Ingersol, and she was the meanest, toughest animal Butch had ever known. Butch guessed if any critter he owned was tough enough to negotiate the steep hillsides it was this mule. He had bought her for 20 *pesos* from a man with a broken leg brought about by a swift kick from the mule.

As Butch began to tighten the cinch, Ingersol laid back her ears and began switching her tail, warning signs that if the cinch was pulled any tighter she might try to break another leg.

Butch needed a tight cinch for riding up and down the steep hills, but he didn't need a broken leg. Keeping an eye on the mule's hind feet he carefully loosened the cinch. Speaking to Ingersol in a kind, soft voice, Butch carefully slipped a pair of hobbles over the hind feet. Then he tied a rope from the hobbles to one of the front ankles. Next he went over to a clump of brush and cut a green stick about four feet long and an inch in diameter. He placed the stick on a rock behind the mule, then returned to Ingersol's side.

As Butch began to tighten the cinch, Ingersol laid back her ears and began switching her tail. Butch ignored the warning signs and continued to pull the cinch tighter and tighter. Finally, she tried to kick him with her left hind foot, but the hobbles prevented the foot from doing any damage. She tried again. As Butch stepped behind her to pick up the green stick, she tried to kick him with both hind feet, but the momentum of the hind legs was broken by the rope tied to the front foot. Butch slapped her across the rump with the green stick, four or five times, with all his might. When she tried to kick him again, he let her have it twice more, bringing the green stick down as hard as he could across her rump. This time she didn't kick back, so he returned to her side and resumed tightening the cinch, hoping she had learned her lesson. When she started to lay her ears back, Butch reached for the stick. Quickly the ears straightened out, allowing Butch to put the stick down and return to the cinch.

With the cinch tight, Butch carefully removed the rope and hobbles. He replaced the halter with a bridle. Before mounting, he pulled Ingersol's head around so she could see what he was doing, holding her head in that position with one rein while swinging into the saddle. He wasn't sure she was broke to ride, and knew that by holding her head so she could see him get aboard, she would be less likely to buck. Butch could feel a hump in her back, but the mule did not buck as she headed down the road after the cattle. By afternoon Butch was riding all over the steep hillsides with no fear of rolling to the bottom of any more gullies. The white mule negotiated the steep terrain with the ease of a goat, never stumbling, sliding or losing her footing.

While Butch had always taken pride in being well mounted on the finest horses, in the name of safety, he was more than happy to swallow his pride and make this white mule his main riding animal, at least in the steep mountain country.

Eventually they reached Puerto Montt where they sold their cattle. Chile was not cattle or cowboy country, too much rain, and too many trees and brushy hillsides. Keeping eight horses and two mules, the outlaws returned to Argentina.

Butch knew the cattle buyer, Apfield, and commissar Tasso would talk freely with authorities. It wouldn't be long until a host of Pinkerton agents, railroad detectives, hired guns from the bankers' association and even the U.S. Cavalry would be invading Argentina in search of the notorious outlaws. Butch knew the search would be intense and relentless, eventually forcing him to leave the country. So he decided to take advantage of a brief window of opportunity, and get as much money as he could before leaving.

After crossing back over to the east side of the Andes Mountains, the outlaws headed north to Neuquen, a mining and farming town on the Rio Negro about 200 miles directly north of Cholila. After robbing the bank, they continued north another 200 miles to the town of Via Mercedes. After cleaning all the *pesos* out of the Mercedes bank, they headed west to the town of Mendoza. There they spent a few weeks studying the express train that went from Mendoza over the mountains to Valparaiso, Chile. After recruiting two *gringos*,

Hank Fowler and Billy Haines, they relieved the Valparaiso express train of some gold bars and three bags of *pesos*.

When relays of horses were used Butch always saved Ingersol for the last relay. Ingersol couldn't run like a horse, but she could glide along on a six-mile-per-hour singlefoot gait through the most rugged mountain country in Argentina. Few horses could keep up with the white mule after two or three hours on the trail.

Butch and his gang continued to work their way north, holding up one more train and four pack trains. By the time they left Argentina, crossing over the northern border into Bolivia they had two pack mules carrying nothing but money.

"Why do we keep doing it?" Etta asked one afternoon. "We certainly don't need any more money."

"To slow down the Pinkertons," Sundance said. "It'll take them years to check out all them robberies."

Butch was more serious in answering her question. He said after this string of robberies was finished he was going to give up the outlaw life for good, and he wanted to be sure he had enough money for the rest of his life.

"That might not be very long," she said. "This is dangerous business, and one of these days one or more of us will get killed, or at least sent to prison. Maybe we should stop while we're still alive and free."

Butch knew she was right. Still he was determined to do a few more holdups. He told himself he needed more money. Besides, he didn't know where to go. He couldn't go back to the United States, and soon it would no longer be safe for him in South America. Maybe he would go Canada, Africa or Australia. He was considering every possibility.

Though Etta never complained, Butch guessed being on the move all the time was taking its toll on her. When Butch suggested she take some of the money and go to Buenos Aires for a while, he thought for a minute she was going to do it.

"I can't," she said, finally.

"Why not?" Butch asked.

"If I left I don't think I would ever see you and

Sundance again." She was fighting to hold back the tears.

"Buenos Aires isn't that far away," Butch said. "We could get together again in a few months."

"Butch, I don't believe you."

"Have I ever lied to you?"

"No. This has nothing to do with trust. It's just a feeling, a strong one, that if I leave I will never see either one of you again. Something is going to happen to stop us from being together again. I'm afraid to go."

"Then stay," he said. The discussion was over.

Upon entering Bolivia they rode to the mountain town of Huanchaca where they rested for a full week. Then they rode west to the railroad where they flagged down a north-bound train. After telling the conductor they were prospectors traveling to La Paz, they jumped their horses and mules into one of the empty freight cars and traveled by train to Bolivia's capital. They stayed two weeks in La Paz, continuing to pose as prospectors. Visiting the many saloons, they gathered information about locations of mining camps, train movements, and bullion shipments. Because of all the mining activity around La Paz, there were a lot of foreigners, including many Americans and Europeans.

With their horses and mules under Harvey's watchful eye in a stable, Butch, Sundance and Etta rode the train to the northwest end of Lake Titicaca, then down to the Pacific Ocean. The country was not to their liking so they returned to La Paz, loaded their horses and mules back on the train and returned to Huanchaca, saddled up their horses and mules, and headed for the mountain mining town of Potosi. A week later they held up a supply train between Oruro and Cochabamba. From there they went west to the railroad, stopping at Challapatta where they began laying plans to hold up the train.

Not liking what they saw, they moved southeast to Cotagaita, a more remote area where the train had to go slow in many places because of steep hills.

They had no trouble stopping the train. Harvey merely jumped aboard the engine while the train was creeping to the top of a steep hill. He pulled a gun on the engineer and ordered the train stopped.

It wasn't until Butch and the conductor were disconnecting the passenger cars from the express car and engine that Butch realized something was wrong. He thought he could hear loud shouting coming from the passenger cars, strong male voices barking orders, military style. He looked back just in time to see dozens of soldiers, armed with rifles, piling out of the passenger cars. The train the outlaws had decided to hold up was carrying a regiment of soldiers. Butch didn't waste any time alerting his companions who raced towards their horses as the soldiers began firing their rifles.

As the outlaws approached the horses on foot, Etta, already mounted, was doing her best to keep the animals calm and under control. Bullets from the soldiers' rifles began kicking up the dust. The moment everyone was mounted, Etta's horse took a bullet in the shoulder and went down, pinning her leg between the wounded animal and the ground. Almost in panic, she was able to work her leg free. Taking a hold of Sundance's left wrist with two hands, she swung up behind him. The hail of bullets continued as they galloped out of range. Probably because the soldiers did not have horses, they made no attempt to follow the outlaws who headed south to San Lucas, then to Sucre.

They abandoned their horses outside of Sucre and entered the city separately so as not to attract attention. After finding places to stay they met at a fountain near the town square to discuss what to do next. All were nervous after such a close call, especially Etta who never before had been so badly frightened.

"I'm not doing this any more," she said. "I can't stand getting up every morning wondering if I am going to be dead before nightfall, or wondering which one of you will be dead. I'm through."

Nobody argued with her. In fact, Butch was amazed she had stayed with them as long as she had. Sundance handed her his money belt, containing his share of the recent holdups.

While in La Paz the outlaws had exchanged all their gold for large denomination currency.

"Deposit the money in the London and Platte River Bank, and get a room at the Hotel Europa," Sundance said. "I'll be along in a month or two. Then we'll go to Paris or Madrid for a few years."

She didn't say anything. She was crying. Sundance tried to reassure her that everything would be fine, but she didn't believe him. Somehow she knew this was the end. She didn't want to go. But neither could she stay. She couldn't do it any more.

Harvey, who had been wanting to return to Argentina, where he thought the holdup business was a lot easier and safer than in Bolivia, agreed to accompany Etta as far as Cordoba. Etta and Harvey left on the morning train.

Chapter 39

After Etta and Harvey left, Butch and Sundance trailed their outfits over to Santa Cruz, a fairly large town in east central Bolivia. They parted with Haines and Fowler too, who figured they had learned enough from Butch and Sundance to make a go of it on their own. They headed into southern Bolivia, hoping to hold up some pack trains, and maybe a locomotive.

Butch and Sundance rented a house at the edge of Santa Cruz, next to a large pasture where they could keep their horses and mules. It didn't take Butch long to conclude that of an estimated population of about 18,000 in Santa Cruz, probably 14,000 were women with little to do other than get into mischief. And about a thousand of them had been going to confession where another priest had been selling the blue-eyed baby doctrine. Most of the healthy men, it seemed, were off working in the mines in the mountains of western Bolivia.

The hill country surrounding Santa Cruz looked like excellent cattle country to Butch, but there were no cattle. The

479

big news in town was the coming of the railroad in a year or two, connecting Santa Cruz with Paraguay and Brazil on the east, and Argentina on the south. Though water was scarce, Butch concluded Santa Cruz would be an excellent place to start another cattle ranch.

What Butch couldn't figure out was why the people in town did not dig wells. There was plenty of water about 30 feet down. Instead, everyone seemed content to rely on rain barrels, and when it didn't rain for several weeks, they paid to have water brought in in barrels from the Piray River, just west of town.

In time Butch and Sundance became restless and began riding over to the mining towns to the west, looking for holdup opportunities. The problem was that other outlaws, like Fowler and Haines, were working in the region too. Butch had received word that Harvey had joined up with a couple of fellows to hold up two banks in Argentina. In both robberies they had killed bank clerks. Butch concluded that not only was Harvey one of the bravest men he had ever met, but also one of the dumbest. Butch had heard that Haines and Fowler had succeeded in knocking off at least two pack trains. As far as he knew no one had been killed in these robberies.

Every bank Butch and Sundance scouted had one or two armed guards standing by the door. Every train they checked out had at least one platoon of soldiers in the passenger cars. Every pack train they passed seemed to be accompanied by cavalry.

"Remember the Pleasant Valley Coal Company," Butch said, one afternoon. "Had my horse not become so excited, it would have been an easy holdup. We got away with $10,000 in gold. I haven't heard of any bandits in Bolivia or Argentina making off with a mine payroll on payday."

"That's because nobody knows when payday is at most mines," Sundance said. "Because there's so many bandits, they don't even tell the miners when they are going to get paid."

"We were able to figure it out at Castle Gate. I suppose

we could do the same here," Butch said.

"Let's try."

They headed out in different directions, scouting various large mines, getting work at or near the mines so they could study how the mines paid their workers.

Butch ended up at a mining camp near Sucre, owned by a pair of wealthy Scotchmen. They seemed to be two of the jolliest men Butch had ever met, so he concluded their mine was prospering, and therefore a payroll robbery would be in order.

Butch told them he was a prospector fallen on hard times, in need of work so he could get a new grubstake to enable him to resume prospecting. The Scotchmen said they didn't need any more men at the moment, but they'd be glad to put him on as a night watchman to help him get on his feet again. They told him he was welcome to eat in the chow tent with the rest of the miners. They even showed Butch their secret store of alcoholic beverages, which included wine, whiskey and beer. They told Butch to help himself whenever he had the urge.

Because Butch was one of the night watchmen, they told him when the payroll money came to camp, so he would be sure to keep an eye out for strangers during those periods. Within a week Butch knew everything he needed to know to take the payroll.

He reached two conclusions. One, the Scotchmen were awfully stupid to trust a relative stranger with information about the payroll. Two, Butch Cassidy could not rob two men who had treated him with so much kindness. A week later, Butch thanked his employers for their hospitality, and moved on, leaving the payroll for the workers.

After regrouping with Sundance in Santa Cruz, the two outlaws decided to check out one of the biggest mines in Bolivia, the Concordia Tin Mines near Tres Cruces, in the mountains east of La Paz.

When they arrived at the mine, Butch used the same story that had worked so well with the Scotchmen. He said he and Sundance were a couple of prospectors who had run out of money and supplies, and were in need of work.

Clement Rolla Glass, superintendent of the mine, said he would give them jobs as teamsters, freighting ore from the mine down to La Paz. Butch and Sundance were pleased, figuring that with the passing of two or three pay periods they would learn everything they needed to know to steal the payroll.

The only problem was that their new jobs didn't last beyond the first Sunday, the weekly day off for the miners. In their wanderings through Argentina and Bolivia, Butch and Sundance were constantly on the lookout for fast horses which they would try to obtain by trading, stealing or honest purchase. In their business a fast, reliable horse or mule was probably more important than a gun.

When they found out the mine shut down operations on Sundays to give the men a day off--a free day for drinking, gambling and horse racing--Butch couldn't resist the temptation to start lining up Sunday match races. He was confident his horses could beat anything at the mine. When some of the miners were hesitant to bet against the new horses, Butch set up a Friday night match race with one of the slower horses in camp and let it beat his horse by half a length. After that he was able to start lining up bets on the Sunday match races.

Guessing there could be some hard feelings after the races, when Butch and Sundance, the newcomers, won all the money, Sundance announced a Sunday morning shooting contest in which he would give a hundred *pesos* to the first man who could outshoot him with a pistol at targets thrown into the air. Each challenger had to pay five *pesos* for the chance to win a hundred. Butch and Sundance guessed that after the miners saw how good Sundance was with a pistol, there would be less chance of the miners complaining when they lost money at the horse races.

When Sunday morning rolled around, Sundance had collected a box full of tin coffee cups from the mess tent. The rules of the contest were simple. After paying five *pesos*, the challenger got to shoot at three cups, one at a time as they were thrown into the air. Then Sundance shot at three airborn cups. If the challenger hit more cups than Sundance, he got the hundred *pesos*. If they tied, they each shot at three more cups.

There were six challengers willing to shoot against Sundance. One of them hit two cups. Three hit one cup. The rest missed every time. On the other hand, Sundance shot all three cups each time. The men at the mine had never seen such accurate shooting at moving targets.

When all the challengers were eliminated, Sundance asked if there was anyone else willing to put up five *pesos* for a chance to win a hundred. By now everyone had gathered around to watch the shooting competition, a total of two or three hundred men. Some of them were urging their companions to shoot against the Yankee.

Finally a hand went up at the back of the crowd. The crowd cheered for the new challenger, but quickly became silent when they realized the new contestant was the other new Yankee, the one who called himself Roy Parker.

Quietly, Butch walked to the front of the crowd. He drew his Colt .44 and squinted down the barrel at an imaginary target in the air. Then he returned the pistol to his holster and folded his arms. He nodded to the thrower to let the first tin cup fly. The thrower hesitated. All the other shooters had held their weapons in the ready position, hammers cocked back, before nodding for cups to be thrown. How could this stranger shoot if his pistol was in his holster? Others in the crowd were thinking the same thing.

His arms still folded across his chest, Butch nodded a second time. It was clear, he wanted the thrower to toss the first cup. After shrugging his shoulders to express his lack of understanding, the thrower tossed the tin cup high into the air.

With a swift, curling motion, Butch's right hand circled his hip, bringing the pistol forward out of the holster. As this was happening his left hand, palm down, swept across his body, meeting the forward motion of the pistol, fanning the hammer on the single action revolver.

Bang, ping. The cup was suddenly spinning like a top as it changed directions. But Butch wasn't through. Bang, ping. The cup changed directions a second time before falling to the ground. A loud cheer erupted from the crowd. Never had these men seen such shooting.

Butch returned his pistol to the holster, folded his arms, and nodded for his second cup. Bang, ping. Bang, ping. He repeated the performance. He returned the pistol to the holster and nodded for the third cup. Again he hit it twice before it fell to the ground.

Scratching his head in amazement, Sundance walked over to Butch. He seemed a little upset.

"I set this up to win some respect," Sundance said, in English so none of the other men would understand. "Not to be humiliated in front of hundreds of men. Here, take your hundred *pesos*, you dirty double-crosser." Sundance reached into his shirt pocket and pulled out the wad of bills he had promised the man who could outshoot him. He held the money out to his partner.

Butch reached out to take the money, but just as his hand was about to touch the bills, Sundance jerked them away and returned them to his shirt pocket. Without an explanation, he turned, faced the thrower, and nodded for a cup to be thrown into the air. The crowd was suddenly silent.

A moment later the cup went high into the air. Bang, ping. Bang, ping. Bang, ping. Three shots, three hits. The crowd went wild. No one thought such shooting was possible had they not seen it with their own eyes. Butch walked up to Sundance.

"Keep your hundred *pesos*. I think we have achieved our purpose. Let's start the horses races." They shook hands.

As it turned out, the shooting competition was too impressive, too intimidating. No one was willing to bet large amounts of money against the two Yankees who performed miracles with their pistols. Perhaps they could perform similar

Chapter 39

miracles with horses. Still, when the racing was finished, Butch had about 150 *pesos* to divide with Sundance.

As they were cooling off the horses, they were approached by a young American. His name was Percy Seibert, and he was an engineer at the mine.

"Glass wants to know if you two are going to pay for all the cups you shot full of holes," Seibert said, after introducing himself. He told them to call him Si.

"Sure," Butch grinned. "How much do we owe?"

"Don't know. You'll have to ask Glass. He's in his office. Wants to talk to you about another matter too." After putting the horses away, the three walked over to the superintendent's office.

"What do we owe you for the cups?" Butch asked as they entered the office. The superintendent ignored the question. First he poured a cup of whiskey for each of his visitors. Then he offered them chairs. When all of them were seated, Glass asked Butch if he had any character references.

Butch hesitated. He wasn't sure what was being asked, or why. "I don't understand," Butch said, wanting Glass to explain.

"Is there someone you have worked for who can confirm that you are dependable and competent?"

Butch mentioned the two Scotchmen he had been working for before coming to the Concordia Tin Mines. Glass knew them. He nodded his approval, then he looked at Sundance.

"The Pinkerton Detective Agency," Sundance said. Butch nearly choked on his whiskey. Had Sundance gone crazy?

"They can tell you all about us," Sundance continued. "We've been involved with them on a number of big bank and trail holdups."

Seibert and Glass were impressed. So was Butch. Sundance continued.

"We were involved in the chases after the First National Bank holdup at Winnemucca, Nevada, and the Union

485

Pacific holdups at Wilcox, Wyoming and Wagner, Montana.''

"You've both worked for Pinkertons," Glass said, awe in his voice.

"I didn't say that," Sundance explained, his voice cool and matter-of-fact. "We were never full-time employees, but the Pinkerton Agency can certainly vouch for our ability with guns and horses."

"Why did you come to South America?" Glass asked.

"All that chasing around with the Pinkertons was getting a little dangerous. Thought things would be more peaceful down here."

"Well, they're not," Glass said. "The mountains around here are thick with thieves. And sooner or later we're going to lose our payroll. Have to bring it up from La Paz every two weeks. Have had a few close calls already."

"Maybe you should hire some Pinkerton men," Sundance said. Butch felt like kicking his partner in the shins. For all he knew the Pinkertons had an office in La Paz. With Sundance planting the idea, maybe Glass would drop in to see them next time he went to the big city.

"I think I've found my Pinkerton men already," Glass said. "As of tomorrow both of you are relieved of your regular duties at the mine. Your wages are doubled, effective immediately. All you have to do is bring the payroll up from La Paz every two weeks."

"I don't know," Sundance said, playing hard to get. "We came down here to get away from this kind of thing." Again Butch felt like kicking Sundance in the shins. The farmer was asking the foxes to guard the chicken house, and Sundance was acting like he didn't want to do it.

"If you agree to guard the payroll, you don't have to pay for the cups," Si joked.

"It a deal," Butch said. "When do we go to La Paz?"

As Butch and Sundance returned to the bunk house that evening they could hardly contain their excitement over their good luck. It appeared the Concordia payroll was going to be tossed in their laps. They were sure this would be the easiest robbery of their entire outlaw career.

Two days later Butch and Sundance accompanied Glass to La Paz. After the shooting demonstration at the mine the previous Sunday, Glass obviously felt the two newcomers were all the protection the payroll needed. With hundreds of workers at the mine, Butch figured the payroll would be at least as big as at Castle Gate.

Glass was older than Butch and Sundance, probably in his fifties. He had worked in the mines most of his life, and didn't have a family, at least not one he talked about. He treated Butch and Sundance like they were his sons, like he had a responsibility to show them the ropes, to teach them. When he tried to share his food and whiskey with them, Butch declined. He remembered how the kindness of the two Scotchmen had softened his heart, and he wasn't about to let that happen again.

Butch was riding Ingersol. Sundance and Glass were on mules too, because the trail was steep and rocky in places. A fourth mule, carrying their bedrolls and some supplies, trailed along without the benefit of a lead rope.

The first night they camped beside the trail. The second night they slept between sheets in a La Paz hotel. The next morning they went to the bank and picked up four sacks of gold which they deposited in the panniers on the pack mule. This was done in the crowded street in front of the bank. It worried Butch that so many people saw them load the gold on the mule. He decided that for his next robbery he would just camp in front of a bank like this and watch the people bring out the money. When the amount looked substantial, he would follow the party receiving the money to the edge of town and there relieve them of their burden. It would be easy, so easy that Butch guessed other outlaws had already thought of it, and some of them had probably watched Glass load the Concordia Tin Mines' payroll onto the mule.

Butch decided he and Sundance had better make off with the Concordia payroll as quickly as possible, because if they didn't, someone else would. He conveyed this feeling to

Sundance, who suggested they do it that same day, at a spring they had stopped at the day before on their way to La Paz.

The plan was to get the drop on Glass while he was drinking at the spring, tie him up, then leave with the four mules. With the spring so close to La Paz, they didn't think it would be very long before someone would come along and untie Glass.

When they reached the spring, Glass stepped stiffly from the saddle and knelt down beside the cool water. Butch stepped out of the saddle and drew his pistol, at the same time cussing himself for the hesitation he felt.

The Concordia superintendent liked Butch and Sundance. He trusted them with his gold. Now they were going to steal it. Butch had a sick feeling in the bottom of his stomach, like he had just gulped down a pan full of wet, mildewy oats. He hated himself for what he was about to do. He guessed if Sundance weren't along, he probably wouldn't do it. That made him mad. Was he getting too soft to be an effective outlaw? He pointed his revolver at Glass' back.

Bang. Crack. Bang.

Someone was shooting from the hillside above the spring. Dirt kicked up at Butch's feet. Water splashed in front of Glass' face.

"Ambush," Sundance yelled as he dove for cover.

Butch grabbed Glass by the belt and rolled the surprised superintendent behind a boulder as another eight or ten shots were fired from the brushy hillside.

Butch and Sundance didn't fire back. They still hadn't seen the enemy, and they weren't sure who the enemy was. Were law officers from Argentina or Bolivia attacking Butch and Sundance, or were they being attacked by common bandits after the Concordia payroll?

"Maybe we should just give them the money," Glass whined. "It isn't worth getting killed over."

"Give them the money!" Sundance exclaimed. "Over my dead body!"

As another flurry of gunshots erupted from the hillside,

488

a man raced from the trees, heading straight for the pack mule.

"They're after the gold," Sundance shouted as he fired at the running man. The bullet hit its mark. The man fell, tried to crawl away, then was still.

The firing on the hillside stopped. All was quiet.

"Bet they're holding a conference to decide what to do next," Butch whispered.

"We'd be crazy to give'm time to work up a plan," Sundance said, holding his hat above the rock to see if someone would shoot at it. No one did. Suddenly Sundance was racing towards the brushy hillside, Butch close behind. They reached cover before a single shot was fired. They guessed there was a good chance the bandits hadn't seen them run to the hill. If they had, there would have been shooting. Butch and Sundance worked their way up the hill, spreading out as they did so.

The bandits saw Butch first, and opened fire, pinning him behind a fallen tree. They were so occupied in shooting at Butch that they didn't see Sundance creeping up on their right flank. Sundance had all five of the bandits in clear view, less than 50 yards away, when he finally opened fire. Two went down before they realized the tables had been turned. The ambushers were now the ambushed. With three of their party dead, the bandits scattered in every direction. After removing the weapons from the dead men, Butch and Sundance returned to Glass, who was still curled up behind the boulder where Butch had flung him.

"Is it over?" Glass asked.

"Last we saw, they were headed for the top of the hill as fast as they could go," Butch said.

"All but three," Sundance said. "And they're on their way to see St. Peter as fast as they can go."

"Let's get out of here before they decide to come back," Butch said. They hurried to their mules, mounted and headed up the trial.

"No telling who else saw us at the bank," Butch said.

"I don't want to camp on the trail. I say we ride all night, keep pushing until we get to the mine." Glass offered no objection. Neither did Sundance, though he was wondering what Butch was thinking. It would be a lot easier to take the payroll from Glass, if they stopped to camp.

As they hurried along, Glass didn't stop talking.

"You saved my life," he said to Butch. "They were trying to shoot me and you risked your life to throw me behind that boulder. Then you both risked your lives going up the hill after the bandits."

"I have $11,000 in my retirement savings," Glass continued. "Take all or part. My way of thanking you for saving my life."

"We don't want your money, just the Concordia payroll," Sundance thought, but he didn't say it.

When Butch and Sundance didn't offer to accept any of Glass' retirement savings, the superintendent said that as soon as he got back to the mine he was going to write a will and name Roy Parker and Harry Longabaugh as the beneficiaries.

Just before dark, as the trail entered a narrow canyon, a perfect place for an ambush, Glass asked Butch if he thought there might be any more bandits after the payroll.

"I know of at least two," Butch said. Sundance gave him a strange look.

"How can you be so sure?" Glass asked.

"Because their names are Parker and Longabaugh," Butch said. Glass stopped his mule.

"I assume you're joking, and that's not a very funny joke," Glass said.

"Nobody's joking," Sundance said. "We hired on at the mine to learn about the payroll so we could take it. You were very accommodating, taking us to La Paz with you. Now if you'll get off your mule, we'll take the gold and be on our way."

"Why did you save my life?" Glass asked, bewildered.

"We may be bandits, but we're not killers," Butch said.

490

Chapter 39

"But you risked your own safety to save my life."

"And I'd do it again."

"If I tried to stop you from taking the payroll, would you kill me?"

"No," Butch said.

"Maybe I would," Sundance added.

"Then go ahead and shoot me," Glass said.

"In cold blood?" Sundance asked.

"In cold blood," Glass said. He didn't seem even a little bit frightened. Sundance and Butch looked at each other. Neither drew his gun.

"You two are the sorriest excuses for outlaws I have ever seen," Glass scolded. "The gold on that mule is worth about $13,000, and you can't even shoot a helpless old man, the only one standing between you and all that money."

"We could tie him up," Sundance said to Butch.

"I got a better idea," Glass said.

"What's that?" Butch asked.

"Why don't we go back to the mine and get roaring drunk, and forget this holdup business? You two will still be in my will, and you can earn a good living as payroll guards for the Concordia."

"Sounds good to me," Butch said. "Somehow it just doesn't seem right to rob a man after you saved his life." Butch rode his mule alongside Glass, reached out and shook the superintendent's hand.

Upon arriving at the mine, they went into Glass's office and proceeded to drink. Seibert, the engineer, joined them. Glass talked and talked about Butch saving his life. Butch talked about his desire to give up the outlaw life, and how the Pinkertons, bank detectives and bounty hunters, with their relentless chasing, wouldn't give him a chance to do it. Sundance grumbled about their inability to pull off the easiest job of their outlaw careers.

Si proposed two toasts. First, to the victory over the bandits at the spring. Second, to a friendship that meant more than $13,000 in gold. All of them drank to both toasts.

491

Butch and Sundance stayed on at the mine. In addition to guarding the payroll, they became the stock procurers for the mine, traveling far and wide purchasing mules, horses and beef for the Concordia Tin Mines. Glass trusted Butch and Sundance, not only with his money, but to make sound purchasing decisions in his absence. Butch and Sundance did nothing to betray that trust. With the passing of time, the bonds of friendship between the four men grew stronger and stronger.

But Butch and Sundance hadn't given up the outlaw life entirely. In their travels, buying livestock for the mine, they were on constant lookout for robbey opportunities. They knew eventually the long arm of the law would find them at the Concordia, and when it did, they would have to move on. Sundance still wanted to go to Paris with Etta, and Butch still wanted to give the outlaw life up entirely, hopefully settle down somewhere. Both needed more money to achieve their objectives.

Finally, they identified a pack train that left La Paz in the direction of Tres Cruces on a weekly basis. Reportedly, the pack train carried payrolls for three large mines. Normally there were four or five guards accompanying the pack train, but no soldiers. Butch and Sundance knew the job would require daring and courage, but they also knew the rewards could be substantial enough to help them retire from the outlaw life in Bolivia.

It was midday when the pack train left La Paz, following lengthy delays at two banks where Butch and Sundance watched as bags of gold were stashed in the mules' packs. It was 3 p.m. the following afternoon, near the head of a deep canyon called The Gorge, that the bandits heard the tinkling of the bell on the lead mule coming up the steep trail. Butch and Sundance had tied their mules at the head of the canyon, and walked down the trial a hundred yards or more to some big boulders that offered excellent hiding places on both sides of the trail.

Finally, the man leading the pack train, made his way

Chapter 39

around the point of a rock on a sharp curve in the trail, directly in front of Butch.

"*Manos arriba*," Butch shouted, stepping from behind one of the big rocks. The hands of five or six men, spaced here and there among 20 or 30 pack animals, went high in the air.

Stepping into view on the rock above, Sundance pointed his pistol at the men while Cassidy disarmed them. Once that was done he began searching the packs for the money. Sundance continued to keep the men at bay with his pistols.

Butch hadn't gone through three or four packs when he became aware of some commotion at the back of the train. He looked up in time to see a detachment of Bolivian cavalry riding around a sharp curve into the open. The officer in charge barked a command. The soldiers drew their weapons and opened fire. Butch and Sundance scurried into the big boulders uphill from the pack train. Braying mules were scrambling to get away from the shooting, some trying to turn around on the steep trail. The soldiers were attacking, moving forward through the mules, firing their weapons into the boulders where the outlaws had disappeared.

"There's too much open country between here and the horses," Sundance said. "If we run, they'll gun us down. If we stay, they'll soon surround us, and gun us down like fish in a barrel."

"Then what do we do?" Butch asked.

"Shoot them before they shoot us."

By this time bullets, which seemed to be coming from every direction, were splattering and ricocheting against the boulders.

Crouching low, Butch peeked around the edge of his boulder towards the trail. Two soldiers were coming around the big rock, not 30 yards away. Butch still had not fired a shot.

"Shoot them before they shoot us," Sundance repeated. He could see Butch, but not the soldiers.

Butch hesitated. He had shot in the general direction of

posses before, but he had never knowingly killed anyone. These soldiers were close enough to see the expressions on their faces. As close as they were, he would not miss.

"It's them or us," Sundance said, sensing Butch's reluctance.

Butch pulled the trigger twice. Two soldiers rolled off the trail, one screaming in pain. Butch felt sick to his stomach. He offered a silent prayer, not out of fear, but a prayer of regret and disgust. He promised if he got out of this alive he would never do another holdup as long as he lived.

Suddenly Sundance was shooting back at the soldiers. It seemed hundreds of bullets were striking the rocks. Butch crept to a tiny opening where he could see a good portion of the trail below. Soldiers were trying to drag away some of the men Sundance had shot. Other soldiers were creeping forward. Butch opened fire.

The battle lasted a good hour before the soldiers began to withdraw. They weren't retreating, just moving back to safer positions. They knew they had the outlaws badly outnumbered, and believed in time the victory would be theirs.

Butch and Sundance decided to start working their way back to their mules, so that as soon as it was dark they could get on their animals and leave, hoping the soldiers wouldn't discover their departure until morning. Together they guessed they had killed at least 14 soldiers, and wounded half a dozen more.

As they were racing to a new group of boulders, all the soldiers opened fire at once. It seemed a hundred soldiers were firing at them, instead of 15 or 20. By the time the outlaws reached the safety of the rocks, Sundance had been hit twice--a scalp wound and a shot through the upper body, under his left arm. The bullet penetrated deep into his chest. Even though there was little bleeding, Butch knew the wound was serious. There was nothing Butch could do but try to make his friend comfortable. Butch fired an occasional shot in the direction of the enemy to keep them away. After seeing so

Chapter 39

many of their companions go down, the soldiers had become much more cautious. Still, they showed no signs of retreating.

"Etta's my legal wife, and has been for many years," Sundance said. Butch wondered why his friend was finally getting around to telling him this.

Sundance pulled an envelope from his shirt pocket and handed it to Butch. It was a recent letter from Etta. Her address was on the outside of the envelope.

"If you get out of this, send her my money belt," Sundance said. Butch promised he would.

Butch knew Sundance was dying. Both wounds were ugly.

"Tell Etta I died fighting, and thinking of her," Sundance said with his last breath. With one last gentle sigh, he stopped breathing. His eyes were still open.

Butch turned away, fighting back the sea of emotion that was filling his heart. As he did so, he saw two soldiers working their way up the ridge to get above the outlaws. The soldiers didn't realize they were so close. Butch shot them both.

Darkness was beginning to set in. Butch waited a few more minutes, said a final goodby to Sundance, then worked his way back to the mules.

Butch rode all night, pushing several miles up a running stream bed, then across miles of slickrock, in an effort to hide his trail. Morning found him at the Concordia mine, exhausted, but unable to sleep. He told Glass and Seibert what had happened. Then he sat down at Glass's desk to pen a letter to Etta. He couldn't do it. Finally he just wrapped up Sundance's belt and wrote Etta's address on the outside of the package. She had had a premonition that something like this was about to happen. When she received the money belt without a letter, she would know what had happened. She would know Sundance's last wish was to send her the money, that he was thinking of her when he died.

"What are you going to do now?" Seibert asked.

"Go where I can find some peace and quiet," Butch

said. "The outlaw life for Butch Cassidy is over. If only they would leave me alone. But I don't think they will, not until I am dead."

"Here they come," Glass said, looking out through the office window. A small detachment of Bolivian cavalry had just entered the front gate to the mine yard. Instinctively, Butch reached for his pistol. Then he returned it to the holster.

"I'm through killing," he said. "Let them do what they will."

Leaving Seibert with Butch, Glass went outside to talk to the soldiers. When he returned a few minutes later, he was smiling.

"Seems a couple of *gringos* were killed in a shootout with soldiers at San Vincente yesterday. They didn't know about the fight at The Gorge. One of the men killed in San Vincente was riding a white mule. They think the dead men might be the two Yankees who shot the tin cups, Parker and Longabaugh. They want me to go down there with them and identify the bodies."

"Hank Fowler and Billy Haines," Butch said. "They were down that way. Fowler had a white mule too."

"I'm going with the soldiers," Glass said. "Stay here as long as you want. I'll be back in a week. If you need to leave, Si will fix you up with an outfit, and all the money you need."

A week later when Glass returned to the mine, Butch was gone. Seibert had given the outlaw a load of supplies for his pack mule, but Butch had refused to accept any money. When Glass asked where Butch was headed, Seibert said the outlaw had said something about following the Beni River northward.

"Who were the dead men in San Vincente?" Seibert asked.

"I told the soldiers they were Parker and Longabaugh," Glass said. "The same men who shot holes in my tin cups."

"Why did you say that?" Si asked.

496

Chapter 39

"Butch said they would never quit chasing him until he was dead. If they think he died at San Vincente, they'll stop. I think Butch is a man ready to be left alone."

"I know a writer in New York," Seibert said. "Arthur Chapman is his name. If he got hold of this story, it would find its way into every major newspaper and magazine. Everybody in the world would think Butch and Sundance died at San Vincente. The Pinkerton files, and everybody else's, would close. Butch would be free to live wherever he wanted, in peace. If they think he's dead, he could even return to the Rocky Mountains, if he wanted."

"Write to that Chapman fellow today," Glass said.

"I will."

The End

Cassidy

Epilogue

Having devoured anything and everything I could get my hands on the last two years that had anything to do with Butch Cassidy, I still haven't found one shred of evidence supporting the claim that he was killed by Bolivian soldiers in San Vincente, Bolivia. A number of newspaper articles were published in 1991 and 1992 concerning the digging up of a grave in San Vincente which allegedly contained the bones of Butch Cassidy and the Sundance Kid. Some of those bones have supposedly been shipped to the United States for further study. Until some hard, scientific evidence, is reported, however, it will be my opinion that the recent box of bones turned up by the San Vincente chamber of commerce is nothing more than a ploy to promote tourism.

On the other hand, there is much evidence that Butch Cassidy not only survived the San Vincente shootout, but returned to the United States to live out the rest of his life in relative peace and quiet. Butch's younger sister, Lula Parker Betenson, in her book, *Butch Cassidy, My Brother,* published by Brigham Young University Press, describes in detail a visit

499

by Butch Cassidy to his family after his return from South America. Many other witnesses, including many of his Lander, Wyoming, friends claim they saw and spoke with him after his return. *In Search of Butch Cassidy* by Larry Pointer presents the most complete body of evidence that he returned to the United States. In addition to testimony of personal friends who knew him before and after South America, there are photos, hand writing analyses, and other evidence presenting a most convincing case.

As for the Sundance Kid, there are many who believe he returned to Fountain Green, a little town in Central Utah where he lived in peace reportedly with Etta Place, until he killed a nearby Mt. Pleasant policeman who tried to arrest him for drunk driving. Sundance allegedly was using the alias, Hyrum Bebee. I personally found the evidence supporting Sundance's return less convincing than the Butch Cassidy evidence, and therefore decided in my book to let him die in South America. In the unpublished manuscript, *Bandit Invincible,* which Larry Pointer believes was written by Butch Cassidy in his later years, Sundance died in the pack train shootout near La Paz.

Sometimes I ask myself why I spent two years of my life researching and writing about an outlaw, a man who refused to conform to the norms of society, a man who achieved fame by stealing. I can't argue with the fact that Butch Cassidy was a thief, successfully robbing nearly 20 banks and trains. But he was a lot more than a thief. He knew how to be a true friend. He knew how to be generous, not only with friends, but with strangers as well, when he sensed struggle and need. He loved people and animals. He took pride in personal skills and accomplishment. As a boy he played the harmonica, built bird cages from willow sticks, sang and told stories to brothers and sisters. As a man he could out rope, out ride, and out shoot nearly all professional cowboys of his day. He was courageous, determined and able to keep a cool head when everyone else was going to pieces. Butch Cassidy made a difference, an impact, sometimes for good, sometimes for bad, but he made a difference. A man like this makes a worthy subject for a book.

As this volume becomes widely circulated, I expect a number of critics will come forward with claims that my book is not complete, that this or that was left out. Let me just say, if I attempted to write about every gun or horse Cassidy ever owned or used, that if I described every bed he ever slept in, every out-of-the-way cabin or hut where he holed up to avoid capture, or if I attempted to describe every conversation with every stranger or friend he ever met, this book would be 10,000 pages long. Butch had so many friends, and ate and slept in so many places that it is impossible to cover even half of the available information. So for those who know something about Butch which was not covered in this book, I apologize for not including it. Still, I managed to grind out 500 pages on Butch Cassidy, more than I have ever written about anybody else.

Someday when I pass beyond the veil, I hope I get the opportunity to speak with Butch about this book. If so, I'm sure he will be able to point out errors. Even so, he won't express his regrets by trying to hit me over the head or swear at me. He'll put his hand on my shoulder and we'll laugh about the stupid thing I wrote about him. That's his style. And I suspect he'll attract a crowd, even there, except, of course, those who were seriously engaged in the banking and train businesses.

Lee Nelson Books Available By Mail

The Storm Testament, 320 pages, $12.95

Wanted by Missouri law for his revenge on mob leader Dick Boggs in 1839, 15-year-old Dan Storm flees to the Rocky Mountains with his friend, Ike, an escaped slave. Dan settles with the Ute Indians where he courts the beautiful Red Leaf. Ike becomes chief of a band of Gosiutes in Utah's west desert. All this takes place before the arrival of the Mormon pioneers.

The Storm Testament II, 293 pages, $12.95

In 1845 a beautiful female journalist, disguised as a school teacher, sneaks into the Mormon city of Nauvoo to lure the polygamists out of hiding so the real story on Mormon polygamy can be published to the world. What Caroline Logan doesn't know is that her search for truth will lead her into love, blackmail, Indian raids, buffalo stampedes, and a deadly early winter storm on the Continental Divide in Wyoming.

The Storm Testament III, 268 pages, $12.95

Inspired by business opportunities opened up by the completion of the transcontinental railroad in 1870, Sam Storm and his friend, Lance Claw, attempt to make a quick fortune dealing in firewater and stolen horses. A bizarre chain of events involves Sam and the woman he loves in one of the most ruthless schemes of the 19th Century.

The Storm Testament IV, 278 pages, $12.95

Porter Rockwell recruits Dan Storm in a daring effort to stop U.S. troops from invading Utah in 1857, while the doomed Fancher Company is heading south to Mountain Meadows. A startling chain of events leads Dan and Ike into the middle of the most controversial and explosive episode in Utah history, the Mountain Meadow Massacre.

The Storm Testament V, 335 pages, $12.95

Gunning for U.S. marshals and establishing a sanctuary for pregnant plural wives, Ben Storm declares war on the anti-Mormon forces of the 1880s. The United States Government is determined to bring the Mormon Church to its knees, with polygamy as the central issue. Ben Storm fights back.

Rockwell, 443 pages, $14.95

The true story of the timid farm boy from New York who became the greatest gunfighter in the history of the American West. He drank his whiskey straight, signed his name with an X, and rode the fastest horses, while defending the early Mormon prophets.

All mail-order books
personally autographed by Lee Nelson

Walkara, 353 pages, $14.95

The true story of the young savage from Spanish Fork Canyon who became the greatest horse thief in the history of the American West, the most notorious slave trader on the western half of a continent, the most wanted man in California, and the undisputed ruler over countless bands of Indians and a territory larger than the state of Texas, but his toughest challenge of all was to convince a beautiful Shoshone woman to become his squaw.

Cassidy, 501 pages, $16.95

The story of the Mormon farm boy from Southern Utah who put together the longest string of successful bank and train robberies in the history of the American West. Unlike most cowboy outlaws of his day, Butch Cassidy defended the poor and oppressed, refused to shoot people, and shared his stolen wealth with those in need. Lee Nelson's longest book.

Wasatch Savage, 135 pages, $6.95

An athletic cowboy from Spanish Fork sets out to become a world champion bull rider. A disillusioned inventor disappears onto the rugged Wasatch Mountains in search of meaning and purpose. This is a story of searching, conflict, romance and superhuman achievement.

Favorite Stories, 105 pages, $9.95

A compilation of Lee Nelson's favorite short stories, including Taming the Sasquatch, Abraham Webster's Last Chance, Stronger than Reason, and The Sure Thing.